KILLER

JONATHAN KELLERMAN

KILLER

AN ALEX DELAWARE NOVEL

BALLANTINE BOOKS • NEW YORK

Killer is a work of fiction. Names, characters, places, and incidents are the products of the author's imagination or are used fictitiously. Any resemblance to actual events, locales, or persons, living or dead, is entirely coincidental.

2014 Ballantine Books Mass Market International Edition

Copyright © 2013 by Jonathan Kellerman
Excerpt from *Motive* by Jonathan Kellerman copyright © 2014 by Jonathan Kellerman

Published in the United States by Ballantine Books, an imprint of Random House, a division of Random House LLC, a Penguin Random House Company, New York.

BALLANTINE and the HOUSE colophon are registered trademarks of Random House LLC.

Originally published in hardcover in the United States by Ballantine Books, an imprint of Random House, a division of Random House LLC, a Penguin Random House Company, in 2014.

This book contains an excerpt from the forthcoming book *Motive* by Jonathan Kellerman. This excerpt has been set for this edition only and may not reflect the final content of the forthcoming edition.

ISBN 978-0-812-99915-0
eBook ISBN 978-0-345-54841-2

Cover art and design: Scott Biel

Printed in the United States of America

www.ballantinebooks.com

9 8 7 6 5 4 3 2

Ballantine Books mass market edition: September 2014

Special thanks to Vicki Greene, Esq.

KILLER

CHAPTER

1

"**I**'m not going to shoot you, Dr. Delaware. Even though I should."

What's the proper response to something like that?

"Gee thanks, appreciate the discretion."

"Hope you don't change your mind."

"Hmm. Sounds like you're feeling . . . homicidal."

When in doubt, say nothing. My job features doubt on a daily basis, but it's good advice for anyone.

I sat in my chair and crossed my legs in order to appear unperturbed and continued to look into the eyes of the person who'd just threatened my life. In return, I received a serene stare. Not a flicker of regret in the flat brown eyes. Just the opposite: icy contentment.

I'd seen the same creepy, inanimate confidence in the eyes of psychopaths locked up in supermax cells. The person across the room had never been arrested.

None of the usual warning signs had been present. No delusions or command hallucinations, none of the bizarre mannerisms or twitchy volatility that can result from too many crossed wires. No seepage of testosterone leading to unbridled violence.

The person who'd just threatened my life didn't have much in the way of testosterone.

Her name was Constance Sykes and she preferred to be called Connie. She was forty-four years old, medium build, medium height, blond turning to gray, with a handsome, square-jawed face, a mellow voice, and perfect posture. She'd been a straight-A student, had earned a B.A. in chemistry, Phi Beta Kappa, summa cum laude, followed by an M.D. at a top medical school, then a prestigious internship and residency and board certification in pathology.

She owned and operated a small, private lab in the Valley that specialized in testing for sexually transmitted diseases and arcane infections, drove a Lexus, and lived in a house far too large for one person. Most people would call her wealthy; she described her financial status as "comfortable."

Every time I'd seen her, including this morning, she'd been well groomed and dressed in quietly fashionable clothing. She wore jewelry but if you spent enough time with her, she'd inevitably remove bracelets and brooches and earrings and stare at them as if they were bits of alien flotsam. Then she'd put them back on, frowning, as if the notion of embellishment was a nuisance but also a responsibility and she was no shirker.

She had her issues, but nothing that had predicted this.

A self-professed loner, Connie Sykes seemed at ease with never having lived with anyone since leaving home for college. Matter-of-factly, she'd let me know she was an expert on self-sustenance, had never needed or wanted or imagined another person in her life.

Until "the baby" came along.

She hadn't gestated the baby or given birth to the baby but she *wanted* the baby, felt she *deserved* to have the baby, had gone to considerable effort and expense to *get* the baby.

That quest had been doomed from the outset, with or without my input, but I'd been paid to offer an expert opinion on her case and Connie Sykes had just learned that she'd most certainly fail in her claim and she was unaccustomed to losing and someone needed to be blamed.

She'd stirred up needless pain but I felt some sympathy for her. My best friend, a gay homicide detective, describes psychologists as reflexive yeah-sayers. (*"Forget Dr. No. You're Dr. Sure-no-problem."*) Of course, he's right. If therapists enjoyed deprivation and prohibition, we'd have studied for the clergy or run for office.

I figured if Connie Sykes called, I'd do my best to offer support, maybe smooth the edges.

She didn't. She just showed up. I had time so I led her to the office.

She entered no differently than before. Settling, straight-backed, butt barely perched on the battered leather sofa the way she always did. Removing her glasses, she placed them in a hard leather case that she dropped into her fine, oversized, Italian drawstring purse and smiled.

I said, "Morning."

She said, "Is it?"

Then her smile died and she cleared her throat, as if preparing to deliver a well-rehearsed speech, and informed me that she wasn't going to ready-aim-fire in my direction. Even though she should.

I kept my mouth shut, figured I was coming across calm as the two of us danced the eyeball tango.

Connie Sykes broke first, smoothing her black gabardine slacks and stroking her purse's whiskey-colored leather. Tapping the bag, she ran her finger over a swell in the leather and smiled wider and waited.

Well-timed comedian, waiting to see if the audience got it.

Implying she'd come with a weapon.

Her finger continued to circle the swell and my heart skipped and my gut churned and the shock must've shown on my face.

Connie Sykes laughed. Then she got up and left the office and continued up the hall.

I always walk patients to the front door. I let this patient find her own way out and locked my office door and pressed my ear to oak until I heard the front door close.

I remained inside the office for a while. A shot of Chivas didn't help much but the passage of time and a shot of rationalization did and eventually I convinced myself she'd just been letting off steam. Given all the court work I'd done, the big surprise was that it hadn't happened before.

A week and a half passed and when I didn't hear from her or spot her skulking around my property or receive any anonymous hate mail or field any weird phone messages, I told myself I needed to forget the whole thing.

What I didn't forget was the battle that had brought Connie Sykes to me in the first place. And while I hoped that she'd file me away as a distant, sour memory, I suspected her loss and grief wouldn't fade for a long time.

If ever.

When the divorce process begins, some people shoot out of the gate like corrida bulls, itching to inflict damage. Others declare good intentions and delay the attack. A small percentage manage to maintain civility, but the default is guerrilla warfare.

Combatants who have children often end up obsessing on the kids. That includes people who don't much care about being parents but lie and say that they do. Admitting apathy about your offspring— going public with those fantasies you've had for years of divorcing the whole *idea* of family life—breaks a lot of social rules.

Parents who couldn't care less about the kids often fight the hardest because it's all about winning.

In the worst of divorces, children become hand grenades. Allegations of neglect, cruelty, and abuse surface, usually false. But when kids are involved everything needs to be checked out. Those are the cases when the courts call someone like me in to offer wisdom.

There's another side to my professional life: working with Lieutenant Milo Sturgis on hideous murders.

That's the easy stuff.

* * *

Back when I left Western Pediatric Medical Center and began private practice, I avoided child custody cases, going so far as to refer away patients remotely likely to become embroiled in legal conflicts. I knew that court work was lucrative but I always had plenty of work, and colleagues who'd struggled to work within the system described it as an unpredictable mess cobbled together by a loose confederation of morons and sadists.

Best interests of the child, indeed.

My practice rolled along nicely: mostly good people bringing in mostly good kids with problems that could be handled short-term. The kind of patient load that can make you feel like a hero and who doesn't like that?

Then a child I was already treating became a custody case. Four-year-old Amy was being raised by a single mother who'd done a fine job, overall, but had come to me for pointers on discipline and development and school placement. The quiet little girl owed her existence to a one-night stand between Mom and a father she'd never met: a then-married, former Washington State trooper fired for taking bribes and suspected of worse.

Said dad had never been in Amy's life nor had he paid a penny of child support. Amy's mom had filed for payments but had never pushed; she was making do and the status quo seemed fine.

One evening her doorbell rang and there he was, trying to grope her and kiss her, leering smugly when she backed away as he served her with papers for a joint custody suit. Recently divorced, he'd been denied contact with his other two children, had been spottily employed since being booted from law enforcement, decided it was time to "get involved with the kid. She kind of looks like me, anyway."

You'd think there'd be no chance of his muscling into Amy's life. You wouldn't be counting on the morons and the sadists.

"Dad" had hired a lawyer with an aggressive streak and that legal eagle had brought in a psychologist whose wordy report strongly recommended fifty-fifty joint physical and legal "sharing," which would entail Amy flying between L.A. and Spokane on a weekly basis. All in "the obvious best psychosocial interests of this child."

The author of that bit of brilliance, a woman named Joan Mort, hadn't met Amy or her mother, relying, instead, upon "well-documented research data on the deleterious effects of paternal absence, particularly for prepubescent girls."

Amy's mother was already scrimping to pay for therapy so I took the court case gratis and wrote my own report. The judge, one of those jurists who actually reads what lands on his desk, called for a meeting in chambers with both attorneys and both experts.

I encountered Dr. Joan Mort as she walked up the court corridor. An older woman with a slight walleye and all the right paper credentials, she had a bouncy step and one of those soft, pseudo-sweet therapy voices that cloys quickly. She gripped my hand with both of hers, said it was a pleasure to meet me, had appreciated my input. As if we were both on the same team.

Once inside, she volunteered to go first. Speaking slowly and clearly, in a well-practiced academic tone that drew heavily on jargon, she managed to couch the absurdity of her argument with apparent scholarship. Made delivering a four-year-old to the mercies of a felonious stranger sound almost reasonable.

Flipping the final page of her report, she patted my hand and smiled reassuringly.

Your turn, sonny boy.

I began with a point-by-point refutation of her little oration, keeping my voice even as I slid into a side lecture on quacks and whores-for-hire willing to say anything for a fee. Using temperate language, of course. ("Superficial so-called evaluations that fail to pay attention to the patient nudge up against scientific and ethical boundaries, at best. At worst they cross those boundaries in a highly destructive manner. I find that inexcusable in any case but particularly destructive and cruel when a child's well-being is at stake.")

Mort and the lawyer who was paying her blanched. So did Amy's mom's attorney.

But the judge was working hard at not grinning. Thanking everyone, he adjourned the meeting. Joan Mort marched ahead of everyone and I thought she'd lost some bounce in her step.

The following morning the judge called and asked if we could meet.

"May I ask why, Your Honor?"

"I'd like to talk to you."

"About Amy?"

"No, that's resolved. In a manner that won't make you unhappy. I'd like to discuss some general issues. If you need to be paid for your time, the court's got a little discretionary fund."

"No need," I said, "but you can buy lunch."

We met at a steak house near the downtown court building, a place Milo frequents when he's testifying or meeting with deputy D.A.'s. His waistline-busting approach to nutrition features enough red meat to feed a bunkhouse full of ranch hands and I've never seen him leave with a doggie bag. The judge, a trim man in his sixties, nibbled a six-ounce rib eye and sipped a martini and told me he liked my style and would appreciate my joining the panel of custody evaluators employed by the court.

I said, "Is Joan Mort on the panel?"

"She is."

"Then forget it."

"It's a list, Dr. Delaware. No list is perfect."

"Granted, but that's a club I'm not interested in joining."

"High standards."

"I try."

"Hmm," he said. "You don't hem and haw like most shrinks."

"So I've been told."

"So you won't consider it? You really should, precisely *because* of people like Mort. There's work to be done refining the system."

"I'm sure there is but I'm happy with my practice and I really don't want to dive into the . . ."

The word I'd been thinking of was "muck" but while I groped for a more appetite-friendly synonym, he said, "Cesspool? Hell, yeah, it can stink to high heaven. But here's the thing: In a few weeks I'm going to be appointed presiding judge and I'm thinking I can clean things up. Why not help me, Doctor?"

"By targeting the bad ones? I'm not a henchman."

"No, no, I'm not asking you to break some code of silence. Just do good work consistently and help raise our standards. Right now the only cases I'm able to ensure get done right are my own. Once I'm presiding I'll theoretically have more control, but in truth, I won't once the other judges get their assignments. Because each of us is a despot in his or her courtroom.

One of my esteemed colleagues would have to rape a goat in the hall to get bounced."

The image made me smile. "The corridors of justice takes on a new meaning."

"Ha."

I said, "Why bother with one new psychologist?"

"Because it's a start. There are other decent evaluators, even some on the panel. But I've never seen anything quite like your level of . . . assertiveness. We can use some serious cojones."

"Flattered, Your Honor, but—"

"Steve's fine."

"Legal work's just not my thing, Steve."

Shrugging, he sliced steak into little trapezoids, ate and drank. A few moments later: "How about this, Alex: You won't need to join the panel, we'll start with me referring cases to you directly. And encouraging my brighter colleagues to do the same. You'll never end up looking like a trial slut because you'll be working for the court, not the parties. As an objective finder of fact."

"All that from the discretionary fund?"

"No, you'll be reimbursed like everyone else."

"By the parties."

"Fifty-fifty, so there'll be no favoritism."

"Steve, when people pay bills, they start to feel entitled."

"I'll make the rules clear."

"On top of that, the bills would be substantial," I said. "Because I think the usual approach—brief interview, a few psych tests, boilerplate report—is a joke. The right way takes time and time is money."

"Your fees are your business."

"I'm talking billing for home visits, school visits, interviews with extended family, friends, anyone I feel is relevant. Travel time, too—charging portal-to-portal, the way lawyers do."

"From the moment you leave your office to the moment you return. Seems fair to me."

"I'd insist on a retainer up front."

"Same answer."

"I'd double my therapy fee. We're talking big bucks, Steve."

He put his fork down. "So you won't be working on any charity cases. Fine, they rarely drag on, anyway."

"The money runs out, the lawyers stop filing."

He smiled. "You don't want to do this so you're attempting to price yourself out of the market. Sorry, Alex, not an effective argument. If someone balks at paying, let them complain to me. And frankly, I hope you get prosperous out of this, I'm all for prosperity. You put your time in at Western Peds. My son worked there as a pharmacist, I know the pay scale. So obviously you did your bit for the public interest."

"You've researched me."

"I wanted to make sure what I saw in my chambers was backed up by substance. You have an impressive résumé, exactly the kind of research experience that'll hold up under cross."

Gin and vermouth disappeared down his slender gullet. "Yes, that was an attempt to further stroke your ego. Did it work?"

I didn't answer.

He said, "You're really that obdurate, huh? Damn shame, you could've made a difference."

He motioned for the check.

I said, "Fine, I'll try it."

"Excellent. How about some dessert?"

"No, thanks."

"Then none for me, either—and put that plastic away, this is on me."

"Not necessary," I said.

"Not necessary but good manners. Something both of us would like to see more of, Alex, in our quest for truth, justice, and the American way."

We left the restaurant and handed our tickets to the parking valet. The judge's drive was a newish, black Porsche 911. When he saw my Seville, he said, "Blast from Detroit's past. You're a loyal fellow."

Before I could answer, he was behind the wheel, gunning his engine. Rolling forward a few feet, he stopped, motioned me closer.

As I leaned in, he said, "Count on Joan Mort to resign from the panel, soon." Big grin. "At least she responds to constructive criticism."

I didn't hear from Steve Yates for nearly two months and figured he'd changed his mind. But shortly after his promotion to presiding judge was noted in the *Times,* he sent me my first case, a dispute between two well-meaning, caring parents whose blood had been heated for battle by a pair of pit-bull attorneys.

I researched the lawyers first, learned they'd both been through messy divorces of their own. Then I met with each parent individually, absorbed more than my minimum daily requirement of vitriol, and made an appointment for the three children.

I found the youngsters well adjusted but understandably anxious. Ignoring repeated phone calls from the lawyers, I brought the parents back in, told them they were good people being led astray and their choice was to switch gears immediately or risk turning their kids into long-term therapy patients. They both took umbrage at that and attacked my argument. The mother went further and questioned my qualifications. Only hostility toward her prevented the father from agreeing.

I persisted and kept taking on the bad-guy role and that nudged the two of them into an ad hoc alliance as *Good Parents*. A few more sessions of that and they'd agreed to persist in their financial battle while keeping the kids out of the fray. I told them that was the least they could do and the three of us grumbled through another couple of sessions that finally produced a reasonable custody arrangement. In my report, I credited the parents' hard work. Judge Yates quoted me in his final judgment, redacted the names of the participants, and distributed his opinion to the other judges as an educational tool.

Surprised at the quick resolution, I realized that some of the five-thousand-dollar retainer I'd taken hadn't been earned. I mailed checks to each parent, received a floral-scented card and a bottle of Armani cologne from the wife, a softcover book on baseball from the father. Accepting gifts in barter was unethical so I gave the cologne to my fishpond maintenance guy, donated the book to a local library.

The next case from Yates arrived a month and a half later. So far, the pace was fine, allowing me plenty of time for my therapy patients.

Number Two was different: a pair of decent lawyers working for a pair of highly obnoxious litigants. An agreement was eventually drafted but I had no faith in its life span. Still, I ended up feeling I'd done my best, had a chance of making a small difference in the life of two already jumpy, compulsive children.

That time, the retainer was more than used up. I didn't bother to bill for the overage.

Eight days later, I got Case Three. Four through Seven arrived in rapid succession and by year's end I'd filed thirteen reports and had a good feel for the system. Such as it is.

The way it works in L.A. County is when opposing parties can't work out their differences quickly, the court mandates mediation carried out by its own employees. The mediators are social workers or master's-level mental professionals and some of them are excellent. However, their workload is massive and the arbitration process needs to be brief. The penalty for failing to reach an easy agreement is nil: Files are tagged as unresolved and sent back for additional consultation by psychiatrists and psychologists on the court panel or an expert agreed upon by both parties.

Or one highly recommended by the presiding judge.

Sometimes that second step helps, often it doesn't. Because asking people who communicate horribly to jointly maneuver the complexities of child rearing is like expecting a chimp to teach physics.

Also, as Yates had warned me, judges retain dictatorial powers in their courtrooms and while some use their authority wisely, others are Ghadaffis in black robes with tenuous links to reality.

When Steve was able to stick with a case, the chance of resolution was excellent. When he needed to punt to another judge, the outcome was a random toss no matter what I did. That should've been enough to make me quit but I discovered that bad outcomes bothered me less than I'd expected, because the happy endings were so gratifying. And even with the nasty ones, I was able to sneak in some supportive therapy for the kids.

But in truth, it was more than that. New situations teach you about yourself. I'd earned a Ph.D. at twenty-four, briefly contemplated adding a law degree, decided white-collar combat wasn't for me. Because my goal was to *nurture,* not to fight.

But, surprise, surprise, matching wits with attorneys turned out to be *fun.* I *enjoyed* a good tussle.

That extended to the infrequent cases when I actually had to testify. The first time—Case Eight—I was nervous as hell and struggled to conceal my anxiety.

By the time I left the stand, I was fighting smugness, and from then on testifying became an enjoyable experience that left me adrenalized. Because most lawyers function well short of Perry Mason. And expecting mental health types to be bumbling wimps, they're ill prepared for self-confidence and assertiveness.

I developed a reputation as a compulsively thorough, hard-to-crack sonofabitch and that led to minimal cross-examination.

That notoriety hadn't reached the senior partner at a top Beverly Hills "family law" firm when he cold-called me regarding Case Eleven. Sterling Stark wasn't directly involved but one of his associates was and he wanted to "weigh in personally."

"About what, Mr. Stark?"

"Read your report, Doctor." A beat. "Don't *like* your report, Doctor."

"Okay."

"You're going to change it."

"Pardon?"

"I want you to change it, Doctor."

"That's not going to happen."

"Don't you want to know how I want you to change it?"

"Nope."

"Not interested at all?"

"The report was accurate."

"Says you. Trust me, Doctor, you'll change it."

"Why would I do that?"

"Because if you don't, I'll subpoena you as a regular witness, not an expert witness. Do you know what that means, Doctor?"

"Tell me, Mr. Stark."

"You won't get paid for your time."

I said nothing.

"I'll tie you up for weeks, *Mister* Delaware. I'll toss

ethical charges into the mix, file and postpone and re-file and re-postpone. You'll end up sitting on those hard benches in the court corridor until your ass turns blue."

"Doesn't sound like fun."

"Far from it, Doctor. Far from it. So do we have an understanding?"

"Hmm," I said.

"When can I expect—"

"Expect nothing."

A beat. "Didn't you hear what I told you? I *warned* you."

"Well," I said. "Give it your best shot. Asshole."

Click.

Never heard from him again.

By the time Dr. Constance Sykes sued her sister, Cherie Sykes, for guardianship of Rambla Pacifico Sykes, a minor female child, age sixteen months, I thought I'd seen it all.

But right from the start, this one was different. As a non-parent, Connie had no rights in family court, no legal avenue to seek custody. The creative solution, per her attorney, was to seek guardianship in probate court, based upon Cherie's unfitness as a mother and the fact that Cherie's "dumping" the baby on Connie for a three-month period was tacit admission of such on Cherie's part.

I'd never worked a probate case, got the referral because Judge Nancy Maestro was the sister-in-law of now retired Judge Stephen Yates and he'd given her my name. The setup I had in family court would transfer easily: As an impartial probate investigator, I'd be working for the court, not the parties.

The case sounded interesting so I agreed to a meeting with Judge Maestro. I was already downtown, wrapping up a week of deposition on a multiple homicide Milo had closed last year. The trip from Deputy D.A. John Nguyen's office on West Temple to the Mosk Courthouse on North Hill was a five-minute stroll.

I found Maestro's court easily enough, well lit and empty, with chambers to the left rear of the bench. Entry was blocked by a broadly built bailiff in sheriff's beige. Thick arms crossed his chest. His eyeglasses were slightly tinted—a pale bronze just dark enough to block out sentiment. As I approached, he didn't move. My smile did nothing to melt his impassiveness.

H. W. Nebe on his badge. Mid- to late fifties, white-haired, a heavy, sun-seamed face that could've been avuncular had he chosen to unclamp his lips.

"Dr. Delaware. I have an appointment with Judge Maestro."

The news didn't surprise or impress him. "I.D., please."

Scanning my driver's license elicited a second visual circuit. "Why don't you take a seat, Doctor."

The previous year a judge in criminal court had been stabbed in his office after hours. Rumors abounded about a love triangle but the case remained open and I supposed Deputy H. W. Nebe's caution was justified.

I settled in the front row of the courtroom—where I'd be stationed if I was a defendant. Nebe took his time with a two-way radio. A muttered conversation out of earshot led him to rotate his bronze lenses toward me and curl a finger. "Okay."

He ushered me through a door that led into a small anteroom. An inner door was marked *Chambers* in chipped black lettering.

Nebe knocked. A voice said, "Come in."

Nebe turned to me. "Guess that means you."

Steve Yates had scored an impressive, oak-paneled inner sanctum, exactly the kind of retreat you'd imagine for a Superior Court judge. Nancy Maestro's chambers consisted of a twelve-by-fifteen, drop-ceilinged, white-walled space set up with paint-grade bookcases, a wood-grain desk with chipped metal legs, unaccommodating side chairs, and a laptop computer. The view was downtown grime under a sky struggling to produce blue.

She got up and shook my hand and sank back down behind the desk. A plump, pretty brunette in her early forties, she favored a broad swath of mauve shadow above each inquisitive brown eye, dabs of peach-colored rouge on the apples of prominent cheekbones. Full lips were glossed glassy. The room smelled of White Shoulders perfume. Two black robes hung from a rack in the corner. She wore a powder-blue suit, an off-white silk scarf draped loosely across her chest, pearl earrings and necklace. Two cocktail rings, one per index finger, but no wedding band.

"Hello, Dr. Delaware. So you're the one."

I raised an eyebrow.

"The smart one. That's what my brother-in-law calls you. He also calls you a few other things."

"The aggressive one."

"That's a fair approximation," said Nancy Maestro. "And maybe that makes you just what we need on this mess. We're talking two total loony-tunes, the one I feel sorry for is the baby."

"Rambla."

"Rambla Pacifico. Know what that is?"

"A road in Malibu."

"You know your geography, Dr. Alex Delaware."

She sat back, drew a couple of mini Hershey's bars from a jar on her desk, offered me one. When I shook my head, she said, "Fine, I'll have both." Chewing daintily, she folded the wrappers before tossing them into an unseen trash basket. "A road in Malibu where the kid was conceived. That's the only fact the two loonies can agree on."

She eyed the candy jar, pushed it away. "Rambla Pacifico. Commemorating the moment. Kid's lucky it wasn't Schmuckler's Bar and Grill."

I laughed.

Judge Nancy Maestro said, "That's the last funny thing you'll hear me say about the case. What do you know about probate court?"

"Not much."

"Most of what we do is uncontroversial. Clearing paper on wills and estates, conservatorships for obviously impaired individuals. Child guardianships arise from time to time but most are uncontested: people happy to ditch their kids, schizophrenic parents, drug-addict parents who can no longer cope, criminal parents with long prison sentences, so control obviously needs to be signed over to grandparents, aunts, uncles, whatever. See what I'm getting at?"

"It's not like family court."

"You couldn't pay me enough to work family, I'd rather do gang felonies than deal with the crap that gets slung when people decide to sever the knot."

She glanced to the side. "How do you do it?"

"It's not my entire professional life."

"You also do therapy."

No sense getting too specific. I nodded.

"Anyway," she said, "let me fill you in on *Sykes Versus Sykes*. Which is really a custody case in disguise and therefore something I wish I could send straight back to family. Better yet, to the circular file. Because it's garbage."

"Then why accept it?"

"Because the law says I have to." She rolled an inch forward. "Can you keep a little secret? Sure you can, you're a therapist. I'm behaving myself because I'm banking on a promotion. What seems like a lateral transfer to Criminal Courts Division. But it's not lateral at all because I'll be supervising huge financial trials. Major banking and investment shenanigans. Money cases are my first love, I worked them as a prosecutor, tried the opposite side of the room for a while as a white-collar defense attorney, then I got appointed to this job. With the understanding that if I rounded out my experiential base, I'd be prioritized for serious corporate felony cases. The last thing I need is controversy—appeals or God forbid reversals. So I accepted damn *Sykes Versus Sykes* and now I'd like you to help me get through it as cleanly and quickly as possible."

"I understand, Judge, but I need to work at my own pace—"

"And *I* understand *that*," she said. "I'm not trying to tell you how to do your job, I'm merely explicating my own priorities: This case *will* move. Meaning I will not grant it a nanosecond more than it deserves. In that regard, objective psychological data will help me achieve my goal. Okay?"

"Okay."

"Sure you don't want any chocolate? It helps the endorphins."

I smiled.

"All right, then," she said. "*Sykes Versus Sykes*. Or as I like to call it, the Harridan versus the Loser. Sykes One—the Harridan—is Constance. A doctor, plenty of money, lives in a seven-figure house in Westwood and can afford every upscale convenience and opportunity for a child. Unfortunately for her, she didn't birth the child in question and would now like to take a shortcut. As in swiping said child from her younger sister."

She rotated her chair to the left, ran a finger along a sculpted eyebrow. "Which brings us to Sykes Two. Cherie. Spotty employment history, a few misdemeanors in her past, lives on whatever she can ladle out of the federal alphabet soup tureen. She co-conceived the child under a Malibu sky but won't name the father. Lives in a ratty apartment in East Hollywood and my guess is little Rambla won't be going to Crossroads or Buckley or Harvard-Westlake." She frowned. "When the kid grows up, she might find herself ladling from the tureen but that's not my concern."

"Cherie's got issues but nothing in her background makes her unfit."

"If only," said Nancy Maestro. "I mean give me some serious anger management issues—better yet, violent acting out. Give me hard-core felonies, major-drug addiction, give me *anything* that puts this child in jeopardy and I've got something to work with and we can all go home feeling good."

"You think the child would be better off with Connie."

Her eyes flashed. "I didn't say that. Once you meet Connie, you'll understand why I didn't say that. I'm just looking for a clear avenue to maximize this baby's safety and security while staying within the boundaries of the law."

"The Harridan," I said. "Connie's got a difficult personality."

Instead of answering, she fooled with the candy bowl. "You have kids, Doctor?"

"No."

"Me, neither. Married young, divorced, grew up. Love my life as it is. Connie Sykes, on the other hand, strikes me as someone who put off personal attachments for her career and now she's stuck living by herself and wants to create an instant family."

"At the expense of her sister."

"Oh, yeah. There's that. The sibling relationship. Or lack of. Which didn't stop Cherie from dumping the kid on Connie while she went gallivanting with some rock band."

"For how long?"

"Eighty-eight days," she said. "Connie's lawyer claimed three months, Cherie's lawyer did a day-by-day count and disputed it. All that took pages of very tedious prose. See what I'm dealing with?"

I nodded. "Did Cherie have contact with Connie or the child during that time?"

"Connie claims she got a couple of phone calls, period. Cherie claims she tried to call Connie frequently, couldn't get through. When Cherie came for the kid, Connie didn't want to return her. There was a scene at Connie's work."

"Medical office."

"More like a lab, Connie's a pathologist. She claimed bringing the kid there was for optimal care: Rather than pawn Rambla off on some babysitter or day care, she had her staff help her 'nurture the baby on a regular basis.' In any event, the showdown was Cherie pushing her way past the staff and grabbing little Rambla."

She grimaced. "The names people stick on their prodge. Imagine if the tryst had been on Busch Drive?"

I said, "Connie got attached, Cherie broke the attachment, they're mortal enemies."

"That sums it up, Doc—Alex okay?"

"Preferable."

"You nailed it, Alex. I'm sure Dr. Connie's going through some major separation anxiety but she's wisely avoided citing that in her suit because the court cares nothing about non-parental adults' emotional issues. Instead, she's contending that Cherie dumping the kid is clear proof that A., Cherie is unfit, and B., Cherie intended for Connie to keep the baby, they had an oral contract stipulating to such and it was only 'low impulse control' that caused Cherie to renege. Connie's also tossing in the usual allegations about Cherie: dope, destructive lifestyle, deleterious environment. The drug part comes from the fact that two of Cherie's busts were for marijuana but those were fourteen and twelve years ago, respectively. Her other arrest was shoplifting when she was eighteen—nineteen years ago. Like I said, give me heroin, crack, crank, HIV-positive, dirty needles, whatever. Pot and sticky fingers is b.s."

"Cherie's alleged character issues amount to zero in the eyes of the law."

"And to tell the truth, she comes across like a much better candidate for motherhood than Connie."

"Warmer?"

"Warmer, friendlier, social. Also, I've seen her with the kid and the kid clearly feels comfortable with her. Haven't seen the kid with Connie because we just began and I'm not sure I want to put a sixteen-month-old through another separation from her mommy. What do you think?"

"You're right."

"Good. I will rely upon your expertise the next time Connie's lawyer hounds me to give her client a chance to demonstrate maternal skills."

"Persistent lawyer?"

"Pain-in-the-ass lawyer," she said. "A young one named Medea Wright, works for Stark and Stark, I'm sure you know what their approach is, talk about black-hearted litigators."

"That could be a problem," I said.

"Why?"

I told her about my experience with Sterling Stark.

"You're kidding," she said. "He was suborning perjury, the old goat. You report him?"

"No, I just shined him on."

"Too bad, you could've created serious problems for the bastard."

"Not my aim."

"Sterling Stark," she said. "Well guess what, Alex: Good news for us, he's dead. Keeled over a couple of years ago while walking to the court parking lot. Big funeral in Hancock Park, every judge got invited. I hear a few even showed up. Anyway, there's no conflict of interest and you are free to deal with Ms. Medea Wright."

"Who's Cherie's lawyer?"

"An independent practitioner out in the Valley named Myron Ballister." She frowned.

"Not a heavyweight."

"Far from it," she said. "I'm sure he's not billing at Stark and Stark levels. Is the playing field uneven? Sure, but Cherie's got the law on her side and Medea's having the time of her life filing ridiculous motions and racking up billable hours."

"Motions you can't just toss in the circular file."

She took another candy. Unwrapped slowly, ate quickly. "Can't wait to get out of this dump, go after some serious criminals. Are you on board?"

"Sure."

"Great," she said. "No kids, huh? That help you retain your objectivity?"

"No," I said. "It's just the way things are."

She studied me. "Married?"

"Almost."

"Engaged?"

"Long-term relationship."

"Take your time with commitments, huh? Why not, life's too short for stupid mistakes. Okay, I'll send you the files."

"A question," I said. "How old was Rambla when Cherie left her with Connie?"

"She had her from six to nine months."

"That period," I said, "the baby began sitting up, probably crept or crawled or even pulled off some early walking. Verbal behavior would also increase—babbling, saying Ma Ma."

"So?" she said.

"It's a fun period for a parent. Connie had a good time."

"That's relevant?"

"I'm trying to get a feel for her experience. To understand why she's pressing her claim."

"Maybe," she said. "But I can't help thinking she just hates her sister's guts."

CHAPTER

4

T wo days after my meeting with Judge Maestro, a court clerk hand-delivered a photocopied *Sykes v. Sykes* file to my home. The six-inch tome contained a mass of motions and countermotions that added nothing to the summary Maestro had given me. I went through every word because skimming is what gets you in trouble when you're on the stand.

By the time I finished, calls had come into my service from Medea Wright and Myron Ballister. Ignoring both attorneys, I emailed the judge and told her I was ready to interview the sisters, contingent upon receipt of my retainer. Estimating what my fees would total, I appended an invoice.

The amount was lower than my typical custody retainer because the case appeared simple: Cherie Sykes had full legal rights to her child unless the court could be convinced she was a clear and present danger to the baby's safety, security, and/or psychosocial development.

Maestro phoned me the following morning: "You're a businesslike fellow, Dr. Alex. Everything up front, no billing?"

"I've found that works best."

She laughed. "Protects you from irate litigants? Okay,

I'll authorize the check and then you can touch base with Wright and Ballister. They're both eager to talk to you."

"They already phoned. I didn't return their calls, don't intend to."

"Why not?"

"They're going to reiterate their paperwork and try to prejudice my judgment. Also, if I spent time with them, I'd have to charge you a helluva lot more. For pain and suffering."

"You have no affection for members of the bar?"

"It's not a matter of affection, Nancy. Life's too short."

The check from the court arrived the following week. I phoned Cherie Sykes's home number, got a recorded message backed by what sounded like slowed-down, garbled Lynyrd Skynyrd.

"*This is Ree. Leave your little message. Ex-oh-ex-oh-ex-oh.*" Giggles.

I decided to give her a day to respond before trying her sister. She phoned my service two hours later.

"Hi, this is Ree! You're the psychologist!" Thirty-seven years old but the tinkly voice and singsong delivery could've belonged to a teenager.

"I am."

"I can't wait to meet you. To finish off with all this bull—with what my sister's putting me through."

"How about tomorrow at ten?"

"You got it! See you then!"

"Do you have my address?"

Silence. "I guess I'd need that. Now you probably think I'm a flake."

I recited the information.

"Do you?" she said. "Think I'm flaky? I'm not, no matter what anyone says. It's just that I'm nervous."

"No one likes being judged."

"Yeah, but that's not the main reason, Doc. It's dealing with my sister. She's a wicked weirdo."

Not so weird you didn't leave the kid with her for eighty-eight days.

I said, "Let's talk about that tomorrow."

"You bet," she said. "We're gonna need to talk about it a *lot*!"

She was five minutes late, flashed a smile as she apologized for "getting lost in all these crazy, winding streets."

My house is a white geometric thing perched atop an unmarked road that rises above a former bridle path snaking northwest from Beverly Glen. Once you've been there, it's easy to find. Until then, good luck.

First-time visitors often comment on the light and views. Cherie "Ree" Sykes stood in my living room and looked down at the floor. I shook her hand. Hers was cold and moist and she withdrew it quickly, as if afraid secretions could betray her.

Tall and strongly built with hair dyed the color of orange soda, she looked every bit of thirty-seven, and then some. The flaming hair was long and braided. The plait reached the small of her back. Feathery bangs looped over a sun-seamed forehead. Earrings dangled from both lobes. The hard cartilage of her left ear was pierced by a black metal stud. The danglers were stainless steel; miniature chain link interspersed with miniature letters. X's on one side, O's on the other.

Tic tac court battle.

Her long, narrow face was graced by high cheekbones. Slightly down-slanted black eyes and a full wide mouth suggested a woman who'd once been beautiful. A diagonal scar across her chin, leathery skin, and deep wrinkles attested to adventurous living.

An indigo tattoo of a snake—from the triangular head, some sort of adder—slid up the left side of her neck. It was a warm day but she had on a long-sleeved, snap-button cowgirl shirt, brown with a black yoke, that looked brand-new. Tight jeans showcased ample hips and long legs that terminated in large, broad feet. Bright green patent-leather sandals with a medium heel added to the five eight genetics had granted her.

Tall, broad-shouldered, rawboned woman with a weathered look that evoked the Dust Bowl photos of Walker Evans.

Except for the body art.

I guessed the sleeves to be a cover for additional ink. If so, they failed to do the trick: Curlicues of blue and red and green cascaded across her hands and spilled over her knuckles. Her nails were blunt and unpolished but minute black chips on some of them said acetone had been applied recently.

Dust Bowl meets Goth?

A woman unfettered by expectation.

I let her stand there for a few moments because it's a good way to see how people deal with uncertainty. She turned and glanced out a side window and exposed yet more tattoo: Chinese characters bisecting the other side of her neck. For all I knew they described a take-out order of Kung Pao chicken.

She turned back. Our eyes met. I smiled. She said, "Great view."

"Thanks."

"I really *am* sorry to be late."

"It's no problem, Ree."

Some people are repelled by easy usage of nicknames; any attempt at premature familiarity. Cherie Sykes relaxed and moved forward as if to shake my hand a second time, caught herself and dropped her arms and said, "Thank you so much for doing this, Dr. Delaware. I really *need* you."

She sat on my battered leather couch and resumed wringing her hands. Red string bracelet on one wrist, studded metal cuff on the other.

I said, "This has to be tough."

"It's hell," she said. "Expensive hell. Even with Myron giving me a discount."

"Nice of him."

"I got him out of the phone book. He probably thought I was nuts, just calling him." She shifted uncomfortably. "He's young. I've never seen anyone in his office, and he uses this young chick—a kid—for a receptionist."

"You're worried about his experience."

"No, no, he's great, he really is—he listens. Like you can tell when someone gets it, you know?"

Her look said she hoped I'd qualify.

I said, "It's nice to be understood."

She sank an inch lower. "It sucks. The whole judging thing. Way I've always seen it, people who are *into* judging others suck the most."

"Like your sister."

Strong nod. "She's always been like that—looking down on me, this is just more of the same." She mouthed a silent obscenity. "She has no life so she tries to eat mine like a breakfast burrito."

She stared at me. "Where did that come from? Breakfast burrito? I never do that—use those whatyacallit—metaphors."

"You feel like Connie's trying to devour you."

"Yes! That's exactly how I feel! You're getting the picture, Dr. Delaware . . . cool name, is it Indian? I've got some Indian in me. Chippewa, or at least that was the story my mom told. You part Indian? You from the state—Delaware? That's one place I've never been to, bet it's pretty. What's it like?"

"Let's focus on you, Ree."

Color left her face. Her bronze-colored makeup was too thick to allow a uniform fade but pale blotches broke out on her cheek and her chin and above one eye. "Sorry for being nosy."

"No problem, Ree. If we stay on track we can get this done as quickly as possible."

"Yeah, of course," she said. "Quickly is good. I hope."

I started with a developmental history. She knew the basics of Rambla's physical and behavioral growth, volunteered little in the way of pride or insight. I've met mothers who seemed more in touch, others who knew less.

Her reports of the child's sleep and appetite patterns were normal. So were Rambla's milestones. That matched the brief report in the file by a pediatrician at a walk-in clinic in Silverlake. A single page using the kind of general language that suggested a fill-in-the-blanks template.

I said, "Is Dr. Keeler her regular doctor?"

More pallid spots. "Not exactly, we see whoever's in that day. It's no problem, all the docs there are good. And Rambla's been totally healthy, she has all her shots, I don't do that crazy stuff with no immunizations. No way, I keep her healthy and safe."

Reaching into her bag, she produced a photo. Probably snipped from one of those four-for-a-buck deals you get at carnival booths.

Ree Sykes holding a good-sized, chubby, dark-haired toddler. Cute kid, cute smile, a tentatively waving hand. But for down-slanted dark eyes no obvious resemblance to her mother.

I said, "Adorable."

"She's my heart." Her voice caught.

I returned the picture. "Describe a typical day for Rambla."

"Like what?"

"What does she do after she wakes up?"

"I change her and feed her, we play."

I waited.

She said, "Then . . . sometimes we just stay in the house and hang out."

"What kind of toys does she like?"

"She's not much into toys, I give her like empty cereal boxes, hair ribbons, that kind of thing—spoons, she's really into spoons, likes to bang them on stuff, it's real cute."

I smiled. "So you guys tend to hang out."

"We go out. I take her shopping. Or we just go for a walk. She's a great walker, really gets off on using her little legs, doesn't want any part of her stroller unless she gets super-tired—I got the safe one. The safe stroller. No recalls on that one. I got it secondhand but it was like in perfect condition except for a couple of little dents at the bottom." She mentioned a brand. "That's a good one, right?"

I nodded. "So you two hang out a lot together."

"Like *al*ways. It's just me and her, we're like BFFs, she's a really cool kid." Her lips quivered. "She's my heart," she repeated, patting her chest.

She flung her braid back behind her head, as if tossing a mooring rope. "I love her *so* much and she loves *me*. The minute I found out I was carrying her, I . . . took care of myself. First thing I did, I got vitamins."

"Prenatals."

She looked to the left. "To be honest—and that's the way I'm gonna be with you, period, Doc, always honest, always—at first it was just plain vitamins, I went straight to the store and bought regulars. 'Cause I didn't know anything about . . . details. But then I went to a clinic. In Malibu, I was working in Malibu back then. Doing what, you probably wanna know. Cleaning rich folks' houses, big places on the beach. Not that I was living on the beach, I was crash-renting in a mobile park, a little past Cross Creek—you familiar with Malibu?"

"I am."

"So you know what I'm talking about. It's mobile but it's nice and clean, I had a good setup." Inhaling, she sat back.

I said, "So you went to a clinic . . ."

"Oh, yeah. And they said—the clinic—I should use special prenatals so I threw out the regulars and bought prenatals. I took really good care of myself. Rambla was born big—eight pounds, eleven ounces." She laughed. The girlish giggle I'd heard on her phone message. "Getting that out of me was an experience, I tell you."

"Tough delivery?"

"It's not something I'd do for fun, Doc, but it was over and I was fine and she was beautiful. Not that I'm saying I deserve an award, you know? For taking care of myself. It's what you're *spose* to do."

"But not everyone does it."

"Exactly! It was important to me. Being pregnant, having a healthy baby. I . . . I made sure."

"Your life changed," I said.

"You heard about that."

"About what?"

"The things I did. Before. Sure, I won't hide it, like I said this is total honesty. So, yeah, exactly, I made changes. Because she's my heart and she's always been my heart and I really don't see why I have to prove it to some judge—what's she like? The judge."

"She seems reasonable."

"Oh, man, I sure hope so—it's so weird, someone I don't know judging me." Laughter. "Guess that's why they call her a judge. You'd never catch me doing that. For a job."

Her eyes moistened. I handed her a tissue. "It's really hard, Dr. Delaware. I never did anything to start this. It's all *her*."

"Your sister."

"Bitch," she growled. "And I'm not going to say pardon my French because that's how I righteously feel, she's a bitch, always has been, jealous of everyone and everything. Can't get a man of her own because she's too damn busy making money and bossing everyone around so now she wants what's mine!"

"You two never got along."

"Never—no, that's not true, sometimes when we were kids we were okay with each other. I mean it's not like we were kissy-kiss or tight. But we let each other be. Never hit each other. Never really fought."

"Constance is seven years older."

"How'd you—oh, yeah, the files. That's right, seven, almost eight so it's not like we were hanging out. There's our brother in between, even though he was a boy I hung out more with him. Not like Connie, she never hung around with anyone."

"A loner."

"Exactly! You hit it on the nose, Dr. Delaware, she's a loner, doesn't get people, doesn't even like people, she's totally more into numbers. Math, science, that kind of thing, she always had her head in the books when Daddy would let her."

"Daddy didn't like books?"

"Daddy didn't like anything when he drank. One beer, he's smiling, two, he's still smiling. Three, he gets quiet. By the time six, seven, eight rolls around he's all red in the face and his shoulders bunch up and you'd better not be in his pathway or you're gonna get rolled over on. Like one of those things they use to flatten the tar when they build roads."

"Steamroller."

"Steamroller, exactly. Not hitting or anything but still looking scary and yelling and breaking stuff. Daddy gets to rolling, you stay out of his way. So, yeah, if Connie was concentrating on a library book and he happened to roll into our room and she was at the desk and he fixed it upon himself to not like that, that book would turn into confetti. And what makes it crazier is he liked to read."

"Sounds frightening."

"It was," she agreed. "It was real frightening but you learn to avoid it, you know?"

"Where was your mother when all this was happening?"

"Quiet drunk. She'd go under quicker than Daddy and just fall asleep."

"You and Connie had a challenging childhood."

"Me and Connie and Connor—he was in between us, Connor learned to be a real good runner because Daddy would yell at him the most. He ran in high school and college. Long distance, he won awards, could go for miles."

"Where does Connor live?"

"Up north," she said. "He's got a nice family."

"When your parents weren't drunk, what were they like?"

"Working," she said. "Mommy secretaried at a trucking company and Daddy drove one of their semis."

"So he was gone a lot."

"Thank God."

"Did he treat you and Connie differently?"

"Hmm . . . I'd have to say yes. Her, there'd be books turned into confetti. Me—truthfully I wasn't one for books, reading wasn't my favorite thing, friends were—having a social life. So there was no confetti."

"Did he take out his anger differently with you?"

"Not really. Truthfully, he didn't do much to me because I'd have to say he liked me the best. Because he'd tell me that. When he was sober. 'Ree, you're the pretty one, you make sure you stay pretty so you can get married. Connie, she's just gonna bury her nose in a book and make like she's smarter than everyone, no man will want that.'"

"So Connie had it the roughest."

"If she'd been friendlier, it could've been better for her."

"Friendlier to your father?"

"To him, to everyone—Dr. Delaware, I have to tell you: That girl was weaned on a sour pickle—that's what Mommy always said. Never smiled, always off to herself, pretending to ignore you when you said something. It's like she thought she was better than everyone else."

"Nose in a book."

"In the library more than she was at home. That meant I had to do extra chores. If Daddy and Mommy were sober, they'd probably gone after her to make her do her chores."

"They were drunk so Connie got to do what she wanted."

"Exactly."

"Did you, Ree?"

"Did I what?"

"Get to do what you wanted?"

"After I left home I sure did."

"When was that?"

Black eyes shifted to the floor. "A long time ago."

"How long ago?"

"I was young, I admit it."

I waited.

She said, "Fifteen."

"You ran away."

"Nope, I just walked out the door and no one tried to stop me." Sudden smile, Death Valley–dry. "They never even reported me missing."

"How'd that make you feel?"

"Did it insult me?" she said. "Maybe if I cared it would've. I knew if they found me it would just be more of the same."

"Avoiding your father when he was drunk."

"That, too," she said. "But I'm talking about how boring it was. Nothing ever happened. I got to wondering if that was what life was gonna be like if I stayed there."

"Out on your own, you had adventures."

She studied me. "I had experiences. You gonna hold that against me?"

"Why would I?"

"Alternative lifestyle, Doctor. That's what her bitch lawyer called it. Like I'm some kind of freak. I just lived my life the way I wanted and didn't hurt no one. So don't judge me for any of that, okay? Please. And how about we talk about right now and not get into the past? 'Cause the past doesn't exist anymore, right?"

"I do need to ask about a few things that happened in the past."

"Like what?"

"Have you and your sister ever had any financial connections?"

"What kind of connections?"

"Has she made substantial loans to you?"

"Because she's rich and I'm not?"

"Because obligations can create issues."

"Well, they're not issues for me. I'm happy with my life, if I wanted to be rich I'd go be rich. I figured it was better to bring joy and love into my life. *She* thought different and look where she is now."

"Alone."

"Alone and all dried up and mean as a wolverine. Not that it bothers her, Doc. She *really* doesn't like people. That's why she became a microscope doctor. So she can sit in her lab and not talk to patients. It was always like that with her. Study study study, no friends, no parties, no fun. You daren't go into her room when the big genius had her nose in the books."

"So no financial entanglements between you."

She fidgeted. "I loaned from her a few times. Small stuff. But I always paid it back. Now look how she's paying *me* back!"

"What do you think motivated her to bring the suit?"

"Hatred," she said. "Pure and evil hatred. I was always the pretty one, I had friends. There was always that hatred."

"Why do you think she chose now to take you to court?"

"Ask *her*."

"The suit was filed two months after you retrieved Rambla from her care. It takes time to hire a lawyer and start building a case, so it sounds like she started the process soon after."

"So?"

"Maybe she started to think of herself as Rambla's mom."

"*Fuck* her and fuck what she *thought*."

I said nothing.

Cherie Sykes yanked her braid hard. "Sorry. It just makes me so . . . she's hurting me, she's really chewing me up inside. It's like she's trying to kill me." Another pat of her breast. "Whatever—yeah, she probably was plotting all along but not because she cared about Rambla, Doc. All she thinks about is herself, she wanted to carve out my heart and watch me bleed but I went and took my heart back and she couldn't stand it and she figured she could tell me what to do and I'd just do whatever because when we were kids it was sometimes like that."

"Connie called the shots."

"She sure as hell tried. And when I was little, I bought into it. Then I got smart." She pushed her head forward. "To tell the truth, one of the reasons I left was to get away from her."

"From being dominated."

"Yeah, and now she figures she can use her money to . . . terrorize me. Her and that rich-bitch Beverly Hills lawyer." She snapped her fingers. "Little Ree didn't play the sucker, little Ree went and got her own legal representation so forget *that*—do you have something to drink? All this talking's taken the spit out of my mouth."

I fetched her water.

"Thanks, Doc. Anything else you need from me?"

"Let's talk about the three months Connie took care of Rambla."

Her jaw jutted. "She keeps saying three months. It was eighty-eight days."

"Fair enough, Ree. Tell me how it came to be."

"I was afraid you'd get to that. Why's it important?"

"Connie's citing it as evidence you wanted her to have guardianship."

She put the cup down hard enough to resonate. "That's fucking bullshit!"

"How'd the arrangement come about?"

"There was no arrangement," she said. "No arrangement at all. I was playing with Rambla and out of the clear blue Connie came over. She was nice—a different Connie. She brought me stuff for Rambla. Baby clothes, diapers—like I didn't have the brains to buy diapers. The ones she brought were the wrong brand and wrong size, but no matter, I said thank you because that's the kind of person I am, I always see the best in everyone. And truthfully, Doctor, I was happy with my life, no reason to be unfriendly."

"Connie was being nice."

"Like for once she cared about someone else, not just herself. She even said I was doing a good job—which is something that bitch lawyer of hers denies. So when she asked to hold the baby, I said sure. Even though she didn't know how to do it right and Rambla started fussing and I had to teach her to unstiffen her arms so Rambla would be mellow."

Black eyes turned to chunks of obsidian. "Big mistake. Teaching her anything. She was already scheming."

"To take the baby."

"What else? She never came over, now she was coming over?"

"How often did she visit?"

"I dunno, like . . . once a week? Whatever. It's not like she was babysitting or really helping. That whole time I never went out even one night, I was taking my obligation seriously. And yeah, Connie tried giving me money."

I said, "Tried? You didn't accept."

"I accepted, why wouldn't I accept? Not loans, gifts. She volunteered, I never asked. No way, not after I already loaned from her and paid it back, I didn't want any . . . what you called it, entanglements. But if she was insisting to give me something and she's got more than she needs and it can help Rambla, why not?"

"So for a while, you and Connie developed a better relationship."

"It was phony, Doctor. Totally phony. I'm a truster, that's part of my problem, I have faith in people more than I should. So when the chance came to travel with L.M.—that's a band, some friends I know, Connie was like, 'Sure, go, have fun.'"

"L.M."

"Stands for Lonesome Moan. They do Lynyrd Skynyrd covers, Sir Douglas, Stevie Ray, original material. I known 'em for a long time, sometimes I do some singing for 'em, help out with percussion, that kind of thing. Local clubs, no farther than Reno. But this time they got offered a tour farther. Two weeks, Arizona and New Mexico, doing lounge shows at Indian casinos. They asked me to come along, do some roadying, do some singing. I was like, Don't think so guys, I'm a mom, now. But Connie was like, 'Go, Ree, it's an opportunity, take a break, no problem, I'll take care of her.' I taught her to be okay with Rambla and by then Rambla didn't mind being with her but even so I'm 'Nah, I don't think so.'"

She crossed her legs, lifted the cup of water, drank it empty. "Connie kept working me, Doc. She's like, 'Don't worry.' And then she . . . I'll be totally honest, okay? She gave me some money. For the road. I figured she was being nice, knew how hard I was working with Rambla, wanted me to catch a break. Now I see what she was up to. Bribing me. Moving me out of the way so she could take over."

"For two weeks."

More of that splotchy pallor. "It stretched a bit. The shows were good, L.M. kept getting more bookings, the bus kept going. But I called in regularly.

Connie almost always didn't answer. The few times she did she always said Rambla was sleeping. So I figured she was fine. So yeah, I did another week. Then another . . ."

Two weeks stretching to eighty-eight days. I tried to keep my face neutral but maybe I failed because she sighed and threw up her hands and tears flowed down her cheeks. "I screwed up bad, didn't I, Doc? Just kept going on that bus and let myself be a little happy."

I said, "What brought you home?"

She dabbed with the tissue. "I should make myself look good by telling you it was Rambla brought me back, just her, nothing else. Myron told me I should say that, he threw words at me that I should memorize."

"What kind of words."

"Separation anxiety, maternal urges. And, sure, that was part of it, I missed her like crazy. *That's* why I kept calling in but with Connie telling me don't worry, keep having fun, it'll be a missed opportunity, you may never get another, she's fine, she loves you as much as ever, she's perfectly fine, I figured . . ."

"There was another reason you returned."

Three slow nods.

I waited.

She said, "I'm telling you the God's truth so you'll see I'm an honest person. So you'll trust everything else I say."

"Okay."

"The reason, Dr. Delaware, is no more gigs for L.M."

"The tour ended."

"And we all came home."

I asked Ree Sykes a few more questions about Rambla's speech, sleep patterns, appetite, fine and gross motor skills. Everything within normal limits.

"She's a wonderful baby."

"Look forward to meeting her."

"You need to meet her?"

"I do."

"Why?"

"Making recommendations without seeing her isn't a good idea."

"She doesn't like being by herself."

"You'll be with her, Ree."

She flashed a strange smile: abrupt, knowing. Hostile. "That's really the reason, getting to know her?"

"It is."

"Okay."

"You think it might be something else?"

"No, no, you're the doctor."

She slid a hand under one buttock. Sat on her fingers as if afraid what they might do if liberated.

I said nothing.

"Fine, I'll bring her in whenever you say."

"Actually, I'll come to your home."

She looked away.

"Is that a problem, Ree?"

"No—okay, okay, I'll be honest. I was thinking maybe you want to see me with Rambla so you can judge if I'm a good mother."

"I'm beginning this assuming you're a good mother, Ree."

"Why would you assume?"

"Because so far I haven't heard anything to the contrary."

"Well you just wait. When *she* comes in you'll hear all sorts of contrary."

"I'm sure I will, Ree."

"You believe me? About her being crazy and a liar?"

"Let's deal with one thing at a time, Ree." I made the appointment.

She said, "Do I need to buy extra toys?"

"Whatever you have is fine."

She flinched. "Well, I guess I'll have to depend on you being smart. No offense. I mean I know you're smart, you're a doctor. You have to be smart to be working for the judge. I just need to have faith."

Out came her hand. She studied it briefly, formed a fist that she rested on her knee. Her neck muscles were as tight as bridge cables. The down-slanted eyes had narrowed. "I guess it can only help. Seeing me with Rambla. How much she loves me—will she have to come in here with Connie?"

"Probably not."

"Probably?"

"Most likely not."

"I don't want her alone with Connie. The last time that happened, Connie tried to take her from me."

"The day you came to get Rambla from Connie's office."

Three hard nods. "Connie got crazy, came at me

like she was going to hit me, like . . . clawing. Like she was gonna get Rambla no matter what. Luckily Winky was there—he's a friend—and I handed Rambla to him and held up my fists."

She demonstrated, face flushed, breathing rapid. "I said you just try it, this isn't like when we were kids, I'll beat your ass. That freaked her out, she didn't know what to say, meanwhile Winky's putting Rambla in the car—in the car seat—and starting up the engine and I make a move on Connie and she steps back and that's when I jump in, myself, and off we go."

"What an ordeal."

"Just to get my own baby, yeah, but I figured that was it. Finito. Couple months later, some guy pretending to be a meter reader comes to the door and serves me with papers—does that tell you what I'm dealing with? My lying rich-bitch lying sister and her lying rich-bitch Beverly Hills looow-yer. I know you're gonna help me, Doctor—so when's Connie coming in to see you?"

"Soon enough."

"You won't tell me?"

"Is there a reason for you to know, Ree?"

"No, guess not," she said. "Actually, yes. There's a reason. So I can know what's going on so I don't have to wake up in the middle of the night with my heart going boomp boomp and I'm thinking terrible things and I can't go back to sleep."

"The uncertainty's tough."

"That's the worst. Almost worse than . . ." She shook her head. Another sudden smile. Soft—seductive. "You could fix all that, Doctor. A word from you and there's a happy ending."

I stood.

"I understand," she said. "You can't tell me. But I'm hoping. What's she like? The judge."

Same question I'd answered before. "She seems like a nice person."

"Sure as hell hope so—'cause you're right, Doc, you're a hundred percent right, it's the uncertainty that's the hell. Not worse than losing, though. And I'm *not* gonna lose. Myron told me in the eyes of the law I've got the winning side."

She studied me for confirmation.

I said, "So next Thursday. Looking forward to meeting Rambla."

She sprang up. "Yeah, sure, I gotta go home. Rambla needs me."

"Who's taking care of her?"

"My friend Winky. Not that he's got to do anything, I put Rambla down for a nap. But she'll be getting up soon, don't want my baby waking up and not seeing her mama. She needs to see me all the time, otherwise she gets to crying."

She ran from the office, was out of the house before I reached the front door.

The following day, I called Connie Sykes's office to set up an appointment.

The receptionist said, "Dr. Connie's been waiting for you. I'll read you her openings."

I said, "How about we start with my openings."

"Oh . . . well, she's a really busy person."

"No doubt." I gave her two options. She said, "Well, I'm not sure about those."

"That's what I've got."

"Well, that could be a problem."

"Call me back and let me know which works better."

"Hold on—one second please. *Doctor.*"

Forty seconds of dead air was followed by the same

voice, softer, tighter. "Dr. Connie says the sooner the better, she'll take that one tomorrow."

"See her then."

"Have a nice day, sir." The ice in her voice shoved that way past insincerity.

Next morning, my bell rang ten minutes early.

I opened the door on two women. A medium-sized, fortyish, square-faced blonde with her hair done up in waves that recalled decades past had to be Dr. Connie. Similar facial structure to her sister but none of the hard-living veneer. She wore gold-rimmed eyeglasses, wine-colored pants and jacket and matching suede loafers, dangled a calfskin briefcase from one unadorned hand.

The right loafer tapped the landing as the woman standing slightly in front of her moved closer to me.

She was younger, late twenties to early thirties. Sixty-three inches of silky-haired brunette with a tiny waist, an assertive bust, and muscular legs, all of that showcased by a sleeveless, figure-hugging white knit mini-dress and aqua snakeskin stiletto sandals. A strand of massive South Sea pearls circled a smooth neck. The dark hair was long and meticulously cut. Bare arms showcased a mini-collection of bangles. Her watch was a diamond-studded ladies' Patek. The teeth in her smile outshone her bling.

Two cars were parked near Robin's truck: cream-colored Lexus sedan, black Mercedes convertible.

I said, "Dr. Sykes?"

The young brunette said, "As the primary component of Dr. Sykes's legal entity, I'm part of this appointment." Thrusting her card at me. Medea L. Wright, J.D.

"The appointment's for her alone, Ms. Wright."

Wright's lovely blue eyes wavered then hardened—

annealed by challenge. "Well, I'm sorry, but that's the way it has to be, Doctor. This is a legal proceeding and I'm the legal professional."

I looked past her, to her client. Connie Sykes had turned to study the pines, sycamores, and coast redwoods that ring my driveway.

"Sorry, Counselor."

Medea Wright said, "This is unacceptable."

I said, "Dr. Sykes, you can come in, if you'd like. If not, our time today is over and I'll talk to the judge about alternatives."

Connie Sykes frowned but kept her eyes on the trees.

Medea Wright stepped even nearer, put herself squarely in my personal space. A little music and we could tango. The aroma of scented powder wafted from her, mixed with grassy perfume. Then a bitter overlay. Adrenaline sweat.

She shook her head. "Obviously, I need to orient you, Dr. Delaware."

"About what?"

"The legal system. Beginning with objectivity and parity."

"Parity with whom?"

The question cheered her. I'd allowed her to lead.

"You've spoken to Mr. Ballister, hence you're obligated to do the same for me."

"I've never exchanged a word with Mr. Ballister."

"He says different."

"Then he's lying."

"Re-ally." She chuckled.

I looked at my watch.

Maybe the movement was what caused Connie Sykes to turn. She faced me. Her eyes were flat, brown, bored. "Medea? Do you think you should be alienating him so early in the game?"

"Dr. Delaware is being presented to us as an objective professional. Should the facts turn out not to—"

"Whatever, Medea. I'm ready to get up and at it, put an end to this travesty."

"Connie—"

"Whatever legal nonsense you're worried about, I'll bear full responsibility. I'm busier than both of you, let's get going."

Wright flinched. "Doctor, do I understand that you're asserting you've had no contact whatsoever with Myron Ballister? Are you claiming that to be true telephonically as well as in person?"

My turn to smile. "I already answered that question."

Connie Sykes stepped forward, swinging her briefcase. Continuing past Wright, she sidled by me, entered the house.

No scent at all from her.

But Wright's vapors were now favoring adrenaline. Her body had turned rigid. As if to reverse that, she cocked a hip, laid two manicured fingers atop my wrist. Lots of body heat. "I regret, Doctor, if anything I've said can be construed as combative. If Ballister really hasn't attempted to poison the well, then there's no reason to . . ."

She waited.

Connie Sykes stood in the middle of my living room, her back to me.

I said, "You're welcome to wait in here, Counselor, but Dr. Sykes and I will be going to my office."

"No, I'll go, I've got more things to do than you can imagine. You're on your own, Connie. Have a nice day, Dr. Delaware."

Second time in twenty-four hours someone who didn't mean it had wished me well. It was starting to sound like a hex.

CHAPTER

6

I led Connie Sykes toward my office. She took long strides, surging past me and continuing beyond the destination.

As I stopped to open the door, she kept going like a dieseling engine, finally realized she'd overstepped and put the brakes on. Not a hint of embarrassment as she retraced.

I held the door for her. She entered as if she knew the place, chose the precise spot on the leather couch occupied by her sister, and pressed her knees together.

No facial movement, no giveaway tics, the brown eyes remained as still as taxidermy. But as I delayed by shuffling papers, she began wringing her hands just as Ree had. Reached for her hair like Ree. No braid to play with; an arched thumb stroked the bottom of a particularly dramatic wave.

"That," she said, "was unfortunate. The little contretemps with Medea. I'd like to believe you won't hold her assertiveness against me."

"No problem."

"No problem for you, but for me, it could be a big problem if she mucks things up. I've already paid her a fortune and she refuses to guarantee anything close to results. Some racket, this law business, no? We caregivers operate on a higher level."

If that was a play for common ground it wasn't backed up by anything close to warmth. She had an odd mechanical way of phrasing her words. Clipped, precise, uniform spacing between words that evoked digital processing.

When I didn't comment, she tried something that might have ended up as a smile if her lips had gone along with the plan. "Think I should fire her?"

"Not my place to say one way or the other."

"Of course not," she said. "You're just Solomon with a Ph.D., trying to figure out how to divide the baby with a minimum of bloodshed."

I said, "Tell me why you brought the lawsuit, Dr. Sykes."

"Why?" As if the question was absurd. "Because I had to. In good faith."

"Faith in what?"

"Faith in optimal child rearing. Dedication to the child. You've met my sister."

I said nothing.

"Soul of discretion, and all that, eh?" Connie Sykes unclasped her briefcase but left it on the floor. "You ask the questions, I give the answers. Fine. But there's no reason to be cryptic. I know that you've met my sister because Medea told me you have. Then again, she was certain you'd talked to that courtroom hack, Ballister. But no matter, even if you haven't met my sister, you've surely read some of the material we've sent you. So you understand what I'm dealing with."

"Which is . . ."

"Ah, there it is," she said, "the classic psychiatric riposte, parrying questions with questions. I learned all about that when I rotated through psychiatry in med school. What was it called—patient-directed dialogue?" She crossed her legs. "Not my cup of tea, psychiatry. Too ambiguous. More shamanism than science. I've heard that psychologists operate at a more data-based level."

I said, "What aspect of your sister are you dealing with?"

"Total irrationality. Part and parcel of her psycho-emotional makeup, I'll leave the specific diagnoses up to you. What may *not* be evident to you, yet, is that she's also what used to be called of low moral character. Back when morality counted and every bad act didn't elicit a disease label. Shall I be specific? She has little or no impulse control. Coupled with a relatively low IQ, the result has not been salutary. In sum, she's incapable of supporting herself financially and psychologically, let alone of raising a child."

She removed her glasses, twiddled them by one sidepiece. "Then, there's the coup de grâce: years of chronic drug addiction and concomitant criminal history."

"What drug is she addicted to?"

"I don't know what currently amuses her. But I can tell you that over the years she's admitted to sampling opiates, cocaine, amphetamines, hallucinogens, you name it. Plus far too much alcohol. Of course she denies all that, now." She twirled a curl. "If I were you, I'd call for a hair follicle analysis. Clear up that nonsense, once and for all."

I said, "Does she have any criminal convictions beyond three misdemeanors?"

"Ah," she said. "So you know about those. Aren't three misdemeanors sufficient evidence of lack of fitness, nowadays? Or have standards tumbled that low? As an expert, I'm sure you're aware that for every conviction there are half a dozen offenses never accounted for. Per the FBI."

"You've been doing your research."

"Am I not obligated to do just that? In the best interests of the child?"

Before I could answer, she said, "Now I'd like to educate you in greater detail regarding my sister's psychiatric profile."

My sister. The child.

In her world, names were a nuisance.

At the onset of every evaluation, I work at keeping an open mind, but impressions form and more often than not they're confirmed by the facts. After a few moments with Connie Sykes, observing the flatness in her eyes, hearing the machine-like diction, I couldn't help conjuring a pathologist perched on a lab stool, observing a specimen on a slide.

I said, "Go on."

"First off, she's an unhealthily dependent individual. And she directs those immature impulses at a particularly unsuitable peer group."

"Bad friends," I said.

"She consorts with low-life degenerates whose poor character matches her own. Specifically, we need to be careful about two individuals. Either one of whom could very well be the child's father."

Withdrawing a manila file from the briefcase, she placed it on her lap.

"We begin with a disreputable man named William J. Melandrano. Aka 'Winky.' Origin of that nickname is still unknown to me but given this person's obvious attention deficit disorder, I have my theories. Sample two is one Bernard V. Chamberlain. Aka 'Boris.'"

She let out a dry laugh.

I said, "You believe one of them is Rambla's father."

"Neither will come forward and attest to such, nor will my sister shed light on the matter, but she's been intimate with both of them over the years. During the same time period, which should tell you something."

"You know this because—"

"I've seen them with her. The way they touched her. My sister *loves* attention." She shuddered.

"Ree won't confirm paternity."

"Yet another indication of poor character," she said. "Isn't knowledge of paternity any child's birth-right? A vital component of a child's proper development?"

"Both these men are bad influences but Rambla needs to know which one's her father."

"If for no other reason than to be wary."

"How did you meet Melandrano and Chamberlain?"

"My sister introduced me to them. Prevailed upon me to hear them." She huffed. "They're alleged musicians. An alleged band called—are you ready for this? 'Lonesome Moan.' The only moaning in question is that which arises upon being assaulted by the noise they create."

"Not virtuosos."

"Good grief," she said, covering her ears. "The entire situation—my sister's milieu—is repellent. For her whole life she's made decisions that have left her bereft of the normal material and emotional nutrients enjoyed by decent individuals. Now she's made the supreme error of delivering a child out of wedlock. I cannot, in good conscience, visit her sins upon her offspring."

"You believe she puts Rambla in danger."

Giving her a chance to use the toddler's name.

"I don't believe it, I know it. Because unlike you and the judge and the attorneys—all of whom are intelligent enough and, I hope, well intentioned—I'm the only one able to draw upon a comprehensive data bank that offers the complete picture."

Her foot nudged the briefcase.

I said, "All those years with your sister."

"Must you do that?" she said. "Paraphrase everything I say? This isn't psychotherapy, it's fact finding."

I said, "What's in the briefcase?"

"The chronicle of a lifetime spent with my sister. May I summarize?"

"Please do."

"I was close to eight when she was born. Soon it became apparent that she wasn't up to Connor and myself intellectually."

"Not as smart as her sibs."

"No doubt you think my remark was unkind. But the facts back it up. I was a straight-A student, graduated as high school salutatorian, and the only reason they didn't make me valedictorian was I hadn't accumulated enough 'social points.' Whatever that means. I attended Occidental College on a full scholarship, graduated with a four point oh, Phi Beta Kappa, summa cum laude, departmental honors in chemistry, advanced to medical school at UC San Francisco, where I also served my internship and my residency in pathology."

"You were always academically gifted."

"Quite. After residency I enjoyed a stint at Harbor General Hospital, then I obtained an executive position with a private lab. Ten years ago, I began my own lab and experienced immediate and consistent success. Currently, I specialize in the analysis of esoteric tropical diseases as well as immune disorders, including but not limited to HIV. My referrals emanate from private physicians and institutions as well as several governmental agencies secure in the knowledge of my total discretion. Since completing my residency, I've earned six figures consistently, have invested wisely, and I enjoy a comfortable lifestyle, including ownership of my own thirty-five-hundred-square-foot house in Westwood. I am able to provide anything a child could possibly desire. A fact my sister was well aware of when she abdicated the care of her child to me for three months while she went gallivanting across the country with Melandrano and Chamberlain and engaged in who-knows-what. It was only after she returned and apparently experienced some feeble variant of maternal *pangs* that she changed her mind and began making a fuss."

She put her glasses back on, sat back.

Long speech and an obvious invitation for me to ask more about the details of the "fuss."

I said, "Tell me about your brother."

"Connor was also an excellent student. Not at my level, but solid A's and B's. He attended Cal State Northridge, obtained a degree in accounting. With honors ... I'm not certain if it was magna or just cum, but definitely honors, I distinctly remember the asterisk next to his name in his graduation program—a ceremony that my sister did not attend, because, apparently, she had better things to do. More like worse things ... in any event, Connor was always a *solid* boy."

"He's an accountant?"

"Much better, Doctor. He's an executive at a firm up in Palo Alto. Very successful. So you see."

"You and Connor," I said. "Then there's Ree."

"She was never close to our level and I'm certain the discrepancy affected her. No doubt that's why she ran away. When she was fifteen. Did she mention that?"

"What led her to run away?"

"You'd have to ask her." Sly smile. "If you already haven't. No, won't fall into that trap, Doctor. Giving you unsubstantiated information—innuendo, rumor. I want you to be certain that when I say something it's based on fact. Why did she run away? Obviously, she was unhappy."

"With family life."

"We had a fine family. If my sister was a poor fit, all the pity for her. But a child shouldn't be made to suffer."

"Tell me about your parents."

"Fine people. Working people."

"What kind of work?"

"Father was a teamster, Mother did bookkeeping."

"You all got along pretty well."

Her eyes narrowed. "You've heard different?"

"Tell me how you remember family life."

Her arms clamped across her chest. One foot pushed the briefcase farther to the side. She said, "Fine, but that's no excuse for *her* behavior. There were three of us, only one turned out immoral."

"What's no excuse?"

"Drinking. They both drank. Not during the day, it never impeded their work, they supported us in fine form during our entire childhoods. We had food on the table, clean clothes, the home was beautifully kept. Mother was a first-rate homemaker. Back when that meant something."

"They drank recreationally."

"They drank to wind down after long, grueling workdays. Yes, it was excessive. No, it doesn't excuse *her* lifestyle choices. I grew up in the same environment and I am a teetotaler. Furthermore, I've never seen Connor indulge in more than a single beer, cocktail, or glass of wine. He says so, explicitly, when waiters attempt to peddle a refill. 'I'm a one-drink guy.' So don't let her avoid responsibility by blaming Mother and Father."

"Did your parents' behavior change when they drank?"

"Not really," she said.

I said nothing.

"I'm telling you, there were no drastic changes, Doctor. Not in a way one would consider unexpected."

"The change was predictable."

"She went to sleep. He did, as well." Tug on a hair wave. "Except for those very few times when his mood got the best of him. In any event, that's not relevant to the current issue: my sister's fitness. Or lack thereof."

I pictured her, sitting at her desk, trying to study. Wondering if tonight books would get turned into confetti.

I'd lived through worse, could well understand wanting to block that out. If she hadn't decided to wrest her sister's child away, she'd never have been forced to confront the past.

But . . .

I said, "Your father's moods changed when he drank."

"Wouldn't anybody's?" she said. "All right, he could get a bit . . . surly. But never violent. No matter what you've heard."

"No child abuse."

"Not one instance. Did *she* claim that?"

"Still," I said, "that kind of unpredictability can be frightening to a child."

"It wasn't unpredictable, Doctor. One knew that when he drank there was a distinct possibility of some sort of mood upset."

Now her lips did cooperate and she flashed me a wide, engaging smile.

"In fact," she said, "the entire issue made me curious. The precise rate of mood upsets. I decided to approach the question scientifically. Began keeping records and attained a result. Thirty-two point five percent of the time he'd grow surly."

"About a third of the time."

"Not about, Doctor. Precisely thirty-two point five. My data collection was meticulous. I went over it, trying to see if I could find a pattern. Day of the week, time of day, any other variable. I came up with nothing and I believe it was at that point that I decided to devote myself to science on a cellular level rather than deal with anything as imprecise as human behavior. So you see, Father did me a favor. By directing me to what has turned out to be a rewarding career path, he proved extremely helpful."

"Lemons into lemonade."

"Now contrast that, Doctor, with *her*. Blaming everyone but herself for her deficiencies. It's fortunate that we're talking about this because it allows you to delineate the difference between myself and my sister: I face reality, she escapes. Well, this is one time she's not going to find that quite so easy, eh? Now, what else can I help clarify?"

"Nothing," I said.

She flinched. Smiled. "I've given you more facts than you expected? Well, that's fine. And here's a written record of all the background material I've just presented verbally, so you can take your time, study carefully, really educate yourself."

A black-bound folder emerged from the briefcase. She placed it next to my appointment book, squaring the volume's edges with those of the desk. "This has been a very *profitable* hour. Good day."

Next step: a home visit to Cherie Sykes and her daughter.

She lived in a studio apartment near Western and Hollywood, a five-hundred-square-foot share of a not-so-great ten-unit building in a marginal neighborhood.

She was ready at the door, beckoning me inside with a flourish. The air smelled of Lysol and I assumed she'd prepped for the appointment.

Not much to tidy. A foldout bed was covered by a thin white spread and dressed up by a couple of batik pillows that looked brand-new. Nearby stood a crib. A well-worn tweed love seat crowded the rest of the tiny room. A two-seater folding table straddled the kitchenette and the front room. Propped up against a space-saver fridge was a vacuum cleaner. In front of the sink was a plastic high chair.

Much of the floor was taken up by a neat stack of toys. A closet door left open revealed stacks of disposable diapers, jars of baby food and "beginner" toddler victuals, boxes of graham crackers and organic "healthy apple juice," a collapsible stroller.

"Kid Central," said Ree Sykes. The tremor in her

voice would've done a Hammond organ proud. The drowsy child in her arms stirred.

I said, "Is she about to nap or just waking up?"

"Waking," she said. "She does it slowly, never cries. Sometimes I wake up and she's standing in her crib, just looking at me. I hold her for a while, let her blossom like a flower."

She stroked dark, wavy hair. What I could see of Rambla Pacifico Sykes's face was plump-cheeked, slumber-pink, dewy with sweat. She had on pink pajamas patterned with cats, polka-dot hats, and beach balls. The way she molded to her mother's chest compressed her face, turning full lips into rosebuds.

I made mental notes. Pretty child. Average size. Well nourished. Relaxed.

Her tiny chest heaved as she sighed. One hand touched Ree Sykes's chin. Ree kissed her fingers. Rambla's eyes remained closed.

Ree said, "*This* is my heart."

I sat on the tweed love seat and Ree perched near the edge of the foldout bed, Rambla still molded to her. The child's breath quickened, then slowed, as she sank into deeper sleep.

"Guess she's still tired," said Ree. "She's a great sleeper, made it through the night at two months."

"That's great. Any change when you picked her up from Connie?"

"You mean did she get worse being with Connie? I'd like to say yeah, but honestly no, she was fine. She *was* real happy to see me, she like *jumped* into my arms. Which I wasn't sure would happen, you know like maybe she forgot me? But she didn't."

"She reconnected instantly."

"Yup." Her eyes shifted to the ceiling. "That's not exactly true. She was quieter than usual. I'd try to kiss her and she'd turn her head. But that didn't last long, maybe half a day and then she was herself."

Medea Wright would probably use that to show Connie Sykes had done a great job of interim parenting. If Myron Ballister was smart, he'd skew it as evidence of the durable attachment between Ree and her child.

I'd note the facts and save interpretation for later.

Ree bit her lip. "I have to say this, Doctor. So you won't think I'm crazy or cruel: I screwed up, okay? By leaving in the first place. By staying away that long. Connie kept telling me everything was fine, it was the first time we—me and Connie—ever did anything together, you know? I liked that. Not just was Rambla taken care of but me and Connie, we . . . whatever."

"You felt Rambla had brought you and Connie closer."

"I could hope. Because we never . . . she always made me feel stupid. I know she's the smart one, but . . . I guess I coulda studied harder but it didn't come easily. Reading, numbers. Everything. It was hard. I did my best but it was hard. Still, she didn't have to make me feel stupid."

Her eyes grew moist. She began rocking Rambla. A small hand grasped the braid and squeezed. "She loves it. My hair. Kind of a security thing, don't you think?"

"I do."

"Anyway . . ."

"You were hoping Connie and you could be closer."

"Because she was acting different. I know now it was phony but how could I tell at the time? I'm a trusting person."

"Different, how?"

"Paying attention to me, Dr. Delaware. Talking to

me like I was a grown-up—like normal sisters. So when she offered to care for Rambla and then she'd always tell me when I called that Rambla was doing great, I deserved a vacation, just go have a good time—it was like she approved of me. For the first time in my life."

"You were encouraged."

"I'm not saying that excuses it. Staying away from my baby-love so long. And yeah, I wasn't being totally honest with you, Rambla didn't jump into my arms, at first she looked scared and my heart just dropped to my feet, like *Girl, you really screwed up, this time. One thing in your life that you love and now you screwed it up.* More like she accepted me but she was quiet. But it didn't take long and she was like melting against me just like she's doing now."

Her eyes lowered to her shoulder. "Touching my braid just like she's doing now. It's like the flame needed to be turned on but once it was, it just kept burning."

She kissed a plump cheek. "I just love you, I love love love you."

Rambla stirred. Opened her eyes. Smiled lazily at her mother.

Spotting me, she gripped Ree tighter. Began whimpering.

Appropriate attachment. Expected separation anxiety for the age.

Ree said, "I usually give her a snack when she wakes up."

"Sounds like a good idea."

I sat there and watched Rambla eat, keeping my distance, careful not to intrude. Ree broke the food up into tiny pieces while delivering an ongoing commentary. ("Organic, Dr. Delaware, no preservatives.")

Eventually, Rambla permitted herself several glances in my direction.

I smiled.

The fourth time she smiled back. I got up, crouched low within inches of her face.

She yelped and gripped her mother.

I retreated.

Ree Sykes said, "It's okay, baby—I'm sorry, Dr. Delaware, she must be still half asleep."

Appropriate, appropriate, appropriate.

The great yeah-sayer.

Rambla quieted but avoided eye contact.

Five minutes later, she allowed me to show her the picture I'd drawn. Smiling face, bright colors.

She beamed. Giggled. Snatched the paper and crumpled it and threw it to the floor and thought that was just hilarious.

For the next ten minutes, I sat next to her high chair and we giggled together.

When I got up, she waved.

I blew a kiss. She imitated.

I said, "Bye bye."

"Bah bah." Plump hand to mouth, flamboyant wave.

I headed toward the front room.

"Now what?" said Ree.

"Nothing," I said, "I've seen enough."

I gave her hand a squeeze and left.

That night I wrote my report. Shortest draft I've ever sent a judge.

The first sentence read, "This well-nourished, well-functioning sixteen-month-old female child is the object of a guardianship dispute between her birth mother and her maternal aunt."

The final sentence read: "There appears to be no reason, based on either psychological factors or legal standards, to alter the child's status. A strong recommendation is made to reject Dr. Constance Sykes's request."

A few paragraphs in between. Nothing that required a Ph.D., but education's what they pay me for.

A week after I sent my findings to Nancy Maestro, I returned home after a run and found Connie Sykes out on my front terrace, sitting in one of the wicker chairs Robin and I leave there when we want to catch sunrise over the trees.

Warm morning; I was sweaty, breathing hard, wearing a sleeveless tee and shorts.

She said, "Nice muscles, Doctor."

"What can I do for you, Connie?"

"Obviously, I'm pretty crushed."

"I'm sorry—"

"I understand," she said, in a softer voice than I'd ever heard. But still, that strange, digital spacing. As if every word needed to be measured prior to delivery. "I knew at the outset that it was a long shot. May I come in?"

I hesitated.

"Just for a little support? You are a psychologist."

I glanced at my watch.

"I won't take up much of your time. I just need to . . . integrate. To talk about my own plans. Maybe adopting a child of my own?"

"Was that something you'd thought about before?"

Her shoulders heaved. "Can we talk? Please? Just briefly but I'll pay you for a full session."

"No payment necessary," I said. "Come on in."

This time she allowed me to lead. Settled in a different spot on the couch. Placed her leather purse to her right and her hands in her lap.

I said, "Morning."

She smiled. "I guess things work out the way they're supposed to. Though I wish I could be more confident about the poor child."

"Rambla."

"She really is in danger, Doctor. You may not be convinced of it, the court may not be convinced of it. I'm not even sure my own lawyer was convinced of it. But I've got superior analytic powers. Always have. I can see things—sense things—that elude other people."

Gone was the soft voice.

Something new in her eyes. A sputter of . . . irrationality?

"So," I said, "you're considering adopting."

She laughed. "Why would I do that? Why would I assume the risk of ending up with something genetically inferior? No, that was just . . . I suppose you'd call it an icebreaker. Gaining rapport in order to build up trust, so you'd let me in. That's your thing, right? Rapport. You sure pulled a fast one on me. Convinced me you understood me and then you went and wrote that I had absolutely no case. Very ethical, Doctor."

"Connie—"

"Dr. Sykes to you," she snapped. "You're 'Doctor,' I'm 'Doctor.' Okay? It's the least you can do. Show me some *respect*."

"Fair enough," I said, keeping my eye on her every movement. "Dr. Sykes, I never—"

"You never, you never, you never," she snapped. "You're *Doctor* Never. And now that poor child is destined to never lead the life she deserves."

Smoothing black gabardine slacks, she lifted her right hand, stroked the purse's fine, whiskey-colored leather.

"I'm not going to shoot you, Dr. Delaware. Even though I should."

Tapping the bag, she ran her finger over a swell in the leather and smiled wider and waited.

Master-of-timing comedian, pausing to see if the audience got it.

When I didn't respond, she tapped the bag harder. Something beneath the leather gave off a dull thud.

Something hard and dense. Implying she'd come with a weapon.

If she had and decided to use it, I was too far away to stop her, blocked by the desk.

Bad situation; I'd let down my guard, broken every rule, allowed her to catch me off guard.

No way to predict something like this.

Lots of victims probably thought that. No excuse for me; the whole point of my training was expecting the unexpected. I'd always figured myself pretty good at that.

The worst kind of assumption: blithe and arrogant.

I studied the flat-eyed, weird woman sitting across from me.

Serene stare from her. Icy contentment. She'd evoked fear, knew it. Had gotten what she'd come for.

The threat was the first time she'd used my name.

A new form of intimacy.

I kept silent.

Connie Sykes laughed. Then she got up and left the office and continued up the hall and I scurried to lock myself in, feeling like nothing but prey.

CHAPTER

8

My true love is a gorgeous, thoughtful, intense woman who cherishes solitude and makes her living transforming wood into guitars and mandolins of great beauty. Sequestered in her studio, she plays her own ensemble of instruments: routers, chisels, gauges and knives, band saw, jigsaw. A roaring table saw that rips through rosewood and ebony like a hungry predator.

Soft flesh versus razor-edged metal. A single slip can lead to horror and Robin lives with hazard every day. But it's my work that has led us to danger.

I sat at my desk, wondering what to tell her about Connie Sykes.

We've been together for a long time and how much I divulge about the terrible things has always been an issue. Robin knows better than to ask about therapy patients. But the other stuff—court work, the murders Milo brings like bloody gifts—is open territory and I fight the urge to overprotect.

I've finally figured out an approach that seems to work: assess how receptive she really is, divulge no more than she wants to know, temper the details.

Working with power tools and avoiding people

doesn't mean you lack insight and sometimes she offers an opinion that leads to a solution.

That's the way it is, now.

Years ago, a psychopath burned our house down. After the shock wore off, Robin recouped quickly, the way she always does, designing and supervising the building of the eye-filling white structure we eventually learned to call home.

Connie Sykes's visit marked the first time, since then, that I'd felt personally threatened by someone sitting on my battered leather sofa.

I'm not going to shoot you.

Technically, a non-threat.

Massaging the bulge in her purse.

Subtle.

Connie Sykes had shown herself eager to use the legal system as a weapon, so maybe the visit was a ploy. Enticing me to accuse her of something, so she could file a spite lawsuit.

A weapon? Ridiculous. I keep tissues, cosmetics, and a cell phone in there. This is defamation and harassment, this man is clearly unfit for the job with which he's been entrusted.

If she tried that, she'd lose. Again. But that wouldn't stop her from convincing herself she had a chance of winning. Because if Connie Sykes believed it, it had to be true.

I could call Milo but drawing him into the mess would just add complication.

I imagined a fine-print complaint against him handmessengered to the LAPD brass. Parker Center was Cover-Your-Ass Central. Milo, always an official irritant operating beyond his official boundaries, would be vulnerable.

Medea Wright, not my biggest fan, would enjoy the process.

Gun in a purse? The complainant is a physician, not a criminal, and this alleged *mental health expert is showing himself to be rather delusional and paranoid, leading to serious questions about his professional competence and qualifications for state licensure. Furthermore, his exploitation of personal connections to the police department in order to exert vengeful damage to the complainant is nothing short of venal.*

If you couldn't get the outcome you wanted, torture 'em with process.

The more I thought about it, the better it explained Connie showing up on my terrace. Bested in court, she itched to squeeze out a few drops of control.

To Connie Sykes, everything was *about* control. That's why she'd tried to confiscate her sister's child in the first place.

To Connie Sykes, winning meant someone had to lose.

Dr. Zero-Sum. I decided the best response to her stunt was none at all. Give her time to cool down.

Even if she forgot about me, she was likely to re-group for *Connie v. Ree, Chapter II.* Because she had the means and the opportunity and the system was receptive to second, third, fourth, millionth chances.

So forget about telling Milo, keep the bear in his den. But I'd let Robin know because the invaded territory was as much hers as mine.

Steeling myself for the walk through the garden to the studio, I poured coffee in the kitchen, drank some but found it bitter, organized my desk, checked files that didn't require inspection, ran out of delay tactics.

Just as I was about to leave the office, I thought of someone else who needed to know.

If Connie Sykes could muster that level of rage against me, what was she feeling about the judge?

I phoned Nancy Maestro. A hard, wary male voice answered, "Chambers."

Familiar voice; the deputy I'd met with the bronze-lensed eyeglasses. H. Nebe.

I said, "Hi, it's Dr. Delaware."

"Her Honor's unavailable. You have a message you want to leave?"

More of the protective attitude I'd seen in court. Not a bad idea, as it turned out. I told him about Connie Sykes.

He said, "Well, that's pretty insane. She do anything else crazy?"

"No."

"*Not* going to shoot you, huh?" said H. Nebe. "Sounds like she got you pretty scared."

"No, just wary."

"Meaning?"

"Watchful. I figured the judge should know."

"Okay, Doc. I'll handle it from this end."

"Meaning?"

"That nutcase shows up again, lock your door and call 911."

I filled a second mug with coffee, carried it down the back stairs to the garden, paused by the pond to listen to the waterfall and feed the koi, continued up the stone path to Robin's studio.

Quiet day, no machine noise. I found her standing over her workbench, face-masked, auburn curls top-knotted, wearing red overalls over a black T-shirt and looking sexy. Vials of varnish and oil and stain flanked her. A HEPA filter whirred at high speed.

Her hand gripped a soft wad of cotton, moved in small, concentric circles. French-polishing the quilted maple back of a seventeenth-century French guitar. One of those petite parlor instruments, high on decoration but low on sound. What used to be called women's guitars, back when women were deemed incapable of making serious music. This one was owned by a man, a collector who couldn't play a note but demanded that everything in his world—including his third wife—be pretty and shiny.

Robin continued working as Blanche, our little blond French bulldog, snored at her feet.

I cleared my throat. Removing the mask and putting down her polishing cloth, Robin smiled and Blanche's eyes began fluttering open.

"The prince brings caffeine. Perfect timing, how'd you know?"

"Lucky guess."

By the time she kissed me and took the mug, Blanche had padded over. Robin retrieved a stick of beef jerky from a jar on a shelf, kneeled to Blanche's level. Blanche took the treat with a soft mouth and held it there until Robin said, "Nosh-time."

Waddling to a corner, Blanche settled and chomped with delicate lust.

I felt a gentle tug. Robin's finger under my collar. "What's wrong?"

No sense asking how she knew anything was wrong, she always did. I told her.

She said, "What a nasty, vindictive person. Obviously, you were right to keep the kid out of her grasp."

"Anyone would've made the call."

"You're the one who did."

We moved to a couch against the wall, sat with our thighs touching.

"So," she said, "you think she might actually do something?"

"Doubt it," I said. "I just thought you should know."

"Appreciate it. So what's the plan? We batten down the hatches and go on red alert?"

"Maybe orange."

She squeezed my hand. "Don't mean to be flip. So you think she was just posturing."

"She's narcissistic and asocial but nothing in her past says she'd ever be violent."

"You going to let Milo know?"

I explained why I wasn't.

She said, "You're making a good point. Okay, for the next week or so—or longer, whatever you think— we'll lock the gate at the bottom of the road, anyone wants to intrude they'll have to do it on foot. And we'll make sure the night-lights are on down there. Be more careful about bolting the doors to the house and when we leave, we'll be extra-watchful."

"Sounds good," I said. My tone said "good" was a foreign word.

Her fingers left my collar, traveled to my cheek.

"What a pain," she said. "You do your job and get *this*. I suppose it was only a matter of time before someone needed a scapegoat."

"My court work bother you?"

"Of course not. You're doing good deeds. Crappy system needs you."

She rested her head on my shoulder. "It's never about the kids, right? Just screwed-up adults going to war. I remember the times I thought my parents were definitely getting divorced."

"That happen often?"

"Two, three times a year. They were always sniping at each other but sometimes the fights got really bad and you could *smell* how much they hated each other. I mean literally, Alex. The house would fill with this feral odor. Then they'd retrench and each of them would try to get me on their side. Dad always paid attention to me so it felt more natural when he got all chummy. But you know Mom. Parenthood didn't exactly rank high on her to-do list so when she started going on about all the things we should do together, just us two girls . . ."

She shuddered. "I didn't argue but ugh."

Untying her hair, she set loose a torrent of curls, brushed tendrils away from her face.

"Eventually, they'd make up and have disturbingly noisy sex and I'd go outside and pretend I was living on Mars. Then he'd be back to showing me how to use a hand plane and she'd revert to her usual icy, selfish self. Terrible thing to say about the person who gave you life, huh? But you know Mom."

My mother had possessed the capacity for tenderness but for the most part she'd been passive, depressed, and unable—or unwilling—to shield me from my father's alcoholic rages.

I said, "We don't pick our relatives."

She laughed. "That crazy woman's sister sure knows that."

CHAPTER

9

For the next week and a half, life went on as usual except for the locked gate and the lights. And the part I didn't tell Robin about: during my morning runs, looking for tree-shrouded spots where someone with a firearm could hide.

To relax myself, I imagined Connie Sykes in combat fatigues and a mud-smeared face jumping out and playing Rambette. The image was ludicrous and my jaws eventually unclenched. By day seven, I didn't need that bit of cognitive behavior therapy. By day ten, I was certain there was nothing to worry about and we could unlatch the gate.

I was about to broach the topic with Robin when the buzzer to that very barrier sounded.

Milo said, "Alex, it's me."

I beeped him in.

He's always hounding me about being lax with security. No comment, now, about the extra precaution.

Preoccupied? Probably a new whodunit.

Dealing with someone else's problems. Excellent; I was ready.

As I waited out on the terrace, a black LTD drove up. The passenger door opened and Milo's bulk emerged.

He wore a navy windbreaker, baggy brown slacks, scuffed desert boots, white shirt, skinny tie. Even from this distance the tie's colors were an intrusion: orange-rind paisley over week-old vegetable clippings. His olive vinyl attaché case swung at his side.

I said, "Morning, Big Guy."

His reply wave was minimal.

Out of the driver's side stepped a short, stocky woman in her thirties wearing a gunmetal-gray suit. Clipped dark hair, full face, excellent posture, as if she labored to stretch above five two. Clipped to the breast pocket of her jacket was a detective shield. She'd left the jacket unbuttoned, revealing a slice of white shirt and smidge of black—the strap of a nylon shoulder holster.

She made eye contact immediately, but we'd never met and her eyes had nothing much to say.

She let Milo lead the way as the two of them climbed the stairs.

Just before they reached the top, he said, "This is Detective Millie Rivera, North Hollywood Division. Millie, Dr. Alex Delaware."

Rivera extended her hand. Her fingers were barely above child-sized, but her grip was solid—a pair of miniature pliers finding their mark and maintaining a hold. On top of that, she'd mastered that thumb-on-webbing trick women learn when they've had their hand squeezed too many times by macho fools.

I said, "Pleased to meet you," and she let go. "What's up, Big Guy?"

Milo said, "Let's go inside."

Typically, he beelines to the kitchen and raids the fridge. Sometimes, when there's an especially knotty puzzle on his mind, he heads for my office and either commandeers my computer or stretches out on the leather couch, where he proceeds to think out loud or gripe about the policeman's lot.

A few months ago I presented him with a gag invoice. Six-figure charge for "years of listening." He looked at it, said, "Will a large pizza do as payment?"

This morning he went no farther than the living room, picking the nearest chair and plopping down heavily.

Detective Millie Rivera settled in an adjoining seat.

I said, "West L.A. and North Hollywood. Sounds complicated."

Milo said, "It's simple, Alex." He motioned to the facing couch.

I sat.

Milo said, "The bad news is someone wants to kill you. The good news is it hasn't happened, yet."

I said, "Constance Sykes."

The two of them looked at each other.

Millie Rivera said, "You're aware of the plot?"

"I'm aware of her anger but never figured she'd go that far." I recounted Connie's non-threat.

Rivera said, "That didn't alarm you, Doctor?"

"I've been looking over my shoulder."

"The gate," said Milo. "In your world that's security?"

Rivera said, "So on some level you figured she was serious. Well, good guess, Doctor. She tried to hire a hit man."

"You got him?"

"No, Doctor. He got us."

"I don't understand."

"You're unbelievably lucky, Dr. Delaware. The only reason the plan wasn't put into action was the person Dr. Sykes hired to kill you only wanted to be a broker and the person *he* turned to just happened to know you." She smiled. "Apparently, there are bad guys who think you're a good guy."

Milo muttered, "The friends we keep."

Rivera looked at him. He motioned her to go on.

"Here are the basics, Doctor. Sykes went to a not-so-solid citizen named Ramon Guzman who works for a company that cleans her offices at night. Guzman has a steady gig, now, but he's gangbanger up the wazoo, spent time in Lompoc for agg assault. At this point we don't know if Sykes actually knew about Guzman's prison record, but since he's covered with tats and looks like a badass, her assuming wouldn't be a stretch. And turns out, she was right because Guzman had no problem getting involved in murder for hire, he just didn't want to do the shooting because—get this—his eyes are bad, he didn't want to mess up. So he took a thousand-dollar down payment from Sykes and turned to one of his senior homeboys, a *gangster prince*. And wonder of wonders, *that* guy called me. I know this joker's entire family, they go way back criminal-wise. But Doctor, this is the first time I've ever been contacted directly by an upper-level bad actor. This one goes by the moniker Effo but his given name's Efren Casagrande."

My eyes widened.

Rivera said, "Obviously he was telling the truth about knowing you."

I kept silent.

"Doctor?"

Milo said, "He thinks he can't say anything, Millie. The old shrink-confidentiality thing." To me: "Guess what, Alex, you're free to express yourself because Mr. Casagrande let us know he was your patient. Though he was clear that it wasn't for a 'head problem.'"

They waited. I said nothing.

Rivera said, "Effo granted you permission to talk to us."

Milo said, "So how 'bout you educate us so I don't find myself writing a eulogy."

I said, "He give you written authorization?"

He cursed. Pulled out his phone, punched numbers. "It's me, Lieutenant Sturgis. Ready for a reunion, amigo? Hold on."

Handing the phone to me.

I said, "Dr. Delaware."

A familiar voice, older, deeper, ripe with amusement, said, "Yo, Doc. Long time. So how's the lifestyle? Looks like you still got one."

"Looks like it. Thanks."

"Hey, you don't think I'd let your ass—let you get with *no* lifestyle? Fuck that, Doc. *Fuck* that."

"Appreciate it, Efren."

"No prob—anyone else listening to this?"

"No."

"Then let me tell you: I'm so fucking pissed some bitch would try to do that, I'm ready to *kill* her ass. You with that?"

I said, "Nope."

Laughter. "Just kidding. Maybe. Yeah, okay, let's both of us hang on to our lifestyles. Let's both of us *represent.*"

"Good idea. How're things going?"

"Mostly up, few downs, haven't been in the E.R. since last Christmas." Laughter. "Too much partying. You know. What can I say?"

"Season to be jolly," I said. "Listen, anytime you want to—"

"Nah, I'm fine. And so are you. Try to stay that way, Doc."

Click.

I handed the phone back to Milo.

He said, "Heartwarming," and hummed a few bars of "Auld Lang Syne."

Millie Rivera said, "Casagrande may be charming but he's suspected in at least five murders. Doctor, you've got to be the luckiest man in L.A County."

Milo said, "Let's keep it that way. Now tell us every goddamn thing about this goddamn crazy lunatic who decided you don't deserve to breathe anymore."

Crazy lunatic. Redundant. It wasn't the moment to get finicky about grammar.

I said, "A thousand down? How much more to complete the job?"

"Four," said Millie Rivera.

"Five measly gees to snuff you out," said Milo. His green eyes were hot. His pallid, pockmarked face was tight with rage.

I couldn't help thinking some of that was directed at me.

CHAPTER

10

B ack when I worked at Western Pediatric Medical Center, my main job was helping children with cancer and their families. But soon I began getting consults from departments other than Oncology, most frequently Endocrinology. And when I switched to private practice, Endo referrals continued.

It's a natural pairing. Glandular and metabolic disorders—growth problems, puberty issues, juvenile diabetes—pose obvious emotional challenges. Diabetes adds an additional hardship because it requires a level of patient compliance—monitoring blood sugar, regulating diet, injecting insulin—that anyone would find tough, let alone a kid.

When diabetic children become teens, it can really get hairy, because adolescence is all about identity, differentiating yourself, breaking away from authority figures. Which isn't to say that all diabetic teens act out medically. Many ease into mature self-management.

Others are like Efren Casagrande.

He came to me as one of those last-resort panic referrals, a fourteen-year-old "exceptionally brittle" diabetic who needed to draw blood multiple times a day and control his food with a level of precision that would faze a competitive bodybuilder. Diagnosed at age eight, he'd been reasonably compliant until the onset of puberty, when his attitude shifted to "Fuck this shit," and he simply stopped cooperating.

During the past half year, he'd ended up in the E.R. thirteen times, had nearly died twice.

His doctor tried to talk sense into him.

Efren listened attentively, claimed he understood.

Blithe lie.

The same applied to pleading by his mother, two older sisters, an aunt who worked as a health care aide and was deemed the family medical guru, a hospital social worker named Sheila Baxter who was damn good and had accomplished wonders with other patients.

Three days after assuring Sheila he'd changed his ways, Efren ended up in a near coma.

She called me the day he was discharged. "Got time for an interesting one, Alex?"

"Anything you can't handle has to be interesting."

She recited the history wearily.

I said, "Want me to be brutally honest?"

She sighed. "Hopeless?"

"I'm always hopeful, Sheila, but I can't perform magic."

"No? Isn't that what mental health's all about? Spells and incantations and head-shrinking voodoo hexes? Heck, Alex, maybe I should break out my Tarot deck, couldn't be any less effective than I already am."

I said, "The lightbulb."

"I know, I know, it has to want to change. Which is fine when we're talking naughtiness in school. But this kid—and he's personable and bright when he's not screwing up—is going to die soon."

"I'll give it a shot, Sheila."

"That's all I can ask for. And guess what? This family can pay, I'm not asking you for charity." A beat. "Which leads me to something else about the family. They're intact in an official sense but the father hasn't been around for a long time. He got sent to Pelican Bay when Efren was three and will be there for twenty more years."

I said, "Pelican's all about serial killers and major-league gangsters."

"In this case, it's the latter. Efren's daddy was a player in the heroin trade."

"Business trumps prison walls, huh? Ergo the family's ability to pay."

"Alex, please don't tell me you just got qualms. Because no matter where the money originates, Efren really needs help and, believe it or not, his mother's a good person. Long suffering, you know? And effective; two older sisters are in college."

"Do I get reimbursed with Baggies of black tar?"

Another sigh. "I would think not, dear."

"Don't worry, then. Qualms are for sissies."

She laughed. "I'm sure Efren would agree. Who knows, you two might actually get a rapport going."

Rosalinda Casagrande phoned two hours later and set up an appointment with my service for the following morning. Precisely on time, a low-riding Chevy painted gold with green pin-striping and a black Aztec eagle emblazoned on the trunk huffed up in front of the house. As its engine continued to pulsate, a skinny kid in droopy duds got out of the passenger side, scratched his saggy-khaki butt, and squinted up at the sun.

The Chevy's engine kept running. Anyone else in the car was concealed by heavy-tint windows.

I stood in full view of the boy. He looked everywhere but at me.

When he began to turn his back, I called down: "Efren?"

Reluctant swivel.

"C'mon up."

He stood there.

I said, "Or don't."

His mouth dropped. "Wuh?"

"We can talk inside or out here." I laughed. "You can even stay down there and we'll yell at each other. Good workout for the vocal cords."

His face aimed up at me.

I said, "Nice wheels. Maybe one day you can drive it."

His lips pretzeled. "I already drive."

"Great."

The Chevy revved loud. The boy flinched. A second clap of gasoline thunder got him rolling his head, as if trying to dispel the noise. Rev number three sent him trudging up the stairs.

By the time he reached the top, the trudge had been replaced by a comical swagger. Up close, he was far from impressive: small for his age, a whole lot more bone than muscle, a chin that could use help, sallow cheeks assaulted by acne. His head was shaved to the skin. A toss of pimples had chosen his scalp for a nesting spot. He had long, soft-looking arms, not much upper body. Smallish feet that he tried to augment with too-large work boots verging on cartoonish. His fingernails were clean and he didn't emit body odor but his clothes gave off that three-day-old must that flavors adolescent bedrooms.

I held out my hand. He looked at it.

Withdrawing, I entered the house and continued to my office without checking to see if he'd followed. I was behind my desk for ninety-four seconds before he appeared in the doorway and gave the room a quick scan.

"You got a lot of things, man." His voice cracked a couple of times. Alto aiming for tenor but a long way from success. On the phone, he could be mistaken for a girl. Hopefully testosterone would eventually come to the rescue. Insulin sure hadn't been there for him.

"A lot of things," he repeated.

The office was free of personal mementos, the way a therapy space needs to be. "Think so?"

"Yeah, those art pictures out there."

"You into art?"

"Nah . . ." He bobbed his head a couple of times, as if adjusting to an internal beat. "You trust me with all that, man?"

"All what?"

He smiled. His teeth were uneven but white. "Your things, man. You got nice things, I was out there with 'em and you were in here, man."

"You want my things?"

"I can have 'em?"

"Not a chance."

He stared at me.

I said, "You can sit."

He didn't budge.

"Or don't," I said, moving papers around and consulting my appointment book.

He continued to stand there.

I said, "Here's how I see the situation. Everyone's getting on your case to be a good boy with your diabetes. It's like a mountain of noise, coming at you all the time. So you tell 'em sure, no problem, but you mean, 'Fuck you, leave me alone.'"

The obscenity caused his head to retract. Black eyes sharpened. A boot tapped.

"Noise, nonstop." I ticked my fingers. "From Dr. Lowenstein, from your mom, Aunt Inez, Aunt Carmen, Aunt Dolores, Ms. Baxter. Maybe a *curandero* I don't know about."

He didn't react.

I said, "Basically, you've got an army of people getting on your case, so you need to defend yourself."

He shook his head.

I said, "I'm wrong?"

"You don't know me, man."

"You've got that right."

"Whatever." The tapping picked up speed. An index finger bumped atop a thumb. A dozen times.

I said, "So now they've got their backs against the wall and they send you to me. You know what kind of doctor I am?"

Grunt.

I waited.

He said, "Head doc."

"Everyone's hoping I can find a trapdoor into your head and crawl in and tell your brain you need to be a good boy. Problem is, even if I wanted to do that, I couldn't 'cause there's no, no trapdoor. Your brain is yours. No one can control you."

"You don't want to?"

"To go into your head?"

Nod.

"No way, Efren. I'm thinking it's a complicated place."

He whipped around, faced me.

I said, "There's a lot going on in your head because you're a lot more than diabetes."

He mumbled. Inaudible but the placement of crooked upper teeth over lower lip suggested something beginning with "F."

He glanced at the couch.

I wheeled my chair back, stretched.

He said, "Why you do this?"

"Do what?"

"Psycho stuff. If you don't wanna . . . if you don't care."

"Once I get to know someone, I care plenty."

He smirked. "You don know a dude you don give a shit?"

I said, "Do you care about people you don't know?"

"I don't care about nothin'."

I got up. "You drink coffee?"

"Nah hate that shit."

"I like that shit, wait here."

Leaving him alone in the office, I took time filling a mug from the kitchen. When I got back he was perched on the arm of the couch.

I sipped. He licked his lips.

"Thirsty?"

"Nah." He swayed.

I drank some more, sat back as far as the desk chair would allow.

One of his hands gripped the couch. A second sway, wider. His eyes began to roll upward. "You got like juice, man?" Weaker voice. Fading.

"Got orange."

"Yeah."

I filled a glass quickly, returned to find him slumped on the couch, pale and sweaty. He drank slowly, revived quickly. I returned behind the desk, worked on my coffee.

Suspending the empty juice glass between his palms, he gave the office another examination. "You make a lot of money?"

"Enough."

"For what?"

"Some nice stuff."

"That like picture you got," he said. "Guys hitting each other."

"That's a boxing print by an artist named George Bellows."

"Cost a lot?"

"I got it a long time ago, so not so much. Also, there are a lot of them. The painting they're based on is worth millions."

"Who got it?"

"A museum."

"Where?"

"Cleveland."

"Where's that?"

"About two thousand miles away."

His eyes glazed. Apathy, now, not low sugar. I might as well have said Venus.

I said, "Too far to walk."

He began to smile, checked himself. "You always work in your house?"

"Sometimes I go to hospitals. Or to court."

He stiffened. "Court? Like a cop?"

"No, I get paid to be an expert."

"About what?"

"Mostly it's people divorcing and fighting over who gets the kids. I get paid to say what I think. Sometimes it's kids getting hurt—like in an accident—and they pay me to say that's a problem."

He stared at me.

"Yeah," I said, "it's a sweet deal."

"Who gets 'em?"

"Who gets who?"

"The kids they're fighting for."

"Up to the judge."

"So what do you do?"

"Tell the judge what I think."

"You're smarter than the judge?"

"I know more about psychology—about how people think and act."

His soft little chin pushed forward. What would've been a jut had he had more to work with. "How?"

"How what?"

"How do people think?"

"Depends on who they are, what's happening to them."

His expression said I'd failed some sort of test.

I said, "Like you, Efren. Sometimes you think you're in charge of the world, you're huge and powerful."

Black eyes remained fixed on me.

"Other times, you think you have no control over anything. It just depends."

His hands faltered. The glass fell to the floor, thudded on my Persian rug. Scooping it up, he said, "Sorry, man."

I said, "It's the same with everyone. Sometimes we're feeling big, sometimes we're small. I get paid to be smart because I've had a lot of schooling and experience. But I don't have magic and I don't have trapdoors."

"What do you got?"

"What people tell me."

"I'm not telling you nothing."

"Your choice."

Head shake. "Right . . ."

"You don't think you have a choice?"

Silence.

I said, "Unlike the other doctors who poke you and probe you and tell you what to do, I won't order you to do anything."

"Right."

"I mean it, Efren. You've got enough forced upon you. I don't want to be part of that."

He looked down at his knees. "You don't want it, huh?"

"What?"

"Being my—doing the doctor thing."

"I want to do my job," I said. "I love my job. And you seem like an interesting guy and I'd be happy to work with you. But to be part of that mountain of noise? No way."

He stood. Hefted the empty glass, put it down hard. "You got that, man. I don't need no more shit."

Zipping past me. End of session.

I figured I'd never hear from him again, was rehearsing my sad call to Sheila Baxter when the service rang in.

"A Mrs. Casagrande wanting to talk to you, Doctor."

"Put her through."

A beat. "Hallo?"

"This is Dr. Delaware."

"This is Efren mother."

"Nice to talk to you. How's everything?"

"Actually," she said, "a little good. Efren test himself twice after he come home from you."

"That's great."

"He still find the candy and sneak but he at least test and take the shot . . . when you wanna see him again?"

"He wants to come back?"

"He forget to pay you," she said. "I give him money, he forget. I send double, okay?"

"Sure. So Efren—"

"He say next week. That okay?"

I found a slot, made the appointment.

Rosalinda Casagrande said, "Thank you, Doctor. Effo say you a mean guy."

"Really."

"That good. To him, you know? Mean is strong. He live all the life with girls, everyone thinks he the little kid, you know?"

"He gets babied."

"I think now he need someone to kick his butt. He come next week."

For the next three months the gold low-rider arrived punctually for weekly sessions. I never set Efren's appointments in advance, offering him a choice each time—requiring him to make the choice explicitly.

But keeping his slot open because he'd become high priority to me. A fact I'd never let on.

With the exception of one instance when he had a cold and canceled personally with seventy-two hours' notice, he opted to come in.

The first few sessions were more question than answer. His questions about me—my education, how much money I made, the places I'd lived. I gave out very little information and my reticence pleased him: Someone who protected his own privacy could be trusted to respect his.

I dealt with the confidentiality issue early on, being clear that at fourteen, he couldn't be guaranteed secrecy. But pledging that I'd never divulge anything he didn't want divulged even if pressured.

"By the cops?"

"By anyone. Why would the cops ask me about you?"

Sly smile. "I dunno. They come in, you tell 'em, right?"

"Wrong."

"What if they busted you and beat your ass?"

"I'd have nothing to tell them." I showed him his chart. "This is what I write every time you're here."

He flipped pages. Read. The identical note every week: "Patient doing well."

He said, "That's bullshit, man. I'm fucked *up*." He laughed. And remained jocular for the rest of the session.

When he arrived looking settled, we talked in my office. When he was antsy, we moved to the garden where he got a huge kick out of feeding the fish and threatened to come back with a hook and line to "catch their asses for dinner."

When he flagged he asked for juice. Soon, he began thanking me for "keeping it nice and cold, man. You got beer?"

"Not for you."

"Awww."

"How about vodka?"

"Really?"

"No."

A couple of times sitting anywhere wouldn't do and we walked. Leaving the property and getting as far as the Glen before returning. Once we spotted hawks circling and I had to disabuse him of the notion that they were those "vultans that eat dead stuff."

I learned about him. The TV he watched, the movies he liked, the foods he enjoyed. A girl in his class that had "like tits out to here, man, and prolly a real hairy pussy."

The subject of his father never came up. Same for his gang heritage. Not a word about the drive-bys in his Boyle Heights neighborhood, including two fatal attacks reported in the papers that I looked up in my Thomas Guide and found to be walking distance from his house.

Same for diabetes.

On the twelfth session, I took the risk.

"Let me ask you something, Effo."

"What?"

"You're a smart guy—more than smart, you're sharp, perceptive—you see things clearly—"

"I know what that means, man." Grin. "Like a college perceptor."

"On top of being smart, you like yourself. Which is good, that's a sign of strength. You also understand all about diabetes. The scientific part."

"All that shit? Keep the sugar smooth, man."

"Exactly," I said. "So how come when they sent you to me you weren't keeping it smooth? I'm asking 'cause I'm curious."

Shifting sideways, he stretched prone on the couch. "Know what I'm doing, lying down?"

"What?"

"I saw it on TV, they say that's the way you spose to do the head-doc shit."

I smiled. "Make yourself comfortable."

He closed his eyes. His breathing slowed and I figured he'd sleep, or fake it, to avoid answering.

He said, "Why'd I do it?"

The eyes opened. He turned sideways. Winked. "It's the diabetes, man. That shit don't fit my *lifestyle*."

I thought: *Lifestyle? You dumb kid, you're lucky you still have a life.*

I said, "Okay, makes sense."

CHAPTER
11

Detective Millie Rivera said, "Looks like you chose the right patient. I never figured Effo could be right about anything but being wrong. When's the last time you saw him?"

"Years ago."

"What'd you treat him for?"

I shook my head.

She said, "I hope it wasn't for his antisocial tendencies. If so, it didn't work, Doctor. He's a serious gangster, climbed higher in the gang after his father died. In Pelican Bay. Know anything about that place?"

"Worst of the worst."

"It's probably where Effo will end up one day, Doctor. Who knows, he might even inherit Poppy's cell."

Heat had come into her voice. Her left wrist rolled up and down a chunky thigh. Working gang detail is an infinite process with infrequent satisfaction.

Rivera turned to Milo. "Big-time killer, now he's a good citizen, go figure."

I said, "You're North Hollywood. Did Effo change his turf from East L.A.?"

Milo said, "He's got a business in North Hollywood."

"Alleged business," said Rivera. "Car stereo place. Where bangers go for boom. We think it's a front. You haven't seen him in a long time?"

"He was my patient when he was a teenager."

"He's twenty-seven, now," she said. "So, ten years?"

"Give or take."

"No contact since then? Even on the phone?"

I said, "I have no ongoing relationship with him or anyone else in the gang."

"Well, looks like *Effo* thinks you have a relationship. If he didn't, Doctor, you wouldn't be part of this conversation. Because Effo's not shy about homicide. Like I said, he's suspected in five and I'm sure there's a whole bunch of stuff we don't know about."

"In those five was he the triggerman or a contractor?"

"Does it matter, Doctor? The point is when he decides people are going to die, they tend to do just that. We've been trying to nail him for a long time. He's integral to the organization and taking him down will be a big deal. Unfortunately, because of *your* situation we have to treat him like he's a good person and that means backing off. Until we resolve *your* situation."

"Sorry," I said. "Next time I'll try to be saved by Batman or the Green Lantern."

She blinked.

Milo hid a smile behind a hand.

I said, "How *are* we going to resolve my situation?"

Rivera said, "By wiping the slate clean of Dr. Sykes."

"What do you want me to do?"

Milo said, "You do nothing, Alex. We're here to protect and serve."

Rivera said, "This—us notifying you—is part of the protecting. But you don't talk to anyone about this, okay? Specifically, you *don't* contact Efren Casa-grande."

I smiled. "Not even to maintain clinical support?"

Milo said, "His ego's doing just fine. Charming lit-tle weasel that he is."

Rivera said, "Doctor, you need to take this seri-ously: Everything stays buttoned up until Sykes is taken care of. Speaking of which, you need to educate us: Is she crazy, or what?"

I summed up my impressions.

"I'm hearing cold bitch rather than outright loony-tuney," said Rivera.

I had a grab bag of diagnostic labels to dip into. Said, "Fair enough."

"She one of those compulsives, Doctor? One try fails, she doesn't give up?"

I said, "When did she solicit Guzman?"

Milo said, "Four days ago."

"Six days after she showed up here."

He nodded.

Rivera was puzzled by the exchange.

Milo said, "Woman takes her time, Millie. Premed-itation, not impulse."

She said, "Smart criminals. Hate 'em."

I said, "She's about organization and planning, so sure, she could persevere. What's the plan?"

Milo said, "Far as Sykes knows—far as Ramon Guzman's telling her—the hit's on and ready to go. We're gonna work with that."

"Guzman's cooperating."

Rivera said, "Guzman, there's another winner. So-ciopath like Effo but minus fifty IQ points. Yes, Doc-tor, he's *cooperating* but only because he has no choice. We can bust him for conspiracy anytime we choose but we're holding off because his arrest could tip off Sykes and leave her untouchable—the word of a lowlife against a rich doctor. Instead, we had Effo bring Guzman to a meeting and then we popped in. At which time Effo informed Guzman he needed to play nice."

She ground her teeth. The fist on her thigh gathered fabric and maybe some skin. "Not that we routinely take the word of people like your prize patient. But we needed Guzman totally submissive and Effo had him over-the-top terrified. Genuine fear, Ramon's too stupid to put on a convincing performance. But stupid can cause problems so everything needs to be kept strictly under wraps."

I said, "After Sykes threatened me, I warned Judge Maestro."

Rivera frowned. "You did that because . . ."

"She wrote the order dismissing Connie Sykes's suit. I figured she might be in jeopardy."

"You informed her, but not the police."

"It didn't seem to reach the level of—"

"It reached a level where you warned a judge."

"I played it as I saw it, Detective."

"And the judge's response was . . ."

"I spoke to her bailiff. He said he'd handle it."

"Well," said Rivera, "right now *you're* the prime target so let's take care of *your* situation and everyone else will benefit."

I said, "Effo wires up, meets with Sykes, you're listening in?"

Rivera slashed air with one hand. "Effo meets with no one. His participation is officially over, no way we'll get that cozy with him, last thing we need is he goes to trial and his lawyer tries to cash in big-time brownie points for heroic law enforcement cooperation."

She scooted forward on her chair. "You need to be clear about this, Doctor: Your situation has created an inconvenience for us but no matter what he's done for *you*, we *will* get him."

Milo said, "Yeah, we're stinging her, but using our own. I borrowed Raul Biro from Hollywood."

I said, "Raul doesn't come across gangster."

"Give him credit, Alex. He's quick on his feet and he can play cold-blooded."

"When's it happening?"

Rivera said, "When we're ready."

"I want to be there."

Rivera laughed.

Milo didn't.

She said, "El Tee?"

I said, "This woman tried to kill me. I want to watch her go down."

Milo said, "Nice to know you've got the revenge gene like the rest of us."

Rivera said, "Well, I need to talk to *my* lieutenant."

"Bill White's a good man, Millie. I'll handle it."

"Fine, your responsibility." She stood. "Nice meeting you, Doctor. Try to stay healthy."

Milo got up, as well, but he left the attaché case on the floor and he didn't follow Rivera.

She stopped. "Something else, El Tee?"

"Gonna stick around a bit. Educate the doctor a little more."

"Ah . . . good luck with that."

We walked Rivera out, remained on the terrace, watched as she sped away.

Milo said, "You're gonna have to chauffeur me back to the station."

"After you educate me?"

He laughed. "Like Millie said, good luck."

I said, "You think I screwed up by not reporting it?"

"My protective instincts say yeah, it's more of your

usual denial. But the truth is, she really didn't threaten you, she just acted nasty. So there's nothing I could've done other than to warn her away. And I don't know her well enough to predict how that would turn out."

"I thought about telling you, figured if you did step in and she complained it could get sticky department-wise."

"No doubt." He smiled. "What a pal."

"So what's Rivera's problem? I got on her bad side without really trying."

"It ain't you, Alex. She's going through a rough patch."

"Gang work burnout?"

"Probably that, too," he said. "But the main thing is an ugly divorce. Her ex is an arson D from Van Nuys. Not a bad guy but he and Millie are going at it. One kid and they're ripping at each other. So Millie's not too high on men, nowadays."

"She told you about it?"

"I have my sources."

Returning to the house, he headed for the kitchen.

Two roast-beef-and-coleslaw sandwiches and half a pint of milk later, he said, "How you doing with it?"

"With what?" Stupidest answer in the world but I couldn't find anything else to say.

"With the pollen count—what do you think?"

I shrugged.

He washed his dish and his glass, returned to the table. "You were pretty much Dr. Sphinx with ol' Millie and I'm sure you had your reasons. But now it's just us Boy Scouts, so feel free to emote."

"I'm all right."

He let that ride. Returned to the fridge and scrounged for dessert.

I repeated that to myself: *I'm all right.* Punishment

for the lie arrived a split second later in the form of a wave of nausea that surged below my sternum and scuttled up to my gullet. My breathing caught, my vision fogged, nausea switched to vertigo, and I braced myself with two hands on the table.

That didn't work, so lowering my head to my arms I closed my eyes, worked at slowing my breathing.

I heard Milo say, "Alex?" As if from far, far away.

My skin turned clammy. My pulse clanged in my ears. My head felt like a chunk of pig iron, barely secured by a rubber spine.

I needed to settle down before the next challenge: updating Robin.

The fridge closed. Heavy footsteps grew louder. I got my pulse down to a fast trot but the vertigo lingered and I kept my head down.

Milo and I have been friends for a long time and all those cases we've worked have probably shaped the way we think because sometimes we seem to be sharing the same brain.

This was one of those moments.

He said, "She back there, working? You sit and relax, I'll deal with it."

A big hand patted my back. Heavy footsteps diminished. The kitchen door closed softly.

CHAPTER

12

Six p.m., the commodious parking lot behind Rubin Rojo's Mexican Hacienda, Lankershim Boulevard, North Hollywood.

Fifty-two hours after Milo and Millie Rivera's visit. My new way of keeping time.

Robin and I had spent most of that period in Santa Barbara, bunking down in a bed-and-breakfast off upper State Street, filling our days with enforced recreation: leisurely mountain walks, strolls along the beach, ocean kayaking off Stearns Wharf, even a spin on the carousel on Cabrillo Boulevard.

Just another couple apparently enjoying one of the loveliest places on the globe.

Robin had taken the news well, though she was quieter than usual. I felt guilty about the whole mess and said so and, of course, she reassured me and moved us on to the next distraction. Sleeping for more than a couple of hours in a row would've been nice, but I made do with minutes at a time.

Now we were back in L.A., Robin visiting a friend in Echo Park, me sitting in the back of Milo's unmarked, with him at the wheel, Rivera riding shotgun.

The restaurant was one of those oversized stucco rhomboids erected decades ago when land was cheap and signage despised subtlety. A proprietor smart enough to own, not rent, had helped it avoid the wrecking ball.

Now ninety years old, Rubin keeps the place for fun, using reasonable prices and mammoth portions to surround himself with smiling people.

Six p.m. is midway through the restaurant's Happy Hour. Tall, overly sweet Margaritas for four bucks. The big parking lot is three-quarters full.

Warm L.A. evening. Gray skies, poor air quality, so what else is new?

The cream-colored Lexus arrives first, driving through the aisles and selecting one of the remaining slots.

Exactly fifteen minutes early.

Six oh three: A gray Ford pickup, rear deck crammed with gardener's tools and bags of fertilizer, one of the hubcaps missing, drives in, takes no apparent notice of the Lexus, parks well across the lot.

In the truck's driver's seat sits North Hollywood plainclothes officer Gil Chavez wearing sweaty work clothes and two days of heavy stubble. Chavez turns off his engine, lights up a cigarette, and trains his camera on the cream-colored Lexus, pushing the zoom function to the max and focusing upon the square-faced middle-aged woman in the car's driver's seat, waiting motionless, her window open.

Her first movement comes at six oh six. Checking her watch.

Producing a cell phone, she texts.

After sending her message—later ascertained to be a reminder to her office manager to obtain more Medi-Cal and Medicare billing forms—she lets out a luxuriant yawn, doesn't bother to cover her mouth. Returning to the phone, she dials up the Internet and examines something later ascertained to be a CNN news feed. Financials.

Later, Chavez will comment on how cool she appears.

"Like she's there for chiles rellenos and a couple frozen Margees."

A few other vehicles enter the lot.

The woman in the Lexus watches them with shallow interest. Glances in the vanity mirror on the underside of the driver's sun visor. Freshens her makeup.

Chavez's camera clicks away. Captures a smile on her lips.

Her phone drops from view. A magazine takes its place.

The zoom can't pick up the title.

Small-print index on the cover.

The periodical is later ascertained to be *Modern Pathology.*

Two more vehicles drive in. The woman watches them briefly. Yawns, again. Flicks something out of the corner of her left eye.

Six fourteen p.m.—exactly a minute early—a ten-year-old black Camaro shows up. Stopping, it proceeds slowly, makes a loop of the parking lot, passes the Lexus. Two additional circuits are completed before the Camaro returns to where the Lexus is positioned and slips in next to the luxury sedan.

The new arrival's passenger window is open, offering a direct view of the Lexus's driver's side. But the square-faced woman's window is closed, wanting to study the Camaro's driver without being studied herself.

Nevertheless, one of the four video cameras concealed in the Camaro's black tuck-and-roll kick in. Captures a close-up of mildly tinted glass.

The Camaro's driver leans toward his open window. A young, slim, handsome Hispanic man with pronounced cheekbones and inquisitive dark eyes, he wears a long-sleeved, plaid Pendleton shirt buttoned to the neck, saggy khakis, and white Nikes. A blue bandanna sheaths his freshly skinned head. Three hours ago, Detective Raul Biro sported a head of thick black hair so luxuriant you could mistake it for a toupée. Now, freshly cholo-buzzed by his partner, Petra Connor, with some makeup added to blend his sun-deprived scalp with the rest of his coppery dermis, he squints at the Lexus.

Expertly applied temporary tattoos litter the top of Biro's hands and meander up his neck. The perfect blue-black hue of prison ink, also provided by Petra, a trained artist prior to becoming a cop.

Left side of the neck: a beautifully drawn blossoming rose in the center of an orange crucifix.

A teardrop under the left eye.

A crudely drawn black hand.

That much ink showing in such limited dermal terrain implies an entire body given over to adornment.

No one expects Biro to have to strip down, exposing the illusion.

He continues staring at the Lexus's driver's window. As if responding to his energy, the glass slides down and the square-faced woman reveals herself.

Expressionless, she studies Biro.

He returns the favor.

Finally, she says, "Juan?"

Biro says, "George. Don play games, lady."

The square face tightens, then brightens. Eyelashes bat. "Good to meet you, George. I'm Mary."

Different voice than I'd heard in my office. Connie Sykes is playing girly-girly with hammy abandon, laying on a Southern Belle drawl that would be comical if I was able to tolerate funny.

Neither Milo nor Millie Rivera has ever heard her real voice. They don't react.

My stomach crawls.

She's enjoying this.

Biro: "Anyone see you?" His voice is different, too. Lower-pitched, East L.A. singsongy, imprecise around the edges.

A refined man of perfect diction slumming for a one-woman audience.

Connie Sykes says, "Of course not." *Of cowass not.*

"You sure."

"I am, George."

Biro says nothing.

"Cross my heart, George. So where do we do this?"

No immediate answer. Biro looks around the parking lot. "Okay, get in."

"To your car?"

"You got a problem with that?"

"Well . . . I suppose not."

"So do it."

Grimacing but bouncing back with a "Shuah, George," Connie Sykes flips her wavy hair.

The first feminine gesture I'd ever seen her display. Absurd and incongruous. Like a tutu on a rhino.

"George" couldn't care less about her sex appeal and Connie senses that and frowns again, as she gets out of the Lexus.

Walking to the back of the black Camaro, she sidles around, takes the passenger handle, finds it locked.

Biro unlocks it with a click. No doubt about who's in charge.

Connie gets in. Fools with her wavy hair. Tries for a warm, flirty smile, comes up with a weirdly repellent twist of freshly painted lips.

Or maybe I'm being too harsh. She does have an X chromosome.

Millie Rivera says, "Creepy bitch."

Biro lights up a cigarette.

Sykes barks a pretend cough. "That's not good for you, George."

Biro blows smoke rings. "Show me the money, lady."

Sykes pats her bag. Same way she'd implied a gun while sitting on my leather couch. "The money's all here, George."

"How much?"

"What we agreed on."

"Let me see it."

Connie opens the bag, pulls out a wad of bills.

Biro says, "What you want me to do?"

"What do you mean?" Sykes has dropped her drawl. "Huh?"

"I thought Ramon worked that out."

"Yeah, right," says Biro. "Do a guy."

"So you do know."

"That's nothin', lady."

"What do you mean?"

"Do can be anything," says Biro. "How you want it?"

"By 'how' you mean—"

"Shoot, cut, break the fuckin' head." He turns to her, exhales a bust of smoke. "They's all kinda do, Mary."

Sykes opens a window and breathes in fresh air. "Would you mind putting that out? You're really asphyxiating me."

Biro, still puffing: "You gonna tell me or what?"

"I assumed Ramon already discussed—"

"Fuck Ramon, I'm here, you're here—you sure you got all the money, lady? You only showed me that bunch."

"Of course I'm sure." Peeved.

Silence.

Connie says, "I'm a busy person. Why would I bother to come here if I wasn't serious." She laughs.

"Something funny, lady?"

"I mean, George, you don't impress me as the type of guy who does things just for fun. Though I imagine it must be fun for you."

Biro stares at her. "You talk crazy, lady. Gonna tell me what you want, or what?"

Connie stares back. Her mouth is set hard.

The atmosphere in the Camaro has shifted and all of us know it.

Milo rubs his face, as if washing without water.

Rivera says, "Uh-oh . . . c'mon, Raul, work it, man."

Biro says, "What, lady?"

Connie says, "I think you're being . . . legalistic, George."

"Huh?"

"Pressing me for details."

"It's your job, lady."

"But you're the pro, George."

"Yeah. So."

"So you decide."

"Everything?"

"Sure. Why not?"

"Suit yourself, Mary. I just figured you'd wanna—"

Without warning, Connie Sykes pushes the Camaro's passenger door open and exits the car. Rather than flee to the Lexus, she returns to the rear of the black car, stops for a second. Seems to be studying something.

Milo says, "What the—she's memorizing the tag?"

Rivera says, "Unbelievable. Ballsy bitch."

Raul Biro speaks, barely moving his lips. "What now, guys? I go after her?"

His tone says that's the last thing he wants.

Milo says, "Stay there."

Connie Sykes walks into the restaurant.

Milo says, "Get out of there."

Biro complies.

Moments after the Camaro exits the lot, Connie Sykes steps out, looks around, approaches her Lexus, takes the time for another check of her surroundings before getting into her car.

Cruising slowly, she's gone.

Millie Rivera curses.

Milo joins her.

My head fills with what-ifs. I keep them to myself.

Driving back to the city via Laurel Canyon, Milo headed for Hollywood Division and the sure-to-be-depressing meet-up with Raul Biro.

Not at the station on Wilcox. Biro, sounding deflated, had no desire to be in the company of Petra or any of his peers.

He directed us to a coffee shop on Sunset near Gower, was already seated at a booth, coffee cup in hand. He'd loosened the top button on the Pendleton, rolled up the sleeves. Clean arms but marked-up hands. Instead of the bandanna he wore a Dodgers cap.

Before Milo, Rivera, and I were sitting, he said, "I know I messed up but I still can't figure out how."

He's an unusually bright and perceptive detective, free of macho self-delusion but confident and self-possessed. Seeing him like this was sad.

Milo said, "That's 'cause you didn't screw up, Raul. She's a paranoid weirdo."

As if he hadn't heard, Biro said, "I did the hard-guy because the department shrink said to." He looked at me. "I would've asked you but they said you were too involved."

I said, "Understandable."

"Would you have done it differently?"

"There's never a cookbook. Milo's right, there was no way to predict."

"Oh, man," said Biro, "what a mess."

"You poor guy," said Millie Rivera. "Losing your hair."

"Don't care about that, it'll grow back," said Biro. "Meanwhile she's still out there—I'm really sorry, Doc."

I said, "Don't worry."

Biro shook his head. "I used to think actors were idiots. Now I'm thinking I'm the fool, need to appreciate them."

A waitress came over. The request for three more coffees made her scowl. "That's it?"

"Nah, that's the appetizer," said Milo. "Bring me a chocolate sundae with hot fudge—you got pineapple sauce?"

"Just peaches and cherries."

"Fine."

"Which one?"

"Both."

"It's extra."

"I'm an extra type of guy."

The waitress left, rolling her eyes.

Biro said, "El Tee, if I eat now, I hurl."

Rivera said, "Well, I can use a sugar rush—maybe I'll also get a sundae."

Milo said, "It's yours I just ordered," and stood, nodding at me to do the same. We left the booth. He said, "Don't sweat it, kids, it'll work out."

"You two are going?" said Rivera.

"I'll be in touch."

"We're finished?"

"In terms of official business? For the time being."

"What do I tell Lieutenant White?"

"I'll tell him."

"What about Guzman?"

"Sounds like he's under control via Effo."

Rivera thought about that. "Okay, what about Effo?"

"Do your thing, Millie."

She looked at me. "How do you feel about that, Doc?"

"If you're asking will I warn him, I won't. But even if I did, would it make a difference? He's got to know you're after him."

Rivera bared her teeth.

The waitress approached with the sundae.

Milo said, "Sweeten your life, kid," and tossed a twenty on the table.

The waitress said, "You don't want this?"

"I like it but it doesn't like me." Patting his gut, he handed her a ten. Her mouth dropped open.

Milo winked at her and we left.

As I reached the coffee shop door, I glanced back at the booth. Neither Biro nor Rivera had moved.

Cop tableau.

My best friend had a surplus of personal power, knew how to use it judiciously.

I should've found that comforting.

Milo started up the car. "In answer to your first un-asked question, I'll take care of the situation. In answer to the second, why bother yourself with the details?"

I let him drive for a while before speaking. "In response to your first answer, how, when, and where? In terms of the second: because it's my life and I need to know what's going on."

He picked up speed. "Fair enough. I'm figuring on a nice direct confrontation with Crazy Connie."

"I'm not sure—"

"Hear me out, Alex. I'm going to surprise her at home, let her know we know everything, scare the hell out of her within legal limits, maybe even get her to do something that allows me to arrest her." Touching his abdomen, again. "I'm not exactly a small target. She makes contact anywhere on this Sahara of Irish dermis, she's toast."

"You'll be—"

"I'm a homicide cop, I get to work any damn homicides or attempted homicides that I choose. Per His Majesty."

"You asked the chief?"

"I posed a theoretical question to one of the chief's sycophants."

"You figured the sting would fail?"

"I figured nothing, Alex. It's the Boy Scout training. Be prepared."

"Connie uses the legal system—"

"Yeah, yeah, she'll get herself a lawyer. But meanwhile, the booking process can go *real* slow, let's see how snotty she is after a stretch in County with some east side homegirls as roomies." Big wolfish smile. "She wants to end your life because you wrote a damn *report*? *Fuck* her. Where does she live?"

"Westwood."

"Address."

"Don't know it by heart."

"It's in her file."

"Yes."

"File's back at your house."

Nod.

"Then that's where I'm aiming this chariot."

Instead of heading to my office, he said, "First things first," and continued through the house and out to the garden and Robin's studio.

She was working the table saw, so the two of us stood just inside the door. When the roar died, she removed her goggles, brushed dust off a rectangle of spruce. "Big Guy."

Milo said, "Hey."

Wiping her hands, she came forward. Blanche followed. "I'd like to say great to see you, Milo, but I'm sensing bad news."

He told her.

She shrugged. "Those things, you never know."

"The perfect woman."

Finally, something I could agree with.

The three of us convened around the kitchen table. Blanche settled at Milo's feet. He scratched her head absently. "If you had K-9 training, pooch, I'd take you along."

Robin said, "Take her where?"

I said, "He's going to confront Sykes."

Milo reiterated his logic.

Robin said, "Makes perfect sense. Thank you." To me: "Really, honey, what's the choice, continue in limbo?"

"I'm not sure this will get us out of limbo."

"What's your approach?" said Milo. "Doing therapy with her?"

I said nothing.

Robin fooled with my hair. "Honestly, Alex, the only other solution I see is you put her out of her misery, yourself." Sly smile. "Or I do it. Come to think of it, I've got all sorts of implements of destruction back at the studio."

Milo clamped his hands over his ears and began humming.

Robin laughed, pulled his left hand free, placed her

mouth near his lips. "And then I fill a bathtub with sulfuric acid, after which I take the bitch and—"

"Save it for the movie version, kid. Alex, get me that address."

I said, "When are you planning to do it?"

"She's a doctor, probably works late, I want to catch her at home, maybe tennish."

"Tonight?"

"You see any reason to prolong this? Gonna get myself a nice hearty dinner, something rib-sticking— hey, maybe ribs, that joint on Centinela—no, kids, don't offer to provide sustenance, I need a little alone time. Collecting thoughts, as it were."

"Ding dong," I said. "Homicide calling."

"Hey," he said, "if she'd succeeded, she woulda met me, anyway."

CHAPTER
14

After Milo left, Robin and I returned to the kitchen table.

I said, "So."

She said, "I suggest we adopt Plan B."

I said, "What's A?"

"Sitting around, our tummies in a knot, waiting for Big Guy to call and tell us what happened."

"Where's your sense of fun? What's B?"

"Enjoy life—maybe a rib-sticking meal of our own. If anyone can clear up this mess it's him, so why worry?"

"You can eat?"

"I'd sure as heck like to try. And please don't ask what happens if he doesn't convince her. We'll deal with that if and when it comes up."

"Fine. Where do you want to go?"

"Let's decide once we're on the road."

"Okay," I said. "Sorry."

"For being a potential victim? I think not, Alex. I think the only one who needs to apologize is that insane monster."

"I live," I said, "with the perfect woman."

"Far from it, darling." She punched my shoulder lightly. "But I'm way better than most."

* * *

We decided on Thai food at a storefront café on Melrose, were finished at nine forty-five. By now, Milo would be at Connie Sykes's place, watching, waiting.

I asked Robin if she wanted to drive around a bit.

She said, "You bet, beats us obsessing."

"Appreciate the kindness."

"What kindness?"

"Using the plural."

"What, you think I'm an Iron Maiden? This is nerve-racking for me, too. I'm just trying to utilize all those coping skills some psychologist taught me."

We cruised west into Beverly Hills, traversing Rodeo, stopping a few times so Robin could check out window displays.

"Name it, it's yours, Tsarina."

"Thank you, Sugar Daddy." Adopting a southern drawl. Unfortunate choice; my gut tightened. I looked at the dashboard clock.

Ten twenty-three. By now, Milo would be—

Robin said, "Let's go home, watch some tube, if he doesn't call by midnight, I'm assuming all is well and our dreams are going to be a lot better than hers."

Ten after midnight. Lights out.

"Love you, babe, thanks for your patience."

"Love you, too, Alex. Everything's going to be fine."

Three minutes later, I was swimming in worst-case scenarios, jumped when the phone rang.

Milo said, "It's me. You're safe."

"You're sure—"

"*Trust* me, you're *safe*. My life, on the other hand, just got a whole lot more complicated."

CHAPTER

15

Connie Sykes's residence was a one-story brick Tudor on a hilly dead-end street between Wilshire and Sunset. A cobbled driveway hosted the cream-colored Lexus.

Nice quiet location, mature trees lining the curb. Walking distance to the U. made it a good fit for a young professor's family, back when professors could afford Westwood. The house was set farther back from the curb than its neighbors, shrouded by shrubs and a four-story deodar cedar. Ideal setup for someone who craved privacy.

A typical custody evaluation would have led me to visit the place. No need for that in *Sykes v. Sykes* and the house had remained an abstraction—an address in a file.

Until now I hadn't realized how close it was to my home: five-minute drive, ten if commuters jammed up the Glen.

Walking distance if you were fit and so inclined.

It would've been easy enough for Connie to take a little hike under cover of darkness. The locked gate at the bottom of my road would have impeded a vehicle but a stalker on foot could've found a way around.

But that wasn't Connie's style; she was a delegator.

Now she was on the receiving end of someone else's plan.

Three black-and-whites parked diagonally across the street kept me well back from the yellow tape. So did a carelessly positioned white coroner's van and one of the black vans used to transport crime scene techs. The sky was black; same for the sidewalk fronting the house save for a single spotlit area near the front door.

I walked to the cops guarding the yellow tape. Jack-and-Jill team, early twenties. Officer Flynn, Officer Roosevelt, neither one impressed by my dropping Milo's name. I wasn't sure checking with him would help; he'd been clear about his preference.

"*No, stay home, Alex.*"

"*You called me.*"

"*To let you know you're safe.*"

Click.

Stepping back from the uniforms, I phoned him. "Reporting for duty, Lieutenant."

He said, "Oh, shit."

"Instruct your minions to let me in."

"Alex—"

"I won't make a mess. Promise. *Mom.*"

"Why the he—"

"I need to see."

He hung up. Moments later, the female uniform, Flynn, got a call on her radio. Looking doubtful, she waved me under the tape.

Connie Sykes lay on her back near the center of her smallish entry rotunda. No center table, just a round rug over hardwood. Imitation Persian, beige and blue and green, plus a splotch of amorphous, rusty red no weaver had ever intended.

A wrought-iron chandelier illuminated her death.

She wore a mocha-colored terry-cloth robe over sensible white flannel pajamas patterned with tiny sky-blue flowers. A white china teacup sat on its side, backed by a yellow evidence marker, around six feet to her right. The cup had landed just off the rug, coming to rest on oak flooring. The surrounding tea stain was a clear amoeba with a gray border.

The terry robe had flapped open, revealing another rusty blotch, dry and crusted, spreading over much of her pajama top. Just above the spot where her navel would be, a five-inch rip was visible in the blood. Clean, straight, horizontal, puckering at the center.

Initial pierce, then a side-to-side slash, laying waste to the diaphragm.

The robe was open because its sash had been removed and used to garrote Connie Sykes.

Her face was gray where it wasn't purplish-black. Her tongue was a Japanese eggplant sprouting from between chalky lips.

A coroner's investigator I knew as Gloria kneeled beside the body, camera around her neck, jotting notes in a little spiral book. Milo watched from a few feet away.

I said, "Stabbed, then strangled?"

Milo said, "In that order. No forced entry, no sign of struggle, all doors were locked when I entered. So she probably opened the door for someone, got stuck, and after she was down, they finished her off with the belt."

"Would the stab wound have been fatal?"

"I look like a doctor?"

Gloria smiled. "Hi, Dr. D., we can't go on meeting like this. No way to know for sure until she gets opened up but if I had to guess, I'd say yes. Go deep enough where she was cut, breathing stops."

I said, "But just to make sure, strangle her." I looked at the sash. No knot, just a loop.

Gloria looked down at Connie Sykes's distorted face. "Up close and personal. Someone sure didn't like her."

I thought: *Not an exclusive club*. Kept silent and struggled to sort out my feelings.

Seeing anyone debased to this extent makes me sad and some of that filtered through.

So no flush of triumph.

But . . .

Relief.

Suddenly I felt calmer than I had in days. Realized how wound up I'd been.

Milo said, "Seen enough?"

I looked past the body. The only room visible was a simply furnished living room backed by mullioned windows. The panes probably afforded a nice view of the backyard; tonight, they were squares of black.

To the left of the corpse was a small powder room, to the right, a coat closet.

A techie emerged from around a corner. "No sign of any burglary or disruption anywhere, Lieutenant. Bobby's dusting her bedroom and her bathroom but my guess is you won't get anything interesting, all the action was right here."

I said, "Taking care of business quickly."

Everyone stared at me. The techie, because he didn't know me; Milo and Gloria probably because I sounded flip.

Milo hooked a thumb. "Let's go outside."

We ducked under the tape and headed for the Seville. Lights in neighboring houses flickered. Three properties south of the crime scene, a large man held a large dog on a tight leash. As we passed, he said, "What's going on, Officers?"

Milo said, "A crime's been committed, sir."

"What kind of crime?"

I expected evasion. Milo said, "Homicide."

The large man said, "Her? She got killed?"

Milo veered toward him. As we got close, the man's porch light created details: soft build, white hair, bushy eyebrows, midfifties to sixty, wearing black velvet sweats. The dog was a tiger-brindle mix, overweight, with a blunt face and bright eyes. When we arrived, it settled on its haunches and breathed audibly. No protective instincts, maybe Lab plus rottweiler, more of the former.

Milo said, "You know Dr. Sykes?"

"I know she lives there," said the man.

"Nice person?"

"Huh . . . she was okay."

Milo waited.

The man said, "I guess I shouldn't speak ill of the dead but *nice* wouldn't exactly be accurate. She kept to herself, sometimes you'd say hi and she wouldn't answer. Maybe she was lost in thought."

"Or unfriendly."

"She never had friends over that I saw, Officer. Fact is, only time you'd hear from her was if she was complaining about someone."

"What'd she complain about?"

"Not cleaning up poop, leaving garbage cans out too long, that kind of thing."

"Who'd she complain to, Mr. . . ."

"Jack Burghoff. Anyone she thought was responsible. One time she knocked on my door and pointed to a pile of poop near her driveway. *Minute* little pile. Not exactly Otis's style, right, Otey?"

The dog let out a wheeze.

Burghoff said, "If only you *did* one-baggers, pal. Otis leaves a souvenir, you're going to need a shovel. Which is what I told Dr. Sykes. She looks at me like I was lying. I just walked away. Any idea who killed her? Was it a gun? 'Cause I didn't hear anything. We're vigilant, someone hears something, they report it."

He stopped. "Was it?"

Milo said, "No, sir."

"Then how—"

"I really can't say at this time, sir. So it was a pretty quiet night."

"Totally," said Burghoff. "Three or so years ago we had a bunch of burglaries, lots of stuff taken. Turns out the creep was a grad student at the U. who decided to augment his fellowship."

Milo said, "Stuart Belize."

"You busted him?"

"My colleagues in Robbery did."

"Nuts, huh? Studying for a Ph.D. by day, breaking into vacant houses at night? Anyway, that's my point. You guys got him because someone on the block reported him—Professor Ashworth, to be exact." Burghoff pointed across the street, at a two-story Spanish. "Which was kind of ironic, no? Professor nailing a student?"

Milo smiled. "What can you tell us about Dr. Sykes?"

"Just what I said, she wasn't too social. Last year we had a block party, everyone getting together, bringing potluck. Dr. Sykes didn't show and she was home because her car was in the driveway just like it is now."

"You're observant, sir."

"Goes with the territory, I'm an artist. Commercial, graphic, run art direction for Intello-fuel. You tell me your name today, tomorrow it'll be erased from my brain. But faces, visual stimuli? It's like life's a movie and I remember each scene."

"Did you happen to observe anything out of the ordinary tonight, sir?"

"Nope, if I had, I'd have called you guys. Only thing I can tell you is the approximate time she got home. I pulled up at seven twenty and her car wasn't there. Otis hadn't been walked yet, so I walked him. After changing my clothes, having a beer, so it was around seven forty and by then her car was there. So around seven thirty would be my guess."

"Would that be a typical time for Dr. Sykes to arrive?"

"Couldn't tell you," said Burghoff. "Generally I'm home by five, Otis is walked by six, once I'm in I don't come out. Tonight I had a late meeting."

The door to the neighboring house opened. A man stepped out. Burghoff waved.

The man walked toward us. Around the same age as Burghoff, shorter, thinner, wearing a white T-shirt and pale blue sweatpants. "Jack."

"Mike."

"What's going on?"

"Dr. Sykes got killed."

"You're kidding." The new arrival looked at us. Milo introduced himself.

"Michael Bernini. Who did it?"

Milo said, "Don't know yet."

"Killed. Wow—hey, Otis."

The dog exhaled as Bernini stooped to pet him.

Burghoff said, "Pretty crazy, huh?"

"I'll say."

"Your turn, Mike. Back to bed, Ote-man."

Bernini had nothing to add. Same for two other residents of the block, an elderly couple and a younger woman in a silk kimono who opined that Connie Sykes had been "basically a hermit," and repeated the block-party story. Speaking with no more agitation or sympathy than had anyone else.

Milo and I continued down the block.

He said, "Late, but unlamented."

I said, "Unlamented could mean a long suspect list."

"I've got a short list. Starting with your buddy Effo or one of his homeboys and ending with the sister."

We reached the Seville. He held the driver's door open. "Facts is facts. Have a nice night."

I said, "You're taking the case?"

"Why wouldn't I?"

"When did you get here?"

"Ten thirty, what's that got to do with anything?"

"You parked, watched her house, mulled about how best to scare her off without creating a problem for both of us. No easy answer to that so eventually you got out and walked to her front door and rang her bell and got no response. Her car was in the driveway so you figured she was in the shower or doing something else that impeded her hearing. Or she'd heard you just fine and was refusing to come to the door. The door has a peephole, for all you knew, she was looking right at you. You got irritated but stayed cautious: Crazy woman, what if she was standing on the other side holding a gun? You took out your Glock, rang some more. Zip. At that point, your choice was to back off completely and continue worrying about me, or to do a little checking. You squinted through the peephole. That chandelier gives a lot of light and you saw her. You cursed, put the Glock back, gloved up, tried the door. If it was open, you'd re-arm and go in. If not you'd start making calls."

"It was locked. So what?"

"You're officially a witness, yet you're taking the case . . ."

"Because I want it. Some muckamuck says I can't do it, fine. You going to suggest that to anyone?"

"Of course not."

Turning his back, he loped back toward the crime scene.

I said, "Talk to you tomorrow."

His response was muted.

I think he said, "Maybe."

At the end of the next day I phoned Milo. No call-back.

With no active therapy cases, my workload consisted of writing up two reports. That left plenty of time for playing with the dog and downtime with Robin.

Robin was busy and Blanche's high-rate behavior was the sleep of the just.

That left plenty of time for thinking.

I felt like calling Efren Casagrande, knew it was wrong.

Ditto, Cherie Sykes.

The following morning at nine, Milo called my private line.

I said, "Lieutenant who?"

"Touchy, touchy."

"How's the case?"

"Moving along," he said. "If you call idling moving. And guess what, you can now get involved."

"What changed?"

"Hour and a half Rivera and I are interviewing your amigo Effo Casagrande. He's a savvy guy, which is to be expected seeing as crime's his chosen career. Has hired a lawyer who's informed us that *Mister*

Casagrande is under no obligation to talk to us. However, *Mister* Casagrande will deign to donate some of his precious time if *Doctor* Delaware is present. Apparently, he misses you. Must be nice to be wanted. Unlike ol' Connie who no one seems to give a shit about. Including her brother up in Silicon Valley who I just got off the phone with. He reacted like I'd given him the weather forecast. Said he'd get down soon as his schedule frees up. Meanwhile, the body molders at the crypt."

"Anything interesting from the autopsy?"

"Nope, stabbed fatally then strangled for good measure. No sign she fought back."

"Given the chance to fight, she would've," I said. "So she was taken by surprise."

"That's the way I see it. Someone who didn't scare her."

"That doesn't apply to Efren."

"But it might apply to Efren's homeboy Guzman because he cleans her office and she's already done business with him. And if that doesn't work out, I've got Sis."

"Have you told her about the murder?"

"Didn't think that was advisable. And obviously you haven't told her, either. So please don't. See you at ten thirty."

CHAPTER

17

I drove to the West L.A. station, wondering what Efren would be like. Thinking back to the session following his lifestyle comment when he'd showed up jumpy and distracted, only to sink down and hang his head drowsily.

That day I said, "Feeling okay?"

"Yeah . . . maybe a little . . . I don't know."

"Confused?"

He shook his head. I got him juice, anyway.

"I'm okay—been thinking about a new engine."

"For the Chevy?"

"Yeah. I get it when I'm sixteen."

"Congratulations."

"Yeah but it's slooooow."

For the next quarter hour I listened to car-talk and watched him perk up. The crate engine he wanted for the low-rider, new speakers to "like shake up your head, man."

Maybe he'd keep the Aztec eagle, maybe he'd replace it with "something more bad."

I said, "Car have hydraulics?"

"Yeah but shit. I'm gonna make it like this." Separating his hands with a three-foot gap.

I said, "Going for the big-time bounce."

"Yeah . . . I said something last time. Lifestyle. You prolly don remember."

"Diabetes doesn't fit your lifestyle."

"Yeah, yeah. So what the fuck was *that*?" Slapping his forehead hard. "I mean what *was* that, man? Like it's it's it's . . . like a *thing*, man? Like it's gonna go *away*, man? *Fuck* that. Fuck that bitch's ass. Her. The bitch."

"Diabetes."

He clawed his fingers. "She's like a lyin' naggin' bitch. Goin' at me, ruh ruh ruh ruh ruh."

"Trying to control you."

"*Fuck* that." He punched a palm. "Fuck *her*. Fuck *all* a them. I make her *my* bitch."

"It's your body," I said.

"Damn fuckin right—I'm like the blood is *good*, man. The blood is red, *mi sangre*, it's like alive, man, you know? Get a little sweet, fuck, I change it, you know? With that insulin shit, it's fuckin' *bullshit*, y'know? It's just sugar."

I nodded.

"*Fuck* them," he said. "I do it *my fuckin' way*."

The following week, he said, "Can't do every week no more. Like maybe two a month, y'know?"

I figured he was getting ready to terminate. Maybe premature, maybe not, but no sense arguing. I had to remain the adult who made no attempt to control him.

I was wrong. When it came to Efren, I got used to being wrong.

For the next thirteen months, he showed up faithfully, never a minute late, never forgetting to bring cash payment. During that time, his mother called five times, a gracious, soft-spoken woman who'd married a psychopath and had possibly birthed a psychopath. Wanting me to know he'd had great checkups, the smoothest blood sugar his doctor had ever seen.

The fifth time she phoned her voice swelled with emotion. She told me I was a miracle worker, she was saying prayers for me every Sunday Mass, could she send a pot of *menudo* with Efren, did I know what that was?

"Know it, like it, appreciate the gift, Mrs. Casagrande. But please don't feel it's necessary."

"No gift, Doctor. A thanks."

"Seeing Efren has been a pleasure."

Silence. "Really?"

"He's a very bright boy."

"I know, I know, so how come he's so stupid?"

I didn't answer.

She said, "Anyway, he's doing good. First I thank God, then you."

I wrote my third follow-up report to his endocrinologist. As with the first two, I never heard back. I knew the doctor as anxious and over-extended, barely coping with the patient load the hospital shoved at him. He did send me three new referrals and they proved simple, compared with Efren.

The *menudo* was delicious, perfect for a chilly November night.

Robin said, "You should mold your practice, darling: patients with moms with culinary skills."

After the last session of the thirteenth month, Efren announced he was moving from L.A., couldn't come anymore.

"Where you going?"

He shifted on the sofa.

I said, "Big secret, huh?"

"Nah . . . Oakland, okay? Anyway, thanks, man. For listening to my bullshit."

"Actually," I said, "you put out very little bullshit."

"Yeah, right."

"I mean it. You were straight."

A sunken chest heaved. A flimsy-looking hand moved swiftly to one eye, then the other. He worried a big zit nippling his underbuilt chin.

Back to the eyes, now. "Got some shit in here, like dirt."

"Smog," I said. "That's L.A."

"Yeah . . . you been to Oakland?"

"Took my licensing test there years ago but not since." Before that I'd trained at Langley Porter, UC San Francisco, supplementing my fellowship's pittance by working as a research assistant on a gang study. Braving some of Oakland's more murderous streets. Blocks that saw more blood than some butcher shops.

Efren said, "License? Like for driving? Why you go up there for that?"

"My psychologist's license," I said.

"Huh?"

I pointed to the framed certificate behind my desk. "That says it's legal for me to do my job."

"Legal? What's illegal for you, man? Doing some gangsta-freak doctor shit?" He bobbed his head. "How you feelin' I stealin' you dealin' we all feelin' getting *real-in*."

I laughed. "Interesting concept."

"You're saying you gotta pay to work?"

"There's a fee, but mostly you need a certain amount of—"

"Oh, man, they pushin' you *around*."

"Not really—"

"You gotta *pay*? To do your *job*? That su-ucks— hey, you ever need help, you say, okay?"

"Help with what?"

"Anyone *pushing* on you." He winked. "Now I got to go. Long trip to El Oco-land. El *Loco*-land."

"You're driving up there?"

"Maybe." Another wink. "Oh, yeah, I ain't *legal* to drive." Laughing, he got up and slouched to the door. Walking back to me, he held out his hand.

I shook it. His bones felt fragile. "Hey," he said. "It's been real, man."

I said, "I'll walk you out."

"No, no, I know the way, man."

"Okay, then. Have a good time, Ef."

"Good?" His eyes slitted. "Ain't gonna be fun. Gonna be *business*."

Now, years later, I reached the West L.A. station twenty minutes early, parked a block away, strolled the distance on foot, kept walking past the building. Figuring if Efren reverted to instinct he'd be on time, if he wanted to strut a bit, he'd keep Milo waiting. Either way, I had a decent chance of seeing him before anyone else got involved.

I'm so fucking pissed some bitch would try to do that, I'm ready to kill *her ass. You with that?*

Nope.

Just kidding. Maybe.

If I encountered him, what would I say?

He was early. Walking south on Butler from Santa Monica Boulevard next to a curvy blonde, the two of them engaged in animated conversation.

He'd grown a few inches but was far from tall. Had added breadth to his shoulders but remained a skinny, loose-limbed figure with all the bulk of a wire hanger.

He wore a long-sleeved white shirt, dark pants, black shoes. Full head of black hair, brushed straight back; adopting the gangbanger coif of a previous era, none of that shaved-head obviousness.

No ink I could see from a distance. His skin had cleared.

I backed into the shadow of the station's façade. Whatever the blonde had to say held Efren's attention. As they got closer I made out details. His face was longer, bonier, with thick black eyebrows and a beak nose bottomed by a faint dark smudge.

Mustache or shadow.

The blond woman was about Efren's age, taller than him by an inch with Marilyn Monroe hair and a shape to match. She wore a fitted red satin blouse, black pencil skirt, crimson stockings flocked in black, silver stilettos that did nothing to slow her prance-like gait.

They were five yards away. The flocking on her legs turned to applique: tiny black roses. A maroon suede briefcase swung from a black-nailed hand.

Gorgeous face, exuberant makeup, gigantic hazel eyes.

The smudge under Efren's nose was, indeed, a wispy 'stache.

I stepped in front of them. Efren's hand shot to a pant pocket. Reflexive move.

He took a second to focus, grinned and grabbed my hand. "Hey, it's my doctor—this is him, Leese. This is the *patron* save my life when I was a stupid sugar baby."

His voice had taken on more East L.A. singsong than before. Hormones had lowered it to tenor. His teeth had been straightened, his smile was radiant, his hair smelled of citrus pomade.

Gangster prince. Same look of easy confidence you saw on Ivy League legacies and showbiz brats.

We shook hands. His bones had laid on some calcium but they still felt flimsy. Nice manicure.

The blonde watched disapprovingly.

Efren said, "*Man*, it's been a long time. How you been *doin'*, Doc—oh, yeah, not so good." His irises turned to lumps of coal. "Bitch tryin' to do *that*. Crazy."

I shrugged.

The blonde said, "Anyway . . ."

Efren turned to her. Her gaze was stony.

"This is *him*, Leese."

Unimpressed, she offered her fingertips to me. As she pulled away, curving black nails grazed my knuckles and I couldn't help but take that as a warning.

She said, "Lisa Lefko, Mr. Casagrande's attorney."

"Alex—"

"I know who you are," she said, consulting a Ulysse Nardin watch rimmed with diamonds. "We need to get going, E.C."

Efren said, "Wait one sec—so, Doc, you sure you okay? I mean psychological."

"I'm fine."

He studied me. "So how're things going for you? Besides all this shit?"

"Great. How about you?"

"Me? Life is be-yootiful, got what they call a thriving business."

I knew but I asked. "What kind?"

Lisa Lefko tensed up.

Efren said, "Car audiovisual." He kissed air, bounced on shiny new loafers. "Top-of-the-line entertainment systems, Doc—hey, why don't you come in, I set you up with something really sick—what kind of music you like?"

"All kinds."

"All kinds, huh? Well, I got systems for all kinds.

We also got a place next door, do custom rims. Got a guy with the best blue squirrel brush in town, does pin-striping it's like *art*. Don't you think, Leese? That stripe on your Jag pretty cool, no?"

Lisa Lefko said, "Lovely. Now, can we—"

"Doc, anything you drive we can make it hyper-bitchin'. What's your wheels now?"

"The Seville."

"Same one?"

I nodded.

"You kidding."

"She's been good to me, Ef."

"Whoa," he said. "That's like . . . historical. Original engine?"

"Third."

"Third," he said. "Caddy?"

I nodded. "New old stock."

"Wow wow wow, that's like antique."

Lisa Lefko tapped a stiletto heel on the pavement. A black-and-white drove past, entered the staff parking lot. She followed its trajectory. So did Efren.

"Cops," he said. "They could use better wheels. Make 'em happier, they stop giving problems to everyone."

Steel in his voice. Lisa Lefko cleared her throat, arched her back advertising her figure, dared anyone to make a comment.

Movie-star face, pinup body, the eyes of an IRS auditor. She reminded me of someone—Connie's lawyer, Medea Wright, another looker with a J.D. not afraid to flaunt.

Lisa Lefko could be Wright's taller, blonder sorority sister. Maybe law schools were looking for a type.

Efren said, "Okay, Doc, let's do this."

Lefko said, "He's not part of it, E.C."

"What you talking about?"

"That's what I was trying to tell you on the way over, E.C. Got a call from that lieutenant. Dr. Delaware's not going to be part of your interview."

"Why not?"

"Police procedure."

"What does that mean?"

"It means whatever they want it to mean, E.C. Bottom line: They don't want him participating."

He turned to me. "You know about that?"

I shook my head. "All I was told was you requested I show up."

"Shit," he said. "They wasting your time, they wasting my time."

Lisa Lefko said, "Before you get too friendly with the doctor, consider that maybe he's closer to them than he is to you, showed up as a sop to you."

Efren said, "Sock?"

She sighed. "Sop. Throwing you a bone."

"Huh?"

"Cops want you here, you wanted Dr. Delaware here. They probably figured you two would talk for a few minutes, then they'd corral you. But now you managed that on your own. So can we go in and get it over?" Turning to me, she continued to address him. "It's not like you have *anything* to tell them, Efren."

He blinked. "Yeah. True." To me: "Good to see you, Doc. Just wanted to make sure you're healthy."

"I am. Thanks."

He hooked a thumb at the station entrance. "Lisa says you work with the cops."

Always did.

I said, "Sometimes."

"Like what, getting inside bad guys' heads?" Smiling.

"Basically."

"You still seein' sugar babies?"

"Once in a while."

"Mostly it's the cops?"

Lisa Lefko said, "E.C., we really need to—"

He waved her quiet, gripped my hand with both of his. "Been real, Doc. Stay healthy."

I waited a couple of minutes before phoning Milo's desk.

Moe Reed answered. "He just started talking to the suspect, Doc. You're supposed to go to his office, video feed's on his computer."

"Right on the desktop?" I said. "New system?"

"Been operative for over a year," said Reed. "This morning he let me show him how to use it."

Clean, beige room. One table, three chairs, no water, no coffee. The table was pushed into a far corner. No physical barrier for psychological protection. Efren sat next to Lisa Lefko. Both of them faced Milo.

Milo said, "Thanks for coming in, Mr. Casagrande."

Efren said, "Hey, my pleasure."

"Okay, let's start—"

Lisa Lefko said, "In this case, start equals finish. Mr. Casagrande has nothing to discuss about anything."

She got up, hefted her briefcase.

Milo turned scarlet. "What the—"

"Mr. Casagrande has nothing probative to offer about any criminal or civil matters and upon advice of legal counsel, he will offer no replies to any questions whatsoever."

Milo leaned toward Efren. "That the way you feel?"

Efren's smile was gone. His shoulders were stiff as he turned to Lefko.

As surprised as Milo.

Lefko said, "That's exactly the way he feels, Lieutenant."

Milo said, "She talks for you, huh?"

Efren said, "Hey, Leese, we can talk about the Dodgers, no?"

Lefko's face was stony.

Milo said, "If you intended this all along, Ms. Lefko, why did we waste time—"

"Good question, Lieutenant."

Both men stared at her. She cocked a hip, tossed hair, switched her briefcase to the other hand. "Ready, Mr. Casagrande?"

Efren shifted in his chair. His laugh was strained.

Milo said, "Adios," and stomped out of the room.

Once he was gone, Lisa Lefko smiled down at her client. First indication I'd seen that she was capable.

Efren sat there.

She said, "Don't say anything, I'm sure the room is bugged."

He didn't move.

"Got some mail for you back at my office," she said. "From out of town."

Emphasis on *town*. Efren's eyebrows climbed. She walked to the door. Held it open for him.

His turn to follow. He did. Moving like a much older man.

CHAPTER

18

Milo flung open his office door hard enough to propel the knob into the wall. Easy fit into the hole he'd established years ago. He yanked the knob out. Plaster snowed on linoleum.

Flicking a black lick of hair off his mottled forehead, he said, "What a fun job, that mouthy little lawyer . . ."

Dropping onto his chair, he set off a chorus of squeaks.

I said, "She's Efren's attorney of record but I doubt he's her primary client."

"Who, then?"

"The greater organization."

"Barbie the Mob Mouthpiece?" He rolled his neck, loosened his tie. "What makes you say that?"

"Efren looked as surprised as you by her sandbag. And after you left, he sat there until she told him she had mail waiting for him from out of town. Sounded like code to me."

Shuffling papers, he shoved them aside. "Probably . . . a total waste of time—at least *you're* happy."

"You're not?"

"What do I have to be happy about?"

I smiled. "My continuing existence."

He stretched his arms wide, crooked the right limb to avoid slamming a wall. Wriggling out of his jacket, he scrolled through email that made him glower.

His office is a cramped, stuffy, windowless closet far from the big detective room. Part of a deal he and a former police chief hammered out after Milo unearthed enough dirt to demolish the boss's personal and professional lives. An urbane, enthusiastically corrupt man, the chief probably figured the room would serve as punishment. I believe Milo regards it as a perk. When it comes to LAPD, he's always been a man apart.

In the old days, that resulted from being a gay detective when the department supposedly had none. It's been years since his locker was stuffed with nasty porn and carved with swastikas. Nowadays the department has regulations that bar discrimination of anyone by anyone based on anything, anytime. What that does to internal attitude is anyone's guess.

What distances Milo these days from his colleagues are an affection for solitude and an allergy to authority. The new chief keeps him on because he's a statistics fan and Milo's close rate is always at the top. But my friend will never rise above lieutenant.

To someone else that might be career stalemate. Milo likes it just fine because most lieutenants work the desk ("Just what the world needs, another pencil-pushing zombie") while he's got the title, the pay, and the promised pension, and can still detect.

Still, on days like this, the room felt like a cell.

He said, "Must be interesting. Having Casagrande be responsible for your continued existence but knowing if it was someone else they'd be dead."

I said nothing.

"Don't want to heap on the cognitive dissonance,

Alex, but what's your take on Ramon Guzman's life expectancy?"

"You figure Efren will tie up a loose end."

"Guzman embarrassed him by improvising. You figure otherwise?"

"Well," I said, "seeing as Guzman was happy to take the contract on my life and Efren stopped it, I'm not going to contemplate too deeply."

"So just let it rest?" he said. "Including Ol' Connie's murder? Seeing as you're not mourning her in any big way."

"Not mourning but I am curious."

"An intellectual thing."

"You feel any personal attachment to her, Big Guy?"

He didn't answer.

I said, "Yet you're working the case. So we're in the same place. What next?"

"What next is I need to learn more about Mr. Casagrande because he remains my prime. Normally, I might be asking you for your insights. Since this is an abnormal situation, I guess we go our separate ways."

"Connie was an abrasive woman. There could be lots of suspects."

"You've convinced yourself Casagrande didn't do it."

"I don't know one way or the other but it might not hurt to be open-minded."

"Okay, then the sister."

I didn't reply.

He said, "What, some patient didn't like her bedside manner so they sliced her diaphragm and choked her out?"

I said, "Bedside manner doesn't apply. She ran a pathology lab, had little or no contact with patients. But she could've ticked off any number of people."

"No forced entry, it was someone she'd open the door for."

"I don't see Efren or gangbanger hit man fitting that description. Her social skills, she couldn't have been a terrific boss."

"The classic disgruntled-worker scenario? Hell, with a net that wide, it could be gardeners, delivery boys."

"I'd still start with those she could've irritated chronically. Any plans to visit her lab?"

"It's on my list."

"I'm free for the rest of the day."

"Oh, sure, tag along, great idea."

"You're on it, no reason I shouldn't be."

"She didn't try to off *me*, Alex."

"Granted," I said. "But her plan failed and my head is clear."

"And now you're directing me away from the two most obvious suspects: Casagrande and the sister."

"Can't speak for Efren but I don't see Cherie as violent. Just the opposite, she's passive, easygoing."

"Not so passive she didn't fight Connie in court."

"She didn't fight, she defended herself. And she won, there'd be no reason for her to kill Connie."

"What if she worried Connie would keep yanking her back to court? Connie someone who'd give up that easy?"

"I just don't see Cherie committing murder," I said.

"Because you know her."

"Because I just don't see it."

He rolled his neck. "Maybe you're right, maybe not. Either way, there's no sense in you getting involved because *I've* got to consider them as suspects and you're not free to talk about either of them."

"I can talk to you about Ree. She's not a patient."

"What is she?"

"The subject of a report. Guardianship cases are public record."

"If you had something on her, you'd tell me."

"You bet."

"She convinced you she was righteous."

"I went in without preconceptions but it wasn't a custody dispute where both parties are presumed to have rights. The child is legally Ree's and Connie tried to use the system to take her away."

"Sounds like legalized theft."

"If she'd succeeded it would've been."

"Which leads me straight back to Cherie. What if Connie did tell her she was in for a long war? That's a dandy motive."

"Fine, check her out," I said. "But we could also have a look at Connie's staff."

"Again with the *we*."

"I'll buy lunch."

"Not hungry."

I laughed.

He said, "I can't stand when you do that."

"Do what?"

"Assume I'm ruled by my digestive system."

"God forbid," I said. "Want me to drive? Think T-bone."

CHAPTER

19

Con-Bio Medical Testing was housed in a gray cube on Laurel Canyon Boulevard between Burbank and Magnolia.

Short drive to Rubin Rojo's parking lot. Connie had been nothing but efficient. I imagined her date book the day of the meet with "George."

1. Analyze a few specimens.
2. Fill out the billing slips.
3. Have a little chat to finalize a hit on that bastard.

Thinking about it made my jaw ache. Picturing her dead body helped a bit.

I'd claimed objectivity to Milo but it would be a while before I could sort out my feelings. The key was constructive denial: convincing myself that she was just another victim, a puzzle to be solved.

As I pulled into the lab's parking lot, I caught Milo studying me. When I turned, he made a show of checking his notepad before exiting the car.

Ten-space lot. The dedicated slot marked *Dr. Sykes Only. Violators Will Be Towed at Their Expense* was unoccupied. The area comprised a nice size chunk of Valley real estate. Milo had phoned the assessor as I

drove over the hill, learned that Connie had purchased the property six years ago for seven figures.

That along with the house in Westwood and the in-
vestments she'd bragged about added up to a sizable
estate. What would Rambla's life have been like growing up Westside-affluent? What would it be like with
Ree?

Milo pushed the lab's front door open and we
stepped into a windowless waiting room. Four black
hard plastic chairs sat on green-blue carpeting with all
the give of Formica. A corner table was piled with
dog-eared throwaway magazines. Overhead light was
cold, buzzing, inadequate.

Facing the door was a sliding window of thick peb-
bled glass. To the right was a knobless door plastered
with bold-typed instructions.

Arrivals were to knock only once then wait until
called.

Payment prior to testing could be imposed "at
Con-Bio's discretion."

No smoking, no eating or drinking, no loud conversation.

The premises had been certified by Cal/OSHA and
a host of additional government watchdogs.

No one certifies friendliness.

Milo tried to slide open the glass. No give. Pressure
on the door was no more successful.

Each of the four chairs was occupied and our entry
caused the quartet of "arrivals" to stir. Nearest to me
was a black man in his seventies with so little upper
body that his belt rested just below his pectorals.
Next to him sat a corpulent white man with frizzy red
hair, wearing a stained orange tank top and greasy
brown shorts that exposed pink limbs crusted with
scabs. A muscular young black man in exercise togs
had pushed himself as far as possible from those two,

which wasn't far at all. Tucked in the corner, a small, skinny white girl with jaundiced eyes and enough facial pierces to make a minimally empathic person wince, hunched tight, with both feet on her chair.

Milo rapped the glass twice.

When no one responded, he added a loud knuckle drumroll.

The older black man said, "They don't like that."

No answer from the other side of the glass but I could make out movement.

Milo knocked hard. His hand was only an inch from the glass when it slid open. A white-uniformed, pudding-faced brunette in her forties said, "Can't you read—"

Milo's badge turned her anger to reluctant civility. "How may I help you, Officer?"

"By buzzing us in."

"Sir, we're extremely busy—"

"So are we."

"Sir, I'll need authorization—"

"From your boss? Unfortunately, she's not here." Milo leaned in closer, lowered his voice just above a whisper. Four heads behind us craned. "And how do I know that?"

The pudding-faced woman stared.

As he leaned forward, the quartet did the same. He whispered: "Matter of fact, we're here about your boss."

"Dr. Connie? I don't—"

He showed her his card again, tapped his finger near *Homicide*. She gasped and slapped a hand over one breast and said, "Omigod. No!"

"Unfortunately, yes."

"Oh, my *God!*"

The older black man said, "Look like someone up and *tight*."

The pudding-faced woman said, "Everyone leave, your appointments are canceled."

Face-Pierce said, "Hey, what the fuck?"

Pudding glared at her. "You heard me. We'll call you to reschedule."

The muscular black man said, "In case you don't realize it, *some* of us work."

Pudding shouted, "Go! Leave! Out!"

The waiting room emptied amid a chorus of curses. Face-Pierce was the last to exit and she gave the door a kick that caused it to rattle.

The pudding-faced woman—*E. Broadbent*, per her tag—jabbed the rim of her desk and set off a hiss. The internal door swung open.

Con-Bio's nerve center was puny: Broadbent's desk and a smaller workstation, unoccupied. A hallway that led to a door marked *Laboratory* and tagged with a hazardous material sticker. A metal chair and table were positioned against the corridor's left wall. Atop the table sat a metal bin holding a phlebotomy kit: disposable syringes, amber rubber tourniquets, cotton swabs, bandages. Directly across from the puncture station was a door marked *Lavatory/Urine and Stool Depository.*

E. Broadbent said, "Now what are you trying to tell me?"

Milo said, "Unfortunately, Dr. Sykes is deceased."

"Murdered?"

"Afraid so."

"Dear God. When?"

"Last night. When did you last speak to her?"

"Yesterday. It was just another working day. I left at six, she was still here."

"Were you curious when she didn't show up this morning?"

"No," said E. Broadbent. "That wasn't unusual.

Dr. Connie doesn't see patients. We don't have patients—do you understand what we're about?"

I said, "You analyze biologic samples."

"We test for diseases, including conditions other labs can't handle. Exotic tropical things. Uncommon toxins. As well as sexually transmitted diseases."

"If they're not patients, what are they?"

"We refer to them as sample donors."

Milo said, "Stains on a slide."

"Well . . ."

"So Dr. Sykes's hours were irregular."

"Not really," said E. Broadbent. "It's not like she was gallivanting, for the most part she was here and she's almost always the last to leave. What I'm trying to get at is she had her own schedule so if she didn't come in it wasn't something anyone would question." She exhaled. "I can't believe this. What *happened*?"

"How about we talk in her office? We'd like to see it, anyway."

"There is no office."

"Where does she do her thing?"

Frowning, she marched up the hall and unlocked the lab door.

That revealed the bulk of the building's floor space, a wide, windowless area filled with stainless-steel tables, microscopes, centrifuges, a mass of things that bubbled and whirred and flashed digital readouts.

One person working, a white-coated, safety-goggled Indian man twirling dials in between gazes into a binocular microscope. Our presence didn't stop him.

E. Broadbent said, "Sajit?"

He waved, continued analyzing.

She pointed to the nearest table. Cleared of medical gizmos, it bore a laptop and a pair of reading glasses.

"That's where she works."

I said, "She conducted all her business there?"

"You bet. Dr. Connie is—was—" She paused to suck in air. "This is so . . . I forgot what I was saying . . ."

"Dr. Connie was . . ."

"Okay, yes, she was efficient. There was no need for frills—who *did* this to her?"

Milo said, "We don't know."

"Well," said E. Broadbent, "maybe I do. But you can't use my name on any report, I refuse to be connected to any more of it."

Milo said, "Any more of what?"

"I'm serious, sir. I will *not* get involved."

"Fair enough," he lied. "Who do you suspect?"

She looked at Sajit. "Let's go outside."

We followed her through the waiting room out to the parking area. A glance at Connie Sykes's unoccupied parking space caused tears to flow down her cheeks. Brushing them away, she quickened her pace, stopped at the high wall that backed the lot.

Removing a pack of Virginia Slims from her uniform pocket, she lit up, inhaled greedily. "I mean it, you can't quote me." Another deep intake of carcinogens. "Okay . . . God, this is so . . . Dr. Connie was embroiled in a legal matter with her sister. Who just happens to be a nutcase and a drug addict. So it wouldn't surprise me."

Milo said, "What kind of legal matter?"

"Custody. Dr. Connie's niece. The sister's the mother but in name only. She has no sense of personal responsibility—she's also a criminal, I'm talking lowlife. The one smart thing she did was the child—a girl, her name is Rambla, she's just a baby, really—she gave her to Dr. Connie when she went traipsing all over the country with some drug-addict musicians. Dr. Connie raised her like she was her own and the poor little thing finally had a chance at a decent life."

Smoking some more, she squared her shoulders. "Everything was going along fine. Dr. Connie had a space set up next to my desk. She provided the best for her. Top-quality baby food, organic milk, you name it. She'd bring her in and that child would sleep peacefully in that crib, just loving her life. We'd give her toys and love and she'd giggle and then Dr. Connie would come out and play with her in between samples, sometimes she'd take her for a stroller walk. She was a well-behaved baby, Dr. Connie was talking about finding the best preschool, a really first-rate place, this baby had it made in the shade and *then* what happens? *She* comes back. All of a sudden, she's changed her mind, is taking the baby back. She thinks she can do that, after Dr. Connie invested all that energy. Like sure, I'm just your babysitter, feel free to waltz in and out."

I said, "So what happened?"

"What happened? A scene happened."

"A scene here?"

"Oh, yes, you bet. The baby's napping away and *she* comes and barges her way in and disrupts everything."

"The baby's mother."

"In name only," said E. Broadbent. "It should be about character not just dropping them out the chute. There's a license to drive, why not for that?"

I said, "Something to certify fitness."

"You bet. If I had kids, I'd want to make sure I was qualified."

"How'd the sister barge her way in?"

"By being sneaky," she said. "She lurked to the side where we couldn't see her then waited until we buzzed in a sample donor and ran in. And mind you, she went straight for the baby, didn't care that the baby was fast asleep. Just ran past me and snatched that little thing up and tried to make her escape. Not *quite.* I stood there and blocked her but then the look on her face, sirs—I'm talking crazy. For the life of me I thought she'd . . . do something. *With* the baby in her hands. I didn't want any problems so I stepped aside and meanwhile Dr. Connie came out of the lab and the two of them had a to-do."

"Did it get physical?"

"No, but it could've if that one had her way."

"She threatened Dr. Connie?"

"Her whole demeanor was enraged. Dr. Connie tried to convince her rationally. *She* wouldn't listen. So of course, Dr. Connie tried to take the baby. And *she* held on even tighter, began screaming—it was ugly, let me tell you. We had a full waiting room, standing room only, donors hearing the commotion. So what could Dr. Connie do? She stepped aside. Then she called a lawyer. And that's why I'm telling you you have to check that crazy lady out."

"Dr. Connie must've been pretty upset."

"Upset *and* angry," said E. Broadbent. "That someone could be so selfish."

"So she sued."

"It cost her a fortune but she had her principles."

"Was the case resolved?"

She frowned. "They brought in experts—the other side. They brought in sleazy hired guns. One of those psychiatrists who already had his mind made up because *she* flirted with him. Dr. Connie was so frustrated, she tried everything. The judge was a fool. Her lawyer was a fool."

"So she lost."

"For the time being."

"She planned to re-file?"

"She talked about it. So that's why I'm telling you: The only person crazy enough to do something this crazy was *her*. You want a name, I'll give it to you: Cherie." She spelled it. "Cherie Sykes, she's been in prison, I'm sure you people have records on her. The baby is Rambla. I can only imagine what her life is now."

Milo copied in his pad. Convincing prop; E. Broadbent nodded approvingly.

"Ma'am, this information you have about the sister's past, did it come from Dr. Sykes?"

"What do you mean?"

"Did you ever have the opportunity to observe Cherie Sykes prior to the confrontation?"

"No reason I would," said E. Broadbent. "Dr. Sykes is—was"—two nicotine hits—"a brilliant woman. A pathologist. The other one? An addict."

"Anything else, ma'am?"

"I don't think you need anything else. Got your work cut out for you."

CHAPTER
20

I drove out of the lot, paused at Laurel Canyon. "Which way for steak?"

Milo said, "No way." Long pause. "Two sides to every story."

"Doesn't mean more than one's right." I headed south toward the city.

"That cuts both ways, Alex. Yeah, she's biased, but that doesn't mean she's wrong."

"She's wrong about a few things."

"Oh," he said. "That. You're absolutely certain Ms. Cher-ree didn't flirt with you?"

I glared at him.

"Just kidding. And despite any bullshit Connie might've handed Broadbent, her observation says plenty: No love lost between the sisters and now one sister is dead. Even if I accept your assessment that Ree doesn't have it in her, she could have a friend who does. Like the kid's da-da. Maybe *that's* why she didn't let on who he was, he's a badass with anger-control issues, she's stuck in a court battle, can't afford to weaken her case. Unfortunately for Connie, Daddy decided to emerge from the shadows to protect his little nuclear family."

"There was plenty of time to do that before the

lawsuit. Would've spared Ree the expense and the stress."

"Ounce of prevention?" He thought about that all the way to Moorpark. "Maybe Daddy was indisposed until recently."

"Incarcerated?"

"It happens once in a while. And his being locked up would give Ree even more reason to not identify him. I'm gonna learn more about her social life. Does that mean she's at the top of my list? She's sure edging up against your loyal patient Efren. Now, kindly chauffeur me back to 310. Regards to Robin and the pooch."

Code for *Don't call me I'll call you.*

He shut his eyes, slumped, allowed his lips to slacken.

I said, "You're really not hungry."

"Only for the truth."

I dropped him back at the station, drove a block, phoned Ree Sykes. No answer, no voice mail.

The drive to her apartment took nearly an hour. As I transitioned from the Westside to Hollywood, blue skies faded to the gray of wet tissue paper, washed with clots of phlegmy yellow where the sun fought to poke through.

Hollywood Boulevard teemed with junkies, tweakers and off-season tourists clogging the sidewalks that fronted shlock-shops, fast-food outlets, and piercing parlors. Pedestrians stepped off curbs with no mind to vehicular threat. Rounding out the mix were odd individuals dressed like film characters jostling for attention and spare change. A black-and-white cruised in the slow lane but the officers inside were distracted by their own conversation.

Turning off onto Ree's street lowered but didn't kill the street noise. A distant steam drill chewed up asphalt and dislodged some small hairs from my inner ear. Someone shouted in Spanish. A truck used its Jake brake and the resulting sound was the biggest rattlesnake in the universe hissing a warning.

I found a space near Ree's ten-plex. The door to her apartment was closed and her blinds were drawn. I knocked. A female voice shouted, "Yeah? What?"

Tough, annoyed. None of the gentleness I'd observed. Had that been an act? Had I made up my mind prematurely?

"It's Dr. Delaware."

The door opened. A woman, not Ree Sykes, said, "Doctor who?"

Midthirties, short, and flat-chested, she wore a brown T-shirt, camo cargo pants, pink-soled lace-up boots the color of blanched asparagus. Black spiky hair evoked a cockscomb. A hexagonal plug protruded midway between her lower lip and her assertive little shelf of a chin.

I repeated my name.

"I heard you. No one's sick, Doc."

"I'm here to see Cherie Sykes."

"Then you're out of luck. She bailed."

"Moved out?"

"Hmm. Yeah, that's another way to put it—hey, are you really a bill collector or some kind of repo dude? 'Cause she left her shitty furniture here and now I got to store it for sixty days. You help me find her, I'll make it worth your while."

I gave her my card.

She said, "Anyone can print one of these," but appeared convinced. "Psychologist? She's got mental problems?"

"The court appointed me to consult on a lawsuit she was involved in."

"Her sister trying to steal her kid? That was actually real?"

"You had your doubts?"

"She's a hippie flake, I took anything she told me with a grain of sustainable granola. She was always late with the rent. Last time I talked to her about it she said she'd forgotten because she was tied up in court. Cried a little, like that's supposed to soften me up. So what do you want with her?"

"Follow-up."

"The case ended? Who won?"

"She did."

Laughter. "Sister was an even bigger loser, huh? Talk about an evil bitch, hassling your own sister for a rug-rat. I mean, you want a kid, have it yourself. Meanwhile Miss Woodstock Flashback owes me for this month and she's bailed, so I'd be totally appreciative if the court system actually did something for a taxpaying citizen and informed me where the hell I can find her."

"You're the manager?"

"I'm the owner, dude. What, I don't look like landed gentry?"

Reaching into one of the cargo pockets, she produced a card of her own. Same vegetative green as her boots. Outsized silver lettering.

DEE N. MARTOLO
REAL ESTATE INVESTMENTS

A P.O.B. that told you nothing about its location.

"Pleased to meet you, Dee." I extended a hand.

She pretended not to notice, looked back into the apartment. "Jo-Jo?"

An older Asian man stuck his head out. Swiffer broom in his hand.

"Take five."

His look was uncomprehending.

"Take a break, J. Be back in ten minutes."

The man smiled and left, taking his broom with him.

Dee Martolo said, "Yeah, this palace is mine. Courtesy *Olea europaea*. That's olive trees—ever hear of Martolo Oil? Don't lie, you didn't. We have groves in Stockton but we don't brand our own. We send it to fancy supermarkets and they put their own labels on and jack up the price. Great-Grandpa planted the groves, Grandpa made it a business, et cetera."

"Interesting—"

"Think so? Then you've obviously never been to Stockton. Actually, the rest of the family agrees with you. I yawn when they start discussing fertilizer so they pay me to stay away by saddling me with Grandpa's cache of 'original Hollywood real estate.' Meaning this dump and a bunch like it. Anyway, where can I find Chelsea Morning?"

"Don't know."

"Then why are we wasting my time?"

"Could I have a look inside?"

"I'm supposed to just let you snoop around?"

"You could give me the extended guided tour."

She laughed. "What's in it for me, Psychologist Dude?"

"The court hears from her, you could be notified."

"You're here because she stiffed you, too?"

"The court paid me in full."

"Well, bully for you, maybe *I* should've gone to shrink school. Got a sociology degree from Fresno State, figured on joining the Peace Corps or something. Then I realized all those Third World types would probably view me the way I view my family—

don't ask. Anyway, our business is finished here, I'm calling my collection agency."

I said, "Just a second inside?"

"Why? What the hell are you after?"

"Follow-up's part of the process. I need to document everything."

"Oh, man," she said. "Bureaucracy—okay, just for a sec, but there's nothing to see."

True to her word, the apartment had been emptied.

I said, "What did you put in storage?"

"Shitty furniture, shitty clothes. The crap in the medicine cabinet got thrown out. Same for food in the fridge."

"What about baby stuff?"

She thought. "Guess there wasn't any."

"No crib?"

"Nope."

"Playpen, diapers—"

"I just told you, none of that. No secret-code messages or UFO photos, either, okay? And no papers to tell me where she went, which sucks big-time."

"Her car—"

"Gone, what do you think, she's walking the streets toting a rug-rat and a box of Pampers?" Another snicker. "Though I guess that could attract a certain type of customer."

"You figure her for a prostitute?"

"Nah," said Dee N. Martolo. "I'm just being mean. That's my thing. So they tell me."

She had no idea when Ree had left and when I asked if I could talk to some neighbors, she said, "Already done it, no one has a clue. I figure she probably cut out in the middle of the night, 'cause that's Deadbeat 101."

"Any idea who her friends are?"

"I don't socialize with the tenants." She brightened. "Just thought of something, one time she gave me a flyer, some of her friends were playing a club. Shit, can't remember the name, too bad I tossed it."

"Was the band Lonesome Moan?"

"Yeah! Thank you, Doctor Dude . . . what *was* the name of that dive . . . something with an astrology thing . . . Pisces? No. Not Scorpio . . . I don't know. But if she's doing the aging-groupie thing maybe I can find her backstage and nail her for what she owes. Be gone, Court Shrink Dude, I have no more use for you."

CHAPTER
21

Lonesome Moan. *The only moaning in question is that which arises upon being assaulted by the noise they create.*

Connie had also sneeringly dropped a couple of names, certain that one of the musicians was Rambla's father. Citing them again in her deposition, as evidence of Ree's lack of fitness.

Winky something . . . Boris . . .

Winky had babysat Rambla the first time Ree came to see me, so not a stretch for him to help her clear out.

I sat in the Seville and played my iPhone. The band had a website, big surprise. The banner photo qualified as vintage, portraying four long-haired, bearded, love-beaded men in their twenties trying to look purposeful and tough and falling far short on both accounts.

The paragraph below boasted that Lonesome Moan's original members were still together and that the band's longevity was *"proof of the soulful integrity of their music. L.M.'s sounds echo the pulsating heartbeat of a nation that lives to party and loves to rock. We breathe fresh life into Skynyrd, Atlanta Rhythm Sec-*

tion, Blue Öyster Cult, Foreigner. Even choice Doo Wop or juicy Hendrix when the stars are aligned."

The site's *Management* link brought up a crudely drawn caricature of a howling wolf. *"We now manage ourselves. Nothin' like freedom!"*

Sample Our Tunes was *"under construction"* but *Who We Are* served up some content:

Marvin "Chuck-o" Blatt: drums, percussion
Bernard "Boris" Chamberlain: bass guitar, saxophone, vocals
William "Winky" Melandrano: rhythm guitar, vocals
Spenser "Zebra" Younger: lead guitar

Maybe the nation had lost its pulsating urge to rock because Lonesome Moan's *Tour Schedule* page was blank but for a single line in red type: *"Virgo Virgo, Ventura Boulevard, Studio City, Monday Nights, 8 p.m. to 1 a.m."*

Slowest night of the week, some clubs choose to go dark. This one put a middle-aged cover band on stage so maybe the management was all about maximizing cash flow and opened early for Happy Hour.

Time to party.

It was just late enough to make the drive to the Valley a test of patience. The traffic mire began within yards of turning north on Cahuenga. I phoned Robin, told her I'd be late and why.

She said, "Her sister's murdered, she splits?"

"Yeah, I know. And I told Milo she didn't have it in her."

"Maybe she doesn't but one of her friends does. Be careful, hon. What's the name of this dive? Is it a biker joint?"

"Virgo Virgo. Don't know about the clientele."

"Pair of virgins," she said. "Maybe someone's into John and Yoko. How late is late?"

"I might get there in forty if I'm lucky. Depending on what I learn, another hour or two."

"Studio City—okay, got the website right here . . . Ventura B. a couple miles east of Coldwater. Doesn't look too ominous . . . that's right near the spaghetti place we used to like. I could meet you for dinner."

"We'd have to return in separate cars."

"So?" she said. "I'll go first, you'll keep an eye on my rear bumper."

"Now you're talking."

She hung up laughing.

Virgo Virgo was a slab of deep purple stucco the width of a double garage. A long time ago someone had tried to dress up the façade with gold stars and crescents. Most had faded to flaking beige.

Happy Hour!!! banner above the door.

Finally, I'd guessed right about something.

The club was a single room with rough pine walls turned nearly black by grime and miserly light. A sprayed ceiling hovered low. A six-stool bar ran along the western wall.

Tucked into a rear corner, a crudely built wooden stage held a battered upright piano, a drum kit, and a mike stand. The bass drum was painted with *L.M.* and the howling wolf logo I'd seen on Lonesome Moan's website.

House band once a week?

Maybe the fuzzy country rock crackling from overhead speakers was the default soundtrack six days a week.

I continued toward the bar. Every stool was taken, four men and two women hunched over their glasses.

No obvious conversation but when I got closer I picked up the low, slow mumbling that ensues when everyone's blood alcohol is far past the legal limit.

The bartender was middle-aged and bald. A skinny face and fat features gave him the look of a tired vulture. His skin managed to be indoor-pallid but UV-wrinkled. His black T-shirt read *Altamont Didn't End It*.

He saw me. "If you don't mind standing."

The barfly closest to me turned around. Big man, basset-faced, pushing seventy. "Belly up, thirsty traveler, we'll give you space." Rising painfully, he shifted his stool just enough to allow me access to the bar. The top was sprayed with a solid inch of resin, yellowed, splotched, nicked, and dull.

I said, "Thanks, next one's on me."

Basset pumped air with a shaky fist. He had on a shiny dark suit, a frayed white shirt, and a limp tie that looped like a scarf over his wilting lapel. A once-square jaw had melted around the edges. He looked like a CEO who'd been drummed for moral turpitude years ago, hadn't changed clothes since the disgrace.

The drinker next to him, a woman with black frizzy hair and an off-center, verge-of-collapse nose, batted her lashes at me. "You treatin' me, too, Good-Lookin'?"

I said, "Fill-ups for everyone."

Scattered applause.

Basset said, "Fine man, indeed!"

The bartender looked at me. "Okay, Rockefeller, what'll it be?"

"Got Sam Adams?"

"Got Heineken." He filled a glass, clopped it down, moved up the bar to take orders.

Chairman Basset said, "You never been here. I know that." Nodding in agreement with himself, as if he'd stated a profundity. "Least not Monday."

I said, "Monday's a special day?"

"Hell, yeah, they're open." He cackled, eyed the stage. "Despite."

The bartender returned, took his glass, shot something from a hose into it. Suds foamed over the rim and landed on the bartop. Basset used his pinkie to pick up precious moisture then licked the digit clean.

I took a sip. The beer was Heineken like I was an Olympic skater. Not quite skunky but getting there.

The bartender foamed up several other mugs. Local etiquette prescribed Gulp, Don't Sip. Maybe that helped the house brew go down easier. I glanced back at the bandstand, asked Basset who the entertainment was.

"No one tonight." He swayed toward me, letting off a yeasty reek and whispering, "Count your blessings, traveler."

"You've heard 'em, huh?"

He blotted me out with a wet cough. Glanced furtively up the bar as the bald guy approached, wiping his hands with a none-too-clean towel. "Not thirsty, Daddy Warbucks?"

I said, "Working on it."

Basset said, "Hey, Chuck-o, you might got you a fan, here. He wants you guys to play."

Bald's eyebrows climbed. "You heard of us?"

Marvin "Chuck-o" Blatt: drums

I said, "Actually, a friend sent me here."

"Who's that?"

"Ree Sykes."

He looked at me with new eyes. Sharper, curious. "How do you know Ree?"

Even if I'd wanted to lie, the trudge to the Valley

plus stale alcohol fumes had sapped my creativity. "She had a court case I was involved in."

Chuck-o's posture stiffened. "You're a lawyer?"

"Psychologist."

"Psychologist," he echoed, as if trying out a new word. "You're the one testified she was a great mom?"

No sense quibbling. I smiled.

He said, "Well good for you, man. Ree talks about you like you're God."

Basset said, "Doncha know all doctors are God? That's why their shit don't stink and they get to suck all the Medi-Cal money outta the federal teat—"

"Lloyd," said Chuck-o, "no politics today, okay?"

The woman with the precarious nose said, "Tomorrow we're doing politics?"

"We're never doing politics, Maggie."

"Yeah, makes sense," she said, showing the few brown teeth she had left. "Double boo on politics!"

Chuck-o turned back to me, flashing the weary smile of an exhausted babysitter. His teeth were perfect, white as milk. "Well, Dr. Psychologist, nice to meet you but sorry, we're not playing till Monday. And if you were hoping to see Ree, sorry again, she doesn't come in regularly. Having family responsibilities and all that."

Maggie said, "That the one with that cute little baby, puts the baby seat top of the piano when she sings?"

Chuck-o frowned at her.

I forced down some beer. "You're in the band?"

"Drums," he said. "But finally I figured out getting the chicks didn't provide long-term security so I became a businessman." Waving his hand around the room.

"Place is yours?"

"This and two others, Sun Valley and Saugus. Got my sons managing."

"Congratulations."

"Making coin is cool, but I still live for the music."

"So Monday."

" 'Less something comes up."

"Ree sings."

"Sometimes we let her do background. Deep background." He grinned. "What the hell, she's a good chick, always been righteous, I'm talking back to high school."

"Nice for her to have that type of support," I said.

"You bet," said Chuck-o Blatt. "When things were sucking and we were all thinking of getting jobs she encouraged us to keep keepin' on, telling us we had talent. And you know, something always worked out—but I don't need to tell you that, you were her witness, you know the kind of person she is."

When I didn't answer, he said, "You hear me?"

I nodded.

"You didn't say nothing."

"She's a nice person."

"Not just nice, good," he said. Steel in his voice. His neck tightened. "You'd know that if you really are the psychologist and not spying for her fucking sister."

I held his gaze, showed him my civilian card. Doctoral degree and a professorial title that looked more impressive than it was.

He said, "Delaware. Yeah, that's you." More lactic teeth. "Hey, man, sorry for being paranoid but Ree figured the bitch was going to keep harassing her."

"Even though the case resolved?"

"You know the system, right? Got the cash, make the trash. Anyone's a rich bitch with a mean streak it's Connie."

He tried to return the card. Lloyd intercepted it, held it between shaky fingers. "Delaware. That was a Union state, not Confederate. But they still had slaves."

Chuck-o said, "That's fascinating, Lloyd."

I regained eye contact. "Is there somewhere we could talk?"

"About what?"

I shot him a conspiratorial look. People like to be let in on secrets but he said, "Sorry, I got customers."

"How about another round on me? Fill 'em up, then give me a couple of minutes of your time."

"This is about Ree?"

"This is about Ree cutting town. I'd like to know that she and the baby are safe."

I waited.

He said, "She split? When?"

"Last couple of days."

"Well, I'm sure she had a reason."

I didn't answer.

He said, "Why wouldn't she be okay?"

"There's been a complication."

"Like what?"

I shook my head. He faced the barflies. "Merry Christmas, this here is Santa Claus, he lost weight and he's here for your drinking pleasure."

Lloyd said, "Santa's a doctor?"

A voice from the end of the bar said, "Adeste fidelis—what kind of doctor?"

The woman next to him raised her glass. "Gotta be Dr. Feelgood."

Lloyd said, "Hear, hear," tried to fist-pump again and lost his balance, nearly toppling from his stool.

I caught him, set him right.

He said, "Meeting you, my good man, is my lucky day!"

* * *

Chuck-o wiped his hands on a soggy towel, stepped through a half door that freed him from the confines of the bar, and pointed to the bandstand. Taking a seat behind his drum kit, he lifted his sticks and ran off a silent paradiddle on his knees before motioning me to the piano bench.

One of the barflies said, "You gonna play a sola, Chuck-o?"

"Not today." Waiting until everyone was back drinking in earnest, he shifted both drumsticks to his right hand. "Let's hear it for substance abuse. Never got into it myself. Not even on the road."

"Teetotaler?"

"Moderate, one cocktail before I go to bed. That's why I own my businesses. Including the land we're sitting on."

"Congrats."

"So what's the complication?"

"Like I said, Ree cut town. I was hoping someone here could tell me why."

"Someone?"

"Maybe Winky or Boris."

"You know Winky and Boris?"

"I was told they were close to Ree."

"We're all close. Like I said, we go way back."

"High school," I said.

"Junior high, actually. For me and Boris. You didn't answer me about the complication. What, Connie's taking her back to court? Yeah, Ree figured she'd do that, said Connie never took no for an answer."

"No chance of that. Connie's dead."

"*What?*"

"Murdered," I said. "Last night. The police are wondering if the court case had something to do with it. I've told them Ree's not a violent person, but—"

"Violent? Hell, no. Ree's got to be the most un-violent chick I ever knew. Connie's dead? And you're asking about Ree because—oh, man, you can't be serious—"

"Doesn't matter what I think, Chuck-o. The cops always begin with people close to the victim. And someone related who's had serious conflict—"

"Oh, no, man, no possible way."

"I went to Ree's place before I came here. Figured I'd tell her about Connie. That's when I found out she'd split. Cleaned out her apartment and stuck her landlady with unpaid rent."

"Geez," he said. "Maybe it was, you know, stress—all the shit she went through. Maybe she needs to breathe."

"Maybe. But on the surface, it doesn't look good."

"Oh, man." He used his free hand to skitter a roll on his tom-tom.

The same barfly said, "Hey, you *are* doin' a sola—"

"Shut the fuck up!"

The man's jaw dropped.

No one else looked back.

Chuck-o Blatt said, "Murdered? This is psycho."

I said, "If you have any way to reach Ree, you'd be doing her a favor by telling her to check in. She can do it through me."

He studied me. "You're sure you're who you say you are? I mean a card can be bogused."

Same thing Dee Martolo had said. Suspicion born of the digital age.

I said, "Got a computer?"

"Why?"

"Go on the med school webpage, plug my name in, and see if the photo matches."

"Fine, fine, sorry . . . I'm just freaked out. So how do you know what the police are thinking?"

"Sometimes I work with them."

"Like what?"

"Consultant. But it's common sense, a woman dies, has a sister who hates her and splits. You'd think the same way."

"It wasn't a matter of hate . . . okay, it was, but Connie deserved it. And trust me, man, Ree's like . . . a . . . cloud. One of those soft clouds, you know?"

"As opposed to Connie."

"Even back in high school Connie was . . . she was a lot older than us. When we were still in junior high, she was in college, doing her fancy college thing. But even before that she had that . . . that superior thing. I'm better than you, go screw yourself."

"Arrogant."

"Everyone couldn't stand her." His eyes got big. "Oh, man. I should probably not diss her too heavy, give you ideas about me." He smiled. "Connie bit it last night? Last night I was with my sons. Cleaning up the place in Sun Valley, had some party idiots rent it for an engagement, they trashed everything. I had to list the damage for insurance, then we cleaned up. Took like till six in the morning."

He stood. "Not that I need an alibi, right?"

"Right."

"But maybe Ree does."

"It would sure help, Chuck-o."

"Yeah, well, Ree'll be fine, don't you worry, man."

I said, "How can I get in contact with Winky and Boris?"

"Why?"

"Ree mentioned them."

"She mentioned me, too?"

"Of course," I lied. "She talked about all of you. What good friends you were."

"So you want to talk to Zebe, too."

"I want to talk to anyone who can help me find Ree."

"I got your card. Something comes up, I'll let you know."

"Appreciate it."

As I turned to leave, Lloyd said, "Another round, Dr. Claus?"

I smiled, put cash on the bar.

Chuck-o Blatt counted. "This is just enough for what they already had."

Lloyd put his palms together prayerfully. "Another libation, good sir? For the sake of the righteous?"

Chuck-o said, "Don't push it, he *ain't* God."

CHAPTER
22

Back in the car, check the phone. One message: Robin.

She said, "No spaghetti, the place closed down."

"I'm out early, anyway, see you in thirty."

"Does early mean no luck finding her?"

"Not much."

"You going to tell Milo you looked for her?"

"He'll find out anyway, so yes."

"Things are getting complicated, darling."

"Life's little challenges."

"Love your outlook," she said. "Okay, I'll cook spaghetti."

Before I began the drive home, I sat parked near Virgo Virgo, working the iPhone and trying to locate William Melandrano and/or Bernard Chamberlain.

A W. Melandrano the right age lived nearby in North Hollywood, but no address or phone numbers were given and 411 had nothing to add. Four Bernard Chamberlains. A man living in Hollywood seemed the most likely. That address was close to Ree's apartment.

A couple of button pushes could instantly tell Milo if either man had a criminal history. The best I could do was try a website that trafficked in mug shots, one of those mean-spirited celebrations of other people's misfortunes, custom-tailored for an increasingly mean-spirited world.

My hopes rose when I learned that a Bernard Chamberlain had been arrested for disorderly conduct three years ago in Tampa, Florida. The next click revealed a shot of a seventeen-year-old boy.

Time to stop fooling around.

Milo answered his desk phone. "Your pal Effo has an unassailable alibi for the time frame of Connie's demise: partying with homeboys and homegirls at a known gang house in Pacoima, thirty people to back him up. Not that I took any of their words for it. A neighbor across the street, old lady terrified of all the scary kids going in and out, takes tons of surreptitious pictures and she captured him coming and going. So congrats."

I said, "Doesn't mean much. You never figured he did it himself."

"True, I've got Millie Rivera nosing around, see if she can pick up any rumors of a contract. But the neighbor's camera cleared up one thing: Ramon Guzman was at the same party. Which might give you pause, Alex. Here's a joker who tried to get you permanently erased and your buddy's still whooping it up with him."

"Efren was a patient, not my buddy."

My voice had risen.

He said, "Onward to Cherie Sykes. I tried to organize a meeting with her through her lawyer but he's at a convention in Palm Springs. Same for Connie's mouthpiece. What do people like that consider continuing education? Learning how to dress a pit bull in designer duds? Anyway, I'm gonna drop in on Ms. Ree, see how she's reacting to Sis's death."

"Speaking of which." I told him what I'd learned.

He said, "You went to her place—"

"Clinical follow-up."

"I see," he said. "Actually, I don't."

"I wanted to check out my initial reaction. See if I'd been wrong about her. She's rabbited so my being wrong is looking damn likely. Obviously, it's time for me to get out of the way and let you do your thing."

"Hey," he said, "no sense beating yourself up. You're the original victim in all this and I'm glad it's someone else's death I'm investigating. She took just the baby stuff, huh?"

"And the baby."

"I'll bring a techie over, see what turns up."

"Landlady already started cleaning it."

"Nothing ventured, but maybe they'll find something."

I said, "The timing doesn't look good for her. And you were right: Even if she didn't kill Connie herself, one of her pals could've. She's tight with that band." I recounted my visit to the bar, gave him Melandrano's and Chamberlain's names.

He said, "Ties that bind. If Connie was right about one of them being daddy, there's motive to spare."

"And Chuck-o Blatt confirmed Ree was definitely worried about Connie taking her back to court."

"Hold on."

A series of clicks. "Nothing on Melandrano but Mr. Bernard Chamberlain of Hollywood, Cal, was busted ten years ago for assault. In Arkansas . . . doesn't look like he served any time . . . photo shows him as a hairy-biker type. Kind of mean eyes. Big guy, too—not that tall but two hundred and fifty el-bees.

Yeah, we're definitely gonna want to make his acquaintance. Melandrano's, too."

"*We're?*"

"Plural intentional, Alex. The situation has now ventured into psych territory—actually, it always was a head-case. So who better than thou to weigh in?"

"Feeling charitable?"

"Yeah, right," he said. "This is work, pal, no room for sentimentality. And guess what? Brother Connor finally had the time to visit Connie's corpse. Flying in for a meet tomorrow. Connie told you he was a tech guy, right?"

"She did."

He laughed. "Depends on what you mean by technical. He doesn't develop chips, he's a porn-meister, been doing it for a long time. Interesting family, no? Okay, let me firm up current addresses on our Lonesome Moaners, we'll check 'em out tomorrow. Meanwhile, Connor Sykes, my place, eleven a.m. I'm assuming you're RSVP'ing yes."

"Black tie?"

"Business attire."

CHAPTER
23

Connor Sykes didn't look like a pornographer.

Then again, what does a smut-maven look like?

For the past twenty years he'd operated under several corporate headings, producing, packaging, marketing, and peddling adult videos and downloads. His advertised specialty was "natural, pillow-bodied women," which seemed to mean buxom bodies untouched by surgeons or tattoo artists. Several of his series trumpeted "the romantic approach." That seemed to mean buxom bodies untouched by bindings, ball gags, and rough handling.

His business attire this morning was that of any successful Silicon Valley magnate: narrow-lapel navy suit, open-necked blue shirt, expensively unpretentious shoes, digital wristwatch. He had neatly trimmed graying hair, bland features, the kind of face that abounds in business-class lounges. If you squinted you could find traces of resemblance to his sisters: squarish head, slightly generous chin. Photographed as a trio, the Sykes sibs would come across more similar than when captured in pairs. As if Connor was the unifying genetic factor tying Connie to Ree.

If he was traumatized by his sister's death, he wasn't

showing it, sitting motionless in the interview room as Milo handed him bad coffee. He tasted, put the cup down. "If you don't mind, I'd like to text my wife. Our boys have a recital tonight and I'm not sure I'll make it."

"Of course, sir."

Sykes produced his phone, tapped briefly, slipped it back in his pocket.

Milo said, "Music recital?"

"Jared plays the viola and Tyler plays the cello. I'm biased but everyone says they're gifted." Weak smile. "If they've got talent it's not from me. Mariko—my wife—was a concert pianist in Japan."

"Ah."

"I try to be there for all their events."

"Well," said Milo, "we'll do our best to get you out of here as quickly as possible."

"Appreciate that, Lieutenant. But it occurred to me on the flight over that if I'm going to have to deal with Connie's remains, it'll take time."

"No need to do that today, Mr. Sykes."

"Oh? Is she still being . . . what's the proper term, processed?"

"The coroner's done but there's always paperwork and that can be handled over the phone or online."

"So I might be able to get back by five?"

"Sure."

Sykes extricated his phone. "Would you mind if I contact the jet company to arrange my flight?"

"No prob, sir."

Another text.

Connor Sykes said, "Appreciate it, Lieutenant. Now, why exactly am I here, if it's not to handle . . . the process?"

"In a murder investigation, information's our

weapon. So anything you can do to arm us would be helpful."

Sykes considered that, fingering a lapel and gazing at the ceiling before resuming eye contact. "That makes sense. Unfortunately, I have no idea who'd want to murder Connie."

Even tone.

Milo was careful not to react. But I noticed the tightening around his eyes. Connor Sykes, eyes back on the ceiling, didn't. "Mr. Sykes, are you surprised your sister was killed?"

Connor Sykes's left eyebrow arced. Puzzlement, not resentment. "Of course I am."

Milo kept silent.

Sykes's face tightened. Working out a tough math problem. "You think I'm being strangely unemotional. I'm sure you're right, it's an issue I have. Expressing emotions. The problem is, I'm unaware of it. Internally, I feel totally dismayed at losing my sister. But showing it doesn't come naturally. My wife's convinced I'm somewhere on the Asperger continuum. Maybe she's right, she knows me better than anyone. I don't feel asocial. For the most part, I find people acceptable. So forgive my strange reaction."

"There's no correct reaction, Mr. Sykes. You just seemed unsurprised."

"Well, I am surprised. I'm extremely surprised. But I don't see how I can help you. Connie and I weren't close. I haven't seen or spoken to her in a while."

"How long is a while?"

"At least twenty years."

"Twenty years."

Connor Sykes said, "Not even a Christmas card. Sent or received. Our family's never been much for formalities."

"What about Cherie?"

"Cherie I saw more recently."

"How recently?"

"Hmm . . . around . . . ten years ago. She showed up and asked for money."

"Did you give it to her?"

Connor Sykes shrugged. "I had ample funds, she didn't, she's my sister."

"What did she need money for?"

"I didn't ask."

"She just showed up."

"At my house," said Connor Sykes. "Eight in the morning, Mariko and the boys and I were having breakfast. We invited her in. She looked bedraggled. As if she'd been traveling hard."

"Was she alone?"

"She was. She asked for a couple of thousand to tide her over. I gave her five. She hugged me and kissed me, said she'd be in touch. Of course, she didn't follow through."

I said, "Of course. You didn't expect her to."

Connor Sykes stared past me. "Ree isn't known for her reliability."

"She's a free spirit."

"Always has been."

I said, "The three of you are quite different from one another."

"That's what Mariko says. She jokes that it's almost as if our births were random events. I'd never thought about that but now that I'm a parent, I see what she means. My boys have traits in common— they're individuals, of course, but there's something that says these boys are brothers."

"As opposed to you and your sibs," I said.

"Yes. So what kind of family produced that?" He shrugged. "Can't see how that could be relevant to what happened to Connie but I'm happy to tell you anything you'd like to know."

"Tell us a bit about growing up with Connie and Ree."

Connor blinked three times and shot me a helpless look. "That's such an open-ended request, I don't know where to begin."

I said, "Start with your parents."

He smiled. Comforted by structure. "Charles and Corinne Sykes met in high school, in Kansas City. That's where we were born—Connie and I. I don't remember it because we moved to California when I was young. Long Beach. That's where Ree was born."

"Why the move?"

"Mother suffered from asthma and chest colds, her doctors said a warm, dry climate might help. Unfortunately, it didn't, she suffered constantly, died when she was sixty of pulmonary problems. I imagine her smoking and excessive drinking didn't help."

Connor Sykes cocked his head like an eager spaniel. "Odd, no? That she'd smoke when her respiratory system had never been strong?"

Placing his hands in his lap, he grew silent. "People are unpredictable . . . does that help? I really don't know what you're after."

I said, "Tell us about your parents' unique qualities."

"Unique," he said, flatly. "I suppose Father could be termed a ladies' man. Do I mean extramarital affairs? Yes, I do. But he never mistreated Mother, nor any of us. Though I suppose the mere fact of infidelity could be thought of as . . . not appropriate."

I said, "Did he drink, as well?"

"He did."

"How did that affect him?"

"Affect? Well . . . he'd turn a bit grouchy. Sometimes he'd shout."

"And your mother?"

"Mother . . ." As if the concept was baffling. "What can I say about Mother . . . she worked as a bookkeeper, got along fine with people but really didn't like them. I know that because she always said so. People were generally stupid. So if I am Aspergian, she might very well be the source."

"How did drinking affect her?"

"She fell asleep."

"A loner."

"Not in the sense of being shy or retiring," said Sykes. "She was an assertive person. She simply preferred to be by herself. But I never felt neglected. In fact, I look back on my childhood as being rather pleasant."

He faced me, hands on the table, shoulders relaxed. "Whether or not my sisters feel the same way, I can't say."

Three sibs, three stories. Not much communication along the way.

I said, "You never discussed your childhood with your sisters."

Connor Sykes said, "Our family was oriented toward doing, not talking."

I said, "From what we've been told, Connie wasn't the most social person."

"Hmm. I suppose that's true—you know, now that you mention it, there *are* certain parallels between Mother and Connie." He tapped his lips with a fingertip. "Yes, definitely. If anyone was like Mother it was Connie. I never really thought about that."

"And Ree?"

"Ree?" said Sykes. "Nothing at all similar between Ree and Mother."

"She liked people?"

"Hmm—well, yes, Ree has always been a friendly person. Lots of friends. So in that sense I suppose there are parallels to our father. He could be quite gregarious when he chose."

"How did your sisters get along?"

"They didn't have much to do with one—" He stopped short. His right hand began to clench, thought better of it and splayed slowly. "These questions, you're not seriously thinking Ree had anything to do . . . No, that's impossible." His eyes passed from Milo to me, back to Milo. "*Isn't* it?"

Milo said, "We don't suspect Ree of anything but due to the conflict she and Connie—"

"What conflict?"

"The court case."

Connor Sykes blinked. "I have no idea what you're talking about, Lieutenant."

Milo summed up. The man across the table seemed to deflate with each sentence. "Why would Connie do that?"

"We were hoping you could tell us."

"Me? Of course I can't. Connie actually sued Ree? For her child? How old of a child are we talking about?"

"Sixteen months."

"Ree had a baby," said Connor Sykes, wide-eyed. "I had no idea. How bizarre that must seem to you. But it's what I've always been accustomed to."

I said, "Everyone in the family doing their own thing."

"Now that I'm a father I see that it can be different. My wife's extremely close to her sister. My sons are friends as well as siblings. But to think Connie would sue Ree . . . to learn that Ree had a child. You've shocked me, Lieutenant. I'm reeling."

His posture implied defeat but his tone was that of a man picking up his laundry. "Still, you can't seriously believe Ree would ever hurt Connie. She's gentle, always has been. I think of her as a flower child born too late. That time when she showed up asking for money, she actually had flowers in her hair, wore homemade clothing, peace sign earrings. It reminded me of a couple of pictures I did—retro hippie themes, love-ins, et cetera. I looked at old magazine photos to get my costumes authentic."

"What was Ree's mood that day?"

"Mood," he said, taking time to decode. "Happy— goofy. The way she always is. She's the only one in the family like that."

Suddenly he sat taller. "Connie actually took Ree to court . . . was the case disposed?"

I said, "Ree won."

"Meaning Connie lost. That would've been tough for Connie. She was always competitive. If there was a contest at school—science fair, essays, spelling bee—she devoted herself to grabbing first place."

"Did she win often?"

"Oh, yes, she was brilliant. Clearly the smartest person in the family. She skipped a grade, sailed into medical school, graduated at the top of—if you evaluated her, Doctor, you probably know all this."

I said, "How did Ree do in school?"

"C's, D's, a few F's. She isn't stupid, it's just that she was all about . . . fun. But never at the expense of others, she always saw the best in others. I refuse to consider she'd ever harm Connie—do you have evidence she was involved?"

Milo said, "We'd like to talk to her but she's moved out of her apartment, left no forwarding."

"I see," said Connor Sykes. He removed a pair of black-framed reading glasses from his jacket, passed them from hand to hand. "That doesn't look good for her, does it?"

"Any idea where she might be, Mr. Sykes?"

"No."

"No hints at all?"

Head shake. "Sorry."

"Is there anything else you'd like to tell us?"

Connor Sykes seemed to take the question seriously. "No."

"Well, sir, on the odd chance that Ree does contact you—"

"That would be odd, Lieutenant. But yes, if she does I'll tell her she's made the wrong impression by leaving and needs to get in touch with you. Now, in terms of Connie, maybe I will have time to process and get back for the recital."

CHAPTER
24

Milo phoned the coroner's office and helped set up an appointment for Connor Sykes. The two of us walked him out of the station, watched him head up Butler Avenue.

Average-sized man moving at average speed.

Milo said, "One happy family."

"Not that we're here to judge," I said.

"I *live* to judge. Wish I could be the jury, too. So Ree never hinted at who daddy is?"

I shook my head.

"May I ask why you didn't press her?"

"It wasn't relevant."

"She was presumed to be kosher until Connie proved otherwise."

"Exactly."

"Connie was certain it was Winky or Binky, late-night fun on the band bus, huh?"

"You have a flair for description."

We headed back inside. He paused at the stairwell. "If the surviving Sykes sister doesn't show up soon, I'll check out the band."

"Easy enough," I said. "Monday night at Virgo Virgo."

He fist-pumped. "Freebird! Meantime I've got a

BOLO on Ree's car and Hollywood patrol's been sent the usual grainy DMV photo. Subpoenas on her phone and her credit cards would be a whole lot more helpful but sibling rivalry ain't grounds for that level of paper so I need to uncover something incriminating about her in order to uncover something incriminating about her."

"Techies get to her apartment?"

"Not yet because Martolo—the landlord—punted to her lawyer who refused entrance just for the sake of being an asshole. I left two messages on her personal line, total stonewall."

"Tell her you'll relieve her of the free storage she's giving Ree."

"Mercenary motive," he said. "I like the way your mind works."

Punching a preset number on his cell, he connected, smiling edgily. "Ms. Martolo? Lieutenant Sturgis . . . yes, I know. I . . . yes, but I thought you and I could work something out without having to go through . . . I assure you there'll be absolutely no disruption or damage . . . nothing will be taken . . . nothing will be cut out of the carpets . . . I see . . . well, I'm sorry about that, that's totally inexcusable but . . . yes, of course, you have every right to be . . . nothing like that will happen with my people, I promise, Ms. Martolo, scout's honor . . . you were? Well, me, too, made it to Eagle, we trustworthy types need to stick together, don't you think? Also—hear me out—if you allow my techs access I'd be happy to take all those personal items you've had to store for Ms. Sykes . . . yes, all of it . . . just what I said initially: quick swabs, dusts, you won't even know they were there . . . thank you Ms. . . . . thank you, Dee. I'll remember you at the next jamboree."

He clicked off, slapped my back hard enough to

rattle my ribs, reached the crime lab, and emphasized the need to move quickly before the property owner changed her mind. Charging the tech crew to look for "any damn thing but without doing damage. You want a fiber, tweeze it out, no slice and dice, I mean it."

After he hung up, I said, "Martolo had a bad experience with the department?"

"Narcotics raided another building she owns. Unfortunately, they had the wrong address, scared the shit out of everyone, including the poor family living in the apartment. Door got kicked in, place was trashed, it took six months and a whole lot of paperwork before she got reimbursed."

"Long arm of the law. So what's next?"

"I try to locate Ree Sykes and you do whatever you want."

"Ree's lawyer might know where she is."

He pulled out his pad. "Who's the lucky mouthpiece?"

"Myron Ballister, office in the Valley."

"What's he like?"

"Never met him."

"He refused to come in?"

"Both lawyers wanted to meet with me, I turned them down."

"Why?"

"I generally avoid attorneys because their only motive is to try to influence me and I want my information straight from the principals. The exception is a custody situation where the parents will have to work together and I think the lawyers can help with that. In a guardianship suit, there'd be no reason. Which didn't stop Connie's lawyer from showing up at her appointment and trying to muscle in."

"You set him straight."

"Her. Medea Wright, works for one of the more assertive firms."

"Think she's worth talking to?"

"You could try but I doubt she'd cooperate."

"Probably the same for this Ballister. But his client's smelling dirtier each day, so let's give it a shot. You remember where in the Valley?"

"Sherman Oaks." I recited the address.

"You memorized it?"

"It was on every court document I read."

"Paper storm."

"It always is."

"You know," he said, "all these years I never knew much about that part of your work. Big-time fun, huh?"

"Bundle of yuks."

We took the unmarked over the Sepulveda Pass. Neither of us talked much during the drive. Milo's face and posture were uncharacteristically static. I had no idea what was on his mind.

I was thinking. Again.

About *it*.

How close I'd come to being a morgue statistic.

Who'd miss me, who wouldn't.

Sherman Oaks is an upscale neighborhood but there's a stretch, where Ventura Boulevard crosses Van Nuys and slithers west, where the ambience dips to fast food, questionable merchandise, and deferred maintenance.

Myron Ballister's office was located square in the middle of that downgrade, on the ground floor of a two-story Band-Aid-colored building slivered between a Farsi-bannered outfit hawking disposable cell phones and a once-grand art deco movie theater converted to a "bargain emporium."

The interior was two units wide but only one tenant deep, with Suites A and B divided by a strip of green-carpeted hallway that died at a pebbled-cement stairway. Ballister's slide-in door shingle said he practiced solo. The door was plywood in need of refinishing. Unlocked.

What passed for a waiting room did double duty as a reception area, with barely enough space for either function. Myron Ballister's staff consisted of a girl around twenty stationed behind a warped desk. Her hair was a whirl of wheat-colored dreadlocks. Two visible tattoos: Tinker Bell cavorting on her left forearm, *Choose Your Weapon* on her right. Her armaments were a two-line phone, a closed laptop, and an iPod playing Pink's "Don't Let Me Get Me."

Milo's badge elicited, "Cops? What's up?"

"We'd like to talk to Mr. Ballister."

"He's at lunch."

"Where?"

"El Padron."

"Where's that?"

"Up the block." She pointed to the left. "Uh no, that way." Aiming right.

"You been working here long?"

"He's my cousin," she said. "I'm filling in."

"For his regular secretary?"

She giggled. "For him. He used to do everything himself, then I came down to go to school and he's like help me look like a lawyer, Amanda, I'll even pay you." She shrugged. Dreads swayed, a ballet of chorizo. "I'm like, sure."

"What're you studying?"

"Aesthetic technology."

"Beauty school?"

She pouted. "It's a lot more. We learn the science of how skin works." She peered up at his ravaged complexion.

He said, "Hopeless, huh?"

"I mean . . . there's always help. You should do moisturizer—no, maybe something actually to dry it up."

"Thanks for the advice, Amanda. What does Myron look like?"

"He's got pretty good skin."

"How old is he?"

"Like thirty."

"What's he wearing today?"

"Um um um um . . . black shirt . . . gray tie . . . he's a little fat but don't say I said that."

* * *

El Padron turned out to be El Patron. Mock adobe, mock Spanish tile, mock leaded glass, mock wrought iron. The logo above the door was a spavined, serape-draped burro eyeing a droopy cactus. The cactus had a disturbingly human face—lewd, squinty-eyed, unctuously malevolent.

Milo said, "Fat, cute, black shirt," and pushed his way in.

The dining room was commodious and dim, filled with blue vinyl chairs and booths and tables molded from the same polyvinyl as the door. Fuzzy-focus bullfight poster prints hung too close together. Mariachi heavy on off-key trombones comprised the soundtrack.

For all that, nice aromas prevailed: frijoles, corn, tomatillo. The beefy sizzle of carne asada.

The host booth was unoccupied. The reservation book was blank. As our eyes accommodated to the darkness, a waitress in an off-the-shoulder peasant dress circled into view. *"Señors? Vaya con dios!"*

Sixtyish, blond, she had an open face owing more to Ghent than Guadalajara.

Milo smiled but looked past her. Only three parties in the big room, all in booths ringing the west wall. Middle-management types drinking Dos Equis and Margaritas, an elderly couple ignoring each other as they shoveled food, a younger couple ignoring their food as they held hands and nose-nuzzled. The young man was fair-haired, wore a black shirt and a gray tie, the woman dark-haired and petite, had on a sleeveless white dress.

Milo told the waitress, "Our friends are over there."

"Okay *muy bueno*. I'll fetch you some menus and while you're looking you want a couple Margaritas we got frozen strawberry on special today it's fresh blended with real fruit?"

He read her name tag. "That's awfully tempting, Louella, but we won't be sticking around long enough."

"You want nothing?"

"Not for now."

We proceeded toward Ballister and his girlfriend. Her back was to us. Ballister's wasn't but he was wrapped up in her, paid no notice as we got close. His light hair was straight, waxy, longish, edging into blond at the tips. Styled for surfer, whether or not he'd ever stepped onto a board.

He had broad shoulders, a long face, big hands. No evidence of obesity.

He and the dark-haired woman continued to link fingers. He was grinning.

Milo stepped up to their booth, announced, "Sorry to intrude, kids," with utter lack of sincerity.

Myron Ballister's pale eyes widened. Up this close he remained lean, the only aspect of his appearance remotely suggesting spare adipose the beginning of a double chin.

"Pardon?" he said. Boyish voice. Smooth brow untrammeled by worry.

Milo said, "Myron Ballister?"

"Uh-huh—"

The woman in the white dress swung around and stared at me. "You? What the hell?"

Ballister said, "Honey, you know these—?"

Medea Wright jerked her small, manicured, bejeweled hand out of his. The other one had already formed a fist.

I made the introductions, explained Wright's role in the Sykes case.

Milo said, "So this is what, a legal conference?"

More likely the aftermath of the convention in Palm Springs. Continuing education, indeed.

Wright grimaced. "I *demand* an explanation—"

Milo said, "You two were on opposite sides, now you're an item? Which came first, work or romance?"

Medea Wright's perfect makeup couldn't hide the color in her cheeks. "That's *your* business? Who the hell *are* you, anyway?"

Milo handed her his card.

"Homicide? What the hell's going on?"

"You don't know."

She drew herself up to the max but genetics limited the drama of the gesture. "If I knew would I ask you?"

Myron Ballister said, "Honey, this is getting weird—"

She showed him her palm. "Don't say a word. Who the hell knows what they're up to."

Milo said, "What I'm up to is solving a murder, Ms. Wright. No curiosity as to who the victim is?"

Wright said, "Either way, you're going to tell me."

Singular tense; Ballister had become irrelevant.

He said, "Oh, man. Someone got killed?"

Without looking at him, Wright said, "That's what murder usually means."

Ballister's face remained blandly surprised. No offense taken. He probably figured he was out of his league in the first place.

Medea Wright pointed at Milo. "Okay, go."

When her gaze faltered, he said, "Your client, Constance Sykes."

She shrieked, *"What!"* Her voice was talons ripping satin. The drinkers at the end of the dining room put their glasses down and stared. The elderly couple paused in their gorging.

Louella hurried over. "Everything okay?"

Medea Wright waved her away. "We're having a discussion."

Louella said, "Well, obviously," and left.

Wright said, "Tell me *exactly* what happened."

Milo said, "A couple of nights ago someone killed Dr. Sykes."

"That's insane." Wright plucked a corn chip out of a lava-rock bowl, nibbled nonstop like a rabbit on meth. Swallowing hard, she pulverized two more chips with power-grinder jaws.

Ballister watched her with awe. Then he turned to us. "You're actually saying—"

Wright cut him off. "That is totally *totally* insane."

Ballister said, "Totally," and reached for her hand. She drew away. "Who did it?"

Milo said, "That's what I'm trying to figure out."

She glared at me. "So why's *he* here?"

"Dr. Delaware works with us from time to time."

"Does he? Doing what?"

"Psychological consultations."

"I know all about his consultations. He's a courtroom regular." She smirked. "You're trying to tell me he just happened to be on call for the police department when a case he had prior involvement with turned . . . bad?"

Milo said, "Actually, Ms. Wright, Dr. Delaware was already involved. On a whole different level."

"What are you talking about? Stop dancing around the facts and spit it out."

He gave her a minimally brutal summary of Connie Sykes's aborted murder plot.

She gaped. "What? That's impossible."

He began to repeat himself.

She said, "I heard you, I just don't believe it . . . this is bizarre."

Milo said, "Believe it, Ms. Wright."

Ballister muttered, "Totally nuts."

Wright said, "You're claiming Connie actually threatened him?"

Milo edged so close to her that she was forced to crane. "No need to defend her, Counselor. She can't be held accountable anymore. So this is the first time you're hearing about the plot."

"Of course! What do you take me for?"

"Well," he said, "maybe just a lawyer doing her job. Or thinking she was. Anything a client tells you is confide—"

"Not when someone's life is at stake, that's revolting and insulting, you're being absolutely . . ." Swallowing whatever nasty adjective she'd intended, she breathed in and out three times, spread her hands on the table. The color had spread below her perfect jawline. She tried to slow her respiration but failed.

High-strung, compulsively combative woman, the kind of temperament that builds certain types of careers but can also corrode the psyche.

She turned to me. "You think I'd actually let something like that happen to you or anyone else? That hurts my feelings. I can't believe you'd actually believe—"

Milo said, "Neither I nor Dr. Delaware believes anything at this point, Ms. Wright. It's my job to ask questions."

"Well, here's your answer: I had nothing to do with anything. And I can prove my moral fiber because when I was aware of possible peril, I did provide notice to the intended target."

I said, "Connie threatened someone else?"

"It didn't rise to the level of—"

"Who?" My voice had turned hard.

She said, "Judge Maestro. Whom I promptly informed, okay? So if Connie had told me anything about you, I'd have informed you as well."

Milo said, "You told the judge but not the police."

Wright's hands were fists again. "Now *you* listen: I was under no obligation to tell anyone because the level of threat was ambiguous. But I did so anyway. At the risk of putting my standing at the bar in jeopardy. Why? Because I'm a moral person. Now, who killed my client?"

Milo said, "What was ambiguous about the threat to Judge Maestro?"

Sharp intake of breath. "Dr. Sykes never came out and said she was planning to harm the judge or anyone else. After the case closed, she phoned me to vent, it's a common after-reaction. And understandable, she was outraged about what she considered a miscarriage of justice. A conclusion with which I concurred. She felt the system had failed her and that the child would suffer. I allowed her to express herself. For closure. The more she talked the more worked up she got and then in the course of her discourse she said she felt like killing someone. Immediately after that, she went on a rant about Judge Maestro, specifically. How biased she'd been from the onset, how unwilling she'd been to have an open mind. It was the association that concerned me."

Milo said, "Wanting to kill someone, then seguing to the judge."

"There you go, Lieutenant. You're *getting* it. Quite obviously, there was no actionable threat. But I warned the judge anyway and if that's not proof of—"

"How did the judge respond?"

Beautiful teeth chewed Wright's upper lip. "I left a telephonic message."

"You assumed she'd receive it."

"I never heard she didn't receive it." She gave another dismissive wave. "I have nothing more to say to you."

"Actually," said Milo, "it was Mr. Ballister we're here to see, not you."

Not being the focus made Wright frown.

"So if you'd give us some time with Mr. Ballist—"

"You want me to leave? Fine! I'm gone." Milo stepped away and she slid out of the booth, stamped off.

Myron Ballister said, "Oh, man."

Milo said, "Sorry to ruin your hot date."

"She's like a Ferrari, zero to a hundred in . . . whatever. What do you guys need from me?"

"How long you been practicing law?"

"Me? Just this year."

"Helluva case to start with."

"I had others before," said Ballister. "A couple."

"Also child custody?"

"No, just . . . coupla traffics . . . one DUI."

"So you don't specialize in family law."

"I'm still trying to figure out what I'm into."

Milo slid into the spot vacated by Medea Wright. I took up the remaining space in the booth. Ballister, hemmed in, eyed the bowl of chips.

Milo nudged it just out of reach. "Who referred Cherie Sykes to you?"

"That's confidential."

"Really? Something silly like that?" Milo inched closer to him.

"Whatever, Craigslist. I have an ad there." Ballister fidgeted. "Starting out's tough."

"Hey, whatever works, Myron."

"Go to Yale like Medea, it's easier."

I said, "You won the case."

"Yeah," he said, as if he still couldn't believe it. "The day after, Medea calls, I'm thinking, *It's fin-*

ished, you lost, now what? But she was different. Friendly. She asked for a meeting. Dinner, near her office. I didn't get it, but, okay, why not?" Baleful smile. "I was hoping she was impressed with my winning, her firm wanted to interview me or something."

"So you guys had dinner."

"Not for long." Ballister's Nordic complexion made blushing a quick process. Sweat beaded his nose. "I'm thinking this can't be happening, she went to friggin' *Yale.*"

Milo said, "A girl who knows what she wants, Myron. Lucky you."

"Yeah." Ballister's shoulders relaxed. He grinned. Now we were just a bunch of guys talking about women. "She says it—the attraction—is because I'm easygoing. Both of her exes were total assholes."

"Sometimes nice guys finish first."

"I like to go to sleep feeling okay about what I did that day. Before I went to law school I worked at a nonprofit for a couple years. Social work assistant, helping farm people get benefits. I ever pay back my student loans I'll go back to that but as an attorney."

"Public interest law."

"Medea calls it public nuisance. She can get a little . . . outspoken."

I said, "You like helping people, so when Cherie Sykes came to you . . ."

"I was surprised. That she'd just do it with Craigslist. I mean traffic is one thing, even a DUI if it's a first offense. But your kid? I told her I'd never done anything like that, maybe she wanted someone with more experience. She said nope, she liked the vibe I gave off."

His smile was gentle. "I figured maybe she also liked the price."

I said, "You actually charged her?"

"A little." Another shrug. "She's not exactly rich, right? Not like her sister, that's what bothered me, her sister having someone like Medea. It wasn't balanced."

I said, "Luckily the law was on your side."

"After I read up on guardianship I realized that. But still, you never know. I figured we needed for Ree to not look like a serious criminal or an outright psycho. Which she isn't—she's a really nice person, am I right, Doctor? But with the system, you never know. When I worked at the agency I saw all sorts of crazy stuff go down, shit that didn't make sense but there was nothing you could do, judges are in charge. When I found out we were getting Judge Maestro I tried to research her, couldn't find any pattern. She wasn't doing much guardianship, period, it was mostly inheritance disputes, conservatorships, whatever. So I just didn't know. Anyway thanks for your report, Dr. Delaware. It really helped."

Milo said, "Obviously Connie sure thought so."

Ballister's brow furrowed. "That must've been scary as hell. I could tell Connie was weird. But like that?"

"Weird, how?"

"She just didn't react normally—like she was part person part robot."

"A cyborg."

Unfamiliar term to Ballister. "Whatever."

Milo said, "A weird woman, Myron. Now someone's gone and killed her."

"Wow. That's totally crazy."

Louella the waitress cruised past, trying hard not to notice us. Milo said, "Pardon?"

She stopped, half swiveled. "Yes, sir?"

He produced his wallet, peeled off money. "Sorry

for taking up space, and sorry for my daughter's out-burst. Hope this covers it."

She took the cash, counted silently. "This is way too much."

"It includes what they had and what we didn't order."

Ballister said, "You don't need to do that."

Louella said, "You're sure? This is *way* too much."

Milo patted her hand. "Sure as I can be."

"You're an angel," she said, and left retabulating her bounty.

Ballister said, "That was cool of you, man, but really it's not necessary to comp my—"

"Paid off my student loans a long time ago, Myron. Let's talk about Ree Sykes."

Ballister's fingertips tapped his glass. "Don't take offense at this, sir, but if you think paying for—"

"No tit for tat, Myron. Just tell me what you feel comfortable talking about."

"I know you're doing your job, sir, but since she was an actual client, I can't divulge—"

"I'm not concerned with anything related to the lawsuit, Myron. Only Ree's feelings about her sister."

"Feelings? Oh, no, no way, man, you can't be thinking that."

Milo was silent.

"Not a chance," said Ballister. "She's just about the most nonviolent person I ever met."

"Maybe, but I still need to talk to her. Unfortunately, she's left town."

"Why would she do that?"

"Good question, Myron."

"Well, I don't know."

"She never mentioned travel to you?"

"No, never. She take the baby?"

"Sure did."

"So maybe it's a vacation. After all the stress."

"After her sister gets murdered."

"No way," said Ballister. "She doesn't have a violent bone in her body."

"I'm sure she seemed that way but I've been doing this job a long time and I still get surprised."

"That would be a huge surprise, man. No way, I can't see that."

"What if she thought Connie would take her back to court?"

"She figured that would hap—shit, forget I said that."

"She expected to be sued again."

"She figured there was a good chance. I told her I'd represent her, we'd win again. And Medea—oh, shit—"

"Medea wouldn't be representing Connie?"

Ballister groaned. "You can't repeat this, man. I'd be toast."

"Deal, Myron."

"Yeah, Medea said she was through, if Connie asked her she'd refer her to someone else. Because the case was a loser. So you see, Ree had nothing to worry about."

"Except a whole lot of emotional stress."

"Even so. She's like a . . . lamb. When I was at her apartment interviewing her she found a spider and picked it up gently and put it outside."

Milo said, "Flower child."

"Exactly."

"Kinda like the Manson Family?"

"Oh, man . . . listen, you have to do your job but trust me, Ree did not kill her sister. I'd bet on it."

Delivering his argument in a new voice: determined, deeper, as if a sudden hormonal surge had annealed him. Maybe he'd master that over time, end up an effective courtroom warrior.

Milo said, "I'm not into betting, Myron, I build up facts. What would help Ree out is having her talk to me so I can eliminate her. You have no idea where she is?"

"None."

"If you did, would you tell us?"

"Probably not," said Ballister. "I'm being honest."

"Best policy, Myron."

"Not really, sir. Not in the actual world. But it's hard to change."

Milo thanked Ballister for his time and he smiled and said, "Sure, guys. Good luck."

But we made no effort to leave the booth and Ballister's smile crumpled and a knot of muscle below his left ear began twitching. He glanced at his uneaten food, toyed with his Margarita glass. Took hold of it and watched ice swirl before forcing another smile and blurting, "What now?"

I said, "In her deposition, Connie mentioned two musicians she suspected might be Rambla's father."

He'd read the deposition, probably a dozen times. But no comment.

I pressed: "What did Ree have to say about that?"

"We never discussed it."

"Really," I said.

"It wasn't relevant," said Ballister. "I guess you didn't think so, either, or you would've mentioned it in your custody report."

"Good point."

He smiled. "Once in a while, I come up with 'em."

I shifted closer. He tried to move back, couldn't, took hold of the glass again.

I said, "Did Ree ever tell you who the baby's father is?"

Head shake. "I asked once, figured maybe it could help her. She wouldn't tell me so I dropped it."

"How'd you figure it would help her?"

"Having a support system," he said. "If the father was a decent guy. And if she could cooperate with him it would show stability and also make it two against one."

"Ree didn't care about any of that."

"She said it wasn't important."

"Or maybe the father's not a decent guy."

"I don't know one way or the other. Anyway, we won, so who cares?"

"But now Ree's gone."

"Her prerogative," said Ballister. "It's a free country."

Milo said, "Sure is, Myron, but if you do hear from her . . ."

"If I did I couldn't tell you."

"Even if telling us was best for your client?"

"Even," said Ballister. "It's all up to her."

"Spoken like a true attorney, Myron. Best of luck to you."

Ballister raised his glass. "Luck to you, too."

Once again, we didn't budge. This time Ballister was resigned. He sucked up ice, chewed slowly.

Milo said, "We're gonna need luck, Myron—oh yeah, one more thing. I need to ask where you were last Thursday, from seven thirty p.m. on."

"Me?" said Ballister. "Oh . . . you've *got* to be kidding."

Milo sat there.

The young lawyer shook his head. "Crazy . . . okay, sure, no prob, where was I . . . what time?"

Milo repeated the parameters.

Ballister fidgeted. "I guess I was with Medea."

"You guess."

"I was with her, okay? Definitely."

"All night?"

Return of the blush. "Yup."

"She'll back you up on that?"

"I think so," said Ballister.

"She might not?" said Milo.

"It could be a problem for her."

"How so, Myron?"

Ballister nudged his glass an inch away. "Here's the thing, she's still married to her second ex, he's a loser, pushing for more money in the settlement, looking for anything he can use against her."

"So her infidelity might help him."

"You never know. Anyway, it's the truth. We were together that whole time. I left her place around six a.m. She's got a concierge in her building, dude in a red jacket, he can verify."

"Where does she live?"

"Century City." Ballister recited the address. One of the better gated developments. A burst of noise made the three of us turn toward the entry. Six new diners entered the restaurant. Beefy men carrying yellow plastic hard hats.

Ballister muttered, "This place does great."

Milo said, "You were with Medea all night and into the morning but she might not want to back you up."

"Her concierge will."

"That's a start, Myron. Puts you in the building in the morning. But better to hear it from Medea—you actually being in her apartment all night."

Ballister's eyes got hard. "Okay, you know what? Medea *will* verify or I'll get annoyed. And that could *really* create problems for her." His entire face was different. As if he'd grown suddenly tougher, older, a force to be reckoned with.

"Listen to you, amigo." Milo laughed. "Thinking like a *lawyer.*"

Outside the restaurant, he said, "His and hers alibis. How romantic."

I said, "You have doubts?"

"Concierges live on Christmas tips but no, not really. There'd be no reason for either of them to off dear ol' Connie."

We headed toward the car. He checked his messages. Only one but important: the crime scene crew at Ree Sykes's apartment. "You're kidding. Any idea whose? . . . okay, yeah, do that. Sooner the better. Thanks."

Click.

"Techies found a single suspicious red stain on the carpet near the foldout couch. Small, maybe an eighth of an inch in diameter, but confirmed as blood, human, O-positive. Which is a lot of people but maybe Connie was one of them. Hold on."

He phoned the coroner, talked to the assistant of the pathologist who'd conducted the autopsy. Moments later, he was giving the thumbs-up. "O-positive."

I said, "Don't want to ruin the party but Ree was Connie's sister, they could very well have the same blood type. And people bleed in their own homes all the time."

"What a therapist you are . . . yeah, sure, but DNA on Connie will tell me one way or the other so I asked for a fast-track, might get results in a week. It comes back a perfect match to Connie, Ree's chemistry doesn't mean a damn thing."

"Good luck."

"You mean that?"

"Why wouldn't I?"

"Your patient being a murderer?" he said.

"I've lived long enough to experience the joy of being conned."

He half smiled. "Does it happen often or just frequently?"

"Don't push it," I said.

As we drove away, he said, "Okay, time to check out potential baby da-das. Let's do Melandrano first because he's got no criminal record, might be more willing to, as they say, cooperate with the authorities. What's his job in the band?"

"Rhythm guitar and vocals."

"Front man. Sneaking out back with Ree?"

I said, "More important, he babysat Rambla when Ree came to see me."

"Mommy enlists Daddy's help . . . a singer, huh? Maybe he'll warble for us."

William "Winky" Melandrano lived in an apartment on the eastern edge of North Hollywood, midway up a treeless block of pleasant, bland structures not far from the upper-crust streets of Toluca Lake.

During the drive, Milo had obtained stats on Melandrano's sole registered vehicle, a thirteen-year-old Ford Explorer, gray at the time of purchase. The SUV was parked in a space at the rear of the building. Still gray, in need of washing, littered with empty cups and Styrofoam take-out cartons and old newspapers and rolled-up clothing.

"No OCD, here," he said. "Okay, let's meet the Winkster. Should we need to build rapport, you can trade gee-tar licks with him."

Humming the first seven bars of "Smoke on the Water," he circled back to the front.

I said, "Get some hair extensions and you've got a whole new career."

"If goose-farts ever become the new big thing in vocals."

The units were accessible through an open staircase. No answer at Melandrano's apartment. Milo pushed the buzzer a few more times, knocked harder, said, "If life was too easy, we'd take it for granted . . . don't think I'll leave my card, just in case he's helping Ree rabbit."

As we turned to leave, a woman with a small boy in tow appeared at the top of the stairs, stopped to study us, continued warily, stopped again.

Young Latina, hair down to her waist, wearing some kind of medical uniform. The child was four or five, sported a Los Lobos tee that reached his knees, rolled-up jeans, kiddie-Nikes. The woman stepped in front of him. Instinctive protectiveness.

Milo said, "Hi, ma'am, police," then offered his warmest smile along with a badge-flash.

She said, "Police is looking for Winky? How come?" A badge on her uniform bore the logo of a drugstore chain over a name in cursive. *L. Vega.*

"We need to talk to him."

"He did something?"

"No, ma'am."

She looked relieved. "He left."

"When?"

"Couple days ago. You sure he didn't do nothing?"

"Really," said Milo, "we just need to talk to him about a friend of his who's missing."

"Oh. 'Cause sometimes he babysits Carlos, he always seemed okay."

"No reason to worry about him, Ms. . . . Vega."

"Lourdes." She looked down at the boy. "Hear that? No worry 'bout Mr. Winky, *hijo.*"

Carlos began shadowboxing.

Milo said, "So Winky left two days ago."

"Around then," said Lourdes Vega. "I went over to ask him to babysit Carlos and he was out."

"So you didn't see him leave?"

"No. I couldn't get help so I stayed home."

"He's your regular babysitter."

"When my mother can't I sometimes ask him. It's easy, him being next door. He plays guitar for Carlos, he's teaching Carlos to play—you like Mr. Winky's guitar, hey, *hijo*?"

The boy nodded gravely. Threw more punches. Eyed Milo as if considering something naughtier. Milo's smile made him scurry behind his mother.

She said, "Winky say Carlos has talent but his fingers got to grow. You gonna do that, *hijo*, grow your fingers so you can play like Mr. Winky?"

No response.

Milo said, "Sounds like he's a good neighbor."

"Oh, yeah. Real quiet and nice."

"What time did you go over and find him gone?"

"It was at night, like . . . nine? I was doing a double shift, picked up Carlos at the day care, got home like at eight, had dinner, Carlos was sleeping, I figure maybe I can go out with my friends, Carlos would be sleeping anyway, Winky could watch TV. I got more cable stations than him."

"His car's here."

"Really?"

"Gray Explorer, parked out back."

"Yeah, that's his," said the woman. "Well, I don't know . . ."

"Who are his friends?"

"Other guys in the band—he's got a band. They dress up."

"Dress up?"

"Like Oldies guys—extra hair, leather." She giggled. "Like a uniform I guess." She plucked at her blouse. "I got to wear one at Health Aid, so whatever."

"These other guys in the band have names?"

"Um, one I think is Chuck, the other's Morris?"

"Maybe Boris?"

"Could be. I didn't really meet 'em ever to talk, I just seen 'em picking up Winky, everyone's wearing extra hair, so I figure they working. They play at a club, Winky said I could come for free."

"You ever take him up on the offer?"

"Uh-uh, I work two doubles a week at Health Aid, Carlos's daddy's in Afghanistan, I'm doing everything myself except when my mother has time but she works, too."

"Super-busy."

"Well . . . I'll get there to hear 'em, I'm sure they're good. I guess. Also, I don't want to bring Carlos to a place like that and Winky can't watch him if he's playing music so I need to wait for my mother to have all night and lately she works doubles, too. At the Farmer John sausage factory over in Vernon."

"Does Winky charge you to babysit?"

"I offered," she said. "He wouldn't take it. Says he had no kids, always wanted a son of his own, Carlos is a cool little dude, got talent, he's gonna make him a little musician." Reaching behind, she ruffled the little boy's hair. "That right, Carlito? You gonna play music?"

Grave nod.

"Know what talent means, *hijo*?"

"I play good."

"That's right," she said, stooping and kissing his cheek. "You're like a genius, my smart baby."

Carlos squirmed. "I'm hungry."

"Okay, okay—anyway, sir, nice to meet you."

Milo said, "One more question: Does Winky have any female friends?"

"Not that I saw." Her mouth constricted. "But he's not like that. I don't think."

"Like what?"

She cupped her hand to the side of her mouth. Mouthed, *Gay.*

"Likes girls."

"I never saw different," said Lourdes Vega. "All he does is teach Carlos guitar. You're not saying I should be nervous?"

"Not at all."

"Good. I mean I figured he was okay. I mean a mother *knows.*"

CHAPTER
27

B ack in the car, Milo got a text. He read, scowling.

"Binchy. Ree Sykes's car just showed up in the lot at Union Station, parking stub puts it there since the night Connie was killed. If she paid cash she's untraceable. Motive, timing, a definite rabbit, and that blood in her apartment says a lot to me, amigo."

I didn't answer.

He started the car. "Just what I need, Mama and baby riding the rails to who-knows-where. Most likely with ol' Winky, seeing as he cut out right around the same time. Talk about a paternity test."

Steering with one hand, he phoned Sean Binchy, ordered him to remain at the train station for as long as it took to show DMV photos of Cherie Sykes and William Melandrano to Amtrak clerks, porters, and security guards. "They've got cameras but with all the in and out, who knows. Nothing pans out, Sean, have a big steak on Uncle Milo then go back and see if the night shift remembers anything. Really work the place. You need help, get Reed. He's busy, draft someone else."

He hung up and drove faster. I said, "Ree kept her

secret all these years, finally told Melandrano he was the daddy."

"Why now?"

"Who knows?"

Thinking to myself: *They're creating a new family.*

He said, "She took a chance he'd be pissed, her keeping it from him all this time. Maybe she risked it because she wanted help in her time of homicidal need."

"The two of them did Connie together?"

"Why not? A tag team fits the crime scene perfectly: Ree knocks on Connie's door, says she wants to talk things over, work out an amicable arrangement. Connie lets her in, before she knows it, Melandrano's there, sticking her in the gut. Connie goes down, Melandrano finishes her off with her own belt. No resistance, no mess, nice and organized. Baby was probably in the car the whole time. Now they're gone, traveling light because they're serious about disappearing."

My head was flooding with what-ifs. So many things to be wrong about.

Taking on a case that should never have been allowed in the first place and nearly dying for it.

Milo rubbed his hands together. "Let's bust up a happy-family road trip."

Pulling over, he got back on the phone, initiating the APB process on Cherie Sykes and William Melandrano. Then he reached Binchy again and checked the progress of the workup on Ree's car.

A few fingerprints in the expected places but no obvious signs of anything suspicious. The vehicle would be towed to the auto lab for a closer look. Once the prints were cataloged, an AFIS search would start rolling.

He pocketed his phone. "Her arrests are dinky and

they predate AFIS, and Melandrano's not in the system. Too bad, I'd love to confirm his presence in the car, start laying the grounds for conspiracy."

I said, "You could send someone to swab his apartment door, see if anything matches."

He looked at me. "If you weren't so helpful I'd be irritated." Brief call to the crime lab before turning back to me. "Someone'll be at Winky's place in a couple of hours, thank you, Perfessor. Okay, let's try to talk to the lucky guy who *isn't* the father, see what he has to say."

Bernard "Boris" Chamberlain's address was on Franklin just east of the avenue's terminus at La Brea. This was the heart of residential Hollywood, a mixed bag of run-down short-term rentals and once-lavish structures from the twenties prettied up to varying degrees.

Chamberlain lived in one of the rehabbed buildings, a multi-turreted, five-story, vanilla-colored fantasy tagged *Le Richelieu* by a calligraphic neon sign dribbling over brass-framed double glass doors.

The lobby evoked the reception hall of an old deco oceanliner with rounded corners and stepped molding tracing the perimeter of a twenty-foot ceiling. The plaster was moisture-spotted. A chrome chandelier was unlit. Puckered brown wallpaper was patterned with calla lilies. The carpet was a patchwork of gray remnants laid down clumsily.

No doorman, no security of any sort. Two brass-cage elevators were each marked *Out of Order*. The directory between the lifts listed B. Chamberlain in Apt. 405.

We climbed.

Ash-colored floors, walls, and doors made the walk up the fourth-floor hallway an ooze through an oversized lead pipe. Milo's knock on Chamberlain's door elicited an immediate, emotionally neutral "Hold on."

The man who opened was middle-aged and bald but for gray side-hairs gathered into a foot of braid that rested atop his left shoulder. His features were meaty and compressed, his skin the color and texture of Muenster cheese. An immense torso balanced precariously on curiously spindly legs. He wore a black sweatshirt with the sleeves cut off to allow tree-trunk arms some room to maneuver, brown velvet pajama pants, Japanese sandals. Behind him was a dim space set up with a barbell on a rack, a pressing bench, a pair of electric basses, and a small, football-colored Pignose practice amp.

Milo said, "Mr. Chamberlain?"

"Yeah?"

"Police—"

"Finally. Those idiots." Chamberlain crooked a thumb to his right.

"Idiots," said Milo.

"The tweakers? Two doors down in 409? Rich kids slumming and slamming. They wear designer threads, have that rotting skin, look like skeletons."

Milo said nothing.

Chamberlain said, "All's I know is Cat and Jeremy, that's what they call each other. All's the directory says is Cat."

Mammoth arms crossed a convex slab of chest.

Milo said, "What have they done to bother you?"

"Done? Same damn thing, over and over," said Chamberlain. "Since they moved in, it's been hell. They're out all day scoring and shooting, come back at three, four, five a.m., mistake my door for theirs, try to open it, wake me up with all the scratching and banging. Company that manages this dive is useless.

Then I call you guys, you send officers over, by the time they arrive it's quiet, they knock on those low-lifes' doors, no one answers, they say they can't do anything. One of your guys had a bad attitude, trying to make me feel I was paranoid. Actually said, 'You live in a place like this, you can expect bad stuff.' So what now, they finally did something violent?" He sneered. "Cat and Jeremy. Living off the parents, shooting everything right up the arm."

"We're not here about that, sir."

"What? Jesus. Then what?"

"Could we come in, Mr. Chamberlain?"

"For what?"

"A few minutes of your time."

"About what?"

"Cherie Sykes."

Chamberlain squinted. "Cherie? She okay?"

"Could we come in?"

Chamberlain's arms dropped heavily. "She *not* okay? Oh, man, don't tell me something bad, it's too early in the day for bad."

"She's fine, Mr. Chamberlain. Could we come in? And I will make sure someone with authority knows about those tweakers."

"Cat and Jeremy," said Boris Chamberlain. "Low-lifes like that, it's only a matter of time, right?"

Milo nodded. Took a step forward.

Chamberlain didn't budge.

Milo pointed past him.

Chamberlain said, "Sure, fine. But there's nowhere to sit."

No false advertising; the front room was devoid of furniture and the adjoining kitchen looked unused. Bottles of protein shake and a blender crowded the counter. A single window was blocked by a blackout shade. A low-watt bare bulb in the ceiling allowed in some drear.

The basses were a four-string Fender Precision that looked vintage and a six-string Alembic. Serious gear, same for the Bassman amp in a far corner. The barbell disks added up to three hundred pounds, not counting the bar. The brown vinyl of the bench was ripped and sweat-stained.

The room stank of exertion.

Boris Chamberlain said, "I'm not much for entertaining. So what's up with Ree—with Cherie?"

"When's the last time you saw her?"

"The last time . . . had to be a couple of weeks ago. Why?"

"What about William Melandrano?"

"Winky? What about him?"

"They both seem to have left town. Possibly together."

"Left? No way. Why would Winky do that? We've got a gig every—we're in a band together. Left? What for?"

"We were hoping you could tell us."

"Me? First I've heard of it. You're sure you've got your facts straight?"

"What was their relationship?"

"Ree and Winky? Friends. We all are. From junior high, we go way back. Why? What's this about?"

"Far as you know they weren't intimate?"

"Intimate?" Back went the arms, closing across thorax. The resulting sound was a side of beef slammed against a meat-locker wall. "I don't really want to be having this conversation."

Instead of replying, Milo produced his cell phone. Punching a preset, he said, "Petra? Milo. Listen, I happen to be here on your turf, got a concerned citizen who's not getting the service he deserves from your blue meanies."

He went on to summarize Chamberlain's woes with Cat and Jeremy. "Yeah, I know Scott, that would be great, kid. And hey, I might be saving you some work, ounce of prevention, you know? These two sound like they'll cause problems."

Boris Chamberlain's mouth had dropped open during the conversation.

Milo said, "That was a Hollywood detective named Connor. She does homicide but she's passing the information along to a narcotics detective named Scott Perugia. Will contact you personally regarding your neighbors. That doesn't satisfy you, you call me." Handing over his card.

"Okay . . . thanks." Chamberlain's eyes dropped to the card. "Homicide. What's going on?"

"We'll get to that but first please answer my questions. Were Mr. Melandrano and Ree Sykes intimate?"

"Did they ever do it?" Chamberlain's cheese-face turned pink. "Yeah, sure, but a long time ago. Fact is . . . whatever." He tapped a foot.

"Ree was your band's groupie?"

"No, no, nothing that tacky. We all knew each other, did some traveling together." Chamberlain's eyes rounded. "Oh, that's what you're getting at. Them hitting the road because they've got a thing? No way, I'd know if that was the plan. What the hell's going on? These are people I care about, if something happened to them—"

"Are you aware of Ree's problems with her sister?"

"Connie? Trying to steal the baby? What a bitch, she always was. One of those brainiacs but you don't have to make other people feel stupid."

I said, "She lorded her smarts over everyone else."

"Megatons of attitude. We had nothing to do with her. No one did, she was a loner. And way older than us. Then all of a sudden Ree comes in looking like someone died, we say what, she says Connie's trying to steal my baby. Ree loves that kid, she'd do anything for it and Connie saying she's unfit? What bullshit. But Connie's got money, she can keep torturing Ree, that's the way the system works."

"Ree's still worried about that," I said.

"Could you blame her? Taking her to court in the first place was evil. Making her go broke so she'll give up?"

"Nasty."

"*Evil.*"

"Winky have feelings about that?"

"We all do, who wouldn't?" said Chamberlain. "Ree's good people. Got a heart out to here." His arms uncrossed and spread.

I said, "Ree's raising the baby all by herself and now she has to deal with Connie on top of it."

"Evil," he repeated.

"What about the father?"

"What about him?"

"If she had a partner it would be easier."

"Yeah. Well, she doesn't."

"You have no idea who the father is?"

"Ree never said."

"Connie had theories."

"Did she."

I said, "Two names came up in her lawsuit."

"Did they."

"You have no idea."

"What're you saying?"

"In court documents Connie named Winky and you as possible fathers."

Pink turned to vermillion. "That's bullshit! No

way. That kid was born like . . . a couple of years ago and we . . ." He trailed off.

I said, "The baby's sixteen months old."

"Even more true. Ree and me haven't been—we were never really like that, anyway."

Milo and I said nothing.

"Oh, man," said Chamberlain. He waved Milo's card. "You got to tell me: Did someone get killed?"

Milo said, "Connie did."

"*What*? Fuck. When?"

"Couple of nights ago."

"Oh, man—you're thinking Ree had something to do with that? No fucking way. Ree's like the most nonviolent person in the world."

"We keep hearing that."

"That's 'cause it's true."

"What about Winky?"

"Winky? Let me tell you about Winky," he said. "Back in the day, Lonesome—the band, we're Lonesome Moan—back in the day we toured all over the country, did a lot of dives. Sometimes we'd end up in situations, you know? People drinking or smoking too much, assholes get hostile."

He flexed a monumental biceps. "Sometimes you need to take care of business." His eyes shifted from me to Milo. "You look like a guy who played some football."

Milo smiled. "Guard."

Chamberlain tapped a bulging pectoral. "Center and D-tackle. Till I discovered Leo Fender. Anyway, what I'm getting at is best defense is offense, back in the day there was some tussling. Me and Chuck and Zebe—those are the other guys in the band—we whaled a few butts. But not Winky. When the shit hit the fan you could count on him being out in the van or some other place where his nose wouldn't get like mine." Rubbing the battered organ.

"Conflict-averse," said Milo.

"Um . . . yeah, sure. What I'm trying to get across is Wink would do anything to avoid bloodshed."

"Even when threatened."

"Especially when threatened," said Chamberlain. "Back in the day it pissed us off, we thought it should be all for one, you know?"

"Like the musketeers."

"Yeah, whatever."

I said, "Winky couldn't be counted on."

"We're getting our clocks cleaned, doing some cleaning of our own, he's out in the van. Okay, he's a small guy, but still."

I said, "How did Ree react to tussles?"

Chamberlain stared. "She's a girl, what could she do? And don't get the idea she was always with us. Sometimes she was on the bus but just sometimes."

"Was she ever around when clocks got cleaned?"

"How would I know?" he snapped. "It's been a long time, who remembers shit like that?"

I said, "What we're getting at is was there a special relationship between Wink and Ree?"

"They're friends, we're all friends."

"Close enough friends for her to call him when she needed help?"

"What're you *getting* at?"

Milo said, "Okay, here's some facts: Ree and Winky got the hell out of Dodge the same night Connie got killed and Ree's car just showed up at Union Station."

"You're kidding."

"Wish I was, Boris."

Chamberlain rubbed his bald head. "I'm sure there's an explanation."

We waited.

He said, "I dunno, maybe they just felt like splitting. It can get that way, right?"

"What can?"

"Life. It closes in."

"Connie gets murdered, Ree and Winky decide to take a random train trip," said Milo.

Chamberlain threw up his hands. "I got nothing else to tell you."

"Else? You really haven't told us much, period."

"That's 'cause all I know is nothing. I mean, you knock on my door, I'm supposed to make shit up?"

Milo said, "Good title for a song."

"Huh?"

" 'All I know is nothing.' "

"Oh . . . yeah, maybe." He walked over to the Fender bass, removed it from the stand, thumbed a rapid run down the neck.

"Nice technique," I said.

"I practice."

Milo said, "Detective Perugia will be calling you today. You come up with any original ideas about Ree and Winky, you call me, okay?"

"Yeah, yeah, sure." Chamberlain began to rotate away from us.

I said, "One more thing: Why do you think Connie suspected you or Winky of being Rambla's dad?"

Chamberlain's body remained in place but his head swung back. "Probably because we used to party together."

I said, "Any other reason?"

"What do you mean?"

"Did anything happen more recently that would—"

"Okay," he said. "Yeah, fine, what's the big deal?" His mouth clamped shut. We waited.

"Okay, yeah, a few months ago we're gigging and

Connie shows up out of the blue. Sits at the back drinking water, pretending to be there for the show but she doesn't give a shit about music, is checking us out, we have no idea why. Obviously it was about Ree. 'Cause Ree was there, too. Behind the bar. Helping Chuck. He owns the place and he also drums so when he's drumming he could use help and that night his regular bartender was out. So Ree's filling drinks and she doesn't see Connie at first. Then the song ends and I look where Connie was sitting and she's gone, I'm thinking good riddance. Then we take our break and are hanging and Ree and Winky are like . . . okay, nothing serious, just a little making out, okay? Ree's affectionate . . . you know. With me and Ree, it's not even that, just a kiss, friendly, okay?"

Vermillion had turned to ruby. "Then *she* appears again and she's watching."

"Connie."

"Guess she never left, maybe she was in the john, I don't know. Whatever, she's there, giving us the stink eye. Like we're maggots. Then she walks out with this creepy-crawly smile on her ugly puss. Soon after, Ree gets served with legal papers."

I said, "You never got served."

"No way."

"Sounds like Connie was the paranoid one."

"Oh, man," he said. "To put Ree through something like that."

"But now Ree's gone, along with Winky."

"Well I don't know about that but no way did either of them have anything to do with Connie. And let me tell you, a lot of people could've hated Connie."

"Not Miss Charming?" I asked.

"Bitch was a total waste of space."

CHAPTER

28

During the drive back to the station, Milo made several fruitless calls to Binchy. A couple of times his driving suffered but who was going to give him a ticket? By the time he dropped me off he was sullen.

Happy to distance myself from the case, I drove home. A shiny white Range Rover was parked behind Robin's truck, tricked out with big wheels and chrome spinners, the windows tinted way past illegal. Efren Casagrande got out of the driver's side and watched me approach.

I said, "Hey, what's up?"

"You're okay with me here?"

"Unless you've switched gigs and are working for the IRS."

"Seriously, Doc. It's cool?"

"You need to talk, it's cool."

He grinned. "You always were the man."

As we walked to my office, I offered him coffee. He said, "I'm good," and settled on my battered leather couch, one knee pumping. Twitches traced his jawline, fleas jumping beneath the skin. I settled behind the desk.

"Here's where it's at, Doc," he said. Waiting for a moment before continuing. "You know what happened but you don't really know what *happened*."

The knee pumped faster.

I said, "You're talking about the hit on me."

"You sound all cool with that, it don't bother you?"

"It bothered me plenty. I just thought it was over."

"Yeah," he said. "That's the thing. It's over but it's like . . . actually I can take some coffee. Cream." He smiled. "Sugar would be nice but not today."

His shirtsleeves were rolled midway up to his elbows. Tiny red nicks dotted his left forearm. Better testing equipment allowed patients to save their fingers. He'd been drawing blood regularly.

When I returned with two cups he hadn't budged. The knee had stopped moving but when I handed him his coffee the jackhammer rhythm resumed, as if his body anticipated the caffeine jolt.

He took a quick sip. "'S good, Doc. I'm okay with coffee, my endo-doc says it can be good at night, y'know? Raising the level when I can't eat so I don't get the hypoglycemia."

"I've heard that."

"I drink a little before I go to bed and . . . anyway . . . I'm doing okay. With the D." Faint smile. "You weren't here, I'd say the fuckin' D."

I smiled. "Don't let me hold you back."

"Sometimes I think of it as a dude, you know? Some motherfucker trying to poison my blood and I'm killing his ass. That's stupid, huh?"

"Not at all."

"There you go," he said. "Just like before, like everything I do is cool with you."

"So far it has been."

His eyes hooded. "Yeah . . . sometimes 's good not

to know everything, Doc." The coffee cup wobbled. "Anyway, why I'm here is about you not me, Doc. What the cops tell you about how it went down?"

"Connie Sykes contracted with Ramon Guzman to kill me, Guzman talked to you, you called it off."

"Okay," he said, shifting his body to the side.

"That's not all of it?"

He drank. "Yeah, the bitch talked to Ramon. And yeah I ended it but not because Ramon told me."

He winced. Turned away for a second. Was that moisture in his eyes? "You get what I'm saying, Doc?"

"It was a close call?"

He put the coffee cup down. "You don't know, man. How close it was."

I figured I was making a good show of staying calm. My mouth tasted of wet copper. My bowels were twisting.

He said, "Ramon's a dumb motherfucker. He *shoulda* told me because he's nothing in the . . . what he did is, he told someone who didn't need to know. That individual told someone else." He bent forward. "Who told me."

"Are you here because there's still a danger of—"

"No, no, I'm telling you because it came fucking *inches* close, Doc, and it wasn't like she—like this person who told me was even saying it like it was a big thing, you know? Not like checking it out with Effo. It was like . . . like bullshit, part of something else."

She. Pillow talk had saved my life?

I said, "It came up in casual conversation." My voice was tight.

He winced. "I'm sorry, Doc. It's like . . . this person, she's joking about how Ramon's asking around to get someone done, gonna pay a thousand to the shooter and keep four, do some rich doctor up in Beverly Glen, up there in the hills, nice and quiet, gonna be an easy job. She's like . . . laughing. What's really funny is Ramon's already got *two* guys wanna do it—like competing to do it, feel me? So now he's bargaining. Who'll do it for nine hundred, who'll do it for eight."

The joys of free enterprise.

I said, "Bargain hunting."

"It ain't funny, Doc."

"I know."

"Sorry," he said. "I guess you're making like it's no big deal so it don't get to you."

"Good guess, my friend. But it's already gotten to me big-time."

"I'm sorry, man, I'm really sorry. I mean I wasn't even listening to this bullshit until I hear Beverly Glen. I ask what kind of doctor, this person don't know, she's just—it's bullshit talk, okay? I call someone else, say bring in Ramon. Those other dudes, too. *Now.*"

His face was an Aztec stone carving. "We had like a meeting. I'm talking a *day* before it was supposed to go down, they were planning to split the money."

My lungs felt limp and boggy. I exhaled. That hurt my chest.

Efren said, "I told Ramon he fucked up big, had to pay. He got a beat-down."

I smiled. "Hope he learned his lesson."

He took a long swallow of coffee, licked his upper teeth. "I'm still thinking about it. Over and over, like a thought gets stuck in your head, you can't let go, it just keeps going round and round. You feel me?"

I said, "It's called a brain-worm."

"A worm . . . yeah, maybe . . . it used to be that way with the fucking D. I was like thinking about it *all* the

time. Before they sent me to you. Then you tell me I'm
not an asshole, I can stop thinking about that shit."

He tapped his temple. "It's like you helped me
un-mess it in here. So it ain't like that with fucking D
anymore but now it *is* like that with fucking Ramon.
I mean, Doc, if the bad thing happened, it would be
like worms forever, feel me?"

And worms would be feasting on me. "I do."

"Ramon *really* fucked *up*." He clicked his tongue.
"So *now* I'm like maybe a beat-down ain't enough."

He sat back, crossed a leg, mimed a finger-gun.

"Not a good idea, Efren."

"Maybe not for you, Doc. But maybe for me."
Mimed trigger pull. Three times. "No more worm."

I shook my head. "Forget it, Efren."

He said, "It was so *close,* Doc. I keep *thinking*
about it."

"We can deal with that, Efren."

"Like what, a pill? I already got enough pills."

"Not a pill. Mental training." That sounded flimsy
and ridiculous.

He snickered. "You gonna *train* me not to take care
of my own problem? Like a exercise? Like a worm
gym class?"

"I can help you stop thinking about it."

"Maybe I don't *wanna* stop, Doc. Maybe I wanna
take care of *business.*"

"Maybe you do. But don't," I said.

"Why the fuck not, Doc?"

"First off, it's wrong."

He stared at me. "You serious? Motherfucker tries
to kill your ass and you're like *save* his ass?"

"He means nothing to me, Efren. If he came at me,
I'd do my best to finish him off."

"With what, a book?"

Years ago, I'd killed a man who'd tried to kill me.

Whatever crept into my voice when I said, "Trust me, I'd take care of business," made Efren look at me as if for the first time.

"So what's the problem, Doc? Stupid motherfucker needs to—"

"I'd have to report you to the cops."

His lips slammed shut. His eyelids lowered. "You'd rat me out? What the fuck for?"

"It's the law."

"All this time you been telling me what I say here is secret—"

"It is secret but there's an exception. It's called the *Tarasoff* warning. A patient tells me he's going to hurt someone, I have to report it."

His legs uncrossed. "That's fucked."

"It's the law."

"It's the law," he mocked. "Like Ramon gave a shit about the law when he tried to kill your ass."

"I know it sounds—"

He sprang up, walked to the door, paused. "What it sounds is *bullshit*, Doc. First you tell me I got a worm in my fucking brain then you're like don't tell me the truth."

"Efren—"

"Exercises? You think I come here for exercises, Doc?"

"Why exactly did you come here?"

He stood there.

"Efren—"

"You tell *me* why I came here, Doc. You're the smart one."

I shook my head.

"Then I don't know, either."

He left the office. Dropped something on the floor and left it there.

I went after him. With his back to me he waved me away, walked faster.

"Ef—"

"We're cool, Doc. Thanks for your time." He began sprinting. By the time I got down the stairs, he was in the Range Rover, peeling out in reverse.

I returned to the house and retrieved what he'd dropped.

Plain white envelope. Inside were crisp twenties. I counted them.

The exact amount I'd charged for therapy, back when he was a kid with lifestyle issues.

CHAPTER

29

I waited an hour before phoning Efren, left a message I knew he wouldn't return.

What, like a exercise? Worm gym class?

Legally, ethically—*technically*—I'd done the right thing steering him away from revenge. That didn't stop me from feeling out of touch.

In a simple world I'd stalk and kill Ramon Guzman myself. Tossing in the two would-be hit men who'd been bargaining for the privilege of ending my life.

Same fate for Connie Sykes, who started the mess. If Ree had taken care of that, I should be cheering her on, not aiding in finding her.

Meanwhile, I'd damaged my relationship with Efren, probably beyond repair. In the jungle he prowled, nuance was a felony.

I was wondering what to do about all of that when my service rang in with a message from Judge Nancy Maestro. Would I be downtown in the near future for a "chat"?

I phoned her chambers. A female bailiff said, "She's in session, sir."

"Will she be out at four thirty, as usual?"

"Give me your name again, sir."

I complied and repeated the question.

"She's over on Commonwealth, sir, you can try there."

The court building on Sixth and Commonwealth handles big-time corporate litigation. Maybe Nancy was finally transitioning to the white-collar trials she craved. The first clerk I spoke to had no idea who she was and I got nudged along a chain of civil servants before a familiar male voice said, "Deputy Nebe."

The tight-ass I'd met at probate court.

Today, he sounded more human. "Doctor, thanks for getting back. Unfortunately, Judge got tied up in meetings, will be back in chambers tomorrow."

Newfound warmth. Maybe he was getting a promotion, too.

"I can drop by in the afternoon."

"Would one p.m. work for you?"

"Sure."

"Good," he said. "I'll tell her."

At twelve forty-five the following day, I was nearing Grand Street when Nancy reached my cell. "Glad I caught you. Listen, I'm running late, got stuck having lunch over in Little Tokyo. Any way you could find your way here? If you haven't eaten, it's on me."

"Yes, on both counts."

She directed me to Ocean Paradise, a place on First Street that I already knew. Second floor of a smallish shopping center erected back when Japan was considered a financial threat. Decent eateries, schlocky souvenir shops, an old-school sushi bar. From time to time, I'd stopped there when testifying downtown.

The ensuing years had left the structure wilted and rain-streaked with a serious vacancy rate, including the space that had housed the sushi joint. One advantage: cheap, ample parking, and I was heading toward Nancy's corner booth ten minutes later.

Ocean Paradise was a small, overly lit room smelling of broiled fish and seawater. A live tank featured dark squiggly things. Nancy was drinking Perrier and chopsticking a bowl of rice topped with crunchy, spiderish pinwheels.

The place was mostly empty, save for three older Asian women and a pair of tan uniforms stationed at a center table. Deputy Nebe, his bronze-lensed glasses at his right elbow, sat across from a woman around his age. Thin but chesty with curly gray hair and rimless glasses, she chewed on a piece of maki. When she saw me she grinned and waved and I realized she was also a bailiff I'd seen before. Gregarious woman assigned to custody court, trying to make everyone feel comfortable during times of stress. I'd never bothered to learn her name.

She kept smiling.

I detoured over.

The woman's badge said, *W. Nebe.* Sergeant stripes on her sleeves.

She said, "Hey, Doc, so now you know the entire family. Has Hank been nice to you?"

"He's been great."

"Sure he has." She laughed.

Hank Nebe smiled weakly.

"Anyway, nice to see you again, Doc. You slated for any testimony with us in the near future?"

"Nothing at the moment."

"Lucky you, it's been crazy. Enjoy your lunch."

I sat down opposite Nancy. She said, "You know Willa?"

"I've seen her in court."

"She and Hank are an example for all of us, been married forever."

"Sometimes it works."

"You happily wed?"

"Been with the same woman for a long time."

"But no paper, huh?" she said. "That's the way it is, nowadays. Gays crave the legitimacy, everyone else wants nothing to do with it. Myself, I wouldn't mind the paperwork, just never found anyone after I ditched the first loser."

She motioned to a waitress and said, "Menu?"

I said, "Not necessary," and when the woman came to the booth, I ordered green tea and a few pieces of sashimi.

Nancy looked at her bowl. "Meanwhile, you can share this."

"What is it?"

"Baby octopus. Kind of brutal, I suppose. Poor little things never had a chance. Which you could say about kids who end up as pawns."

I laughed.

"People are so fucked up," she said, with sudden fire. "I guess if you can't tolerate it don't go into my profession. Or yours. Especially yours. How do you deal with it?"

"Do the best I can, then make sure I have an outside life."

She thought about that, seemed to turn gloomy. My food came and that snapped her out of her funk. "*Bon appétit*. So why did I ask to talk to you? Because crazy Connie Sykes wanted to have me assassinated and I recently found out she's been murdered. As you can see, that could complicate my life at an extremely inopportune time."

"The promotion to white collar."

"Waiting for the promotion to be finalized—talk about legal limbo. Meanwhile, there's all sorts of nonsense to go through, that's what I was doing at Commonwealth, yesterday."

"Interviewing?"

"Paying homage to the presiding. Big-money cases are a different universe, Alex. Wider in scope, more serious consequences. And with the Feds looking at everything nowadays, the slightest hint of impropriety can be an issue. Not that I've done anything wrong vis-à-vis crazy Dr. Connie."

I said, "She tried to kill me, too."

Her chopsticks faltered. A baby cephalopod tumbled to the table, rolled a bit, stopped belly-up. "You're kidding."

"Wish I was." I told her about the attempted hit.

"Shit," she said. "What a maniac." She shot me a crooked smile. "Are you the one who got her? Just kidding."

I ate a piece of sashimi.

"Sorry, I'm just jangled. She actually wanted *both* of us? Anyone else on her hit list?"

"Not that I know about."

"Wow. I need to get my head around this—what the hell was the matter with her?"

"Obviously lots."

"C'mon, be specific, you're the expert."

"I didn't evaluate her in depth, Nancy."

"Why not?"

"All I needed to know for your case was that her claim had no merit. Didn't take long to discover that."

"Obviously. Crazy lunatic—talk about a waste of court time. You have no idea how much stuff I see in probate that's utter crap, people filing paper just because they can. I can't wait to be out of there."

Lifting the fallen octopus, she regarded it with what might have been compassion. Then her face got hard and she popped it into her mouth, chewing audibly. Wiped her lips. "So, what have the cops learned so far, Alex? About the late, unlamented Connie."

"Not much."

"If there was much, would you tell me?"

"Depends."

"On what?"

"How close to the vest the cops wanted it."

Her head flicked back. Her smile was icy. "Fair enough, Alex. But just tell me one thing: Is there a chance this is going to blow up in my face?"

"Why would it?"

"What I just said: the merest hint of impropriety."

"Why would being a potential victim constitute impropriety?"

"Okay," she said. "I'll keep it simple: Lunatic wants to kill judge, then said lunatic dies violently? *I* know I'm blameless as a lamb but cops are suspicious types, once they go nosing around in my personal life and the media finds out, I become a *story* and there goes my transfer."

"I don't see why that would happen, Nancy."

"Then you don't understand the way things work," she said sharply. "Sorry, I didn't ask you here to give you attitude. I'm just a little edgy. Pivotal point in my career and *this* happens."

I said, "I haven't heard about any intention to question you."

She smoothed her hair. "So you are involved in the investigation."

"Not formally."

"What does that mean?"

"From time to time I'm asked to weigh in on cases. This is one of them."

"Even though you're directly involved."

"Not anymore," I said.

"What do you mean?"

"Connie's dead. It's over for both of us, Nancy."

She shuddered. "When I found out she was after

me, I nearly lost it. I get this anonymous message on my private line, freak out, and immediately tell Hank." Glancing over at Nebe. "Needless to say I wanted her busted immediately for making terrorist threats, was hoping someone in the D.A.'s office would see it that way. Hank asked around and found out she'd just been murdered. I mean this is too bizarre, Alex. What the hell's going on?"

"Wish I knew."

"What about the sister? She under suspicion? Because after what that bitch put her through, can't say I'd blame her. Pardon my loss of objectivity, but when someone desires to slay me it affects my personal feelings."

"Mine, too, Nancy."

"There you go, common ground," she said. She moved as if to touch my hand, thought better of it, ate another octopus. "If you had to guess, would you say it *was* the sister?"

"I honestly don't know, Nancy."

"Would you be opposed to checking with your cop contacts?"

"Do my best."

"Appreciate it." She called the waitress over, asked for two cups of sake. When they arrived, she raised her glass. "Time for a toast: to the demise of our mutual threat."

I said, "Bottoms up."

CHAPTER

30

I drove away from Little Tokyo. Milo called as I crossed Olive Street.

"Where you hiding? Been trying to reach you."

"Just had a strange lunch with a judge."

"That so? Well my bit of strange is Winky Melandrano showed up this morning. Actually, he's been there for a full two days, it took time to I.D. him."

"*There* being—"

"The crypt. Refrigerated. I was looking at the homicide roster, noticed a white middle-aged John Doe killed in North Hollywood a few nights ago, went over and made the I.D."

"A few nights ago is shortly after he left his apartment."

"Looks like he never got on that train."

"How'd it happen?"

"Meet me at my office. If you've got time."

"Nothing but."

A stack of photos sat to the left of Milo's computer: William Melandrano's pre-autopsy death shots.

Small, dark-mustachioed man with thinning hair. No wounds on the front of his body. Blood-matted strands at the back of his head were parted to reveal a single, smallish bullet hole.

Milo said, "There's your 'what.'"

I said, "Twenty-two caliber?"

"Good guess but actually a .25, just took a call from the pathologist. Sometimes they exit. This time the bullet stayed in his head—if you take a close look you can see the swelling here."

He pointed to a spot on the corpse's brow. Barely visible; I'd have missed it.

"Guess he had a hard skull. Poor guy. 'Where' is a couple of blocks from his apartment, nice quiet residential street. He took a stroll and got waylaid."

"Any sign he was lured?"

"That would be my guess." He wheeled his chair back. "A witness saw a woman leaving the scene. Old guy who lives in the house near where the body was found. He wears a hearing aid but it was working well enough for him to make out the pop when no one else did. This was about ten p.m., he was going to bed, went outside to check, saw a 'lady' walking away. No running, moving nice and relaxed, so he thought nothing of it. The next morning, another neighbor found the body. Empty pockets, no I.D., no money, no cell phone."

"Apparent robbery gone bad."

"Apparent but I'm betting not. More like a good way to delay identification, give her more time to run."

"One shot to the brain stem," I said. "That's pretty polished."

"Maybe, maybe not," he said. "People watch cop shows, it's like homeschooling for amateur criminals. Maybe our hippie hippie chick isn't all peace-love-Woodstock."

"What business would Ree have to take care of with Melandrano?"

"He was the dad and that made him a potential threat. As in he sues her for custody."

"If she was worried about that, why would she tell him he was the father?"

"Maybe she didn't, Alex. Maybe he figured it out by himself. Or found out some other way."

"Like?"

"How about Connie convinced him? Suppose after she lost the first round she tried to enlist him as an ally? Promising if he helped her win he'd have full parental rights, maybe even a nice cash payment. Connie's pattern was using her money as a weapon."

"No one's reported any conflict between Ree and Winky."

"The people you deal with in family court once loved each other."

I said nothing.

He said, "Connie's main premise was Ree was a crappy mother—what if she convinced Winky that Ree was mistreating the kid? And for all Connie's nuttiness, she could've ended up with science on her side."

"She got Winky to take a paternity test?"

"Or at least to try. Hell, she had a lab, could've run it herself. And maybe that's what really threatened Ree and caused her to act. All of a sudden, her big secret's blown and Winky *is* mad she never told him. A sister suing in probate is one thing. A co-parent dragging her to family court? Unlike Connie, Winky would have the law on his side."

"Boris Chamberlain didn't indicate Winky knew anything about paternity."

"Who says Winky confided in Boris? Look, Alex, I know this is tough. You went to bat for this woman, don't want to see the kid orphaned. But I have to look at facts on the ground and they tell me Ree Sykes has been clearing away the competition and now she's headed for parts unknown. Add to that a .25. Know what some guys call it? A girl's gun."

"Are you open to an alternative explanation?"

"Like what?"

I told him about my lunch with Nancy Maestro. "She was definitely pumping me for info. Wanting to know how your investigation's going. I walked away with a weird feeling."

"Weird enough for a reasonable alternative?"

"How about this: Maestro went after Connie before Connie could get to her."

"We're talking a sitting judge committing homicide, but fine, let's go with that. Now, what motive would Maestro have to go after Melandrano?"

I had no answer for that.

He said, "Peace-love-Woodstock," and shook his head.

"So now we're making Connie's murder a one-woman job, not a tag team."

"Would two people have made it easier? Sure. But hell hath no fury like a mommy scorned and this mommy was scorned plenty by her own flesh and blood. All Ree had to do to get Connie to open the door was say she was ready to reach an agreement over the kid. Ree had that non-violent image going for her. The last thing Connie would expect is baby sister sticking her in the gut. Meanwhile, I just checked the state of Boris Chamberlain's health, seeing as he's potential daddy number two."

"He was healthy yesterday."

"True but it pays to be careful. And happily the Bore-man is live and well and pumping iron like a maniac. That's per Scott Perugia and his Hollywood narc buddies who are keeping an eye on Chamberlain's building as we speak. Because, guess what?

'Cat' and 'Jeremy' turned out not to be rich kids from the Westside, they're rich kid felony *fugitives* from New York with warrants for dope, bomb building, and embezzlement from Cat's daddy's law firm."

"Wheels of justice," I said.

"Sorry about how it's shaking out on Ree, Alex."

"Any progress finding her?"

"The APB pulled in a ton of mommy-kid reports but nothing valid. The staff at the station didn't recognize Ree and there's no record of her buying a ticket. Time to put the marshals on it, anyone can find her they can."

He dialed a number, reached someone named Jed, started off with catching-up banter before seguing into the specifics of Cherie Sykes's rabbit. Then he said, "Doing it right now, amigo," and began pressing keys and sending attachments.

I got up. He didn't notice. I left.

Denial can only go so far and by the time I reached home I was certain I'd been conned by the best.

Not the first time, probably not the last. No big disgrace. Anyone can be snowed.

Anyone's not entrusted with children's futures.

Maybe it was time to take a break from court cases, work on sharpening my perceptions.

So, of course, the first message my service gave me was from a family court judge, one of the better jurists, named Marvin Applebaum, wanting me to take on a "complicated one."

The operator said, "Something funny, Dr. Delaware?"

"Pardon?"

"I gave you the message and you started laughing."

I said, "Just trying to see the bright side," and hung up.

*   *   *

I called Nancy Maestro's chambers and got Deputy Hank Nebe.

"Doctor," he said. "Enjoy your lunch?"

"I did. You?"

"Oh, sure. What can I do for you?"

"Judge Maestro had questions about the Connie Sykes investigation. I'd like to fill her in."

"You can tell me, sir, and I'll pass it along."

"No need, have her call me."

"Suit yourself, Doctor. But if something's personally relevant to the judge, it's best that she know it sooner not later."

"Nothing earth shattering," I said. "If she's interested, she can call."

"I'll pass that along, sir."

Nancy phoned two hours later. "New development?"

"The police are looking seriously at Ree Sykes as the prime suspect."

"Oh, great," she said. "And I'm the one who ruled in her favor, here we go, another stupid judge story. Has the media glommed on?"

Profoundly self-centered response.

I said, "Not at all."

"Well, that's good, fingers crossed."

"On balance, it's likely to work out well for you, Nancy."

"How so?"

"You're the one who ruled in her favor," I said. "Someone like that, it's nice to be on their good side."

"That's true," she said, brightly. "Thank you, you cheered up my day. Ciao."

A day went by, then another, with no contact from Milo. I figured it would stay that way for a while. I figured I was fine with that.

On the second day, Judge Marvin Applebaum made a second attempt to reach me. Figuring he deserved a personal turn-down, I called his chambers. He answered his own phone. I realized that so did most of the judges I worked with.

Unlike Nancy Maestro who shielded herself with staff to fit the outsized ego she'd displayed at lunch.

I said, "What's up, Marv?"

"I know you like the complicated ones, so here goes—"

"I can't take any case right now, let alone something complicated."

"Oh? May I ask why?"

"It's been a little hectic."

"Work?"

"Work, life in general."

"I see," he said. "Can I cajole you by offering minimal effort and maximal compensation? As in, this is a deal you can't pass up?"

"Minimal effort on something complicated?"

"You bet. Because—psychologically—it's a slam

dunk. The complication comes from the principals."
He named a movie star and an A-list film director.
"Seven years of so-called marriage, kids, splitsville,
surprise!"

Last year I'd dealt with multiple murders involving
a pair of screen gods. Marv couldn't be blamed for
not knowing that. Like so much to do with Hollywood, the media had learned only what the powers-
that-be dictated and the details remained under wraps.

I said, "What makes it a slam dunk?"

"He's a decent dad, she's a harridan with a serious
drug-abuse history."

"What do you need me for?"

"To say exactly that couched in nice psychological
polysyllables. You know how it is, Alex. If I don't call
in an expert I'm vulnerable to accusations of shoddi-
ness."

"I'm your psychological rubber stamp."

He chuckled. "At your highest hourly rate. But
wait, kids, there's more: He's shooting a picture in
Cambodia, has the tykes there. Creature comforts on
the set are a little iffy so he's willing to bring them to
Singapore for you to evaluate."

"Iffy environment but okay for the kids?"

"Hey, maybe he wants them to live like real people—
that's a plus, no? If not, consider that in your evaluation. Consider anything you want. So you'll do it,
okay? Singapore Air first class is *the* best, Jeannie and
I treated ourselves a couple of years ago for our anniversary trip. For a hotel, demand the Fullerton Bay.
They've got those toilets that warm your kiester then
wash it with a delicate spray."

"Very enticing, Marv."

"Okay," he said, "I'll list you as the evaluator of
record."

"It's really not a good time for me to—"

"Listen," he said, "you don't need to make a decision now. I got them to bifurcate money and custody, we're talking a month at the soonest, could be later if the financial issues don't get ironed out. I'm just trying to button down details early so I can take my own vacation before we start crunching numbers."

"Going back to Asia?"

"I wish," he said. "Napa Valley, Jeannie's into wine, now. Why're you so gun-shy all of a sudden?"

"Just finished a case in probate and I think I got conned big-time."

"Probate," he said. "You're talking that guardianship thing with the crazy sisters."

"It's public knowledge?"

"One of my staff was talking about it, said one of the litigants got murdered, the other's the prime suspect. I think it shook her up."

"Nervous staffer?"

"Newbie, a clerk. Anyway, that was obviously an outlier, Alex, so don't beat yourself up. And all the more reason to make haste returning to your roots here at family, where misery *doesn't* love company. In terms of Singapore, they've got this botanical garden, hundreds of orchid varieties growing like weeds. Granted the weather sucks but it's clean and safe, there are casinos, you can take a vacation at the studio's expense."

"The studio's paying the bills."

"You bet. They don't want anything blocking his creativity."

"Will I be listed on the credits?"

He laughed. "You know, I could probably swing that—maybe assistant producer? If you produce something I can use. If you say no, I'll go down the list and we both lose out. Guess who's up?" He named two psychologists on the panel. Mediocre hacks. "Either's likely to screw up, meaning both sides will end up hiring private consultants and it'll drag on for forever. That sound good for the kids, Alex?"

"Give me a couple days, Marv."

"Fair enough. You know us wise men, we're all about fair."

Nancy Maestro had asked me if the media had glommed onto Connie's murder and I'd said no. But the story was traveling the courthouse rumor mill even though it hadn't reached the press.

Logging onto the family court website, I key-worded *applebaum* and got Marv's page, complete with his chubby avuncular headshot and smaller photos of his staff. His aides were an administrator named Mary Johnson, a bailiff named Lionel Wattlesburg, both long-time vets whom I knew, and a young, thin-faced, dark-haired woman named Kiara Fallows, identified as the clerk. Phoning the administrative number got me Wattlesburg on the line.

He said, "Hey, Doctor. You doing that you-know-who case for us? Maybe win an Oscar for best supporting shrink?"

"Maybe, Lionel."

He whistled. "Gonna be fun."

I said, "Is Kiara Fallows around?"

"Nope, quit, she notified this morning. Been here maybe three months. Kids today, no staying power."

"Job stress?"

"Didn't ask her," said Wattlesburg. "She's coming in for her check today or tomorrow. Want me to give her your number?"

"Not necessary."

"I agree, Doc. Screw quitters."

* * *

The following morning, I phoned Marv and told him I'd take the case if I could bring Robin to Singapore at the studio's expense.

He said, "Hmm. That could be tricky—maybe if you go business instead of first? But who knows, they could kick in the entire shaboom, let me inquire."

"How many kids are we talking about and how old are they?"

"Two boys, four and six. I'll make the call, try to score you two sleeping compartments in first, maybe even a suite at the Fullerton."

"Thanks, Marv."

"You'll be thanking me even more once you're there. Someone robs or steals they cane his ass, then they toss him in jail. You can't chew gum, the side-walks are clean enough to eat off."

"Orderly," I said.

"The things I see every day," he said. "I appreciate that."

Twenty minutes later, he was back: "It's all set, the works, but I can't tell you when because a ton of new financial motions from both sides just landed on my desk. I'll keep you posted."

I walked through the garden to Robin's studio with two cups of coffee, stepped into relative quiet. She was hand-sanding a rosewood guitar back, power tools dormant. Blanche snored from her dog bed in the corner.

Robin said, "I'm getting spoiled." Wiping her hands, she took my face in her hands and kissed me. Blanche's eyes fluttered open. Stretching and yawn-ing, she toddled over. I fetched her a Milk-Bone and she did the coquette bit, cocking her head to one side and smiling.

I put my arm around Robin's small, tight waist. "You'll be thanking me more once you're in Singapore."

"Pardon?"

I told her about the trip.

She said, "You're serious."

"You bet."

"Talk about perks. Wow. I have heard it's an interesting place."

"Orchids grow like weeds and if you're naughty they whup your butt before slamming you into a cell."

"I promise to be good. When exactly are we talking about?"

"A month at the earliest, likely later."

"A month . . . I'll check my project list. How long of a trip?"

"Work will probably be a few days, we could stay longer if you want, take a side trip somewhere."

"They're flying you there just to evaluate a kid?"

"Two kids."

She laughed. "Well, that explains it." She tousled my hair. "This is very cool. My baby is such a *genius*, people lay down big bucks for his *wisdom*."

I said, "Here's some freebie wisdom: Buy low, sell high, look both ways before crossing the street, don't talk to strangers, never eat anything larger than your head."

She said, "Gosh, what a lucky girl I am."

I scanned the news fruitlessly for anything on Connie and Ree. Maybe what went on at the court building stayed at the court building.

On the afternoon of the fourth day since I'd heard from him, Milo dropped by looking preoccupied, didn't bother with greetings as he continued toward the kitchen. After the usual fridge-scrounge, he stood over the sink committing assault and battery on a loosely assembled, wet sandwich of leftover chicken, veal shoulder, Bibb lettuce, coleslaw, potato salad, and sliced tomatoes. All of that stuffed between three slices of rye bread past its prime. A beer rinsed it down. Washing and drying his plate, he sat down.

I said, "Greetings."

"Yeah, yeah, I've been incommunicado. 'Cause there's been nothing to communicate."

"There is now? You found her?"

"If only. For an amateur she's done a damn good job of disappearing. No credit card or ATM or cell phone usage, no credible sightings anywhere along a whole bunch of Amtrak lines, no applications for welfare or any kind of assistance for herself or the kid. The marshals checked women's shelters near the major train stops and nada. If she was in the obvious places, their street-sources would tell them. So now I'm wondering if the whole car-at-the-train-station was a ruse, she never left, is crashing with a friend, maybe an old hippie from back in the day. She ever mention anyone like that besides the Lonesome Moaners?"

"No."

"I called her brother—Mr. Porn. He denies hearing from her but I didn't take his word for it, had his local PD do a few drive-bys past his house, looking for diaper boxes, any sign she and the kid were holed up there. Nothing. And now I've got additional reason to believe she's still in L.A.—Hollywood, in particular. Last night someone tried to shoot Boris Chamberlain."

"You're kidding."

"Wish I was."

"Hollywood narco wasn't watching his building?"

"Hollywood narco had just *stopped* watching his building—funny thing 'bout that, huh? Shortly after eleven p.m., they raided and busted the charming Cat and Jeremy. Around an hour later, ol' Boris must've been feeling confident because he went out for a jog, crossed Franklin, started trotting up toward the hills. He didn't get far before a car drove by and boom boom boom. Three shots, three close calls, Chamberlain drops to the ground, rolls into some bushes, plays dead. If the shooter was planning to come back to check, they changed their mind when a bunch of residents turned on their lights."

I said, "Any shell casings?"

"Three 9mms."

"Not a .25."

"So she's got more than one gun, figured a bigger load would be better from a distance."

"North of Franklin at midnight isn't exactly safe jogging territory."

"Granted, not the smartest choice but Chamberlain told me he ran there all the time, figured his quote unquote 'build' would discourage a mugger, it always had. With the tweakers being out of the picture, maybe he was starting to see the world as a kindly, loving place again." Small smile. "Always a mistake."

"Anyone get a good look at the car?"

"Nope," he said. "Too dark, it all happened so fast, blah blah blah. Needless to say, Chamberlain's freaked out, planning to visit his folks in Vermillion, South Dakota."

He rubbed his face. "This is some dragon-lady we're dealing with, Alex. Maybe Connie was onto something when she sued her."

I said, "So the working theory is Ree stalked Chamberlain while his building was being monitored by Hollywood narco and struck as soon as they left."

"Why not? No better time for Hollywood narco *not* to notice," he said. "When's the best time to break the speed limit, kiddo? When the cops are busy giving someone else a ticket. Ree watched the tweakers being taken away, spotted Chamberlain come out for some late-night exercise? Sounds perfect to me."

"It depends on her driving a second vehicle."

He put his hands behind his head. "Gee, that would be tough."

I said, "Okay."

"You still can't accept it, huh?"

"I accept it. No point crossing from denial into stupidity." Mouthing the words but even I could hear the rote-quality. And the resentment.

He said, "Okay, I just ate your grub, so I'll be temporarily open-minded. Is there something about this chick, psychologically speaking, that'll make me think better of her? And I don't mean all that love-beads bullshit. I never trusted the whole flower-child thing. I'm in Asia, they're having love-ins."

I shook my head. "Nothing new to add."

"Then unfortunately I'm gonna stick with the basics as I see 'em, Alex. The Sykes family was a breeding ground for psychopathology. Connie was a thoroughly unpleasant person with homicidal tendencies and Ree is an outwardly *pleasant* person with homicidal tendencies. She's also a helluva lot better at killing people than her sister because she observes Rule One: Want something done right, do it yourself. Unfortunately for me, she's also good at staying under the radar, so hopefully she won't consider anyone else an obstacle."

"Why would Chamberlain be an obstacle?"

"Same reason as Winky: He could be Rambla's daddy and Ree defines bliss as single motherhood."

"Can't be him and Winky," I said. "She'd know."

"Would she, Alex?" His smile was unsettling. If he wasn't my friend I wouldn't have liked him.

I said, "Guess not."

"I mean I don't want to be accused of a dirty mind, but let's hope the kid wasn't conceived during a Malibu gangbang. If that's the case, there's a whole slew of horndogs with targets on their foreheads."

32

Two days after the attempted murder of Boris Chamberlain, the case hit the news.

The L.A. *Times* devoted two paragraphs to "what LAPD sources describe as the emotional fallout from a heated guardianship battle." Focus on the Sykes sisters, no mention of Chamberlain or Melandrano. TV offered similar content in the usual short-attention-span spurts, along with a DMV photo of Ree Sykes.

The newspaper byline was Kelly LeMasters, once a *Times* staff reporter, now a freelancer and writing a book. That volume was based on the movie-star homicides Milo and I had worked on last year. After a rocky beginning, LeMasters and Milo had forged a working relationship; no mystery about the identity of her "sources."

Milo's motivation was obvious: a woman that dangerous on the lam, going public was the logical step. No reason to feel sorry for Ree. Still . . .

I'd been struggling to accept her as a multiple murderer but maybe the real issue was that she'd fooled me completely. I knew that mental health pros were no better than anyone predicting violence, emphasized that when teaching forensic psych to gung-ho grad students.

In the case of *Sykes v. Sykes,* I'd manage to convince myself I was different.

Delusions were everywhere.

I took a punishing run up Mulholland and two miles beyond, staggered home drenched, aching, wheezing like a chain smoker.

After showering and dressing, I checked my messages. Perfect time for there to be none.

Three in ninety minutes, the joys of success.

A judge I respected far less than Marv Applebaum wanted to discuss—big surprise—an "unpleasant" custody case. A "professional career consultant" offered to "grow your practice beyond your wildest dreams, Doctor!" A Clara Fellows had left a call-back number.

I decoded the operator's error: Kiara Fallows. The clerk who'd taken leave from Marv's court. Wondering why she'd called, I tried her first.

A soft, whispery voice said, "This is Kiara."

"Dr. Delaware returning your call."

"Who?" she said. "Oh. Yes. Deputy Wattlesburg said you needed to talk to me?"

I'd told Lionel not to bother. The old courtroom vet being helpful?

"Nothing urgent," I said. "I was just curious how you knew about the Sykes case."

"The what?"

"Deputy Wattlesburg said you'd mentioned a guardianship suit in probate court—"

"Oh," she said. "The two sisters. I guess I did—he's annoyed with me. Lionel. For quitting. When he told me you called he also let me know I'd blown a big opportunity, working for the county, the benefits, the pension."

"Did the Sykes case have something to do with your leaving?"

"It did kind of freak me out," she said. "Someone getting killed over a child? But no, the main reason was it's too far for me to drive. The gas mileage, I wanted something closer to home."

"Where'd you hear about the murder?"

"People talking."

"At the courthouse?"

"They're always going on about something there."

"Okay, thanks for clarifying."

"That's it?" she said. "You were just curious?"

"I was involved in the case as an expert witness, am still trying to make sense of it."

"*That's* scary," she said. "Being a part of it, I mean. Someone going nuts and you could never tell they were dangerous. Like that workplace violence you hear about, no way to predict who's going to go off the deep end. Hey, could I ask you a favor? Being a doctor, you wouldn't happen to know of anyone who needs an office manager or something like that? I'm real good at planning and organizing."

"If I think of anyone I'll let you know."

"Thanks. And good luck to you. Figuring out the craziness, I mean."

I was tackling Joe Pass guitar solos, doing damage to "Satin Doll," when Milo rang in.

"Looks like we got her, Alex. Skid Row, walking distance from the damn courthouse. I was right about her never leaving town. She parked her car at Union, somehow got another set of wheels that she used to drive-by Chamberlain, maybe ditched that, too."

I said, "Criminal mastermind."

"You know as well as I do, amigo. It ain't that hard to be bad."

"How'd you find her?"

"The tipoff was the kid," he said. "How many healthy-looking women with well-nourished toddlers you gonna see at an SRO flophouse? Minutes after her face hit the tube we got three separate sightings. I'm outside the building right now."

"Congratulations."

"Listen, I know this isn't the news you wanted so if you turn me down, I won't blame you. But with the kid involved, the possibility of this turning into a hostage situation is bugging me. Your knowing what makes Mama tick—I could use you here."

"Where's here?"

"The King William Hotel, Los Angeles and Fifth. We'll go in as soon as I decide to. Your arrival will help clarify that decision."

The return trip to downtown was brain-sapping, the usual rush-hour slog turned toxic by morons texting and vicious reactions to vehicular slights, actual or otherwise. After witnessing countless one-finger salutes, window-muted snarls, red faces, and bulging eyes, I wondered what it would take for a traffic jam to turn into a terrible headline.

No way to predict.

Had the world grown meaner? I'd spent most of my adult life dealing with worst-case scenarios, was probably the last guy to ask.

By the time I made my way through the box canyons created by darkened downtown office buildings, the sun had set. As I crossed the western border of Skid Row at Main, the sky was the color of sputum and the streets were strips of lint pied by inkblot shadows and animated by the lurch and stagger of impaired human beings.

The homeless shelters were as fully booked as Oscar

after-parties. Piles of trash, makeshift tents fashioned from garbage bags, and shopping carts teeming with scabrous treasure landmarked pockets of improvisation.

I turned onto Los Angeles Street, spotted Milo two buildings north of the King William Hotel. The flop was a seven-story clot of gray brick, once grand, now soft around the edges and scarred by grime. A private security guard who looked ready to enter middle school stood out front, rendered superfluous by Milo's presence and the four Central Division squad cars positioned twenty yards north. Just beyond the cruisers sat a large, square-edged dark shape.

One of the armored Lenco BearCats used by SWAT as a "rescue vehicle." "BearCat" was a fittingly macho moniker but its true meaning was Ballistic Engineered Armored Response Counter Attack Truck. Lovely hunk of military hardware affording safe transport for officers. Also, an armory on wheels. I pictured the King William's struggling frame shuddering under a barrage of high-tech killing power. Seven stories collapsing as easily as any gunshot victim.

The department owned a fleet of SWAT trucks. Only one had been dispatched to tonight's gig. I tried to see that as a promising sign.

Milo saw me. His finger-wave lacked energy and his posture was bad.

When I reached him, he said, "You made decent time," and waved a key. "She's up on the seventh floor. I figured I'd keep it maximally mellow by leaving the shock troops down here and knocking on her door myself. She opens up, she's unarmed, it's over. She resists or ignores, it gets complicated, but still it's just a single woman and hopefully being with the kid will prevent her doing anything stupid. My question to you is should I use a ruse on her—building manager checking out a pipe—or play it straight?"

I thought about that. Shook my head.

His eyebrows rose. "Nothing in her psyche says one or the other?"

"Apparently, her psyche's virgin territory for me, but if I had to guess, I'd say fool her. Anything to keep her relaxed and avoid confrontation."

"You figure she'll come to the door packing?"

"Who knows? But even if she doesn't, a gun's likely to be in the room. And we're talking a small room, if it's a typical SRO. That could mean easy reach."

"True," he said. "Had a look at similar rooms, they're all the same according to the desk clerk. Eight by eight . . . Mommy with a .25 and a 9mm, wonderful. Anything else you think would be helpful?"

"If she doesn't buy the ruse and stonewalls, I'd be happy to talk to her."

"You read my mind," he said. Twitchy smile. "Then again, they trained you to do that."

The final plan was the SWAT truck would glide past the King William and position itself closer to the building but remain shielded from view by a neighboring ten-story flop named the Pegasus. All officers to remain inside.

Four of the Central uniforms would keep the area free of gawkers, though given the nature of the residents, unpredictability was a more serious factor than usual. A fifth cop would replace the guard out front, three others would keep an eye on the back of the long-incapacitated fire escapes that traced a theoretical escape route down the back of King William to a putrid alley. The hotel's elevators were already on lockdown.

"Those mofos are always broken anyway, rez-dents

use the stairs," said the desk clerk from behind his Lexan window. Milo and I were the only ones who'd entered the building, both of us in Kevlar vests. The lobby was large but empty, high-ceilinged and blue-gray, reeking of industrial-strength bug spray, chronic disease, scorched tobacco.

The clerk was an immensely fat man in his fifties named DeWayne Smart whose bulk threatened to spill out of his bulletproof booth. His shift was two to ten p.m. His job consisted of collecting cash and vouchers for daily to weekly stays, handing out keys, squinting with suspicion. He'd been one of the three tipsters who'd called in on Ree Sykes, had just re-confirmed her identity after viewing her DMV shot.

"Yope, thas her," he said, slipping the photo back through the slot.

"She checked in two days ago."

"Yope. There a cash reward?"

"We'll see," said Milo, looking at the key. "No number on this, you're sure it's 709?"

Smart exposed a maw of broken, brown teeth. "That's the Presidential Suite. She got a nice view."

"You have no central phone line."

"I told you," said Smart, peeved. "All the rez-dents get is what they bring with 'em."

"She bring a cell phone?"

"How should I know?"

I said, "What's she been like?"

"What do you mean?"

"What's her attitude, has she said or done anything unusual?"

"I never seen her since she checked in," said Smart. "She went up, never came down. How long's this gonna last?"

Milo said, "Till it's over."

I said, "Residents have what they bring. What did she bring?"

"No idea," said Smart.

"She have luggage?"

"Louise Veeton—I'm in here, don't go out to examine, they pay, they go to their rooms." Smart laughed. "Maybe she come out at night, like a bat." He flapped his arms. Shoulder fat rippled.

Milo said, "Okay, we're going up."

Smart crossed himself.

Milo laughed. "There's a vote of confidence."

"Huh?"

Milo copied the gesture.

Smart said, "Yope, whatever it takes."

A brown door, so overpainted it resembled a melting chocolate bar, led to the stairs. The stairwell walls were pea-green plaster, much of it corroded to warped lath and specked with black mold. The steps were marble, once white, now splashed gray and brown and yellow and colors I couldn't categorize. Wooden banisters had long given way to vandals, the sole evidence of their presence an occasional splintered post.

We climbed.

Odors varied from floor to floor but the predominant strains were stale piss, ripe vomit, burning sulfur, and more of the nose-stinging bug spray. Clumps of belly-up roaches, water bugs, silverfish, and horseflies attested to the efficacy of the spray. What had finished off the rats moldering on levels 3, 4, and 6 was hard to ascertain. One of the rodent corpses was still fresh and bloody and oozing and some opportunistic creature had ripped open its belly and feasted on the entrails. Maybe a cat. Maybe a who-knows-what.

The mess caught Milo's attention and he stopped

for a moment and swabbed his forehead with a handkerchief and tried to even out his breathing.

He'd been panting since level 2, pores working
overtime, hair plastered to his skull as if he'd just
showered.

I remained dry. Maybe the run up the Glen had
leached me of body fluid, maybe I was in decent
shape. Fitness *didn't* account for a mouth full of cotton and eye sockets that ached each time my attention
shifted.

When we reached the door to the seventh-floor corridor, Milo unsnapped his holster and used the handkerchief to glove his hand as he turned the doorknob.

The knob came loose, clattered down the stairs.
Milo stuck his finger in the hole that remained, managed to slide the bolt, pushed.

The hallway on the other side was long enough for
an LAX arrival terminal. More rotting walls and
acrid stench. A runner of perforated red rubber carpet padding traced the center of a floor paved with
tiny white hexagonal tiles. The doors were black
slabs, scores of them, numerically identified by stick-
on labels.

One of them opened and a man in a soiled wife-
beater and boxer shorts emerged, smoking, clutching
a pint bottle. Shaved head, prison tattoos, long chin
beard tied in several knots, zits where ink didn't dom-
inate. Smoke rose around him and settled like a cloud;
no ventilation.

Milo flashed the badge and waved him back inside.
The man gave the thumbs-up and complied.

We kept walking, stopped two doors short of 709.
Swabbing his brow again, Milo motioned me to stand
back and moved forward on crepe soles. He put one
hand on his Glock, used the other to knock lightly.

A dull thud resulted. Under the black paint, the

door was solid timber, installed when wood was cheap and the hotel hosted residents who mattered.

Repeat knock. No answer.

He tried again. Music filtered from someone else's room. Mariachi remixed to hip-hop.

Milo cleared his throat and stepped close to the door. "This is Leon from downstairs. I need to check your heater." He'd turned his voice gravelly. Louis Armstrong at his most jovial.

The look on his big pale face was anything but. *Hello, Dolly, I come to bust you.*

He stood tall, all traces of fatigue gone. Seconds passed. He ticked them off with a finger on a wrist. He was about to knock again when the door cracked. *Thump-rattle.* Held fast by a chain.

He grinned, "Hey there, can I come in?"

No answer that I could hear, but he must've sensed danger because he jammed one hand in the crack and kicked the door hard. The chain gave way with the sound of crepe paper ripping and he had to keep one hand on the door to prevent it from falling onto him. Awkward but he forged in, gun pointed.

A female cry—fear mixed with the shock of betrayal—was followed by a bleat of terror, high-pitched, horribly rhythmic.

Not an adult sound.

A baby wailing, ragged, terrified.

Then: scuffling, grunting. The slap of flesh on something hard.

Then, just the baby.

I went in.

Milo had her down on the ground, face to the scarred wooden floor of the cell-like room. The single bed was barely wide enough for one person. The baby lay on top of it, resting on a gray sheet, faceup. That was good, less chance of SIDS.

No crib, no other place to sleep. That was bad. Sleeping with an adult risked rollover suffocation.

The baby had good lungs, howling nonstop.

An angry little boy.

Milo hadn't noticed. He brought the woman to her feet.

She was around Ree Sykes's age and height but thinner than Ree and rawboned where Ree was soft. If you weren't looking too closely, you might not notice the discrepancies. All I could see were the discrepancies: narrower hips, smaller chin, longer legs, larger hands.

Hair can always be modified and this woman had altered hers from whatever she'd been born with to shoe-polish black. Chopped brutally at the ends and half the length of Ree's red-blond curls. I wondered what had led DeWayne Smart and two other people to be so sure.

The pulse in Milo's neck raced as his error gut-punched him.

The woman remained still but low guttural warnings emerged from rapidly moving lips. She began grinding her jaws, setting off unnerving squeaks. Her lips curled into a terrible smile. She snarled. Looked ready to spit.

Milo tightened up and did nothing but watch her.

The woman laughed. Opened her mouth, revealing more gap than tooth, and let out a deep, sexless sound that ended with a high-pitched cackle.

That startled the baby. His tiny body quaked, he keened louder, began pummeling the sagging mattress with heels and fists. All that panic rolled him nearer to the edge of the bed but packages of disposable diapers were stacked tight between that side of the mattress and the wall, creating a safety berm. Or they'd ended up there because there was scant space anywhere else.

Milo said, "I'm sor—"

The woman said, "Fhh!" and tried to kick him.

"Ma'am—"

"Fhhh!"

Keeping my eye on the baby I scanned the room in fast-action spurts.

Gray, urine-stained walls, three-drawer raw-wood dresser with the bottom drawer missing. More diapers and a white plastic purse on top. Floor space taken up by stacks of formula and baby food. Adult nutrition in the form of generic canned goods: spaghetti, stew, soup, vegetables. A box of crackers served as a platform for a large, red, vinyl-bound Bible.

To the left of the dresser was a clear view into the doorless adjoining bathroom. The toilet lid hosted a small, foldable camper's stove fueled by a cake of Sterno. A manual can opener sat on the rim of the sink.

The fuel in the stove was reduced to a thin sheet of purple wax. Cooking in here posed a serious risk of fire and carbon monoxide poisoning. Maybe the latter explained why the bathroom window was propped open by two cans of chicken noodle soup. Or maybe that was just an attempt to air out the stench.

The baby continued to wail. The woman on the floor competed to fill the room with noise, cursing wordlessly, shaking her head and hissing each time Milo tried to apologize. That prolonged her confinement and every second of confinement kicked up her rage.

Plain woman, gorgeous child. Rosy-cheeked, towheaded, wearing a fuzzy blue one-piece.

Milo said, "Ma'am, please try to calm down so I can uncuff—"

The woman screamed. The baby turned scarlet and began rolling in the opposite direction, toward the unguarded edge of the bed. I snatched him up. Solid little thing. He fought me, arching his back, retracting his head and thrusting it forward. Making contact with my cheek.

Two points for the little bruiser.

I said, "There, there."

He screamed louder.

Maybe he'd reached the volume where his mother's tolerance ended because suddenly she stopped fighting, said, "Cody. Be still!" Speaking softly in that special maternal rhythm. But the anger lingered in her voice and that did nothing to calm her child and he continued to twist violently in my arms.

I said, "Hey, little buddy." His tears splashed onto my face. I wrapped my arms around his tiny torso, kept his arms safely pinned, began whispering in his ear. " 'Sokay Cody, 'sokay Cody, 'sokay Cody."

Matching the pitch and rhythm of his cries, over and over, my best reassuring drone.

With babies, it's not what you say, it's how you say it. He shuddered, his body stiffened. Finally he began yielding to the primal comfort of the hypnoidal mantra.

Milo said, "I'm going to take off the cuffs, but you need to remain calm, ma'am."

The woman cursed silently.

He gave her a few more seconds. She said, "Free me, I'm doin' your bidding, you bastard."

Once liberated, she shot toward me, grabbed the baby from my arms.

Cody let out a single, forlorn cry of relief and buried his head in her bosom. Holding him close, she shrank back to the wall of diapers, pointed with her head. "Go! I shall be rid of you!"

Milo said, "I really am sorry, ma'am."

The woman clutched Cody tighter. He mewled.

"Go, you are cursed!" Her eyes were blue, blood-shot, compressed by hatred.

"We're going to leave, ma'am, I just want to make sure—"

"*No! Don't tell him!*"

"Tell who?"

The woman smiled. "Like you don't *know*, you bastard. He *sent* you!"

"Ma'am, I'm sorry for what happened but I really don't—"

"Him!" she said. "He that would be blessed but is cursed. He that eats of the Paschal and sullies his maw with the blood of innocents."

Milo looked at me.

The woman began growling again. On cue, Cody cried but this time she was able to still him with a steel-edged hiss. Freeing one hand, she lifted her blouse and I wondered if she'd begin nursing to flaunt her maternal rights. Instead, she stopped just short of the pendulous bottom of her right breast.

A scar, puckered and stitched as subtly as a base-ball, rose diagonally from the outer left edge of her rib cage, wandering across her chest and ending mid-sternum.

I said, "He did that to you."

The woman stuck her tongue out at me. Cody was transfixed by the gesture, staring at her, eyes wide and questioning. Extending his own pink bud and experi-menting with a run across his lips.

His eyes were an identical blue hue to his mother's. Other nuances of facial resemblance began cropping up: narrow chin, wide brow, large flat-to-the-skull ears. If he lived long enough, this chubby tot would end up a tall, rawboned man. Lord knew how his genetics and upbringing would affect his personality.

His mother turned back to Milo, keeping her scar in view. "He *sent* you. Be *gone.*"

Bitter and hostile, but relieved by suspicion confirmed. The corners of her mind tucked as neatly as her bedsheet.

Because surrender to uncertainty could be more frightening than death.

Milo said, "Ma'am, we were just following up on a—"

"Ma'am? I am *She*!"

Cody whimpered.

She rocked him. Spoke to his left ear. "Shh shh shh shh shh shh shh shh shh shh."

Miraculously, that quieted him down.

Milo spotted the white plastic purse and headed for it. "Ma'am, I'm just going to check your I.D.—no, no, don't get upset, obviously he didn't send us or I'd know who you are."

The woman said, "Hmm," contemplated that logic, continued to rock her child.

Milo opened the purse, found a black plastic wallet, shuffled through the contents, examined a driver's license. Before he closed the purse he slipped in a couple of twenties.

The woman spat. "Cursed by thy blood money."

Milo said, "Actually, it's holy money, I got it at church."

"Liar!"

"Save it for yourself or buy Cody a present."

"No! Remove the filthy pelf! You bring the leprosy of the crumbling wall upon the flesh of the anointed!"

Milo removed the money. The woman's eyes dropped to his gun. Her forehead grew smooth. Big smile.

Keeping his distance, he waved me to the door, backed toward it, saying, "Sorry for the inconvenience."

Just for good measure, the woman screamed louder.

When we finally reached the bottom of the stairs, Milo said, "When you write your memoirs don't put that in." Trying to make light. His hands clenched and opened, over and over. His mandible protruded. An assembly line of lumps rolled along his jawline.

We crossed the lobby of the King William, continued past DeWayne Smart's booth. Smart called out, "Hey!"

Milo circled back to Smart's window. "What?"

"So where is she?"

"Not our suspect."

"That sucks," said Smart. "For you, not her." Laughing. His jowls were wine bladders.

"You're a comic philosopher, DeWayne?"

"I—"

"When you look in the mirror, do you see Brad Pitt? That's how accurate your I.D. was."

"I—"

"Be sure to fill that prescription for bifocals. Toss in a white cane for good measure."

"I—"

"Yeah, you."

* * *

Back on L.A. Street, Milo distracted himself from failure by taking charge of small details. Clearing the scene with a series of clipped commands, checking if the APB on Ree Sykes had produced additional credible sightings, not surprised when the answer was no. Texting Moe Reed, he told the younger detective to rip up today's arrest form, keep fingers crossed for a second opportunity. "And maybe pigs will indeed pilot fighter jets."

When nothing else remained to be done, he stood watch as the cruisers and the BearCat drove away. As the last official vehicle departed, Skid Row residents began to materialize in the darkness. A glance from Milo sent several of them back inside but enough gawkers remained to set off a buzz. Then snickers.

Milo motioned me toward his unmarked and we left. Inside the car, he said, "Oletha Dreiser. Wheeling, West Virginia 26003." Talking to himself, not me. Repeating the info, as if practicing a lesson, he began running her through the databases.

Nothing on Dreiser at NCIC, no wants or warrants locally or statewide, no missing persons reports filed.

"Not a criminal," he said, with some regret. "Mama and child in that dump isn't much better than wanderers in a manger, huh? We find Daddy Joe, we can build a crèche."

I thought: *Where are the wise men?* but held my tongue.

"So," he said, pulling out a dead cigar. "She's psychotic, right?"

"Probably."

"So time to call protective services."

I said, "Not necessarily."

"Why not?"

"Depends on what they can offer."

"You think she's fit to raise a kid?"

"Is it an optimal situation? No. But on a basic level, she's doing an adequate job."

"Because she feeds him?"

"Because he's well nourished, outwardly healthy, appropriately developed, and clearly attached to her. Because ripping him away from her and stashing him in some shake-of-the-dice foster home will be traumatic for both of them and could do more harm than good."

"Even if she is well past poco-loco."

I said, "Even with that."

"You're a tolerant guy."

"I know the system. It's always a matter of least-terrible."

"She's also got a bit of a temper—"

"She had good reason to be angry."

He frowned. "So I do nothing."

I said, "Let's be realistic: Even with a formal diagnosis of schizophrenia, unless there's clear evidence that she poses an imminent danger to the baby, no court will take him away from her. Hell, even dangerous psychotics don't get treated now that the Feds consider them another persecuted minority. What you *can* do is try to teach her about carbon monoxide poisoning and find her a small crib—anywhere that the baby can sleep safely other than right next to her. That will eliminate the risk of a rollover suffocation."

"What carbon monoxide?"

I told him about the cooking stove. "Though she did have the sense to prop the window open."

He said, "The bathroom. Didn't look in there. Brilliant—okay, so who do I call for all this safety education if not the caseworkers?"

"There's a juvey detective at Pacific I've worked with who's smart and practical. She'll know who to contact at Central. Want me to try her?"

"That would be nice."

I reached D II Monica Gutierrez at her home in Palms. She promised to have her counterpart at Central, D II Kendra Washington, check out the situation first thing tomorrow, see what could be done on Oletha and Cody's behalf.

"But you know, Alex, all we can do is advise her. Unless there's a clear threat."

"I wasn't suggesting you take the baby."

"Well, that's good," said Monica. "Because we've got far too many babies with no one to care for them."

I hung up and summarized for Milo.

He said, "Yeah, yeah, I got the gist," and gazed up at the seventh floor of the King William.

I said, "Sorry it didn't pan out tonight," and opened the passenger door.

He said, "Are you really?" Then: "Mea culpa, that was uncalled for."

I said, "No sweat," but his apology bypassed my brain and stuck in my gut and I felt myself bristling.

Wishing him luck, I headed for my car.

Driving home on streets emptied of rage and steel, I thought about the quandary posed by Oletha Dreiser and her baby.

Family unification at almost any cost was a long-standing doctrine at social services originally motivated by compassion but powered now by budgetary restrictions and the soulless grinding of a bureaucratic machinery that viewed kids as case numbers.

Short of obvious life-threatening danger, no court would sever Oletha's attachment to Cody. I'd seen people far more impaired than her entrusted with parenthood.

The fact that too many kids died in foster care

didn't help, either. Last year, the toll had been three babies at three separate temporary homes. One was a neglected influenza, the second remained undetermined but was suspected to be a smothering. The last was a confirmed homicide committed by the foster mother's gangbanger boyfriend.

A deputy D.A. had described that killing to me as a "big-time oops."

Despite all that, Mommy as murderer would change the rules fast; Ree Sykes could forget about bureaucratic inertia as a shield.

Why had she taken the risk?

Once Milo caught up with her, what lay in store for Rambla?

I wondered how the two of them were coping with life on the run. Were they holed up in a sad little room like 709 at the Prince William, cooking with Sterno?

I wanted to believe Ree was too safety-conscious to put her child in jeopardy. That got tougher as I thought about the cold elimination of two human beings. Trying for an even three.

Winky Melandrano had served as Ree's babysitter. Had she brought Rambla the night she ambushed and shot him?

Facts were piling up against her but I still had trouble reconciling that level of callousness with the woman I'd evaluated.

Devoted mother. Appropriate. Nurturing. I'd believed all that enough to put my endorsement in writing. But what if maternal devotion had degraded to a competitive blood sport?

The prize, twenty pounds of innocence.

Maybe . . . but even if I'd glossed Ree's character, the motive Milo was ascribing to her seemed flimsy. If her goal was having Rambla to herself, why not simply disappear?

Because Connie was relentless and had the money to fund a long battle and needed to be taken care of first?

Fine, but that didn't explain going after Melandrano and Chamberlain, men described as Ree's lifelong friends.

Occasional lovers.

A wild night in the Malibu hills?

Complicated . . . if Ree wasn't a killer, why had she vanished?

Maybe her disappearance hadn't been voluntary. What if someone viewed *her* as an obstacle? The obvious candidate was Rambla's father. Brought into the game by Connie.

But if Connie had discovered his identity, why hadn't she named him in her court papers?

And why focus on Winky and Boris?

Because naming them as possible fathers had nothing to do with the truth, it was just another ploy to cast Ree as a dissolute, sexually indiscriminate groupie.

If so, it was possible Connie had made a fatal error. Igniting a frightening man's paternal urges, leading him to clear the deck of competition.

Connie out of the way, then Ree. Doing it quickly so that Ree's disappearance would cast her as a suspect.

Easy enough to accomplish. So was leaving Ree's car at the station, misdirecting the cops on a fruitless search.

A good planner. Meticulous.

But:

You left a speck of Connie's blood on Ree's carpet. An iota that flaked off shoes you thought you'd cleaned thoroughly.

You're not quite as smart as you think you are.

Dad.

The more I thought about it, the more I liked it intellectually. And hated it emotionally because of what it implied for Ree. And Rambla.

Child as Holy Grail. Property to be coveted, just like all the other crap cases I'd fielded in family court.

If I offered any of this to Milo, he'd point out that I had no evidence.

Neither do you, Big Guy.

No sense getting into it with him.

Also: I hadn't a clue where to take it.

Morning can bring clarity or confusion. By six a.m. the following day I was experiencing a strange mixture of both.

I woke up thinking about Lonesome Moan, couldn't shake the feeling that the band had occupied my dreams.

No nocturnal music video; Ree's long-lived friendship with all four members was the issue.

Half the quartet had been marked for murder, the other half left out of the crosshairs.

Did that make Chuck-o Blatt a target? Along with the guitarist I hadn't met—Spenser "Zebra" Younger?

Or was one of *them* Rambla's dad?

I thought of Blatt's protectiveness when we'd talked about Ree.

If you really are a psychologist and not spying for her fucking sister . . .

You know the kind of person she is. You hear me? You didn't say nothing.

She's a nice person.

Not just nice. Good.

Aggressive sort. Suspicious—he'd held back giving me anything of substance until I proved my identity. Had ended up supplying a rationale for Ree's disappearance: *Ree figured the bitch was going to keep ha-rassing her.*

Unlike his bandmates, Chuck-o was a hard-nosed businessman who'd managed to parlay gig money into ownership of three bars. Whom I'd watch handle an array of serious drinkers with effortless dominance.

Boris Chamberlain had his muscles and Blatt was built soft, but from what I'd seen Blatt was the likely alpha in the band. And alphas were all about protection, so who better to turn to when you were feeling threatened?

Especially if your relationship with the alpha had produced a child.

Then there was the matter of Zebra Younger, a total question mark.

If either man was in danger, warning them was the right thing to do.

If one of them was Rambla's murderous daddy, additional face-time would be interesting.

Either way, time for a return visit to Virgo Virgo.

At eleven a.m., I drove into the Valley. One parking spot was available across the street from the bar, situated ten yards west with a gently oblique view.

Papered over the *Happy Hour!!!* banner was a new announcement.

CLOSED UNTIL FURTHER NOTICE

I remained in the Seville, playing my phone as I tried to find personal data on *marvin blatt*. Nothing. I tried *charles, chuck,* and *chuck-o.* The last led back to the Lonesome Moan website and I was figuring out my next step when a man approached the bar's front door.

Seventyish, basset-faced, shiny blue suit well past salvation, white dress shirt, droopy tie.

The boozehound with a penchant for history—Lloyd. Maybe he was also into current events. As I got ready to sprint across the street, he pulled on the bar's door handle. The door swung open and he stepped in, exited moments later toting a brown paper bag too small to conceal the bottle it held. Full fifth of something amber, glass neck reflecting sunlight.

He stood there, talking to someone inside Virgo Virgo. That person stepped closer. Chuck Blatt's soft face caught sunlight.

I watched Lloyd reach into his pocket and draw out cash and try to pay Blatt. Blatt shook his head and patted the older man's shoulder, then retreated and closed the door.

Lloyd waddled away, jaunty, bearing his treasure.

My turn.

Chuck-o stood behind the bar, boxing up liquor. The stage was empty. Blatt's drums were gone. A solitary bulb lent the bar the ambience of a root cellar.

I said, "Donating the inventory?"

Blatt stopped working and studied my approach. Plucking a bottle of Crown Royal from the shelf behind him, he eased it into a carton atop the bar.

I said, "Just saw Lloyd—"

Blatt placed his hands flat on the bar. "Lloyd's an untreatable alcoholic, drinking's what he does, he considers it his profession. That's why he doesn't make heavy six figures selling insurance anymore. That's why I've stopped trying to educate him. So if he comes in jonesing for Jackie-D, what do I care?" He looked around the room. "It's all over, anyway."

"Because of Winky."

His teeth clacked together. "Well, shrink-friend, it's kind of hard to rock anyone's world when your singer gets murdered, don't you think? You here to tell me something about that? Like who ruined the world by offing one of the coolest, most gentle human beings ever to set foot on this godforsaken planet?"

Reaching into the box, he yanked out the same whiskey he'd just carted and flung it across the room. The bottle hit the wall behind the empty bandstand, shattered, and skittered down the plaster. Shards landed on wood, tinkling like a harp glissando.

Chuck-o Blatt said, "Fuck this world and the assholes who live in it." Turning away, he snatched a fifth of vodka from the shelf and boxed it.

I said, "Thank God Boris got away."

He turned toward me, eyes blazing. "*What?*"

"You didn't hear about it."

"Hear what?" Suddenly he came around from behind the bar, arms bent and bunched, fists lofted at nipple level. "Don't dick around, pal, this isn't a game. You got something to tell me, *tell* it."

I told him about the attempt on Chamberlain.

He sagged. "What the *fuck's* going on?"

"Wish I knew."

"You think *I* can tell you? Only reason I found out about Winky is my check—the money I give him for the Monday gig—was still magneted to his fridge. The idiot was terrible with finances, I'd have to bug him to cash the damn things so my books would be straight. Cops took the checks, figured I was his employer so they came here to tell me—some big fat guy just lays it on me: Your pal's been shot to death. I just about had a heart attack, I mean I really thought I was seizing up."

Slapping his chest. "Then I realize he's there because he either suspects *me* or he thinks I can answer his prayers. Winky's murdered and I'm supposed to know *who*?"

The door opened. A man stepped in and headed toward us. Bumping along laboriously using a pair of elbow-mounted metal crutches.

Middle-aged and thin, he had neatly parted white hair and heavy eyebrows to match, wore an oxford blue buttondown shirt, pressed jeans, white sneakers.

He maintained his dignity with a determined smile as he struggled. Glanced at me briefly but made pro- longed eye contact with Blatt.

Another regular angling for free booze? Neat and clean preppy garb didn't shout desperate alcoholic but I was well past the point of generalization.

As he got closer, I saw that his eyes were bloodshot and his bony face was pale—an unnatural pallor that left his skin almost translucent. As if he'd been drained.

Chuck-o exhaled and said, "Hey, man." The new arrival hobbled to the nearest chair and sat down la- boriously, took some time laying his crutches on the floor.

Once settled, he gave me another look.

Blatt said, "This is the shrink I told you about, man. Helped Ree in court but now he's doing some kind of police thing, came here to pump me for infor- mation I don't have."

The neatly dressed man's scrutiny continued. His eyes were brown and mild. "That so."

Chuck-o said, "Doctor whatever-your-name-is, meet the best slide guitarist this side of Johnny Winter— Spenser Younger aka the Zebra Man. Reason for that is his ax of choice is a black-and-white-striped Strat. That's a Fender guitar, should you not be educated in the way of strings."

I held my hand out. "Alex Delaware."

Spenser Younger offered me five limp fingers. "Anything new on Winky?"

Chuck-o Blatt said, "What's new, Zebe, is someone tried to off Boris, too."

Younger gripped the sides of the chair with both hands. His upper body trembled but the denim-clad sticks that claimed to be his legs remained inert. "Good God. You've got to be kidding."

Blatt said, "Wish I was, man."

"That's crazy, Marv, that's just too nuts." To me: "Someone tried? Meaning Boris is okay?"

"Fortunately."

"Jesus. What happened?"

I told him.

Zebe Younger said, "Oh, man, jogging at night in Hollyweird, yeah, that would be Boris."

I said, "Confident because of his muscles?"

"Ten years ago, he was totally out of shape. One day he changed. Told me he was tired of getting turned down by chicks and made a resolution to get buffed and boy oh boy, did he. He was always strong, played football in high school. But still. The transformation."

Massaging his wasted left leg.

Blatt said, "Guy's a monster, hundred-pound curls with each hand."

Younger said, "We should go see him, Marv. Give him support."

I said, "He's left town."

Chuck-o placed his hands against his temples and lowered his head. "What the hell's going on?"

His shoulders shook.

Zebe Younger said, "Marv?"

When Blatt looked up his cheeks were tearstained. When he spoke, his voice was constricted. "Stupid

Boris. Muscles up the wazoo matters? Bullet's gonna laugh all the way in."

"Aw, man," said Younger. He eyed the few remaining bottles.

Chuck-o said, "Sure, man, name your poison."

"Love to, Marv, but the doc says there's interactions with the new meds."

"They got you on new meds? Awesome, man, you're gonna be jogging before you know it."

Younger smiled. "Sure, training for a 10K." To me: "Got what they call a rare degenerative neuromuscular condition, basically I'm melting. Hereditary, one of my uncles had it, he lasted eight months. But now they've got better meds, I'm four years in and the fingers are still working."

Chuck-o Blatt said, "Winky, now Boris. That's why you're here, Doc? You're thinking someone wants to genocide the band? What for? That's nuts."

Spenser Younger said, "I've heard of bad reviews, but c'mon." He laughed. Turned serious. "Yeah, that is ridiculous, Doc."

"Crazy ridiculous," said Blatt. "Who the hell's doing this?" He stared at me. "Cops have no idea?"

I said, "Sorry, no."

Younger said, "Winky was the nicest guy, it makes no sense. If it wasn't just a street shooting, which is what I assumed."

I said, "I'm wondering if it had something to do with Ree's court case."

"How so?"

"Winky and Boris were both named as possible fathers in Connie's legal papers."

"Connie," Blatt broke in, "was a stone psycho cunt so anything she said was either psycho or total bullshit. I mean there's no way. Like I told you the first time you were here, any partying Winky or Boris did was a long time ago."

I looked at Younger. Impassive.

Finally, he said, "We're all past the partying stage."

I said, "Obviously, Ree wasn't—"

"Because she had a kid?" said Blatt. "That's not partying, that's what chicks do, they have kids. It's a hormonal thing, you're a doctor, you know that. If it was partying, all she had to do was terminate like . . . the ball was in her court."

I said, "Like she did before?"

"Like nothing," said Blatt. "Her business isn't yours or mine or anyone's."

Spenser Younger said, "I'm still not getting what being a father has to do with getting killed."

"Exactly," said Blatt.

Both of them waited.

I said, "A theory has come up. Someone wants Rambla to themselves and is trying to eliminate the competition."

Both men looked puzzled. Tears pooled in Chuck-o Blatt's eyes. He wiped them away violently, pulled out a bottle of gin, twisted the cap off, swigged and grimaced.

Spenser Younger said, "I guess I could see that kind of nasty with someone like Connie, but—oh, man, I wasn't even thinking about Connie, she's another victim, isn't she? This is crazy."

Blatt said, "Like I keep reminding everyone, Connie was a psycho bitch, anyone could hate her. Winky? Just the opposite, he was fucking Sara Lee, you couldn't not like him."

Spenser Younger nodded. "And he always wanted kids." His eyes saucered. "Oh, man, I never told anyone because he swore me not to, but now . . ."

He reached for the bottle in Blatt's hand, said, "Screw side effects," and took a swallow.

"Winky couldn't have kids," he said. "Low sperm count. Even a long time ago, he had a chick—remember Donna, Marvie?"

"The redhead," said Blatt, outlining a female hourglass.

Younger said, "She loved Winky, would've done anything for him. Kept begging him to knock her up, this was I don't know—twenty years ago. When we took the bus through Ohio?"

"Rock on, Cleveland," said Blatt, without joy.

"Winky finally agreed but it never happened," said Younger. "One day he asks me to drive him to some place—the Cleveland Clinic, big-time medical situation. I'm doing the driving because his license wasn't renewed, he couldn't get an out-of-state rental. I drive him to the clinic, he goes in, comes out, real quiet. I'm thinking he's got some bad disease, he says nope, don't worry, just routine. Then he clams up. Couple weeks later he's looking real down and we're all pretty . . . remember that sensimilla we used to take with us on the road?"

"Hundred-proof," said Blatt.

Younger smiled. "So Winky and I are both getting high as an asteroid and he goes on one of those weed-speeches, tells me the test was for his sperm count and guess what, it's lower than low, he'll never be a daddy. Then he cries, then like he's forcing himself to get happy, he gets happy, and the topic never comes up again."

Blatt had stared at him throughout the monologue. "No shit. Poor Wink."

Younger turned to me. "Anyway, he's not the dad, Doc, and if Connie thought so she was off by miles."

"Connie was always full of shit," said Blatt.

I said, "If Connie made a mistake, someone else could've."

"Like who?"

"That's what we're trying to figure out."

"Well you won't figure it out here," said Younger. "Hell, why not just ask Ree?"

"Shortly after Winky was shot, Ree left town."

"Shortly after? You're making it sound suspicious."

I said, "Whenever someone splits without notice the police take it seriously."

"They think *she's* behind all this shit?"

"You guys don't watch the news?"

"What for?" said Blatt. "News is all bullshit."

"Hear, hear," said Younger, raising the gin bottle.

I said, "Ree's face was all over the nightly broadcast. The police consider her a person of interest in Connie's and Winky's murders."

"Person of interest?" said Younger. "That mean suspect?"

"A rung lower," I said. "Suspect minus hard evidence."

"That's totally absurd." His laughter was unforced.

Same for Chuck-o Blatt, though his "Ha!" was tinged with anger. "Yeah, sure, two of the coolest, gentlest people on the planet, one's dead, the other takes a trip which is her God-given unalienated right, so the stupid cops think she did bad stuff? Give me a break."

I said, "That's why I'm trying to come up with an alternative explanation."

"Yeah, well, whatever." Blatt curled his finger at Younger. Younger passed him the bottle, said, "I wish I could help you, Doc, but one thing for sure: It wasn't Ree. She's too good a person."

Blatt downed two swigs, put the bottle down on the counter hard.

I said, "Thanks, guys."

"An alternative explanation," said Blatt. "Maybe it's just some fucking maniac shooting people."

Younger said, "Who just happen to be Winky and Connie?"

Blatt said, "Yeah, that is lame . . . okay, maybe he's right." Turning to me. "Maybe you're right, it has something to do with the kid. But what? Fuck if I know. I mean she's a cute kid but what's the big deal? It's not like she's an heiress or something."

"Hey," said Younger. "Wouldn't that be something, Ree partied with a rich guy and now he's worried about getting soaked, so he takes care of business."

"Yeah, right," said Blatt. "On Lifetime network, tonight."

Younger said, "It could happen, Marv. Ree named the kid Rambla, said because the conception was in Malibu. What's Malibu? Rich folk."

"If that ain't the truth," said Blatt. "Million bucks for an ounce of sand."

I said, "You guys remember anyone specific from Malibu?"

"Hell, no," said Blatt. "It's not like we're in that world."

I turned to Younger.

He said, "Can't remember the last time I was even at the beach." Blinking. "Now that I lost my taste for surfing."

"You surfed for shit, anyway," said Blatt.

"Yeah, I did."

"I was even more for shit. Couldn't stay on the fucking board." Slurred words. Third swig.

Younger took the bottle. "You were beyond for shit, man. You were the fourteenth level of hell filled with elephant shit." Burp.

"Yeah but gimme skins, I'm fucking Krupa incarnated." Blatt laughed. "Put me on a fucking board and I'm super-spazz—oh, man, sorry."

"Cut it out, man," said Younger.

"Cut what out?"

"Being sensitive, I like you just the way you are, as an asshole. Me and Mr. Rogers."

"Mr. Rogers liked jazz."

"Mr. Rogers was cool."

"Miss him," said Blatt.

"Miss everyone," said Younger. " 'Member we were in that motel in Harrisburg, watched Mr. Rogers when we were loaded, he had this guy playing a D'Angelico Excel? Handyman whoever, he's supposed to be a janitor and he's got this twenty-grand guitar and he's bopping off notes like Tal Farlow?"

"Handyman Negrino," said Blatt.

"No, no . . . Negri." Younger beamed. "Handyman Negri, cool dude."

"Mr. Rogers," said Blatt. "Go know."

I slipped out of the bar just as the topic segued to Captain Kangaroo.

Musicians are performers but unless Blatt and Younger were trained actors it was hard to see them as suspects.

I supposed Younger's disability wouldn't have stopped him from shooting a gun, maybe even stalking Boris Chamberlain in a handicapped-fitted car. But his shocked reaction to the attempt on Boris had come across genuine. Same for Chuck-o Blatt.

I drove back home, checked my messages. The judge I'd ignored wondered if his message had slipped through the cracks. I phoned his court, told his clerk I was unavailable to take the custody case.

The only other call was another from Kiara Fallows. Probably following up on her job search. I made coffee, sifted through mail, as I phoned her.

She said, "Thought I'd let you know I remembered."

"Remembered what?"

"Who was talking about that case. It was a lawyer. Suit and tie, not a uniform. A bunch of them were walking up the hall, discussing it."

"Okay."

"I think he was Hispanic," she said. "Or maybe Middle Eastern. Hope that helps."

"I'll pass it along, thanks. Any luck with your job search?"

A beat. "Uh, no, still looking. Did you find someone who wants someone?"

"Not yet, I'll keep you posted."

"Sure," she said. "That would be great."

Curious call. Reviewing it only made it feel stranger.

Why had she phoned a second time to offer me useless information? Why did the question about her job search seem to throw her?

I did a little background on Ms. Kiara Fallows.

The Internet gave up four people with that name: a sixty-two-year-old woman in Queensland, Australia, a fifteen-year-old girl in Scarsdale, New York, a college junior at Barnard studying abroad in Sri Lanka, a toddler who appeared in kiddie beauty contests in Tyler, Texas.

More scrolling brought up articles on allowing fields to go fallow and other biblical wisdom for the modern age. The raising, butchering, and marketing of fallow deer for the gourmet meat trade. I was about to log off when I found it.

Two words, conveniently yellow-accented, embedded in a seven-year-old article in the *Ventura Star*.

Teen Charged with Framing Teacher

By Harris Rosen

A Ventura high school junior has been accused of planting narcotics in the backyard of a high school teacher with whom she'd had conflict. Desiree Kiara Fallows, 17, was charged with falsely reporting a crime

and released to the custody of her aunt and uncle, both
L.A. County Sheriff's deputies.

The alleged plot involved placing a bag of marijuana
under rosebushes on the property of a tenth-grade science teacher who'd threatened to fail Fallows in biol-
ogy. Shortly after, Fallows phoned in a tip to Ventura
narcotics detectives, directing them to the stash and
claiming the teacher was a drug addict who behaved
inappropriately in the classroom.

Police contacted the teacher who allowed them access
to his yard and expressed surprise when the drugs
showed up. A subsequent search of his house failed to
produce any additional narcotics and he passed a
polygraph test. The teacher informed detectives of
suspicions that the caller was Fallows, a ward of the
state housed in a group home and bussed to Ventura
High as part of a state-funded re-integration program.
The teacher further stated that the girl had threatened
to "ruin him." Further investigation of Fallows's story
uncovered physical evidence supporting her involvement in the hoax, leading her to confess.

Although Fallows will legally be an adult by the time she
goes to trial, sentencing is expected to involve psychological treatment rather than incarceration. The teacher
has no plans to pursue the matter further.

Seven years ago made Desiree K. Fallows twenty-
four now, consistent with the face on Judge Applebaum's page.

I searched for more on the story. No follow-up. No
matching Facebook or MySpace pages under Desiree
or Kiara.

That made Fallows the only twenty-four-year-old

woman in the developed world forgoing the social network.

No surprise if you had something to hide. Were sitting in prison.

The plotting teen had been a ward of the state. Nearly eighteen as a sophomore suggested learning problems. Not exactly the scholarship of someone who'd qualify for a plum job in Superior Court, when budgets were strained and hiring was sparse.

Still, seven years was ample time for change and if Desiree K. and Kiara the Clerk were the same person, scoring the position could mean she accrued no adult criminal record.

Could because people slip through the cracks. Last year three cadets at the police academy had been expelled due to gang associations and unreported felony convictions.

If a troubled girl had matured to the point of finding employment in the court system, why had she quit soon after? Blaming it on fuel consumption seemed flimsy in retrospect. But maybe I was making too much of two brief conversations.

Still, the story of Kiara Fallows's attempted setup of her teacher was creepy and neither of her calls seemed purposeful.

There was also the matter of Fallows's hem when I asked about her job search. As if reminding herself of a story she'd told the first time.

Back to the con? But she and I had never met, so what was the goal?

Perhaps all of it boiled down to nothing and I was just distracting myself from the Sykes mess.

I went over both conversations, searching for something to decode, came up with nothing more than a hinky feeling.

A girl devious enough to plant dope and call in a

false lead. Not your garden-variety rebellious adolescent.

By the fourth go-round my head was pounding.

One more try. Search for something out of context, some tell.

Then it came to me:

Dressed like a lawyer. Suit and tie, not a uniform.

Way too much detail.

A misdirect, diverting me from someone who *wasn't* a lawyer? Who *didn't* look Hispanic or Middle Eastern?

Subtle at first glance, but clumsy when you examined it closely. What psychologists call over-inclusiveness. It's a pattern found in some schizophrenics and in many compulsive liars. The inability to leave things as they are, the smidge of self-destructive overreach.

That was *perfectly* consistent with an adolescent able and willing to set up an elaborate frame.

I reviewed the call, looking for other diversions. Found the biggie.

Not a uniform.

So look for someone *in* uniform.

And that led me straight to a throwaway line from the *Ventura Star* article.

Aunt and uncle, both L.A. County Sheriff's deputies.

The type of connection that could help score a plum job in Superior Court.

I'd just witnessed a husband and wife in matching tan uniforms. Eating Japanese food.

One of whom had daily access to the court record on the Sykes case.

I began typing like a demon. This time Facebook yielded a prize.

The personal page of Willa Nebe, smiling and upbeat, eager to share her taste in music with her eleven friends. Ditto, a snapshot from her road trip last summer to Arizona.

Along with husband Hank.

And niece Desiree.

The three of them, posing in sweatshirts and jeans, backed by red rock.

Willa, wearing a Dodgers cap and her usual grin, holding a supersized soda. Hank in a ten-gallon hat, eyes shielded by bronze lenses, hulking and saturnine.

Niece Desiree ("who I think of as my daughter") positioned between them physically and emotionally: daring a smile, but the twisting of her lips was tentative. More than that: wary. A crooked, uncomfortable smile. Stiff shoulders. Eyes drifting to the side.

Expecting deception at any moment because she lied as easily as she breathed and figured so did everyone else?

That could make the world a threatening place. Lead you to make pointless phone calls just *in case*.

I studied Fallows's face. Thin, clear, pretty, but for the tension.

Young woman with a more-than-casual interest in a guardianship case that had nothing to do with her.

Aunt and uncle . . .

I'd told Lionel Wattlesburg not to bother giving her my name. The old bailiff was a sensible fellow yet Kiara claimed he'd ignored the instruction.

I reached him at Marv Applebaum's courtroom.

"Hey, Doc."

"I'm going to ask you a strange question, Lionel. Would you do me a favor and keep it to yourself?"

"Now you got me intrigued, Doc. Sure."

"Kiara Fallows called me yesterday, said you told her I wanted to talk to her."

"That's kinda bizarre," said Wattlesburg. "What happened was I ran into her when she came in for her check, asked her how come she was quitting. She said the work environment was unhealthy. I said how so? Her answer was too many criminals around."

He laughed. "Criminals, big shock, seeing as it's a Superior Court, huh? I guess that annoyed me—another spoiled little quitter, so I gave her a hard time about being a fraidy-cat. She got all huffy and stomped off. But no, I didn't mention your name, Doc, so I have no idea why she'd call you. What'd she want?"

"Looking for a new job, did I know anyone who was hiring."

"Typical, this generation. Well, anyway, Doc, she didn't get it from me, I pride myself on being discreet. Have to be, all the crazy things I deal with every day."

Put another lie on the fire.

Framed as sociopathic thinking, both of Kiara Fallows's calls made sense.

First, she'd pretended to offer me information but her goal was finding out what I knew about the Sykes sisters. Failing at that, she'd hung up frustrated. And like most antisocial types, delay of gratification was a problem for her.

That led to her big mistake: the second call.

Trying to steer me away from the Nebes.

At their behest? Or was it Little Miss Devious's bright idea?

More important: Why?

Either way, she'd screwed up because she didn't know me well enough to grasp how the *obsessive* mind deals with frustration.

Dig, dig, dig, dig, dig.

Keep digging.

Rinse and repeat.

Eons in the future, some historian in a cyber-garret will aim a laser-cognitive gizmo at a sensory-digital receptor whatchamahoosis and record an obvious but profound truth:

In the twenty-first century, privacy died.

I found no address for Desiree Kiara Fallows but a residence for Henry and Willa Nebe popped up in fifty-nine seconds: Zillow listing of their one-family property on Haynes Street in Van Nuys, complete with square footage, purchase price, property tax, and a color photo.

The structure was a two-story beige smudge partially blocked by vine-crusted chain link. Padlocked gate, gigantic pine obscuring another chunk of façade.

Occupants who *liked* their privacy.

Tough luck.

Robin entered the kitchen just as the sun was setting. Her eyes drifted to the car keys in my hand.

"Need to take a short drive back into the Valley."

"This hour you'll hit crazy traffic." As I weighed

that, she smiled. "You're doing that thing with your hands," she said.

I looked down at my fingers. Curling rapidly, as if touch-typing air. I stilled them.

She said, "Didn't mean to make you self-conscious, sweetie."

"Do I do it a lot?"

"When you're keyed up. I used to think you were mentally practicing guitar."

I touch-typed the back of her neck, ran my fingers down her spine, drew her near and kissed her.

When we broke, she said, "Now you're getting me thinking about fun. When will you be back?"

"Let's eat dinner first and then I'll go. That should clear the roads."

"Have you cooked? Me, neither. So either we pull a Milo and forage, or we go out."

"Either way."

She laughed. "I look like Milo to you?"

Two hours later, nourished by a boozeless Italian meal, I was back on the Glen heading north. Take rush hour out of the equation and the trip from Bel Air to Van Nuys is a short hop. Van Nuys to the court complex downtown is a bit longer but a routine commute for lots of people, including Kiara Fallows's aunt and uncle. Her avoiding the drive seemed even sketchier as a motive.

Deceptive at seventeen, no reformation at twenty-four? How did that connect to two murders?

No matter how hard I tried, I could produce no answer.

When all else fails, snoop.

The beige blur was a narrow, characterless rectangle on a poorly lit block north of Victory Boulevard. Proportional to its neighbors in style and size, unremarkable in every way. That part of Van Nuys had begun as white working class, shifted to majority Hispanic. The Nebes had probably moved in years ago, decided to stay put.

Dark windows on the ground floor, whiskey-colored glow behind a shade on the second story.

A convoy filled the driveway: light-colored Ford Focus nearest to the gate, darker Toyota in the middle, a third compact nudging the garage door, too remote to identify.

I positioned myself as I had when visiting Virgo Virgo, several car lengths oblique from dead center. Distant enough to avoid being obvious, near enough to track movement.

No movement for an hour. I filled the time iPhoning for more info on either the Nebes or Kiara Fallows and added nothing to my pile of ignorance.

Seventy-two minutes in, the light on the second story went out and I was about to leave when the front door opened and a figure left the house.

Hank Nebe, dressed in sweats, unlocked his front gate and slid it open. Slipping into the light-colored Focus, he backed onto the street, pointed the car west, drove past me.

I watched him come to a complete stop, despite the absence of any other vehicles. What a law-abiding guy. The Focus turned left.

I started my engine.

Nebe drove to an all-night convenience store on Victory and Sepulveda. I parked at the far end of the lot and watched. His in-and-out, exposed by plate-glass windows and bleached by fluorescence, took eight minutes.

First stop, the beer case. Two six-packs of Miller Lite. Next stop, the cereal aisle. A yellow box suggested Cheerios. Economy size.

Nebe headed for the register. Okay, nothing ventured.

But before he reached the cashier, he veered to another part of the store.

Something ventured.

I followed him back home. For a law enforcement pro he was an easy tail, exhibiting curiously little vigilance, even when passing a street corner teeming with underaged teens hooting and dancing and drinking out of paper bags.

Sailing right past the group without a glance. The confidence of a man used to wielding authority? Or maybe for Nebe off-the-job meant just that.

As he turned onto Haynes, I hung back and switched off my headlights, waited several minutes before cruising into my former parking spot. The Focus was back in place, the gate was locked, Nebe was nowhere in sight.

I stuck around for another hour. The windows remained dark. Late-night grocery run but any snacking had to be taking place at the back of the house.

Another hour of zero and I was gone.

Before going to bed, I tried to reach Milo, got only voice mail. At eight the following morning I tried him again. He answered his desk phone.

"Sturgis."

"Morning."

"Got your messages, was just about to call. If it's progress you're after, you picked the wrong detective."

"I've got some new info."

"About Ree?"

"Maybe."

"This point I'll take anything. Go."

I told him.

I heard a drawer opening. Slamming shut. "Hold

on." The *click click* of typing. "Nothing on this Fallows kid, she may have acted out seven years ago but she's been clean ever since."

"She still has a penchant for lying," I said. "Heard about the Sykes case from her uncle but tried to steer me away from him."

"Maybe she regretted opening her mouth to that other bailiff, didn't want Unkie to find out and hassle her about it."

"The case was public record, Nebe's free to say what he wants."

"Still," he said, "there's the law and there's the unwritten rule: Keep your mouth shut."

"Maybe, but what gets me is Fallows keeps exhibiting the same type of clumsy deviousness as when she set up her teacher. Manipulative scheming mixed with stupidity. Like claiming Wattlesburg passed my message to her when I could easily verify that."

"Sure, but no reason for her to think you'd check up on her."

"Fair enough," I said. "But when we did connect she really had nothing to offer and it was clear she'd fibbed originally about a job search. I checked her out because she twanged my antenna, Milo. All she had to do was keep her mouth shut. Not doing so is classic mediocre psychopath."

"Mediocre?" he said. "What do the good ones do?"

"Run for office."

He laughed. "Okay, you convinced me, little Miss Kiara has personality issues. Now how do I connect that to the murder of two people we have no evidence she ever laid eyes on?"

"She may never have met Connie and Ree but I'll bet she heard plenty about them from Hank Nebe. He's a cranky sort, I can imagine him coming home from court, jaded and disgusted. Maybe she got the same from Aunt Willa, who's worked family court for years. For both Nebes, observing parents at their worst would've made it easy to conclude that people like that were unfit to rear kids. For some reason it came to a head with *Sykes Versus Sykes* and the family decided they could do a better job."

"They stole the kid? Aw, c'mon."

"Hank Nebe did a late-night run for diapers, last night."

Silence.

He said, "Disapproval leads to multiple murder and kidnapping? Jesus, Alex. And why Melandrano and Chamberlain?"

"The scenario fits *perfectly* with Melandrano and Chamberlain being targeted. Your motive's been correct all along: clearing the deck of competitors. And both of them were named in court as potential fathers. Hank Nebe would know that. He might also be aware of the threat Connie posed to his boss. Because Medea Wright didn't speak to Maestro directly, she left a message. And unlike some judges, Nancy's not big on answering her phone. Every time I've tried to reach her, Nebe's on the other end."

"Bailiff going the extra mile for the boss . . . it's crazy, Alex. And how does Kiara figure in?"

"She's part of the family unit. They're pooling pathology. And maybe that's why she quit her job: Willa and Hank work full-time. They'd need someone to care for a sixteen-month-old. But they couldn't exactly advertise for an au pair."

"Reforming the system," he said, "one dead person at a time. This is totally out of left field—farther, out on the street a mile from the centerfield bleachers."

"I know it sounds wild, but Nebe's pushing sixty, Willa's way past childbearing age, and he bought diapers last night. Maybe I'm dead wrong and they've got a daughter or son with a baby but nothing like that showed up on their vacation photos. Just the two of them and Kiara."

"Kiara could have her own baby."

"She could and maybe the nastiest thing you'll find in their house is the diaper pail. Only one way to know."

"Ph.D. surveillance ace," he said. "You went out on your own, huh? Don't be insulted but are you sure Nebe didn't spot you?"

"If he had, he would've cut his shopping trip short."

"Beer, cereal, diapers," he said. "Something for everyone. All right, stay put."

Ninety minutes later, he was at my door, ignoring Blanche when she trotted out for the usual greeting.

Nothing in his hands. He held them pressed to his sides. His eyes were active and bright. "Just talked to the detective who arrested Fallows for the hoax. He barely remembered the case other than 'Oh, yeah, that kid was tricky.' No file because it ended up as a juvey case and juvey records are confidential. I also found Rosen, the reporter who wrote the story in the *Star*. His first comment was 'Not exactly the Manson family.'"

"So nothing," I said.

"On the contrary, he remembered little Kiara quite vividly. Spooky kid, absolutely no remorse, uncommunicative, maybe a little depressed, in his opinion probably a sociopath. He interviewed her, did research on her background, but the case settled so he never wrote any of it up."

"What's her background?"

"Druggie parents, neglect, abuse. Daddy spent more time incarcerated than at home, Mommy brought home random men, some of whom took a *liking* to Kiara. Of course most of this came from Kiara, no complaints were ever filed. But I did locate her father's criminal history. Roger Walter Fallows, confirmed lowlife. Even with that, two older brothers turned out okay, both joined the military and stayed in."

"How serious of a criminal was Dad?"

"Drunk and disorderly, batteries, assaults, minor-league drug sales. He fancied himself an outlaw biker but was never in a club. A week after his final parole he and Kiara's mom were out riding near Pomona and he crashed his chopper into a freeway divider. According to what Kiara told Rosen, the brothers never came home for the funerals and that made her feel deserted. She got sent to a group home. Then a tougher one, after she kept escaping."

"Then she got arrested and Uncle Hank and Aunt Willa stepped in."

"Guess they needed some motivation."

"I can see Nebe distancing himself from a criminal relative, but Willa's more social, maybe she convinced him to step up. Do they have any children of their own?"

"Nope. Same for Kiara. I know, I know. Diapers." He began pacing the living room, stopped and bent and rubbed Blanche's knobby head. She smiled with vindication, nuzzled his trouser cuff.

He said, "God help me, you come up with what sounds like *Twilight Zone* stuff and it starts to make sense. But two boxes of Pampers? Not exactly grounds for a warrant—my tummy hurts, got grub?"

Not waiting for the inevitable answer, he made the inevitable trek.

Moments later, inhaling slices of dry salami dipped in the mayonnaise jar, he said, "If you're right, I wonder where they buried Ree."

CHAPTER

37

Rather than face the notion of Ree's interment, Milo opted for half a box of cookies. I let him create chocolate dust for a while, then said, "Let's get hold of the Nebes' work schedules."

"Why?"

I told him.

He called D.D.A. John Nguyen's secretary, who didn't have access to court personnel records but thought she knew someone who did. That source, a clerk in Human Resources, had retired but her replacement was easygoing and Milo got the data.

Not bothering to write it down because the answer was straightforward: Deputies Henry Wallace Nebe and Wilhemina Waters Nebe were both assigned to the day shift five days a week.

I said, "Someone has to stay home with Rambla."

He wiped his lips. "Kill Auntie, kill Mommy, kill Possible Daddy One, go after Possible Daddy Two, meanwhile the kid's handed over to Scheming Niece? Now, how do I get into that house to verify Rambla's presence?"

"Watch and hope for an opening. Maybe she'll take the kid out for a walk."

"What's the layout for a watch?"

"Quiet, residential, no cover. But you could take advantage of it being predominantly Latino."

He smiled. "Use Raul, again? I'm sure he'll be thrilled."

I said, "Actually, he might appreciate the opportunity. Redemption and all that."

A call to Biro's captain at Hollywood produced a turndown. Raul was busy with a fresh shooting, couldn't be spared.

I said, "You could try Millie Rivera."

Milo said, "I could try a lot of people, the department's a multicultural haven."

But he phoned Rivera, switching to speaker. "Millie? Milo. You in the mood to be a star?"

She said, "At what?"

He told her.

"Just watching? Any chance of bang-bang?"

"Not that I see."

"Not that you see," said Rivera, "or definitely no?"

"All I need is for you to observe a house. If we're lucky and you spot the baby, we move in and you don't need to be part of it."

"Too bad," she said. "I like action."

Milo said, "So you're in?"

Rivera said, "There is a complication. But you know, it could work out okay."

The brown van with the grimy stick-on sign reading *Ramirez Tile* over a 213 number was in place at five twenty a.m. The number traced to an actual side business run by two Central detectives, brothers who did home renovation on weekends.

Mike Ramirez had agreed to lend the van, laughing. "Sure, maybe we'll get some customers."

Steve Ramirez said, "Economy the way it is, we'll take criminals as customers."

Milo and I hunkered down behind tinted windows drinking bad coffee and avoiding the donuts he'd picked up an hour ago.

At six fifty-four, Deputy Hank Nebe left his house in full uniform, motoring slowly in the Focus, which turned out to be light gray. Making the same full stop and heading for the 101.

At seven oh two, wearing street clothes, Deputy Willa Nebe drove off in the dark gray Toyota.

Same destination, same schedule, perfect opportunity for a car pool. Maybe after all these years the Nebes no longer desired each other's company. Maybe, like millions of Californians, they equated being behind the wheel with personal freedom.

The third compact, an older white Nissan, remained in the driveway, nosing the aluminum door of a single garage. Registered to Desiree Kiara Fallows, at an address in Oxnard where Fallows hadn't resided for years.

The landlord there remembered her. Loner, total slob, always late with the rent, vacated with no notice, good riddance.

The view from the dash-mounted cameras in the van was narrowly focused on the front of the beige house but managed to capture a sliver of the vehicle.

No movement by eight thirty. The donuts were nearly gone. The two I'd eaten felt like cement in my gut.

At eight forty-five a.m., Milo made a call and Millie Rivera, hair tied in a bun, wearing green leggings and a baggy white blouse that concealed her Glock, wheeled a stroller east on Haynes Street.

Belted comfortably into the pram was Rivera's five-month-old son, Jorge. The picture she'd passed around at last night's planning meeting showed a smiley baby with sharp black eyes and chubby mocha cheeks. Rivera's estranged husband, the Van Nuys arson detective, was also a major in the National Guard, currently working as an MP in Basra.

When Millie was on duty, her mother took care of the baby. "She loves it and Jorge's fine with it but I'm always feeling guilty, that's why I took a couple of unpaid days."

Milo said, "Appreciate the flexibility, kiddo."

"Hey," said Rivera, "spend time with my angel and get a paycheck? I *love* to multi-task."

Fifteen minutes into Millie's slow-stroll surveillance up Haynes, Jorge's whimpering filtered through the mike in the van. Millie braked the stroller, unbelted him, peeled off a blue blanket, and took him out.

Hugging and kissing him, she spoke into the tiny clip-on mike affixed to the inner seam of the baggy blouse's front yoke.

"Hey you cutie, yeah yeah, *mijo*. What a *good* boy." Soft laughter. "Best assignment I ever got, El Tee."

By nine forty-five, still no movement from the beige house. Rivera had covered half a mile of working-class Van Nuys streets, stopping to give Jorge a bottle. "Rather do it the old-fashioned way, El Tee, but this blouse would mean a striptease and my gun would show."

Milo said, "There's a mixed metaphor for you, kid."

She laughed again. "Superwoman on duty. When do you want me to circle back?"

"Go another half block, then turn around."

"You got it—oops, I'm *smelling* something. Oh, Jor-ge, you did a big one—yeah, El Tee, definitely, got to find a spot—okay, okay, calm down *mijo*—El

Tee, there's a little park up ahead. Don't see any junkies so I'm gonna use the bench to take care of this toxic waste situation."

Milo said, "Nothing happening here, anyway."

He yawned. Ninety seconds later, the front door opened and Kiara Fallows stepped out wearing a black blouse over blue jeans, dark hair tied back in a pony.

Better looking than her photos would lead one to believe. A seriously pretty young woman, swinging a purse, walking with a jaunty step, the trace of a smirk curling glossed lips.

Alone.

We watched her get in the Nissan. Gunning the engine, she shot out to the street in reverse, oblivious to cross-traffic. Speeding west, she neared the stop sign Hank Nebe respected.

She didn't.

Moe Reed, stationed near the 101 on-ramp, called in. "She just got on, east, same as the other two, maybe she's also heading to court."

Milo said, "Follow her, Moses. And keep me posted."

Ten minutes later, Reed made contact again. "She got off in Burbank, riding stable near Griffith, looks like . . . yup, she's pulling in . . . paying."

"Girls and horses," said Milo. "You in the mood to play cowboy?"

"Tried it last year with Liz, made me sore and bow-legged for a week. How about I watch from a distance, El Tee? There's a good spot."

"Sure." Humming "Home on the Range," Milo phoned Rivera.

She said, "One sec, got my hands full . . . stop *squirming, mijo* . . . sorry, El Tee, he got a little . . . productive, take me a sec to finish up here . . . hold *still* . . . sorry. Time for another pass?"

"Don't bother, your gig's over."

"You're . . . kidding . . . ecch, *mijo*—El Tee, it's a little intense here . . . I hear you right, I'm done?"

Milo explained.

She said, "I could still do another pass, maybe she'll come back and we will get a glimpse of the kid. That happens, I could try to make contact, be friendly, everyone loves Jorge, he's a good icebreaker."

"She went horseback riding, Millie."

"Oh. Can't remember the last time I did that. Oh, yeah I do. Never. So, that's it?"

"Thanks, kid. Far as I'm concerned you put in the full two days."

"Aw, El Tee, not necessary."

"Sure it is," he said. "The gig began with last night's meeting. And don't tell me you weren't planning into the wee hours last night instead of getting your beauty sleep. I'm putting in for your overtime."

"Ha . . . thanks, I really mean it. Anything I can do from home—some sort of research?"

"We're fine, Millie."

"So I should just book?"

"You and Junior. Enjoy."

"All that talk, no action," she said, regretfully. "Ecch, *mijo*. *Again?*"

Milo reached for another donut, had second thoughts.

I drank cold coffee in the van as Milo made a show of sealing the donut box and tossing it to the back of the vehicle, well out of reach.

"Cognitive behavior therapy." Lightness in his voice, considering the situation. Then it was gone and he was glaring at the beige house.

"Way I see it," he said, "there are two possibilities, both bad: One, there's never been any baby in there and I'm back to zero. Or there once was a baby in there but we're not seeing anyone take care of it because it no longer requires care."

I said, "How about a third option: Rambla's alive and healthy and Kiara left her alone because she's a flake and a sociopath and doesn't think about long-term consequences."

"Taking a break from babysitting for an encounter with Mr. Ed?" Another long look at the house. He phoned Reed.

"What's the situation, Moses?"

"She paid for an hour, rode up into the park."

"Let me know when she heads back home."

"You bet."

Milo turned to me. "An hour ride, maybe you're right, she's just taking a breather. God, I hope you are and the worst that happens is the kid gets hungry or scared or needs a diaper change."

Worst case for Rambla. Her mother was another story.

I said, "Likely neglect would give you justification for entry."

"Maybe to look around but not to break down the door."

"Fair enough." I got out of the van.

Kiara Fallows hadn't bothered to lock the gate behind her. Before we stepped onto the property, Milo checked out the street. No one around but that didn't exclude neighbors watching from inside their homes. If so, they'd see a couple of guys in sweatshirts and jeans. Milo had added a black baseball cap with a warped brim that made his face look crooked. I'd taken an empty toolbox that had come with the van.

Milo said, "Ready to set some tile?"

"Actually I tried my hand at it years ago."

"Summer job?"

"My first house."

"Fun?"

"Not as much as this."

We walked up the empty driveway and ducked into the backyard. Small and basic: a square of grass mowed to gray, a rusted barbecue tilting in a far corner. No greenery other than a thirty-foot ficus hedge climbing along all three borders. That afforded complete blockage of the adjacent lots.

The house needed painting. The composite roof could've used patching. Every window was shielded by old-fashioned venetian blinds but the back door leading to the kitchen featured a small, four-light window that afforded a clear view inside.

Milo climbed the three-step porch and peered in.

"Milk carton and bowl on the counter . . . guess Kiara didn't clean up her breakfast dishes . . . nothing scary that I can see . . . and no evidence of anything kiddie-related."

Stepping down, he said, "You look and tell me if I missed something."

I obliged. "You didn't."

We circled the house again, looking for spy-space between the blinds. I found a tilting slat on the eastern wall that offered a slice of master bedroom: queen-sized, knotty-pine four-poster, matching night-stands and dresser, cheap overhead fake-Tiffany lamp, wall-to-wall carpeting.

Returning to the yard, we searched for signs of disturbance. No hint of excavation, no recent break in the turf, and the hedges hadn't been monkeyed with.

Milo circled the house a third time, pausing every few yards to press his ear to the wall.

He returned frowning and forming a zero with thumb and forefinger, leaned against the garage, began kicking the bottom of the wall absently with the heel of one desert boot.

Each thrust of his foot released dust from the grass that spurted and settled. "I'll get Binchy to watch the place tonight but don't get your hopes up high."

"No chance of that."

"My pessimism's finally rubbing off?" he asked.

"Reality's rubbing off."

His shoe impacted stucco a couple more times and then he realized what he was doing and looked down and saw the smudge he'd left. Kneeling, he used his handkerchief to wipe the stain.

Lightening the gray smear but unable to erase it. Frowning, he straightened.

As he stuffed the handkerchief back in his pocket, faint sound emerged.

From inside the garage.

Bump.

Muted, barely audible.

Long pause.

Bump bump.

Both of us turned and faced the garage. Milo kicked again, harder.

Immediate response: *bumpbumpbumpbumpbump-bumpbump.*

Then a new sound, terrible, muffled, high-pitched.

Milo shouted at the wall: "Hold on!"

More percussion. Droning—a wail.

We hurried to the side door that opened from the garage to the yard. White-painted wood, simple brass knob.

Second glance said not simple at all: no external hinges, no visible lock, and when Milo tried to turn the knob it didn't give. He pulled, pushed. Immobile.

The bumps from inside the garage sped up. Still muted but insistent, a terrible drumbeat.

Milo kicked the door hard.

Not a hint of shudder. None of the vibration you'd get with wood, alone.

Braced from behind by something substantial.

Positioning his mouth close to the seam of the door, he shouted: "Ree Sykes? Police."

Storm of bumps.

"Just hold on!"

We ran to the driveway, tried the aluminum garage door. Like its smaller wooden cousin, no outward security apparatus but at least these hinges were in sight. Still, no budge when Milo tried to pull the panel up. Operated electrically? Or something else holding it in place?

He said, "Need tools," and ran to the unmarked. I stayed behind, studying the door. Corrugated aluminum. Hanging an inch or so higher on the left side. I got down on the driveway, used the gap to peer up. Saw the inner wall of gray behind the metal. Grout at the base. Vertical seams. Cement block. Fresh enough to give off the yeasty odor of wet sand.

Newly constructed prison.

Milo returned with a crowbar. I showed him the barrier and he cursed and we hurried back to the wooden side door and searched for a fissure. The door was set tight into the jamb and when he tried to insert the bar it slipped. After several failed attempts and a narrowly avoided encounter between the point of the bar and his knee, he pulled out his Glock.

Something else strange about the doorknob: no surrounding plate, just brass sprouting from wood like a weird, shiny fruit. Dummy knob, a handhold with no function. But the convex surface posed a serious risk of ricochet and so did the door if it was backed by metal.

Muttering, "Whatever," Milo stepped back, aimed at the wood around the knob, and squeezed off a shot. The bullet entered the wood with a dull *chunk*.

No bounce-back, minimal splintering.

None of the ping or rattle you'd get with metal. With any surface harder than the bullet.

As if he'd shot a block of cheddar.

He fired at the opposite side of the knob, then above the brass and below. Creating a ring of perforation in the wood.

The sound from within the garage had ceased as the crack of the gun repeated. Conspicuous noise on a quiet day in a quiet neighborhood. Someone might call the cops. Dandy.

He jiggled the knob. Some give, but not enough.

Bang bang bang.

A new sound seeped from inside the garage, keening and rhythmic like a fire alarm.

A child, gasping, crying.

Milo yanked the knob, putting his weight into it and bracing himself with a foot on the wall. The dummy knob shot loose and he tumbled backward, landed on his butt. I would have helped him but he was on his feet quickly and I had better things to do. Picking up the crowbar, I inserted it into the hole the knob's exit had created.

I hooked, pulled hard. Still no give to the door. On the other end of the hole was a panel of medium brown. Grained. Plywood. But plywood didn't explain the *chunk*. Sticking my finger into the hole, I poked around. Touched something worm-like.

"There are wires in here. It's probably activated by a remote."

"Careful, it could be a booby trap." Placing his mouth near the hole, he shouted, "Ree, this is the police, we're going to get you out of here so bear with us but we found wires behind the door. If it's a booby trap, tap once. If not, tap twice."

Bump. Bump.

"Okay, good. If it's safe to mess with the door, tap once. If not, tap twice."

Bump.

"Good. If the door is operated by a remote, tap once."

Bump.

"If the remote's in the hou—"

Hard bump.

Milo ran to the kitchen door.

That one was easy to pry and he was back in a couple of minutes, brandishing a black plastic module sporting a single square white button.

Standard cheapie, adaptable to anything running on a circuit.

One finger-push and we were in.

The bullet-burying barrier behind the door was a sandwich of two foam mattresses divided by one sheet of plywood and backed by another, the entire contraption framed with two-by-fours.

One side of the frame was hinged to the inner surface of the doorway. Operated by a solenoid wired to a high rafter. Crude but effective. Sound-resistant.

Sound damping didn't end there.

The walls of unfinished garages that accompany houses like the beige structure are usually wood beam and tar paper. These walls had been surfaced with carelessly grouted block. The result was a dingy cruel space, barely illuminated by the single bulb dangling from the peak of the rafters.

A room that should've been clammy but was warmed well past stuffy by a space heater glowing in a corner. A porta-crib sat in the opposite corner. Eyebolts driven into the block hosted sampler-type homilies dangling from piano wire.

Children Are For Loving

**THE GREEN TREE OF LIFE IS NURTURED BY
THE FOUNTAIN OF CARING**

Families Are the Glue;
Love Is the Craft

Ree Sykes, hunched, gaunt, limp-haired, wild-eyed, at least ten pounds thinner than the last time I'd seen her, stood well away from all that wisdom, as close to the center of the garage as she could manage. Clutching Rambla tight to her bosom. Her rusty hair had been chopped short and ragged. Rambla's dark tresses had also been clipped. No obvious wounds or outward signs of abuse but the little girl's cheekbones were too pronounced for those of a toddler.

The room stank of baby poop and applesauce. A steel garbage can overflowed with soiled paper. Next to the crib was a portable latrine. Three rolls of toilet paper sat on the floor next to a package of disposable diapers. Same brand Hank Nebe had purchased last night.

The crib was within Ree's reach but the space heater wasn't due to the stainless-steel ankle band and matching chain that formed her umbilicus to the garage's eastern wall.

Six feet of chain; a two-step universe. Links running out a maddening foot and a half from the padded door.

The ankle encased by the band was swollen and thatched with scratch marks, testimony to a vain struggle to free herself. Scabs on the scratches said she'd given up days ago. Soon after being taken captive.

The setup was Predator 101 but her captors had made a tactical error by shackling her close to the wall adjoining the yard.

Allowing *bumpbump* to filter through.

Despite the heat, Ree Sykes trembled, naked under

a pale blue cotton nightgown. The kind you get in the hospital.

Rambla wore pink fuzzy pajamas with feet. Snot mustached her upper lip.

I said, "We're here for you."

Both of them screamed.

CHAPTER

40

I approached slowly.

Rambla brightened with recognition. Then her little face clouded and constricted. Shuddering, she jerked away from me, clutched her mother.

Cody in the fleabag, now this.

Both kids reverting to primal survival impulse, genetically encoded eons ago: *Make yourself small.*

As Rambla fought to burrow into her mother, Ree capped the child's head with a protective hand.

I backed away.

Ree's eyes bounced around. "They're *crazy!*" Her voice quaked like that of an old woman.

"I know—"

"We need to go *now.*" Lifting her shackled leg. Rambla trembled and mewled.

I glanced back at Milo. On the phone. "Soon."

I stood there, making sure to pose no threat to anyone.

Rambla hazarded a peek at me. I smiled. Her lips vibrated and tears streamed out of her eyes and tiny fingers began clawing her mother's nightgown.

"C'mon, now," said Ree. "Baby-dolly's okay baby-dolly okay, 'sokay . . ."

Rambla mumbled, "Nuhnuhnuh," and broke into sobs.

Ree looked at me. "I can't help her."

I said, "You're doing fine."

"We need to *go.*"

"We'll get you out of here."

She clutched Rambla tighter, rocked faster. "*Both* of us."

"Of course."

"I *mean* it."

"So do I, Ree. You're her only mother."

She studied me. "You," she said. As if seeing me for the first time. "You *hold* me."

Mother sank into my embrace but daughter cried harder, letting loose tears and gasps and sprays of mucus that glazed my sleeve.

Ree's comforting chant lowered to a mechanical drone. " 'Sokay, baby dolly, 'sokay . . ."

I focused on Milo's phone conversation, 911 request for Fire Rescue, specifying bolt cutters, a "freed hostage situation." Then the lieutenant at Van Nuys station.

Rambla never stopped crying.

When the sirens sounded, Ree Sykes said, "That's beautiful."

With both victims hustled away in an ambulance and an army of techs ready to do their thing, the entire property became a crime scene.

Milo and I returned to the unmarked. Leaning against the van and kicking the tire the way he had with the garage wall, he followed up with Moe Reed.

Reed said, "Didn't call you, El Tee, because she's not coming back there right now, drove into Burbank, Marie Callender's, she's having lunch. That gave me a chance to look into her car. She's a slob, but no baby stuff and nothing overtly weird."

"She dining alone?"

"So far. I'm out in the parking lot, in position to see if that changes."

"Whenever you're ready, take her down, Moses."

"Re-ally," said Reed. "So you got the evidence."

"Got everything." Milo filled in the details.

"Whoa. And I missed the party. Okay, so she's my loose end, I'll tie her up."

"Any indication she's packing?"

"Not unless she's got something small in her purse."

"One of our vics was killed with a .25."

"I'll remember that, El Tee. Congratulations."

"For what?"

"Live victims."

Next call: SWAT lieutenant Byron Bird, using a secure tactical band. Bird answered with a growling, "Yeah?"

Milo said, "I could use your help."

"And here I was thinking you were offering me tickets to the game," said Bird. "Let me give you some deep background, friend: Been up since three a.m., shitload of time wasted on a false-alarm dope raid. So don't even talk to me about work, Milo. Going to the gym."

"Got something more therapeutic than bench-pressing, Byron."

"Like what?"

Milo told him the situation. Bird said, "Two tan-shirts, Lordy Lord. Where exactly at Mosk?"

"Family and probate."

"Familiar with both those purgatories. Two divorces and my mother's will. Okay, I'm déjà-vu-ing the layout in my head, those halls full of civilians . . .

my thought is we need to be *subtle*. That's French for just enough foreplay."

The takedown team would be sixteen of Bird's physically strongest officers in plainclothes.

"Eight for him, eight for her," said Bird. "Last thing I need is my new girlfriend getting on me for the sexist thing."

Laughing his way through the planning but not pleased at substituting muscle for staggering firepower. But getting any sort of a weapon into the court building without triggering a commotion would be tough, let alone showing up with the heavy artillery the swatters preferred.

The final arrangement: each of the sixteen officers would be limited to a single 9mm handgun concealed by a blousy shirt and relegated to last resort.

The primary weapon would be human bulk: blitz-swarming the Nebes after they left their respective courtrooms. As long as the bailiffs ventured far enough from onlookers to minimize collateral damage.

If the hallways were packed, the arrest would be postponed for a safer time and place.

"Just what I need," said Bird. "Another pud-yank marathon."

"Be optimistic, Byron."

"Why?"

"I got live victims."

"Good for you—but you also got those two dead ones so don't be going all positive-thinking on me."

Hank Nebe, exiting Nancy Maestro's chambers an hour after the SWAT team was in place, went down easy.

"Shoulda seen the look on his face," said Bird, radioing in the all-clear. "Like a geek who crapped his pants on a first date. Then he gets all smirky, don't even try to talk to me, I want a lawyer. Not my problem, he's on his way to Central Booking. That should get interesting, no? Man-in-tan processed by his compadres. All those *po*-lice-loving gangbangers."

Milo said, "I think that's called irony."

"It's called ef-you justice, Milo. You have any indication he did something to that baby?"

"Not so far."

"'Cause if I knew he did something like that, I might've aimed a well-placed kick," said Bird. "Either way he's evil. Probably need to call in a shrink for your vics."

"Thanks for the tip, Byron."

"Okay, back to you when we nab *Missus* Evil."

Ten minutes later, Bird was back on the line: "Got a problem, Milo. Her court got recessed two hours ago, some kind of stomach bug hitting the judge."

"She show up?"

"We're still checking."

"Her car's not in staff parking?"

"No sign of it yet. We're covering every inch of the structure, including the visitors sections. Something happens, I'll let you know."

Milo hung up and rubbed his eyes. Settling behind the wheel of the unmarked, he pushed the seat back and stretched. I got in the passenger side.

I watched him fidget.

"What's on your mind, Big Guy?"

"What Byron said, any indication the baby was abused?" His laugh was bitter. "Other than being locked up in a garage with her mother shackled to the wall?"

He phoned Reed again.

"No change, El Tee."

"Yes, there is, Moses. Look out for the aunt. Her court recessed and she left the house in civvies, so it's possible she never made it to the court building. She's a deputy, *is* likely to be packing."

Reed said, "Appreciate the warning, El Tee."

Milo clicked off. "No, he doesn't, but that's one of the things I like about the kid."

"Respectful."

"I prefer deferential. Bet he always ate his vegetables." He yawned, placed the cell phone on the dash, rolled the back of his head along the seat. Tugging his tie loose, he closed his eyes. "Hope to hell this doesn't drag on."

Just as he began to snore, I said, "Doesn't look as if it will."

The Toyota was a dark gray blur at the far end of the block.

Rolling toward us at moderate speed. Coming to an abrupt stop well short of the hubbub fronting the beige house.

Swinging a quick three-pointer, it sped off.

Yanking the seat forward, Milo started his engine, jammed his foot on the accelerator.

No match between the Toyota's four cylinders and the unmarked's police-enhanced V8. Within seconds we were riding the compact's rear bumper.

The driver—female, head topped by the curly do I'd seen on Willa Nebe—hooked a squealing right turn and raced along a side street lined with bungalows.

Milo stayed on her tail, NASCAR comes to Van Nuys. An errant pedestrian would be doomed but walking in L.A. is generally relegated to gym machines and this time that worked out fine for the citizenry.

L.A.'s also delinquent about maintenance unless some crony of the mayor or a council member has a sweetheart contract, so the asphalt was scarred by potholes and the Toyota hit a big one and bounced

straight up and swerved left and rocked before settling. For a moment I thought that would end the
chase.

The Toyota straightened, surged forward making
an ugly sound. Sped faster.

Smooth sailing for three blocks before a cul-de-sac
changed things.

The Toyota took the only option: quick left turn,
barely short of the dead end, onto another side street.

Milo re-glued the unmarked to the Toyota for another four blocks of straightaway.

This time people were crossing: two women pushing strollers.

Bracing himself, he slowed. The Toyota didn't bother
to and the women jumped back, wide-eyed and open-
mouthed, avoiding obliteration by inches.

Milo looked everywhere, then forward, gunned his
engine, narrowed, finally closed the gap. His gun remained holstered. In the movies, cops and bad guys
race at Indie speed while shooting at each other. In
real life it's all cops can do not to die behind the
wheel.

The Toyota's bearings looked shaky but it kept
going. Off in the distance, a stream of cross-traffic
filled the horizon.

Van Nuys Boulevard. Once the pursuit moved to
the busy thoroughfare, the risk factor would change
in terrible ways.

If the Toyota made it to the freeway, we'd be on
every local station's live cam and anything could happen.

The little gray car raced for escape. One block shy
of its goal, an obstacle rolled into view.

Massive, unpleasantly green steel hulk lumbering
from the right on six wheels.

City garbage van. But no cans out at the curb so this wasn't pickup day.

Yet there it was edging along at fifteen per.

I made out a sign on the truck bed's ridged flanks: tree clearance program, credit to the district's councilman.

No sound of sawing, no evidence of arboreal work, no foliage sprouting in the bed.

Let's hear it for sweetheart contracts.

The driver, oblivious, was doing something that caused him to look down.

Texting.

The Toyota hit the rear of the truck head-on, full speed. The sound was surprisingly restrained. Dull and squishy, heavy-on-the-plastic Japanese engineering surrendered to heavy metal.

By the time we got out of the unmarked, the truck's driver, a paunchy guy with a drooping white mustache, his phone still in his hand, was on the pavement staring at the upended accordion that had once been a vehicle.

Milo checked the Toyota's front seat but there was no need to. The car had compressed to half its normal length, the entire front section now shared space with the rear.

What remained of Willa Nebe was curly gray hair flecked with pink pudding above a sodden lump of something that might've been chuck steak had it been able to hold itself together.

"I couldn't stop," said the driver, to no one in particular.

Milo glanced at me. "You wanna do therapy, be my guest."

CHAPTER
42

Processing the Toyota would take a long time, beginning at the crash site and ending at the motor lab. But inspecting the car's trunk was instant gratification: the hatch had shot open on impact.

Inside were three weapons: Housed in canvas cases were a semi-automatic 9mm Sheriff's Department duty-authorized Heckler & Koch P2000 subsequently tied to the shell casings left at the Bernard Chamberlain shooting scene, and a similarly sanctioned 12-gauge Remington 870 pump shotgun.

Wrapped in a white tea towel embroidered with pink roses, and wedged into a blood-pooled corner of the crash-distorted compartment, was a smaller handgun with a short nose that made it appear more grip than barrel.

Taurus PT25, later I.D.'d as the firearm used to shoot William Melandrano in the head.

No current registration for the little gun but its serial number was traceable: wrested from a mentally unstable man attempting to smuggle the pistol and a hunting knife into the Mosk Courthouse, presumably to inflict damage upon the ex-wife who kept dragging him back to family court for more child support.

Following confiscation, the gun had been placed on

a shelf in a basement storage room, part of a cache destined to be destroyed in an official county meltdown. Among the bailiffs given access to that room was Hank Nebe, who'd earned a month's worth of taxpayer-funded overtime by supplementing his courtroom chores with yawn-inducing sentry duty.

On advice of counsel Nebe had nothing to say about that, or anything else. Fifty-six days into his incarceration at County Jail he was beaten severely and raped by fellow prisoner(s) unknown. That, despite being sequestered in a high-power, protective security cell.

Kiara Fallows remained equally mute. So far, her stay in the women's wing at the jail's Twin Towers had been uneventful, but for a report that she was "making friends quickly."

Ree Sykes had plenty to say.

CHAPTER

43

Statement of Cherie Sykes (victim)
    re: Defendants H. W. Nebe and D. K. Fallows

Penal Codes
    182 (Conspiracy);
    187 (Murder);
    664/187 (Attempted Murder);
    206 (Torture);
    207 (Kidnapping);
    236 (False Imprisonment);
    273a (Abusing or Endangering Health of Child)

Location: Undisclosed
    Present: Deputy D.A. John Nguyen
    LAPD Lieutenant Milo B. Sturgis
    Dr. Alexander Delaware (victim's psychologist)
    Court Reporter Deborah Marks

Mr. Nguyen: So why don't you just tell us everything in your own words. Take your time.

Ms. Sykes: It all happened quickly. I knew him—the husband bailiff, Nebe—from the court and he always seemed kind of mean. But I never thought he'd—anyway, him I knew, her I didn't. The wife. So when she showed up at my apartment at night wearing a bailiff uniform and saying I needed to sign court papers I had no reason not to believe her. Even though it was late, I figured they worked all kinds of shifts, I mean what did I know, she seemed nice, she had a uniform. And a gun . . .

Anyway . . . I went looking for my glasses, I'm always misplacing them. So I could see what I was signing. Because after all that time in court, listening to lawyers I learned one thing: You have to dot your i's and cross your t's. I'd left them in the bathroom. For putting on my makeup. So when I was looking for them in there, she waited out front and she seemed nice and friendly and Rambla seemed to like her and while I was looking for my glasses she asked if she could pick Rambla up and I said sure and then when I finally found my glasses in the bedroom and came back out, all of a sudden there's two of them. Her and the younger woman and now it was the younger woman who was holding Rambla and Rambla didn't like her, she must've had a bad feeling about her, kids are like that, they can tell.

(23 second pause for Ms. Sykes to compose herself)

CS: Sorry. Okay. So the young one had Rambla and Rambla was struggling and then all of a sudden she puts her hand over Rambla's mouth and on top of the shock about everything I got scared that she was pinching off Rambla's nose so I yelled at her to let Rambla breathe which I know sounds kind of strange, I should've had a problem with her having Rambla in the first place but I was just thinking my baby needed to breathe.

So she shows me Rambla's nostrils are clear but she doesn't let go of Rambla and I make a move to get Rambla and the older one—Willa—she's shoving me back and pointing a gun at me and then before I know it she spins me around and handcuffs me and puts a gag in my mouth.

(32 second pause, Ms. Sykes drinks water)

CS: So . . . we all leave the apartment, this is like a nightmare, I'm thinking it can't be happening. But it is, it's crazy, it's like

a bad dream out of nowhere and I'm figuring my sister's behind this, at that point I didn't know, I mean I never knew—
what had happened to my sister—until you guys told me
after you . . . liberated me. Us. So at that point . . . anyway,
we get outside I'm still figuring I can alert someone but it's
late, it's dark, no one's out there and they parked their car
real close to my building so it doesn't take long to get to it.
They shove me in the trunk and I'm thinking you've got no
car seat for Rambla, Rambla needs a car seat.

(14 second pause)

CS: Where was I—

Dr. Delaware: A car seat.

CS: The drive took, I don't know . . . it seemed like forever . . .
I worried the whole ride, then we got home—their home, not
mine—I saw them take Rambla out of the car seat. So they
brought it. Which was good, at that point I just wanted anything to be good. They had diapers, too. Mine. My baby
stuff. So. Okay. I thought they were going to take her and kill
me but at least they cared enough about my baby . . . then
they put us in the garage. So they didn't kill me. So at least
we're together. So what's the point? They uncuff me and
chain me up to the wall with this like animal trap thing but
they let me hold Rambla the entire time they're doing it and I
can reach Rambla's crib but if I put Rambla down and she
decides to crawl far from me there's nothing I can do.

Mr. Nguyen: Did that ever happen?

CS: No. Not once. Not one single time. Rambla stayed right
next to me.

(26 second pause)

Dr. Delaware: You talk about them putting you in the garage. Is
it still Willa Nebe and Kiara Fallows?

CS: Oh. No. When we got there he was there also. The one I
knew from the court. Those glasses of his, hiding his eyes.
That really shocked me. Two bailiffs are doing something like
this? But then I figured it out they were married. And crazy.
Anyway. Rambla never left me. She never stopped wanting

me. No matter what they said about me being a terrible mother. A terrible person.

Dr. Delaware: They told you that.

CS: All the time. Over and over. That was their reason. They knew what I was. From their work. Being in court, day after day. Hearing about miscreants and bums. That's what they called it. Miscreants and bums and lowlifes who didn't deserve to have kids. When so many people who deserved kids couldn't.

Dr. Delaware: Like them.

CS: That's what I assumed. Then she would come in and it got crazier.

Mr. Nguyen: She, being . . .

CS: The young one. Kiara. She was the scariest. I guess. I mean they were all scary, but her . . .

Dr. Delaware: She was especially scary.

CS: Because the other two—Willa and Hank—at least they said they cared, they had a reason for being crazy, some sort of crazy moral judgments, their work, I don't know. But at least they gave me a reason. With her it was clearly a joke, she couldn't care less. A mean joke, she'd come in, bring the food, that was her job, bringing the food and emptying the toilet but she'd always do it in a mean way. Spill food. Spill you-know-what out of the toilet and make sure I saw it and I had to clean it up because with Rambla crawling around it was disgusting. And she'd always make sure it was just far enough so I could clean it but I had to stretch and hurt my ankle, you know?

Dr. Delaware: Sadistic.

CS: Definitely. Also, what she'd say to me was sadistic. I mean with Willa and Hank it was always a test. The test, that's what they actually called it. I was being examined. To see if I was fit. That gave me hope. At least at first. That I'd pass and they'd let me go. But of course . . .

(2 minute pause)

CS: I'm sorry, I was just thinking about what could've happened. I try not to think about it. Even though you tell me it's okay to think about it, Dr. Delaware, it'll get better. I mean I believe you, I trust you, from the moment I met you I had a good feeling about you. And now . . . thank you so so so much. And you, too, Lieutenant Sturgis. (laughter) And you, too, Mr. Nguyen. I guess you're all fighting for me. (more laughter) I guess I should thank you too, miss. For taking notes. For putting my words down for posterity. Anyway . . .

Dr. Delaware: You had hopes you'd pass the test—

CS: And they'd let me go and that would be that. But down deep I knew. I mean I knew who they were. How could they let me go? And then I'd think about what would happen to Rambla. Someone else raising her. Because they judged me. And then she'd come in. Kiara. Not only would she spill stuff including from the toilet. She'd laugh and sneer and totally ignore Rambla. And then—the second day I think it was—she told me what the real plan was. That Rambla was for her. The other two were her uncle and aunt but they raised her so they were more like parents. But they were shitty parents. That's what she called them. Strict and controlling and shitty, she hated them, one day she was going to take care of them. And then she winked and her face turned into this evil wink. Like she meant it. But like try to prove it. And then, the second day, she said, "They want her for me." She never even looked at Rambla or smiled or was nice to Rambla. "They want her for me." Her uncle and aunt are figuring a child will teach her responsibility. She laughed about that. A lot. Then she did it again. That evil wink.

(14 second pause)

CS: Okay, deep breath. Like what you taught me yesterday, Doctor. Deep deeeep breath . . . okay. Okay . . . so then she tells me one day Rambla will be hers and she can do anything she wants with Rambla, she doesn't give a shit about kids, kids are a pain, maybe she could train Rambla to do circus tricks, make some money from her. Wink wink. Then

she says, So guess what, bitch? It'll all be up to me and
there's nothing you can do about it.

Lieutenant Sturgis: Did you ever tell this to Willa or Hank?

CS: I thought about it. Then I figured she'd just say I was lying
and they'd punish me, maybe by taking Rambla away. I figured I had to behave myself. For my baby.

(90 second pause)

Mr. Nguyen: Are you okay to continue?

CS: That's really it. I mean they locked me up and tortured me
and I knew they were going to kill me and take my baby and
then you showed up and liberated me and I'll forever be
grateful, if I ever have another baby it'll be named after you.
If it's a boy. If it's a girl, I'll figure something out . . . maybe
Alexa. Maybe Mylie.

(Laughter from JN, AD, and MS)

CS: I mean that was as unreal as the whole experience. Being
liberated. I mean it really was.

Mr. Nguyen: So they made it clear that the primary reason for
abducting you was to take control of your child.

CS: Well . . . I mean the other two claimed it was the test. But
after the beginning—maybe the first two days—they stopped
coming in and it was just her.

Mr. Nguyen: Kiara Fallows.

CS: Yes. Like she'd been made the one in charge. Like it was
part of her training. Bringing the food. Giving and taking. She
became God. Evil goddess. And she made it clear she was
in charge, she even called me that. I'm sorry, you wouldn't
know what "that" means. A problem. She called me a problem. Said they were clearing away problems so she could
learn to be a good mother. Then she laughed. And spit. Not
on Rambla but at Rambla. Rambla understood, kids understand. It was getting to the point where each time she'd
come in with the food my baby would scream. And she liked
that. Kiara. Rambla would scream. And she'd laugh.

Milo and Nguyen agreed that Ree needed to know about Winky and Boris. That I was the one to tell her.

The day after she gave her statement, I returned to the suite at the small hotel in West L.A. that had been set up as her recuperation space. A detective named Ray Roykin sat out in the hall, playing with his iPad. No need to check my I.D., I'd been here when the refuge was set up and Roykin had received his orders from Milo.

Rambla slept in the crib set up in the living room. Ree lay on a neatly made bed reading *People* magazine.

I let her chitchat for a while and when I figured the timing wouldn't get any better I told her.

Over the course of an hour, she went from shock to craving details to racking sobs to survivor guilt. Rambla woke up after twenty minutes and Ree was able to fight back her grief and tend to her child. When Rambla was back asleep Ree said she also needed to rest. I told her I'd be back later in the evening, sooner if she needed me.

She said, "For sure I will need you. I put her down at seven, she's like clockwork. So anytime after that."

"She's settled back to a schedule."

"For the most part. I guess it wasn't as bad as it could've been. Them leaving her with me, I mean."

I wondered how long that would've lasted before the Nebes decided Ree had failed the motherhood test.

Maybe Ree was thinking the same thing, because when she walked me to the door, her hands were shaking.

I held them.

She said, "This is going to sound materialistic but I'm going to sue. Not just them, the whole Sheriff's Department. And the county for running the courts like that, and anyone else we can think of."

"You've hired a civil attorney."

She blushed. "Myron called. He's ready to take 'em all on. Can I count on you to be there for me? Just to tell them I'm a good mother and that Rambla's a good girl and to describe what they did to me?"

"Of course," I said. "We also need to make sure you and Rambla are doing as well as can be—"

"Therapy," she said. "You bet. That'll be part of the settlement." Smile. "Maybe I'll have so much money you won't be able to get rid of me."

I smiled back. "I can live with that."

She leaned forward, planted a hot, brief kiss on my cheek. "Sorry if that was inappropriate but I feel I need to . . . touch you. Not in a sexual way. To connect. To thank you, I mean right from the beginning you could see the truth."

"Glad I could help."

Her mouth turned down. "Poor Winky. Thank God Boris is okay—I tried to call him but he didn't answer his phone. Guess I'd be the last person he'd want to talk to."

"Not your fault, Ree."

"I keep telling myself that."

"It's true."

"I know, I know. But I can't help—guess it's like you said, it's going to take time. And we'll have plenty of time if Myron gets what he says he can get. Not that I'll let it change me. Getting rich isn't the point. Living kindly and honestly is. Winky knew that. He was such a good friend. So gentle. And now I'll never see him again."

No mention of the other murder victim.

She sagged against the doorway.

I said, "Ree, seeing as we are going to be dealing with all of this, it would help if, at some point, you could tell me everything."

"What do you mean?"

"You just said Winky had nothing to do with any of it. I took that to mean—"

"He's not—wasn't Rambla's daddy? No he wasn't. That wouldn't have been so bad, but Winky couldn't have kids. So now you're wondering if Boris was. The answer is no, again. But that begs the big question, right?"

"It does, Ree."

Her cheeks puffed. She reached for her braid, touched air. Frowned. "I didn't tell not because I was afraid or ashamed, Dr. Delaware. I did it to be kind. Because *he* doesn't know and if he found out, it would change things. For him and for other people."

"His family."

Nod.

"He's married."

Slower nod. "A good man who"—she chuckled—"strayed. That's how he put it. After it was over. I thought nothing of it but he felt guilty, said he'd never done anything like that before."

"You believed him."

"I did," she said. "I still do. It was one of those crazy things. The bar at Moonshadows. He was there because he'd had a fight with his wife. I was there because another guy had dumped me and I was feeling low about myself and we just started talking and he was such a total gentleman and a sweetie. Older, the kind of manners old guys have."

She shrugged. "We decided to take a drive. Up Rambla Pacifico. In his car because it was much nicer than mine. What you'd call a luxury car." Impish smile. "But don't ask. We drove and talked, then we came to a spot with a gorgeous view of the ocean and we parked and talked some more."

She looked to the side. "I can't even tell you how it happened, Dr. Delaware. Both of us were surprised. He felt worse than me. Said he'd strayed. I ended up comforting him. Next month, I had no period. But I said no way. Second month, I took the test and there it was, a little pink dot. So how do I know it was him? Because that stretch of time was a famine for me. He was the only one. Plus she looks like him. Like his other kids. He showed me pictures. At the bar. They're grown. Successful. He's got a great situation. Loves his wife, that night they had a fight. Why should I ruin all that?"

"You haven't talked to him since?"

"Not once," she said. "I did do one of those stalker things. Driving by his house, I knew where he lived because he showed it to me, a real beautiful place not far from where we parked. He showed me because he was feeling sad, saying he put so much into it and now it seemed his wife was tired of it, needed a change, he hoped that didn't mean she was sick of him. But that time, driving by his house, I saw them. Him and his wife, she's a beautiful woman and they were walking together, arm in arm. So that's it. He strayed and I ended up with a treasure. I love him in a certain kind of way for giving me that treasure and

I'll never do anything to hurt him. In fact, I'm proud of myself. For being there for him when he was sad. For comforting him when he said he'd strayed. I feel I helped him, was there at just the right time."

She smiled. "I guess you'd know something about that."

CHAPTER
45

The criminal cases against Hank Nebe and Kiara Fallows would take months, maybe longer, to prepare. Sixty-seven days after his arrest, Nebe suffered a second jail assault and was transferred to a "location unknown" that I knew to be a federal lockup in New Mexico. Matrons at the women's wing said Kiara Fallows had become a "queen bee" on her tier and was also being considered for transfer.

Then Fallows's lawyer phoned John Nguyen. His client was ready to "come clean" in exchange for cooperation from the D.A. That translated to a predictably self-serving summary: Uncle Hank and Aunt Willa had murdered Connie Sykes with minimal assistance from Kiara. Yes, she'd accompanied Willa during the abduction of Ree and Rambla, but no, she had no idea what was going to happen, as Willa had simply said there was "court business to take care of."

Subsequent examination of Willa Nebe's duty Oxfords revealed minute traces of Connie's blood and that fit with the speck she'd carelessly left behind at Ree's apartment. A couple of knives found in Hank Nebe's nightstand could conceivably be the murder weapons but no definitive proof would be possible.

Nguyen told the lawyer he'd weigh his options. He

told Milo and me Kiara's chance of avoiding serious prison time was "significantly lower than arctic temperature in Hades."

Myron Ballister wasted no time filing his deep-pockets civil suit. I was returning from my third deposition at the downtown law offices of the white-shoe firm defending the county when I spotted Judge Marvin Applebaum leaving the building with a good-looking brunette his age.

He didn't notice me until I waved.

"This is my wife, Jean, Alex. Honey, Dr. Alex Delaware, one of our custody consultants."

Jean's handshake was a cool gift of fingertips.

Marv said, "Now that I think about it, honey, if you don't mind."

She grinned. "So what else is new," and walked out of the building.

When the revolving door stilled, Marv said, "Our estate lawyers have offices here, we're trying to figure out how grateful our progeny will be if we do things the right way." He turned grim. "That Sykes woman, some mess, huh? Can't believe Willa was involved, you work with someone all those years . . ."

I said, "She put on a good show."

"She was like one of those sitcom moms from the fifties. Bringing fresh cookies. I figured she had a brood of her own back home. Turns out she didn't. Damned lunatic. What was it, like one of those crazy ladies cuts open the womb of another woman to steal the baby?"

"Something like that."

"Nancy Maestro's *really* freaked out. But Nancy overreacts to everything. Anyway, nice to see you."

I said, "About Singapore—"

"Pardon? Oh, that. Sorry, I should've told you, deal's off, they've reconciled. At least for now."

"That's good, Marv, because I'm going to be tied up for a while on Sykes, was going to beg off."

His eyes wandered to the revolving door. Outside, Jeannie Applebaum smoked a cigarette. "Well then everyone's happy. Ciao."

hree months after the liberation of Ree and Rambla Sykes, Detective Millie Rivera called and asked to speak with me.

Remembering she had a small child—Jorge—I figured she had a developmental question or two.

"Sure. When did you have in mind?"

"Actually," she said, lowering her voice, "I'm right outside your gate."

She came in dressed for detective work: brown pantsuit, hair pinned tight, open jacket revealing her side-arm.

In my office, she said, "Nice place. Okay, no way to soften this. Efren Casagrande's dead. Murdered. I didn't want you to find out indirectly and think I didn't respect your situation. 'Cause I do. Not just for what you did for that woman. For your overall demeanor that I kept giving you grief about. He was your patient, I had no right."

I thought: *What the hell happened.* My mouth wouldn't go along with asking.

Rivera said, "And now he's gone and I'm feeling kind of like a nasty bitch. Even though everything I said about him was true, I know you liked him, Doc, but trust me, he did a lot of terrible things."

"I know he did."

"He told you about it?"

"No," I said. "But I kind of figured it out."

"Yeah. Guess you did. Anyway, sorry for the attitude. My line of work, you kind of fluctuate between victory and frustration, know what I mean?"

I nodded.

"I mean it's not like your situation, Doc. Working with basically good people, trying to make them better. What I do—to catch rats you have to crawl into sewers. So it changes you. Not that I'm calling Effo a rat. Truth is, he was honorable. For his situation. An intelligent individual. In a different family, who knows what he would've been able to accomplish?"

"Agreed."

"And I don't say that about all of them, Doc. Most of them are morons. And cowards. Needing the gang because they can't live competently as individuals. Like Ramon Guzman."

"He killed Efren?"

"That's the word out," said Rivera. "Not that I can prove it. Or do anything about it because he's dead, too. One hour and fifty-three minutes after Efren's murder, drive-by in front of his house. Has to be some sort of payback record."

"What happened to Efren?"

"He was at an after-hours club, Cesar Chavez Avenue, what my folks called Brooklyn Avenue back when they and the Jews were living there, tell the truth they miss the bagels. I mean it's not like they socialized with the Jews but the Jews didn't shoot anyone and there were great delis—whatever."

She picked at a cuticle. "Efren was at this club. Along with his posse, partying. And then Efren doesn't look so good, says he has to go to the bathroom, give himself a shot, and his homeboys say we'll go with you, Jefe. Because that's the way it always is, he was like gang royalty. But this time Efren says no, I'm fine, and leaves by himself. When he doesn't come back for a while, they go looking for him. He's not in the bathroom, they can't figure out where he is, keep looking and finally go out the club's rear door and he's lying there in the alley, got a syringe and a vial next to him, they assume he O.D.'d on his insulin. Which is a big surprise because Efren was always careful with his dosage. Then they take a closer look and there's blood underneath him and they turn him over. Two holes to the back of his head."

"Ambushed and executed," I said. "You're pretty sure Guzman did it?"

"Yeah, because Guzman got beat down bad by Efren and then he got shot right after Efren. It's all in-house, Doc, the typical craziness I deal with day in and day out."

"Makes sense, Millie."

"I'll be investigating," she said. "I probably won't learn anything."

She got up. "I probably won't care, either." Laughing. "If I do care and I get all depressed, can I come by for an appointment?"

I said, "Have your people call my people."

She laughed harder. "Your people, huh? Not sure I want to know too much about them. Anyway, I wanted you to hear it from me."

"I appreciate it."

"You liked him."

"He was my patient," I said.

Then I walked her to her car.

Read on for an excerpt
from Dr. Alex Delaware's
next chilling case . . .

MOTIVE

A Novel

by

JONATHAN KELLERMAN

Ballantine Books
New York

CHAPTER
1

My closest friend, a homicide lieutenant, won't calculate how many murders he's closed, claiming nostalgia is for losers. My rough guess is three hundred.

Most of those have been the typically sickening mix of tragic and mundane.

A pair of drunks pounding the life out of each other while equally besotted witnesses stand around cheering them on.

An errant knife flick or gunshot putting the period on a domestic spat.

Gangbangers, some of them too young to shave, blasting away through the open windows of scruffy cars.

It's the "different" ones that bring Milo Sturgis to my door.

Katherine Hennepin's homicide easily qualified as different but he'd never mentioned her to me. Now he stood in my living room at nine a.m. wearing a dust-colored windbreaker, brown poly pants, and the face of an overgrown, guilty kid. His olive attaché dangled from one massive paw. Pale, pockmarked, big and paunchy, black hair limp and in need of trimming, he sagged like a rhino who'd lost out to an alpha male.

"Doctor," he grumbled. He uses my title when amused or depressed or uneasy. That covers a lot of ground.

I said, "Morning."

"Apparently it is." He trudged past me into the kitchen. "Sorry."

"For what?"

"What I'm going to offer you. As in tall glass of warm skunky beer."

Stopping short of the fridge, he sank into a chair and unlatched the green case. Out came a blue binder like so many others I'd seen. Your basic LAPD murder book.

Hennepin, K. B. had been opened three months ago.

Milo said, "Yeah, it's old news. Didn't think I needed to bug you, 'cause it was obvious." He growled. "Don't take any stock tips from me."

He sat as I read.

Katherine Belle Hennepin, thirty-three, a bookkeeper at a mom-and-pop accounting firm in Sherman Oaks, had been found in the bedroom of her West L.A. apartment, strangled to unconsciousness and stabbed to death. The blowup of her driver's license photo portrayed a thin-faced, fine-featured woman with caramel-colored hair, a sweet smile, and freckles. Sad eyes, it seemed to me, but maybe I was already biased.

I knew why Milo had shown me the love shot before the death photos. Wanting me to think of her as a person.

Wanting to remind himself.

Rosiness and pinpoint blood dots around the ligature mark but far less pooling and castoff and splotches than you'd expect with thirty-six stab wounds suggested the killer had choked first, slashed second.

A few blood drops and a tamped-down section of carpeting indicated the murder had begun in the hallway just outside the kitchen, after which Katherine Hennepin had been dragged to her bedroom. The killer then positioned her atop her twin mattress, lying faceup, head propped on a pillow. She was found covered, head to toe, with a blanket taken from her linen closet.

The pose the killer had chosen—arms pressed to her sides, legs close together—suggested peaceful repose, if you didn't consider the gore. No obvious sexual positioning and the autopsy confirmed no sexual assault. Milo and Detective I Sean Binchy had gone over the apartment with customary thoroughness and found no evidence of burglary.

An empty slot in a knife block in the kitchen fit the heaviest butcher blade in the set. The dimensions of that high-quality German utensil synched with the coroner's description of the murder weapon. A careful search of Katherine Hennepin's apartment and nearby garbage bins failed to turn up the knife. The same disappointing result followed a canvas of the quiet middle-class neighborhood where the victim had paid rent for two years.

No fingerprints or blood were lifted that couldn't be traced to Katherine Hennepin. The lack of foreign blood was another letdown; knife-murderers, particularly those engaging in overkill, often lose their grip on blood-slicked hafts and cut themselves. Despite the apparent frenzy of this attack, there'd been no slip.

I turned the page to a new set of photos.

In the dinette off the kitchen, the table was set with

dinner for two: a pair of lettuce side salads, later determined to be dressed with olive oil and vinegar, plates bearing grilled salmon filet, rice pilaf, and baby string beans. An uncorked bottle of medium-grade pinot noir stood to the right of a small floral centerpiece. Two glasses held five ounces of wine each.

That and no forced entry and everything else about the crime scene—no break-in, theft, or rape, obvious overkill postmortem attack, shrouded victim, opportunistic weapon—suggested a killer well known by the victim, driven by nuclear rage.

Milo's interview of Katherine Hennepin's employers, an octogenarian pair of CPAs named Maureen and Ralph Gross, uncovered a stormy relationship with a boyfriend, a chef named Darius Kleffer.

Someone with excellent knife skills.

I read on.

Katherine was described by the Grosses as "lovely," "sweet," and "shy." Ralph Gross termed Darius Kleffer a "damned lunatic" and his wife concurred. Twice the ex had "barged in" at the office, "ranting at poor Katherine." The first time, he obeyed the Grosses' command to leave. The second time he didn't, hovering around Katherine, trying to convince her to leave with him. The Grosses called the police but "the lunatic" left before the black-and-white arrived.

Research into Kleffer's background revealed two arrests for battery on fellow drinkers in Hollywood clubs, both charges eventually dismissed. His volatility, the notion of a chef cooking dinner for two, and the fact that Kleffer lived close by in North Hollywood seemed to wrap it up, and I understood Milo's confidence in a quick close.

He drove to the apartment. Kleffer hadn't lived there for three months and he had left no forwarding. A

week of searching failed to locate him and Milo was
surer than ever he'd targeted the right quarry.

Obvious.

Until it wasn't.

I put the binder down. Milo kept staring at the table-
top.

I got up and poured a third cup of coffee. The first
two had been savored at seven a.m. with Robin, before she took our dog to her studio out back and resumed carving a guitar top. I drank, offered a cup to
Milo.

"No, thanks."

"All of a sudden you're into self-denial, Big Guy?"

"Catholic's a genetic trait," he said. "Atonement
must at least be attempted."

"The big sin being . . ."

He didn't answer.

I said, "I would've come to the same conclusion on
Hennepin."

"Maybe."

"Maybe?"

"You have a different way of looking at things,
Alex."

"I digest facts the same way you do."

He didn't answer.

I said, "You can beat yourself up all you want but
Kleffer looked perfect."

"Until he didn't."

I pointed to the blue folder. "There's nothing in
here about why you scratched him off."

He said, "Haven't done the paperwork yet." His
smile was sadder than tears. "Okay, I'll sum up . . .
confession being good for the soul and all that. You're
right, couldn't have asked for a better suspect than
Kleffer, I'm looking for him everywhere, no dice, fi-

nally his name pops up as a little yellow stripe on a Google search. He was on a video, pilot of a show that never actually ran called *Mega-Chef*. Working on the team of some Michelin-star Chinese genius. The filming was in lower Manhattan, but even months before that, Kleffer was living in New York and no airline had a record of him flying out of there. Same for car rental companies. Borrowing a friend's wheels is a possibility but I never found evidence of that. Amtrak was also a consideration if Kleffer paid cash for his ticket, except that for five days before the murder and three days after the murder, he's verified present and accounted for working at an East Village restaurant and then bunking at a hotel where the show put up contestants. One of those dorm situations, three roommates who didn't much like him but still vouched for him. So did the show's producers and everyone else I spoke to. The guy's got an army of alibi confirmers."

I said, "Did you speak to Kleffer himself?"

"I tried, got no callbacks. I know that's weird, his girlfriend is slaughtered and he's not curious. So yet another reason for him to twang my antenna, but unless you can find some way to alter the laws of physics, he's not my guy."

"Does he have any evil friends? Someone in L.A. who'd do him a favor?"

His green eyes widened. "That's what I mean, you think differently. Except I already thought of that and so far, no buddy willing to do something like that comes up. No one who considers themself Kleffer's friend, period. He is not Mr. Popular."

"Unlikable and a knife pro," I said. "How often have you seen thirty-six wounds with no slippage?"

"I know, I know . . . any insights?"

"If the killer wasn't Kleffer, the crime scene's still worth reading."

"Someone else she knew."

"And planned to have dinner with. Any idea if she cooked the meal?"

"No evidence of cooking in the apartment but it could've been cleaned up. You're thinking she had a thing for chefs, following Kleffer with another culinary psychopath."

"Or just one of those guys who likes to impress women by cooking for them. A new man in Katherine's life would explain why Kleffer showed up at her work irate."

"Mystery boyfriend? I'd love it but no one has surfaced. I checked and rechecked with the neighbors. Kleffer's the only man anyone ever saw coming and going and not much of that. These are people who work all day and mind their own business. Binchy and I went through the place, and you know how OCD Sean is. We found no indication of romance in her life."

"When's the last time she and Kleffer talked on the phone or emailed?"

"Way before the murder—he left for New York six months ago and they stopped talking before that. The rest of her records didn't say much, either. Mostly she emailed her employers about work-related stuff— a lot of it after hours, poor thing was a diligent type, they really loved her. The rest of her calls and emails were to her family. Lighthearted stuff, happy birthday, anniversary. She's from a big clan in South Dakota. Parents, grandparents, a great-grandmother, five sibs, nieces, nephews. A whole bunch of 'em came down to take care of the body and to get educated by me. Thank God the department doesn't have teacher ratings. There I am, facing a room full of well-mannered, decent folk and giving them zilch. And they were nice about it, which made me feel shittier."

He raised his arm and brought his fist crashing toward the table. Stopping just shy of contact, he dangled his fingers a millimeter above the surface. "If there is no secret boyfriend, maybe you're right and a buddy of Kleffer was dispatched to carve her up." He got to his feet. "Okay, thanks for the coffee."

"You didn't drink any."

"It's the thought that counts." He paced a few circuits, returned. "What do you think about the meal being staged postmortem? Some kind of sick joke?"

I thought about that. "Sure, why not? If Kleffer did contract the killing, a mock trial could be a way of putting a stamp on it."

"I cooked for you, you dumped me, now you're dead meat."

"You do have a way with words."

He rubbed his face, like washing without water, loped to the coffeemaker, poured, took a sip, dumped his cup in the sink. "Nothing wrong with it, sorry, my gut's raw."

I said, "How many Hail Marys for wasting caffeine?"

"Add it to the tote board. How's Robin?"

That sounded obligatory. A kid trained to say the right things.

"She's great."

"The pooch?"

"Charming as ever. How's Rick?"

"Putting up with my foul temperament since I began working Hennepin." Dropping the murder book back into the green case, he left the kitchen, paused at the front door. "I should've come to see you sooner. Don't know why the hell I didn't."

"I haven't come up with much," I said.

"Maybe if you'd been to the scene—"

"Doubtful."

"Whatever. See ya."

I said, "Hope something develops."

Nothing did.

Two weeks later, he phoned to say the case was officially back-burnered, no trace of anyone or anything linking Katherine's death to Darius Kleffer, no other suspects.

I didn't hear from him for another twenty days when he phoned, sounding adrenalized.

"Progress on Hennepin?"

"New case, amigo. This time you're on it from the git-go."